She rose from her chair as he stood stunned. "Can you forgive me, Jamie?"

He ran his hands through his hair. How could he say he forgave her, when he was the one at fault? But everything she was saying made him think—hope—

"And if my persistence in keeping you at arm's length has ruined any chance that you could still want me—"

That thought blew away the fog that seemed to have engulfed him. Not want her? "Never," he said, and caught her around the waist, pulling her hard against him. "Never think I don't want you." He kissed her, meaning it to be quick because there was more to be said between them, but she put her hands on the sides of his face and held him, kissing him back in a way that almost made his heart stop.

Talking could wait.

Also by Caroline Linden

SIX DEGREES OF SCANDAL
LOVE IN THE TIME OF SCANDAL
ALL'S FAIR IN LOVE AND SCANDAL (novella)
IT TAKES A SCANDAL
LOVE AND OTHER SCANDALS

THE WAY TO A DUKE'S HEART
BLAME IT ON BATH
ONE NIGHT IN LONDON
I LOVE THE EARL (novella)

YOU ONLY LOVE ONCE
FOR YOUR ARMS ONLY
A VIEW TO A KISS

A RAKE'S GUIDE TO SEDUCTION
WHAT A ROGUE DESIRES
WHAT A GENTLEMAN WANTS

WHAT A WOMAN NEEDS

Caroline Linden

Six Degrees of Scandal

AVONBOOKS
An Imprint of HarperCollins*Publishers*

This is a work of fiction. Names, characters, places, and incidents are products of the author's imagination or are used fictitiously and are not to be construed as real. Any resemblance to actual events, locales, organizations, or persons, living or dead, is entirely coincidental.

First Avon Books mass market printing: April 2016.

ISBN 978–0–06238978-7

16 17 18 19 20 OPM 10 9 8 7 6 5 4 3 2 1

To my mother, who always
encouraged my love of books.
I miss you, Mom.

Six Degrees of Scandal

Part One

Do thou snatch treasures from my lips,
and I'll take kingdoms back from thine.

—Richard Brinsley Sheridan

Chapter 1

1806
Sussex

Olivia Herbert knew James Weston was a rogue the first time he winked at her, one fine Sunday morning in August when butterflies were riding warm drafts of air through the open door of St. Godfrey's and Mr. Bunce the curate was droning on and on as if he meant to put every person in the church to sleep.

She was staving off the urge to do just that by watching the butterflies. James Weston, it turned out, was watching her. As her gaze followed one butterfly—a delicate white one with spots of blue on its wings, who swooped and glided effortlessly on the hazy air—it connected with James's. His family was sitting in the next pew over, and when their eyes met, the impudent boy winked at her.

She looked away at once. Not only had he caught her woolgathering, wishing she could flit about the church and out the door like that butterfly, but it was probably a sin to wink in church. With some effort she tried to focus her mind on the sermon, but within moments a bee flew overhead, and once again, quite independently of any wish to be well-behaved, her eyes tracked the insect as it buzzed away, right toward the Weston pew.

This time when he caught her eye, he grinned. Slowly he raised one hand, and with small, cautious movements, pretended to flick the bee as it flew by. Then he screwed up his face and mimed being stung, shaking his finger and sticking it into his mouth.

Olivia couldn't help it. She smiled, and a tiny giggle shook her shoulders. His grin grew wider, and he wiggled his eyebrows at her.

A sharp jab in her side made Olivia hastily jerk her gaze back to Mr. Bunce, whose voice had settled into a low drone, as if he, too, were falling asleep. Beside her, Mother glared from the corner of her eye. Olivia repressed a sigh. Ladies didn't giggle in church, and Mother was determined that Olivia would be a lady.

Mother didn't even wait until they reached home. Her scolding began as they walked to their carriage after the service. "Olivia Herbert, what were you thinking? Laughing in church! What a common, hoydenish thing to do."

"I'm sorry, Mother."

"And making eyes at that boy." Mother didn't grimace, but her tone dripped with distaste. "Those upstart Westons."

"Upstarts they may be, but well-heeled ones." Father spoke for the first time, giving Olivia a measuring glance. "She could do worse."

Mother gasped. "Thomas Weston is an *attorney*. I want better for our daughters, Sir Alfred."

"You've got to be practical, madam." Father waited as the footman helped them into the carriage. "Our girls won't have much to attract a noble husband."

"Only their beauty." Mother's gaze softened as she looked at Olivia and her younger sister, Daphne. "A lady's face, along with her sweet temper and amiable disposition, are her greatest assets, girls."

"Yes, Mother," piped up Daphne. "I'll make you proud and marry a royal duke!"

Mother laughed gently. "I'm sure you will, my beautiful darling." It was already clear that Daphne took after her mother. Olivia wasn't sure if she took after her father or not; Father was often preoccupied with rank and money, and he was very fond of wagering on the horse races, none of which appealed to her. But at the same time, Olivia didn't share her mother's keen interest in fashion or ladylike accomplishments. She supposed she might as she grew older, but at the advanced age of ten she wasn't much interested in sizing up potential husbands.

A tapping beside her broke into her thoughts. She glanced out the window and saw the boy who had lured her into trouble, grinning as he crouched out of sight next to the carriage. "Do you walk in the woods?" he whispered.

Alarmed, she shook her head, even though she did walk in the woods every chance she got. Telling him that would only cause her more trouble.

Disappointment flickered over his face. "Oh

well." He stepped back. "Good-bye, then." He walked back to his family. Olivia eyed them curiously. The father was tall and lean, and his wife was very pretty, with a gloriously beautiful gown. Two girls about Daphne's age stood beside her, although the blond girl was fidgeting in boredom and ran up to her brother as he approached them. He laughed at whatever she said, the carefree sound floating back to Olivia's ears. Neither of his parents reproved him for laughing on Sunday.

The Herbert coachman finally snapped his whip and set the horses in motion. Olivia watched the Westons as the coach drove away. Upstarts they might be, but they looked like happy ones.

She had almost forgotten the impudent boy several days later, when she finished her lessons and was able to slip out of the house. Mother wouldn't approve, but Mother had gone into town to the dressmaker, and Miss Willets, the governess, was fond of sneaking a glass of sherry and having an afternoon nap when Mother was away. This suited the girls quite well. Daphne retreated to the nursery with her dolls, where she fashioned new dresses for them out of scraps of Mother's discarded gowns, and Olivia stole a book from the library and headed for the woods. Mother said Shakespeare was vulgar and too exciting for ladies, which made Olivia eager to read his plays, even though she was forced to hide away to do so.

There was a quiet little glen not too far from Kellan Hall, the Herbert home, with a fallen tree and enough sun to be pleasant without being hot. Settled on the tree, with her feet propped on a nearby stone, Olivia had just reached the magnificent scene where Romeo revealed himself to Juliet and professed his love in words that would rend the heart of any sentient being . . . when someone spoke behind her.

"I thought you didn't walk in the woods."

She gave a little scream and dropped her book. "You—you," she spluttered. "I am not walking!" It was a stupid thing to say, but he had interrupted at a very inopportune moment. Would Juliet return Romeo's love?

"Oh, did you come into the woods by carriage?" He jumped over the tree trunk and scooped up the book. "*Romeo,* eh? Do you like it?"

She glared at him and reached for the book. "Yes."

He handed it back. "It wasn't one of my favorites. My sisters wanted to act it out, but Penelope kept giggling when she was supposed to be dying."

Olivia's eyes widened. Dying? Which character died? She hoped it wasn't Juliet. "Don't tell me any more!"

"I liked that *Henry V,* though," he went on. "Smashing good battle. I'm James, by the way. James Weston."

She gave him a reproachful look. It wasn't proper for a gentleman to introduce himself to a lady, and he ought to know that, even if he wasn't a gentleman. "I know."

He grinned. In the sunlight his brown hair had an auburn hue, and his eyes were sharp and lively. He couldn't be much more than thirteen or fourteen, but he was already tall in Olivia's view. "And you're Miss Olivia Herbert of Kellan Hall."

"Yes." She lowered her gaze to her book, hoping he would go away.

"So," he said after a moment, "if you only walk in the woods to find a place to read, you must know about the waterfall."

Her eyes stopped taking in the words on the page. "Waterfall?" she asked, intrigued in spite of herself.

He tilted his head and gave her a sly smile. "I can show you."

Slowly she closed the book. "Is it far?"

"No."

And before she knew it, she was following him along a winding track through the trees, to where a small stream splashed over a fall of rocks. It was no taller than Olivia herself, but it brought a smile to her face. She'd lived at Kellan Hall all her life and never discovered it.

James pulled off his boots, and then his stockings, and then—to Olivia's shock—he climbed up and stood on the highest rock, letting the water foam over his feet and wet his breeches. "Don't you want to climb up?"

She looked longingly at the rocks. The thought of water running over her feet and ankles was tempting, but not worth it. "I'd get wet, and my mother would be displeased."

"Pity that. It's great fun."

Slowly she looked down at her shoes and stockings. Maybe if she held up her skirts, very high . . . But that would also be improper. "I'd better not."

"Oh," he said in disappointment. "You're a coward."

Olivia's eyes widened. "How rude!"

He shrugged, kicking at the water and sending a spray over the grass. "I can tell you want to get up here but you won't."

"I'd get all wet . . ."

"So walk around until your feet and skirt dry. That's what my sisters do."

Olivia stole another look at the frothing stream. "Your sisters climb up there?"

"And they're even younger than you. But if you're too scared . . ." He started to climb down.

Her mouth firmed. She was not scared. "Those rocks are slippery. I don't want to fall."

He grinned as if he knew he'd won. "I'll hold your hand."

And he did. Olivia peeled off her stockings and slippers, folded up her skirts as high as she dared—all the way above her knees—and carefully stepped into the water. She gasped at the cold initially, but it was a hot day and soon the water felt blissful. James held her hand as promised and coaxed her to stand on the topmost rock at the edge of the waterfall. She balanced on the wide flat stone and a grin spread across her face. The water rushed over her toes and ankles and she thought she'd never done anything this daring in her whole life. "How did I never discover this?"

Still holding her hand, James laughed. "Good girls stay at home."

"So I'm a bad girl for coming out here?"

"No," he said. "A curious girl. I like that kind."

That allayed Olivia's moment of worry. Curious

didn't sound so terrible. She exchanged a tentative smile with James.

When their feet had gone numb, he helped her climb down and back onto the grass.

"Do you play dolls still?" he asked as he put his boots back on.

Olivia shook out her skirts, relieved to see that she had kept dry except for a small spot on one side. "Sometimes."

"Good. Follow me." He started off.

"Mr. Weston!"

He turned at her indignant cry. "Call me Jamie. James if you must. You might as well come meet my sisters, who drove me from the house today with begging me to play dolls. My mother said I had to entertain them but they don't like the way I play dolls." He made an aggrieved expression. "Why can't a doll put on a fine dress and then have a sword fight with another doll? What else have dolls got to do all day?" He shrugged. "You probably know better how to do it the way they want."

"But—I can't—"

"Why not?"

"I can't go into town without permission," Olivia finally said. Privately she was curious to meet the Westons. Her parents didn't view most of the local families as their equal, and Olivia and Daphne weren't allowed much contact with other children. And even though she didn't spend as much time with dolls as Daphne did, she wasn't immune to wanting to see the Weston girls' dolls, which were sure to be much finer than anything at Kellan Hall. But if Mother saw her, she'd be in such trouble.

He grinned as if sensing another victory. "We don't live in town anymore. We took possession of Haverstock House this week, right over the hill."

Her eyes popped open. Haverstock House was the finest house in the county, and lay between Kellan Hall and town. It belonged to the elderly Earl of Malke, who rarely visited since his wife's death. Now the Westons owned it?

"I expect my mother will call on your mother soon, now we're neighbors," he went on. "Will she let you come visit then?"

Olivia doubted it. "Perhaps."

Jamie Weston flashed his confident grin once more. "I'll wager a copper penny she will."

To Olivia's mingled delight and surprise, Mother herself brought up the Westons that evening. "Haverstock House!" she exclaimed. "They've bought Haverstock House! Everyone in town is speaking of it. What is the neighborhood coming to, Sir Alfred?"

Father grunted. "I hear Weston paid a very pretty sum for it. Lord Malke's steward mentioned wagons of new furnishings from London."

That gave Mother pause. "Indeed!"

"I told you: well-heeled." Father glanced at her, sitting quietly in the corner stitching her sampler. "Their boy seemed to like our Olivia."

Instead of protesting that she was only a child, Mother turned to look at her as if struck by a new thought. "Did he . . . ?" But although Olivia was curious to hear what her mother thought, that was the last of the conversation.

Within days, true to Jamie's prediction, Mrs. Weston came to call on Lady Herbert. Olivia only saw her leaving, but the next day Jamie himself came to Kellan Hall. He greeted her mother very politely, even charmingly, and then glanced at Olivia. "I've come to escort Miss Herbert to Haverstock House."

Olivia barely managed not to goggle at him like a fool, but her mother was beaming. "Yes, of course. Olivia, fetch your bonnet. Mrs. Weston has invited you to visit her daughters, and I consented. Good society is so important to raising young people with manners and decorum!"

"Yes, ma'am," she managed to say, even as her heart jumped. She ran for her bonnet and pelisse.

Jamie grinned as they left her house. "I told you my mother would call."

Olivia couldn't keep back an excited laugh. "I just didn't know it would result in this!"

From then on she was permitted to visit the Westons almost at will. Daphne was also invited, but she went only a few times, and stopped entirely after getting into an argument with Penelope Weston over whether ladies should be allowed to drive carriages. But Olivia was soon fast friends with both Abigail and Penelope, who became as dear as sisters to her as the years went by.

Jamie was there as well, although less frequently as they all grew older. He wasn't sent away to school as most boys were but had a series of tutors and instructors. Mr. Weston traveled frequently on business and often he took his son with him. Olivia thought that sounded dull, but Jamie said he enjoyed it immensely.

"It's far better than sitting at home learning Latin verbs," he told her. "I'd much rather visit shipyards and manufactories and see how things are really *done*. Even visiting the bankers is more intriguing than any mathematics exercise."

She had to smile. "When you put it that way, perhaps I agree."

He laughed. "It's all in the way I put it! You're much too easy to persuade, Livie. You'd let yourself be tempted into all kinds of bad behavior, wouldn't you?"

Only by you, she thought. He'd been able to lead her astray since that first morning in church. "I don't know what you mean," she told him. "I'm a very respectable girl."

"And yet I like you anyway," he replied gravely.

She put out her tongue at him and he pulled one of her loose curls, just like any brother and sister.

Chapter 2

When Olivia was fourteen and Jamie seventeen, he went off to Cambridge. By then she was spending more time at Haverstock House than at home. Finances had grown tight at Kellan Hall, and Sir Alfred was only too happy to let Olivia take French and dancing lessons with the Weston girls. That way Mr. Weston paid for her lessons, and when she returned home she was expected to teach Daphne. Her sister complained bitterly about having no dancing master of her own, and Lady Herbert consoled her by buying her finer new dresses than Olivia, despite Sir Alfred's warnings about economy.

In time the Westons noticed. More than once Mrs. Weston gave Olivia a bonnet or a dress, declaring that she had ordered it but then changed her mind or gained too much weight for it to fit. She begged Olivia to take them off her hands. From the triumphant smiles Abigail and Penelope wore whenever she accepted, Olivia guessed that it was a conspiracy. Still, as her dresses from home got tighter and shorter, and her bonnets shabbier, she was grateful. It was obvious that the gifts were well within Mrs. Weston's means. Haverstock House, as grand as it was to begin with, had been transformed into the most elegant and modern house in all of Sussex. Abigail said her parents were talking of moving to London permanently, if they could find a suitable house. Olivia instinctively knew this didn't mean a modest house they could afford; it meant a house fine enough to tempt Mr. Weston, who was now—if one could believe the rumors—one of the wealthiest men in southern England.

She quailed at the thought of losing her friends. The Herberts were not going to London, even though Olivia would soon be old enough for a Season. Lady Herbert had spoken of it for years, planning first Olivia's and then Daphne's debut into the best society, where they would naturally collect a number of eligible suitors and make fine matches. From time to time Sir Alfred rumbled a protest, but Lady Herbert was set on it, and Lady Herbert's will generally ran roughshod over her husband's. The only problem this time was that there really truly was no money.

The summer Olivia turned seventeen, the hints of impending disaster grew ominous. Creditors came to Kellan Hall and demanded to see Sir Alfred, who spent more and more time in his study, the door stoutly barred. Lady Herbert stopped going into town to shop, and instead spent that time sighing over fashion periodicals. One by one servants left or were sacked, and the house grew threadbare. All Daphne's pleas for new dresses were brusquely refused. And every day Olivia quietly slipped away to Haverstock House, where

Jamie had come back from university, now tall and filled out and more handsome than before.

However, he was no less discerning and direct. "What's wrong at home, Livie?" he asked one day as they walked into town, where Mrs. Weston had sent her son on an errand. Abigail and Penelope had been squabbling all day and were confined to their rooms to compose essays on familial affection, so Olivia decided to walk with him. Except for brief visits home, Jamie had been gone for three years. As much as she loved Abigail and Penelope, she'd missed him a great deal. It felt right to walk with him again.

"Why would you think something is wrong?" Olivia affected astonishment. The Westons had never asked, and she had never spoken, about the circumstances at Kellan Hall. She didn't want anyone to know how her family was sinking. It must be clear to anyone who looked closely, but that didn't make it less mortifying.

"I heard things." He wiggled his eyebrows at her. "How bad is it?"

"Now where would you hear things, James Weston?" she asked in exasperation. "You've only been back in Sussex a fortnight!"

He vaulted over a fence and held out his hand to help her climb the stile. "It's no secret that Sir Alfred has abused his credit with every merchant in town. My parents are worried about you."

"Oh? I hadn't heard."

He gave a *tsk* and shook his head. "You're not a good liar."

"I'm not rude enough to call someone a liar to her face."

He didn't laugh, as she'd expected. "I hope you won't lie to me."

His tone gave her pause. The truth was, she didn't lie to him. It was impossible anyway, for he could always tell when she tried. "I don't," she said softly. "I can't. So I wish you wouldn't ask me about home."

He studied her face a moment. "It's that bad?"

Olivia closed her eyes and nodded.

"Well." He seized her hand. "We ought to have some fun."

"But your errand!" she protested as he pulled her off the path into the woods.

He waved it off. "This is more important."

Through the woods he led her, past the waterfall, along the stream to the pond in the meadow where they all used to fish and swim before he went away. But today they had no poles or bait. "What now?" she asked, shading her eyes against the glare off the water.

He pulled off a boot. "Let's go swimming."

"No!"

"Why not?" His other boot came off and he shucked his coat. "We've swum here for years."

"That was long ago!" Olivia watched in shock as he took off his waistcoat and began untying his neck cloth. What he said was true, and yet . . . It was different when they were young. Obviously they'd all grown up—but as he stripped, she became exquisitely conscious of how much *he* had grown.

"Have you forgotten how to swim?" He pulled his shirt over his head.

Olivia took a step backward. Heaven help her,

she wanted to go swimming with him, but she also felt the wickedest urge to throw her arms around him. She couldn't tear her eyes off his bare chest, and her lungs seemed to be squeezed in a giant fist. Jamie had been a handsome lad, and was now a devilishly attractive young man. "No."

"Coward?"

"I am not," she retorted by instinct. One learned quickly that being a coward was not permissible with the Westons.

"Then into the water with you, dressed or not!"

She shrieked and danced away from his grasp, then took off her dress and stays. She hung them on a nearby tree for safekeeping and peeled off her stockings and shoes. Jamie had already removed his trousers and dove headlong into the pond, wearing only his drawers. Olivia waded in and soon found herself dunked, splashed, and goaded deeper into the water. They laughed and swam, until Olivia tried to put a lily pad on his head. Jamie vowed revenge and took chase, vowing to throw her into the deep end of the pond.

He finally caught her and trapped her, her back against his chest. Olivia shrieked and flailed. He yelled as she splashed them both, and lashed his other arm around her. "I got you!" he crowed. "I win!"

She was laughing so hard tears streamed down her face. "You cheated!" She writhed once more, knowing it was hopeless, and when he tried to grab her tighter, his hand slid over her breast.

They both went still, panting heavily from the skirmish. Tentatively his fingers moved, swirling over her flesh. Under his thumb her nipple rose firm and eager. Olivia shivered.

"Livie," he whispered, his voice somehow deeper than usual, and then he kissed her nape.

Her breath caught. Who would have guessed that a boy's lips on the back of her neck could feel so exciting? Her back bowed and her head fell forward. She shut out the little voice in her head warning that this was unbecoming behavior for a baronet's daughter, and gave herself over to the thrill of being worshipped.

His lips moved over her skin. "I shouldn't kiss you," he whispered next to her ear. "I know it, but I don't want to stop, Livie . . ."

She twisted in his embrace. "Don't stop." She wound her arms around his neck and exulted as his mouth claimed hers almost before she finished speaking. It was everything a girl's first kiss should be: gentle and sweet and given by the boy she loved.

His arms shifted, lifting her higher. She giggled until he kissed her again. Buoyed by the water, her legs rose and curled around his waist. His shoulders heaved, and his hands went to her hips, pulling her tightly against him, and Olivia felt the contact with some astonishment. She broke the kiss and raised her head. Jamie met her gaze, his own eyes wide and clear. His mouth was set in a firm white line and he seemed to be having trouble controlling his breathing.

"I'm going to walk out of the pond," he said in that too-deep voice.

If they got out of the water, her soaked chemise would cling transparently to her body. Already she could feel his skin through the thin linen. He was warm and solid and still held her as if he feared to let go. This was truly unbecoming—even immodest—behavior, but without a word she nodded.

He sloshed out of the water with long, careful strides. Olivia's heart skipped a beat as the breeze blew across her wet skin and made her shiver. Jamie noticed, but he didn't laugh or tease her. As soon as he reached the thick tall grasses a few feet from the water, he lowered himself to his knees, still holding her wrapped around him. "Livie," he said, his hazel eyes boring into hers, "if you want to put your dress on, you should run and fetch it."

"If I don't?" she whispered.

He swallowed. "Then I'll kiss you again and again."

A smile broke across her face. "I want you to." He blinked, and she blushed. "Please."

So he did. They tumbled into the sun-warmed grass and explored each other with gentle touches and caresses that grew increasingly bold. He made her giggle and she made him squirm. In the warmth of the day their undergarments dried quickly, which caused her chemise to ride up until his hand landed on her bare knee.

"Livie." He seemed mesmerized by the feel of her skin. He traced the shape of her knee, his fingertips swirling over it. "Livie, do you know about making love?"

"Ah—oh," she said awkwardly. Elizabeth Miller, who was only a year older than Olivia but already married, had regaled a number of young ladies in town about the secrets of wedded life.

"A—a little. Have you . . . Have you done it?" Her face grew hot just asking the question.

Jamie blushed, too, all the way down his neck. "No." He drew a delicate line along her thigh, nudging the chemise higher. "I think of doing it with you, though, all the time. You've grown up so beautiful."

Her heart seemed to swell with happiness. No one at her house thought she was beautiful; that was Daphne, the golden child. And this wasn't just anyone telling her she was beautiful, it was *Jamie*, whom she'd loved since she was ten years old. "I love you, Jamie," she blurted.

He looked at her, not astonished but pleased. "And I love you. Have forever."

She gasped, then gave a laugh of pure delight. "You do?"

"You didn't know?" He sounded wounded.

"You never said!"

He grinned, his hazel eyes sparkling at her from underneath the wild tangle of his still-drying hair. "I just did." The grin faded. "And I can't stop thinking of you. All the time I was gone, Livie. I missed you."

"I thought making love was something only married people did," she said nervously. Elizabeth's stories of great pleasure and shocking delights echoed in her mind. It was tempting—so very tempting—but also daunting.

He didn't seem frightened in the slightest. "I always knew I'd marry you someday. You're the best girl in England, Livie."

Olivia's mouth fell open. "You—you want to marry me?"

Jamie winked. "Of course I do!" She scowled, and he tried to subdue his cocksure grin. "I should have asked with more dash. Or with poetry. Girls like poetry, don't they? 'If only you will marry me, how very happy we will be.'" Olivia snorted with laughter. He gathered her closer. "'If you decide to answer yes, I would then take off your dress.'" His fingers ran up her thigh again as she gasped in exaggerated indignation—and a deep and primitive pulsing excitement. "'You have the finest bosom in Britain, and I would like to kiss your skin.'"

"That's horrid!" Olivia was laughing so hard she could hardly speak.

"I hope you mean the poetry and not the sentiment." He caught her as she tried to squirm away, holding her against him. The motion sent his hand sliding up her leg, higher and higher until Olivia abruptly froze. Her heartbeat roared in her ears. His fingers were right there, brushing a very private place, and for a moment the tantalizing touch made her breath catch.

Jamie had also gone still. Slowly, gently, he ran his fingertips over her skin, gliding up the inside of her thigh but stopping short. Olivia's whole body twitched as those fingers trailed back down. He started to tug her chemise hem down. "I'm sorry, Livie—" he began, his voice hoarse and strained.

"No." She twisted to face him. "I want to marry you, too." She placed her hand against his bare chest. "I do, Jamie. *Yes.*"

He threw back his head and gave a whoop before snatching her against him, even as she laughed. He held her close and kissed her neck and face profusely until she beat on his shoulders with her fists. "Stop," she gasped between peals of laughter. "Stop!" He did, and she caught her breath. He was so handsome like this, tousled and bare-chested, and she'd never felt so happy. "Make love to me."

His gaze sharpened. "Truly?"

She nodded, her heart bursting with love. Her father would give permission—the Weston wealth would ensure that, if nothing else—and then she would be a Weston, with Jamie to make her laugh and kiss her senseless and satisfy this new craving of her body. "I want you to make love to me."

"Far be it from me to refuse a lady." He pulled the drawstring on her chemise. "The fellows at university said it takes practice to do this properly."

"If you don't know how it's done," she began, but he cut her off, sliding over her and pressing a kiss on her mouth. The feel of his body on top of hers stopped any other protest.

"I'm a quick study," he promised, and then he set about proving it, learning which touches made her giggle and which ones made her twist and sigh in longing. Her chemise came off, then his drawers, and under the bright Sussex sun he made love to her. It was joyful, if a little awkward, and hurt a bit at first, but he cradled her against him and moved so tenderly she clung to him until he shouted and flung back his head in ecstasy. And when he realized she hadn't found that same rapture, he started all over again, testing and tormenting every inch of her skin until he learned the secret and left her weak and trembling and absolutely dazed with adoration for the young man holding her.

"Oh my," she gasped as he collapsed on the ground beside her. "Oh my, Jamie. That was . . ."

"Brilliant?" He opened his eyes a little and gave her a triumphant, lazy smile. "I agree. Just wait until we've got some practice."

Later he walked her home, hand in hand, and told her his plans—as usual, Jamie had a plan, and it was a grand one. He'd been learning from his father and wanted to make his own investments. Mr. Weston had promised him a generous amount of capital, and Jamie said he could provide for a wife within a year. Olivia blushingly agreed they would wait, although not perhaps without more of that wonderful lovemaking, and he left her with a scorching kiss at the lane to Kellan Hall. Olivia barely felt the overgrown lane under her feet: she was in love, engaged to be married, and everything in life was perfect.

Her mother caught her returning to the house. "Olivia Herbert! What happened to your dress?"

Olivia blushed—it had spent the afternoon flung over a tree branch, and looked it.

"And your hair!" Her mother peered closer and frowned. "What were you doing at Haverstock House?"

"Oh." She cleared her throat. "Jamie was sent into town, and I walked with him . . ."

"And where did you walk that you come home looking as though you've been rolling in the grass?" exclaimed Lady Herbert. And then she stopped. Her eyes went wide and her mouth opened in a silent O. Before Olivia could say a single explanatory word, her mother seized her arm and hurried her into the nearby parlor, closing the door behind them. "Did that boy take liberties with you?" her mother demanded. "Do not lie to me."

Happiness still sizzled in her veins. When she married Jamie, she wouldn't have to live with her parents anymore, and hear how much her mother preferred Daphne's looks to hers, or listen to her father complain about the cost of two daughters. She would have a home with someone who loved her—a whole family of people who loved her—and she need never return to Kellan Hall. "I'm in love," she boldly said. "And he loves me, Mother."

Lady Herbert caught her arm in a fierce grip. "Did he tumble you? You have the look of it about you."

Olivia felt her face grow hot. She pulled loose of her mother's hold. "He wants to marry me."

"Does he, now?"

"Yes, and I know Father won't refuse, because Mr. Weston's promised Jamie a very handsome sum now that he's finished his studies at university." Lady Herbert fell back, blinking. Olivia felt invincible. "I'm engaged to him, Mother, and I begged him to make love to me. I know he's not the viscount you used to dream I would wed, but you've still got Daphne. Perhaps Mr. Weston will be generous in the settlements and you'll be able to take her to London for a Season as you always hoped."

Instead of shrieking or scolding, Lady Herbert clapped her hands together. "Olivia," she choked. "Oh, my dear! You'll be the saving of us!" And she threw her arms around her daughter.

For the next few days she was her parents' favorite child. Lady Herbert kept her at home, saying she must make the young man come to her. Daphne, who had already been promised a Season as a result of Olivia's impending marriage, was loving and sweet. Even Father clasped her in his arms and called her "dear child," promising to wait at home every day until Jamie came to ask his permission.

The only thing that came to Kellan Hall, however, was a note. Olivia's heart fluttered as she tore it open and saw Jamie's familiar handwriting, sharp and sprawling from the speed with which he wrote . . . that he was leaving for a few weeks and going into Wiltshire to see a canal where his father was considering investing. He closed the note with his usual farewell, and if he hadn't written her name with the O looking vaguely like a heart, she would have thought it was a letter from any passing acquaintance. Still, she trusted him, so she put the letter aside, and when her parents asked why he hadn't come yet, she told them the truth. Truth, she had been taught from birth, was virtuous, and obedient children never lied to their parents.

But before long, Olivia realized that was precisely the worst thing she could have done.

Chapter 3

Her father barged into her room two days later. "Did you lie to me?" he demanded.

"What? No!"

He raised his hand as if he would strike her, but only curled his fingers into a trembling fist. "About the Weston boy," he snarled. "I've just been to Haverstock House and Thomas Weston has no idea his son is engaged to marry you."

Olivia gaped, more at her father's fury than at Jamie's actions. Jamie had never lied to her. "But—no, Father, he did. I swear to you! Perhaps he didn't tell his father yet, but I'm sure when he returns he'll explain everything—"

He slapped her. "He's not expected back for weeks, perhaps months! When is this wedding to take place?"

"Not for another year," she cried, cowering away from him. "We agreed—he won't have enough income until then—"

"I cannot wait a year!" He grabbed her shoulders. "Did he put a babe in your belly?"

"I don't know," she sobbed.

Sir Alfred pushed her away, and she toppled

onto the bed behind her. "If he has, this will all end well," he muttered. "If not . . ." He shook his head and stalked from the room.

Olivia huddled in stunned silence on her bed. Jamie must have forgotten to speak to his father before he left, or not been able to, or not thought it urgent. If only Mother had let her go to Haverstock House as usual . . .

She scrambled off the bed and flung open her desk, dashing off an impassioned letter. A few tears streaked down her sore cheek and blurred the ink, and when she read it over, the words were illegible, incoherent, or both. Jamie would think she'd gone mad. Olivia hesitated, then ripped the page in half and took out a fresh sheet. She dried her eyes and took a deep breath, and wrote a much more civilized letter asking when he would be home. She didn't want to tell him of her father's furious rant, so she simply wished him luck in his journey, and signed it with her name—taking care to make the O look like a heart, to show her love.

Feeling better, but still anxious, she walked to Haverstock House. Nothing was in uproar there, so Mr. Weston must not have taken alarm at her father's visit. She was at Haverstock so often, the butler merely told her where to find Abigail and Penelope. They were in the garden, Abigail dutifully sketching a rose and Penelope plucking the petals off another.

"There you are!" Penelope cried at her appearance. "You've abandoned us for over a whole week now!"

"I'm sorry." Olivia sat down at the table where they worked. "Did you write your essay?"

Penelope rolled her eyes. "Yes, horrid thing. Mama made us read each other's aloud at dinner that night, and Jamie laughed at mine."

Olivia twitched at his name. "I'm sure he didn't mean it. I—I understand he's away from home now?"

"Thankfully," murmured Abigail, still sketching.

"All the way to Wiltshire," Penelope added with satisfaction. "He won't be home for months."

"Oh?" Her voice rose an octave. "Why so long?"

"Jamie doesn't go anywhere directly," said Abigail. "The last time Papa sent him somewhere, it took him over a fortnight to arrive. He kept stopping off to see interesting libraries or inventors along the way. And once he gets to his destination, he wanders off. I daresay he won't spend half his time at the canal; he'll find his way to see the boat builders' workshop, and the bankers' offices, and landowners who live nearby. Papa says he does a good job investigating, but he takes forever at it."

"Good riddance," Penelope declared. "He's been like a caged bear this week! Three weeks in Sussex, and he couldn't wait to be off." She put down her ruined rose. "Livie, are you ill?"

"No," she said faintly. "I just . . . I had a question to ask him. Could I write to him?"

Penelope shrugged. "Who knows?"

Olivia wet her lips, which were bone dry. "Is your mother home?"

The girls directed her to the morning room, where Mrs. Weston rose to greet her. "How are you, Olivia? Your father was here this morning."

"I know."

"He was quite agitated, and hinted at a match between you and James. Neither you nor James ever mentioned such a thing to either of us, and Mr. Weston didn't know what to say."

Put that way, neither did Olivia. Jamie hadn't told his parents. His sisters said he was wild to be out of the house. Had she imagined the whole thing?

At her dismayed silence, a slight frown touched Mrs. Weston's brow. "I didn't mean to upset you. Mr. Weston put your father off because he didn't want to presume there was more affection between you and James than he knew. You're both so young. We would never encourage a match between you if your hearts were not engaged."

"No, I—I am fond of Jamie," she said in a faltering voice. "Very fond, Mrs. Weston."

"I see." The older lady's eyes were keen and direct, so like her son's. "Did he make you any promises, Olivia?"

Her composure wavered. "I'm not sure," she said softly.

Mrs. Weston smiled and clasped her hand. "I wouldn't be disappointed, my dear. You're like a daughter to me already! James couldn't do better than choose you, and if you love him in return, you would have my blessing—and Mr. Weston's as well."

That made her feel marginally better. She took a deep breath and pulled out her letter. "Could I send this to Jamie? I didn't know he would be gone so long . . ."

"Of course. We'll make this right. Give me your letter and I shall send it to him, along with one of my own. Weston men can be oblivious to all outside their immediate interest unless something smacks them in the face."

Gratefully Olivia handed over the note. By the time she reached home her confidence was restored. Jamie would get her note and come home; he would speak to his father, then to her father, and everything would be fine.

Except it was not. A week later no reply had come, nor had Jamie. Another week passed the same way, and Sir Alfred abruptly told them to pack. They were going to Tunbridge Wells the next day. No explanation was given, and no opposition was tolerated. The whole house felt quiet and tense as they obeyed, and the atmosphere didn't improve when they reached Tunbridge. In fact, Olivia was just as happy not to speak to her parents at all, until she discovered the reason they had come to town.

One evening a gentleman named Mr. Walter Townsend dined with them, and the next night he brought his son Henry. Henry was an amiable fellow, moderately handsome and not too tall, who chatted merrily with everyone. Olivia was seated next to him, and when dinner was over and her father asked how she found him, she agreed that he was very charming.

"Very good," said Sir Alfred. "You're to marry him Monday next."

Olivia thought she'd misheard him. "What? No—I'm engaged to Jamie Weston! I cannot marry someone I only met tonight!"

"You can. Walter Townsend is an old friend of mine from university. His son needs a bride, and you need a husband." He fixed a hard look on her. "Especially one who won't mind that you're not as fresh as you look."

She felt a rise of panic in her chest. "I won't!"

"Thomas Weston said his son is too young to marry. The boy himself told you he wanted to wait a year. Why do you think he did that? He only wanted under your skirt, Olivia." He shrugged as she recoiled. "It's not just him, it's all men. You were a silly fool to let him, and now you've got to pay the price."

She sat gaping. By now she knew she wasn't carrying a child, which meant there was no reason not to wait until Jamie returned. But then . . . *I cannot wait a year,* her father had said. This wasn't about her honor at all. "How much is Mr. Townsend offering for me?"

Her father scowled. "None of your concern."

"I think it is." Her voice rose shrilly. "Why must Mr. Townsend resort to buying a bride for his son—is he a lunatic? Will I end up murdered in my bed?"

"Don't be ridiculous. Henry's a good man in need of a wife to settle him." Her father turned to go, but paused. "And the answer is four thousand pounds. A handsome sum that will save Kellan Hall."

When Olivia went to her mother, the answer was the same. Lady Herbert's only consolation was an offer to buy her bride clothes in Tunbridge Wells. The marriage contract was signed, the days sped by, and Olivia prayed every night that Jamie would arrive in time. If he appeared even a moment before the wedding service was done, she would run away with him, and damn the marriage contract. She sent a second note and then a third, but deep in her heart she feared there wasn't enough time. Wherever he'd gone, her letters weren't catching up to him. She lay awake at night plotting how she would refuse to speak during the ceremony, but her father had taken care of that. The curate was paid well and he plowed right over her stubborn silence. With a bemused look, Henry slid a ring on her finger, and it was done.

Four days later Jamie arrived. Olivia heard his voice, echoing urgently through Henry's small house, and then she heard him pounding up the stairs. He burst into the drawing room, dusty and disheveled and wild-eyed. "Tell me it's a lie," he demanded. "Tell me . . ." His voice died as she deliberately folded her hands to show her ring.

She'd had four days to prepare for this. Four days to acquaint herself with the knowledge that Jamie would never be hers, that the stolen day by the pond in the woods was a halcyon moment of bliss, not a portent of her life to come. So far Henry didn't seem a bad sort—he was so charming, everyone liked him immediately, and he had a generous allowance from his father—but he would never be Jamie.

And part of her blamed Jamie for everything. He'd made her a vow, then carelessly walked away without securing her father's permission. If only he'd come to see her father right away. If only he hadn't gone rambling about the countryside without so much as a farewell visit. If only he'd stayed in posting inns where her letters could have reached him. But he hadn't, and now she was paying for it.

"How do you do, Mr. Weston?" she said evenly. "Won't you sit down?"

"No!" He strode across the room, stopping only when she took a step backward. "*Why*, Livie? What happened?"

The anguish in his voice was real, and it tore at her heart. Whatever else he was guilty of, Jamie did care for her. Her composure wobbled. "My father arranged the match. He was concerned for my reputation."

He flinched as if struck before his horrified gaze dropped to her midsection. "My God. You're not—?"

"No!" She glanced uneasily at the door, but a helpful servant had closed it behind Jamie. "I'm not carrying your child."

Relief flooded his face, followed quickly by angry confusion. "Then why such haste? Even if he feared such a thing, *I* should have been the one he turned to."

"But you weren't here," she said tightly. "You left without a word of where you would be or when you would return."

He flung up his hand in a gesture of impatience. "I only intended to be gone for a few weeks. I wrote and told you so."

"But you gave him no reason to wait!" Her temper was fraying. "You never came to ask his permission—"

"As if he would have refused," Jamie scoffed. "We both know he would have squeezed my father for every last farthing and fetched a curate as soon as the contract was signed."

It was true, and it made her furious. "Oh, you know he would have consented, but still you couldn't be bothered to speak to him? What does that say about you, James Weston?"

He flushed. His mouth compressed. "I didn't know he was so anxious to marry you off."

"Neither did I!" She pressed her hands to her face, which burned with anger and humiliation. "You didn't even tell your parents . . . Perhaps you didn't really mean to go through with it, and that whole day was a lark to you—"

"Don't say that," he interrupted. "I meant every word I said!"

"But those were only *words*, Jamie—they were not binding, and they couldn't be exchanged for money!" She was breathing hard now, vibrating with agony. "That's all my father wanted—the money. If you'd been there, he would have got it from you, but you weren't, so he got it from Mr. Townsend. And I'm married to someone I don't even know."

Jamie stared at her, looking stunned and angry and very young. For the first time Olivia felt like the older and wiser one of them; it seemed as though she'd aged a decade in the last week. "I didn't know. You—you didn't tell me!" Growing agitated again, he plunged one hand into his pocket and pulled out her letter, crumpled and stained. "I was all the way to Wiltshire before it caught up to me—my mother sent it to the wrong inn. You didn't hint at anything like this! Livie, you only asked when I planned to return home. If my mother's letter hadn't scolded me, I wouldn't have taken any alarm at all. I turned back but I would have raced like the wind had I know how urgent it was . . ." He shook his head, frustrated and perplexed. "Olivia, we talked about waiting a *year.* I didn't think there was any rush to speak to your father. I wanted to establish myself first."

"You'll have plenty of time now," she replied before she could stop herself.

Jamie's eyes flashed. "You never told me how bad things had become at home. I knew your father was in debt but I'd no idea he was this desperate."

Olivia gave a despairing laugh. "Well. That hardly matters now."

The wild, mad light went out of his eyes. All the light, in fact. He stared at her ill-fated letter for a moment, running his thumb over it to remove the creases. "No. I suppose not."

For a long moment, so long it seemed to last an eternity, they stood in silence. Olivia's fury had vanished and now she had to blink back tears. The urge to fling herself into Jamie's arms and beg him to take her away was almost overpowering. She knew it would be fruitless, and unfair to Jamie, but at this moment, when her life seemed to be ending just when she'd thought it was about to begin, she felt she would gladly throw away any chance of respectability if only they could be together.

"Jamie," she began, then stopped. She mustn't think of him that way any longer. "Mr. Weston. I hope we can remain friends. Anything else between us"—her voice shook, and she paused—"would be improper."

In the days since her wedding, she'd had time to

think about whether she wanted to shut Jamie, and all the Westons, out of her life. It might be easier, but they had been everything to her for years. Her own family had never loved her as much as the Westons did, and now she could barely stand to think of her parents.

But to keep her friendship with Abigail and Penelope, she would have to maintain a civil relationship with Jamie. The only way she could do that was to keep him at arm's length, now and forever. To lose her love was terrible, but to lose everyone she cared about was unbearable.

She'd told herself this several times over the last few days, and wept each time. Odd how it hurt far more now that she had to tell him.

"This is not how I hoped our relationship would change," she went on, forcing out each word, "but what's done is done. It would be best if we kept our regrets to ourselves."

He raised his head. His eyes were dead when they met hers. "Yes. If that is what you wish, Mrs. Townsend." The name sounded leaden and ugly on his lips, and sent another spasm of anguish through her. "I apologize for disturbing you. As you say, what's done is done." He paused, his gaze searching, almost as if waiting for her to beg him to carry her away with him. And Olivia's resolve wavered. God help her, if he said they should run off, propriety be damned . . .

"I suppose that's all there is to say," he said instead. "Good day." His steps sounded heavy as he turned and left.

A few minutes later Henry strolled in. "Who was that?"

Olivia had retreated to the window. Below her, Jamie collected the reins of his horse and swung into the saddle. Without once looking up, he turned and rode off. Pressure built inside her chest until she thought she would suffocate. He was leaving, and all her hopes and dreams lay in ashes in his wake. She laid her palm against the pane of glass as if she would draw him back to her side

"Are you unwell, Olivia?" Henry asked absently. He was reading the racing report and didn't even glance at her. "Did the fellow upset you?"

She swiped a stray tear from her cheek. Down in the streets below, Jamie turned a corner and disappeared from view. "No," she whispered in reply to her husband's question. "I'm fine. It was only an old friend."

And nothing more. Never anything more.

Part Two

They know not I knew thee,
Who knew thee so well—
Long, long I shall rue thee,
Too deeply to tell.

—Lord Byron

Chapter 4

1822
Gravesend, Kent

The clock above the clerk's desk had stopped, and so had time itself, in Olivia Townsend's estimation.

"Will Mr. Armand be much longer?" she asked. Her back ached; she'd been sitting on the hard wooden chair for hours. She had no idea how many, because the clock had stopped, but it felt like a dozen at least.

"I don't know," replied the clerk without looking up from his task. "He's a very busy man, madam."

Olivia supposed that was true. While she had been sitting here, at least three other clients had come and gone, each one shown directly into Mr. Armand's private office on arrival. The clerk had bowed and simpered for them, but otherwise he left his stool only to put more coal on the fire or to fetch a mug of ale from the tavern across the street. Since the fire was across the room from her and he hadn't offered to fetch her a drink, neither of these actions improved Olivia's opinion of him. She was beginning to imagine snatching the quill out of his hand and breaking it before she stormed into the inner office and confronted the solicitor. The last client had left some time ago and no other had appeared. Unless the clerk lied to her, Mr. Armand had been aware of her presence, and duly ignored it, since midday.

The clerk turned a page, his pen scratching endlessly across the ledger. He must be transcribing a history of the world, Olivia thought in aggravation.

"Would you please remind him that I am waiting?" She didn't bother hiding the edge to her words.

The clerk peered at her over his glasses. He was an older man, paunchy and graying, and there was no mistaking the disapproval in his glare. "He is aware of it, madam."

"I think he must have forgotten," she exclaimed. "I've come in response to a package *he* sent *me*. He was my husband's solicitor for many years—"

"Mr. Charters was your husband's solicitor, Mrs. Townsend," interrupted the clerk. "Mr. Armand merely took over the practice."

"If he no longer handles the work, he may as well deliver all my husband's files and records to me." Olivia smiled at the clerk's dour expression. "Since my husband is dead, I'm sure they're only collecting dust. Give them to me and I shall be on my way without troubling Mr. Armand."

He turned back to his writing without the

courtesy of an answer. Olivia's fraying patience snapped. She stood up just as a door at the end of the room opened. "Mrs. Townsend," said the gentleman in the doorway. "Won't you come in?"

Forcing down her temper, she dipped a polite curtsy and went past him into a large but disordered inner office. Pale rectangles on the walls marked missing pictures, and bookcases stood empty. Mr. Armand murmured an apology as he dusted off a chair for her. "I apologize for the delay. I did not expect you to come yourself."

That softened her irritation somewhat. "Of course. But I was astonished to learn you have some of my husband's papers. Henry has been dead for almost two years now. I confess myself very eager to reclaim anything of his."

"Indeed," said Mr. Armand slowly. "Mrs. Townsend . . . Did you not receive my letter? The second one?"

"Why, no," said Olivia after a startled moment. "Only the one."

He sat behind his desk and looked pained. "Mrs. Townsend, I sent you a book—"

Olivia nodded, every scrap of her attention focused on the solicitor. "That's why I'm here."

That book was why she had dropped everything to come to Gravesend in winter. After Henry's death it became more and more obvious that he had kept secrets from her, very large and significant ones. That alone didn't surprise her; their entire marriage had been rather distant, like two acquaintances living in polite proximity. Henry never confided in her about his affairs, and since the bills were always paid, Olivia never pressed.

She'd supposed they were living on his inheritance from his father, which had been substantial.

But when Henry died, her income inexplicably dried up, even though there should have been an annuity to provide for her. The solicitor, Mr. Brewster, could only tell her that the accounts were empty and her annuity had been canceled. He had no idea where Henry drew his funds, and without Henry himself, those funds seemed to vanish. As the money disappeared, so did Henry's purported friends. Olivia hadn't minded that; she knew she was nothing like her charming and gregarious husband, and his friends had no time for a widow of plummeting income and status. In fact, she wished all of Henry's friends had drifted away, but one in particular—Viscount Clary—refused to go away, and that had started all her troubles.

Her pulse spiked just at the thought of him, threatening her composure. With some effort, Olivia focused her attention on Mr. Armand. Three weeks ago, out of the blue, she had received a package from him with a letter indicating that he had taken over the practice of the late Richard Charters, who had apparently been one of Henry's solicitors, and had discovered the enclosed book in Mr. Charters's files labeled with Henry's name. The book looked for all the world to be part diary, part ledger, with a steady stream of payments in Henry's distinctive handwriting. The recipients were only identified by initials, though, and the notations were very suspicious.

Thanks to Lord Clary's intimations, Olivia had begun to suspect her husband was up to something illicit, even illegal, and this book seemed to confirm it, if not explain exactly what those activities were. If she could decipher what Henry had been up to and how Clary was involved, it should help her turn the tables on the viscount and persuade him to keep his distance from her.

Or so she hoped. If not, she had no idea what she would do.

Mr. Armand shuffled his feet and scratched his chin. "About that book, yes. It's been a monumental task sorting out Mr. Charters's files. He practiced for over forty years, you see, and maintained quite a stock of information for his clients—"

"I understand," said Olivia quickly. "You must be eager to be rid of it. I'm here to collect anything my husband left in Mr. Charters's possession." There must be more than the diary. There had to be.

"Ah. . . . You see, Mrs. Townsend . . ." He paused. "I ought not to have sent you the book at all. It was done in error, and if you would be so good as to return it—"

"What?"

The tips of his ears flushed at her exclamation. "Quite right, you're surprised; I apologize profusely. It had fallen from one crate into another, probably whilst being moved, and therefore I didn't immediately comprehend the nature of the information within."

"What is that nature?" For the first time Olivia was devoutly glad she'd left the book hidden at her leased cottage. For a while she had considered bringing it along, in case Mr. Armand offered to help her understand it, but some instinct had made her conceal it beneath her floorboards. She'd expected Clary would be the one seeking it, though, not the solicitor who sent it.

Mr. Armand gave her a placating smile. "I must insist, madam, on having it back."

"No," she said indignantly. "*I* must insist on claiming my husband's property. If he left a debt, I'm prepared to pay it." Her palms were damp. She'd borrowed a large sum of money from Penelope Weston for just this purpose, but she still hoped she wouldn't have to use it. She had absolutely no idea how she'd ever repay her friend.

"It's not about a debt. As soon as I realized the mistake, I wrote to you, requesting its return."

Olivia's jaw firmed. "It contains my husband's handwriting. Do you deny it was his?"

"I see this conversation is upsetting you, as I feared." He held up one hand as she opened her mouth. "I sincerely apologize for my error in sending the book and unsettling you. Mr. Charters kept his clients' information strictly confidential, and he meant that protection to extend beyond the grave. That book was in a box of items that Mr. Charters instructed should be destroyed upon his own death."

The floor seemed to drop from beneath her. "Mr. Armand," she said carefully. "If I had any idea my husband left personal and private belongings with Mr. Charters, I would have claimed them months ago. Those papers belong to *me,* not to Mr. Charters or to you. Please tell me you have them still and can give them to me now."

The solicitor leaned forward. "Madam, you do not understand. The papers were to be kept confidential. Mr. Townsend must have wished it so, or Mr. Charters would not have left such an instruction."

"That is your assumption," she replied. "I promise you, sir, that my husband would not want to keep them from me." Olivia had no idea if it was true or not, but she wasn't about to tell the solicitor that. Henry hadn't been the best husband but neither had he been a terrible one. She *was* certain Henry wouldn't want Clary to intimidate and hurt her, and now this mysterious book, and any other papers that clarified it, might be the only way to stop him.

"Nevertheless, Mr. Charters's instructions were quite clear: everything was to be burned. And it was."

She blinked. "You burned it already?"

He nodded. "And I must ask for the return of that book, so it can also be destroyed."

Olivia stared at him in disbelief. "You can't be serious."

"Mrs. Townsend, I only want to spare you any trouble. Mr. Charters's notes indicated that anything related to that book would be at an end with Mr. Townsend's death, which means it can only cause you upset and renewed grief. I recommend you return it to me and put it from your mind."

No. Not an answer to her prayers but only another mystery, another question that couldn't possibly have a good answer. Stiffly she got to her feet. "I cannot do that, sir." If Henry had been entangled in something so terrible that he wanted all proof destroyed after his death—something Lord Clary may also have been deeply involved in—there was a chance the viscount would speak to Mr. Armand about retrieving that book. And if Clary traced her to Mr. Armand's office . . .

She had to throw the solicitor off. He thought she was a woman easily led and susceptible to emotion, so she might as well ladle it on. She pulled out a handkerchief and bit the inside of her cheek until tears welled up in her eyes. "I think you misunderstand the nature of a woman's grief, Mr. Armand. Far from wishing to forget everything about my husband, I cling to his memory. Anything of his, even those things so mundane you obviously think no one could care about, is more dear to me than ever because it was once his, and he's now lost to me forever." Not only that, it seemed Henry would take his secrets to his grave, and leave her to face the consequences. Henry himself grew less and less dear to her every day, but she would have given almost anything to see his papers that might solve her current problems.

Olivia let some hysteria creep into her voice. "If you ever lose someone so beloved, you'll understand what I feel! My husband's papers belonged to me, and you had no right to destroy them—certainly not peremptorily. I would say the same thing to Mr. Charters, if he'd had the decency to notify me that he had them. I cannot approve of a solicitor who would deprive a widow of her husband's property, and I wonder what Mr. Charters was trying to conceal by burning it!"

Mr. Armand rose as well. "Mrs. Townsend," he said in a voice filled with both condescension and warning, "you are impugning an honorable man. I fear you are overwrought—"

"Perhaps I am," she cried. "I am dreadfully disappointed that my dear husband's last belongings were destroyed without my permission. Good day, Mr. Armand."

She pressed her handkerchief to her mouth and walked out of his office, ignoring the clerk's smirk as she snatched up her cloak and left. The nasty little fellow must have known all along that his employer would give her bad news.

Outside, the bitter wind sliced through her dress. Olivia tugged up the hood and pulled on her gloves. An entire day wasted, and even worse, she didn't know what to do next. She'd read part of Henry's book, but it was infuriatingly mysterious—her hopes were pinned on whatever papers the solicitor had. Surely they must have contained a wealth of information about the money, all that money that Henry noted so carefully. And if that much money had gone through the solicitor's hands, she reasoned, he must know more about it. Well, it seemed Mr. Charters *had* known much more, and now Mr. Armand had burned the evidence. She'd better read the book more closely, since it appeared to be her only source of illumination.

The town was buttoning up for the night. Lamps glowed in windows along the main street, and the smell of roasting meat made her lift her nose more than once. She had purposely taken a small cottage out of town, but now her rumbling stomach and cold hands made her heart sink; she had a long walk ahead of her before she would be savoring her own dinner by a cozy fire. She hunched her shoulders against the wind and started up the road headed north, toward the coast.

She heard the footsteps behind her as she reached the last turn toward her cottage. She caught her breath and listened: it was a heavy tread, a man in boots whose longer stride was gaining on her. It could be anyone hurrying home after a long day, and yet . . . Her heart nearly stopped and her lungs felt crushed as other possibilities streaked through her mind. If Lord Clary had somehow found her, followed her, and discovered her here alone, in this narrow lane at the edge of town . . .

Her hands fisted in the folds of her cloak. *No, no, no.* If she let herself think too much of that, he would win. The man had spent months trying to seduce her, with increasing degrees of coercion and intimidation. If he'd tracked her to Gravesend in the middle of winter, he wouldn't be refused again.

Now her blood was running and her feet sped up as anger flowed freely through her veins. She was so tired of this—a decade of her life had been ruined by men manipulating or forcing her into doing what they wanted her to do, with no thought at all to her wishes. First her father, then Henry's father, blasted Henry himself, that unctuous solicitor, and now the devil incarnate, Lord Clary. Olivia had had enough.

She hated Clary. He hated her, too. If he didn't want under her skirt so badly, he probably would have already engineered some sort of "accident" to dispose of her. For all she knew, he'd finally got over wanting her and now just wanted to get rid of her.

An abandoned building was just ahead. It had

once been a gatehouse, but the tall fences keeping people from the marshes behind it were long gone, and the cottage itself was crumbling into rubble. Just beyond it lay the way to her rented cottage, up the winding path and over the hill. But in the desiccated remnants of the overgrown hedge, the moonlight picked out a familiar and welcome shape: the handle of a shovel.

Her eyes riveted on it. The thick shadows swayed and fluttered with every burst of wind, and if she looked away she might never locate that shovel again. Footsteps still followed behind her, not gaining but not receding, either. Perhaps her pursuer was waiting until they were unquestionably out of sight of the town; once she rounded the gatehouse a sprawling hawthorn hedge would hide her from sight of every window in Gravesend. Not that anyone would be watching, but there would be no hope of help, let alone rescue. This lane was deserted, dark and lonely with a frosty wind blowing in her face. Clary could do what he willed with her and no one would even discover her body before spring.

But that shovel stood there, haphazardly propped against the stone wall. She said a quick prayer it still had a blade and wouldn't fall apart the moment she touched it. Things tended to do that when left out in the open air this near the sea. It was her only hope, though, and she meant to use it in any way possible.

She waited until she was only a few steps away. Thus far she'd moved at a brisk walk but no faster; now she bolted, letting her cloak fly out behind her. Fearful that the shovel would be stuck in a mass of undergrowth, she seized it and yanked, almost stumbling when it came free without protest. She whisked around the corner of the house and flattened herself against the wall, trying to still the loud rasp of her breath.

The footsteps paused. She gripped the handle, her heart pounding viciously and her eyes fixed on the place in the lane where her pursuer must step if he meant to follow her. *Go away,* she silently begged. As much as she wouldn't mind seeing Clary dead, she didn't know if she had the stomach to beat him to death herself.

He spoke. The whining wind blew away his words, scattering them among the clattering of the bare branches, but it was unquestionably a man's voice. His steps crunched closer.

Cold sweat trickled down Olivia's temple. She raised the shovel as one might hold a cricket bat. Her arms shook, and she clenched her jaw to steady herself. *Only one of us can walk away from this,* she reminded herself. If she swung at him and missed, Clary would probably kill her on the spot with this same shovel.

The light faded as a cloud blew across the round face of the moon. She would be harder to see, but so would he. Olivia carefully braced her feet for balance, wishing the man would either prove himself innocent and walk away, or prove himself guilty and come around the damned house. Standing there waiting, poised in terror, was torture.

A step, then another. A tall, shadowy shape appeared around the corner of the house. His hat shielded his face, but there was just enough moonlight to gleam on the barrel of the pistol in his hand.

Olivia sucked in a deep breath and swung with all her might.

He was tall and standing on the path, while she was not as tall and stood in the hollowed shell of the cottage garden. The shovel cracked squarely into his arm with an impact that almost knocked her off her feet. The pistol flew out of his hand and into the darkness. The man cursed and doubled over. Frantically Olivia jerked the shovel back, bringing it up to take another swing. She had to keep him from locating the gun.

"Stop," he cried, flinging up his hands as he collapsed to his knees. "Wait!"

Arms raised, heart racing, Olivia registered the voice just in time to keep herself from slamming the shovel into him again. Not Clary. Not anyone who would hurt her, in fact. "J-Jamie?" she stammered in disbelief.

He tilted back his head as the cloud drifted past the moon and gave her enough light to see his face beneath the brim of his hat. "Good evening, Livie," said James Weston with a crooked smile. "Lovely to see you again."

Chapter 5

Not for the first time, James Weston wished he could wind back the years and beat some sense into his younger self.

Ten years ago none of this would have happened. Olivia would have been happy to see him. She wouldn't have kept dangerous secrets and she wouldn't have run off alone on some mad, risky scheme. Ten years ago she would have come to him before her circumstances grew dire, and asked for help because she trusted him.

Of course, ten years ago she *had* done that—and he failed her. Even worse, it seemed she was still suffering the consequences of that failure. Jamie had suspected that all along, but not until tonight had he realized just how much she was suffering. He didn't blame her for attacking him with a shovel.

Olivia dropped it as if the handle scalded her hands. "What are you doing here?"

Jamie climbed back to his feet. "Looking for you," he said, shaking his arm. It was tingling and weak from the elbow down, and he could barely feel his fingers.

Her breathing wheezed with panic. "How did you find me?" She retreated into the deepest shadows, her face stark white. "Who knows where I am?"

That fear nicked him where it hurt. He knew whom she feared. His sister Penelope had told him an incredible story about Viscount Clary pursuing Olivia for unknown, but unmistakably sinister, purposes, and for once she hadn't exaggerated. Olivia was terrified, even all the way out here in lonely Gravesend. And that meant Jamie had failed her yet again, because Penelope also told him that Olivia tried to see him before she fled London. She was out here alone, reduced to defending herself with a shovel, because he hadn't been there when she needed him.

"No one," he said in reply to her question. "Penelope gave me a few clues, and I made some guesses."

"And that was enough for you to find me." She drew a rough breath. "I must have made a mistake somewhere . . ."

"You're overlooking the chance I was fiendishly clever," he said mildly.

As brief as a flash of lightning, a reluctant smile crossed her face. Some of the tension drained from her rigid figure. "My mistake."

He gave a nod. "I didn't think you were hiding from me."

"No," she murmured. "Did I hurt you?"

Jamie peeled off his glove and held up his hand to the moonlight, flexing his still-numb fingers. "My penmanship won't be the same for a while."

"I'm sorry."

"So am I." He winced as he pulled the glove back on. "You have a strong swing, by the by. Where did the pistol go?"

Her eyes widened. "Oh! I don't know. Over there, perhaps." She pointed across the road.

"Since I presume you were merely alarmed, and I'm not the person you're hoping to kill, we'd better find it." He stepped into the dried grass that rustled along the opposite shoulder of the lane and paced back and forth, his eyes sweeping the dark ground.

"If you hadn't followed me like a murderer, with gun in hand, I wouldn't have hit you." Olivia joined him as he waded into the growth.

"I only drew it on the chance there was something—or someone—else out here giving you fright." A glint of metal caught his eye, and he bent down to retrieve his pistol. "I did call your name, hoping to set you at ease."

"I didn't hear it over the wind."

Jamie didn't doubt that. The wind had been picking up since he spotted Olivia, hurrying through town with her hood pulled over her face. It whistled through the barren trees and made the area seem even more desolate and isolated than it was. "No matter. You ought to defend yourself against anyone who follows you in the dark." He checked the pistol and slid it back into his pocket. "Aren't you going to invite me in for a cup of tea?" It was rude, but he had no intention of letting her brush him aside.

Olivia hesitated, then sighed. "Of course."

He fell in step beside her and they walked in silence. The path climbed, and in the distance he could hear the sea. When they crested the hill, revealing a humble little cottage near the edge of the marsh, the wind gusted strong enough to make Olivia stagger. Jamie made a motion toward her, but she put her head down and burrowed into her cloak.

The closer they got to the stone cottage, the less he liked it. It sat near the edge of a low cliff overlooking the ocean—or really the mouth of the Thames, where the broad open water of the estuary narrowed into the familiar river that rushed through London, some thirty miles away. A rambling hedge and a few scrubby trees served to break the wind, but the cottage itself stood alone, commanding a good view of the river.

His steps slowed as they reached it. Olivia fumbled in her pocket, but Jamie raised one hand to stop her. "It's quite lonely out here."

"I know." She pulled out the latchkey.

"Are you sure it's safe?" The cottage was isolated and difficult to find, but once located, there was no help within sight.

She gave a bitter huff of laughter. "Not at all, but it's no worse than anywhere else, I suppose." She motioned at the door. "I leave a scrap of wool in the door. If it's still there when I return, I assume all is well."

There was a bit of blue cloth peeking out at the latch. Jamie was not reassured. "Then you don't object if I have a look around, in case someone decided to use a window instead of the door?"

She opened her mouth, then simply shook her head. Jamie took the key and let himself in, his pistol in hand. It took only a few minutes to visit every room in the tiny house; there was one on the ground floor and another above it, up a narrow stair that was almost a ladder. Every window was either wedged shut or boarded over, and there was no place anyone could be concealed, lying in wait, not even under the bed. That explained why she wasn't more concerned.

When he returned to the main room, Olivia had stirred up the banked fire and lit a pair of lamps. "How did you get this place?" he asked.

"It's a fisherman's cottage." She took the kettle to the water barrel in the corner and filled it. "He was lost at sea several weeks ago. His widow hasn't given up hope yet and doesn't wish to sell the cottage, but she moved her family into town. It was too lonely, I expect, and too hard to live here without him." She hung the kettle on the hook over the reviving fire. "Fortunately for me, she was happy to let it for a few weeks."

Olivia still wore her cloak, and Jamie felt no interest in removing his coat, either. It was quite cold in the cottage, and he noticed the stock of wood was low. "I'll get some more wood. We may need more than one cup of tea."

Outside he scanned the terrain. Split wood was piled not far from the cottage, but he walked past it to the edge of the cliff and peered over. Ten or twelve feet below, a narrow path unfurled through a salt marsh, the tidal grasses rising and falling like a wave in the relentless wind. The sea was a distant black expanse, broken only by the crests of waves catching the moonlight. At high tide, Jamie wouldn't be surprised if shallow boats could glide right up the edge of the cliff. He had a feeling this cottage had been used for more than fishing.

He loaded his arms with wood. It bothered him that Olivia had come all the way out here. She might feel safe because of the isolation, but if Lord Clary discovered her, he could easily accomplish whatever ill will he wished. Jamie resolved never to leave her here alone. He let himself back in and stacked the wood just inside the door.

"Would you like some dinner?" Olivia had set out two cups for tea, and now she uncovered a plate to show some slices of meat pie. "Humble fare but it smells good," she added with a tentative smile.

In the light of the reviving fire, he finally got a good look at her. It had been nearly two months since he'd had the opportunity to do so. Olivia had made a point of hiding any upset or distress, even when Abigail and Penelope reported in hushed tones that they thought her situation was growing strained. But there was no concealing how pale and drawn her face had become, and the sight sent a bolt of worry through him.

"Tea will be enough for me, thank you," he said. He'd had a hearty meal at the inn before heading out to find her, and if anyone needed an extra slice of meat pie, it was Olivia. "But I insist you have your dinner."

Her face eased gratefully. She put a slice of the pie on a plate and set it on the grate to warm, while the kettle began to steam. She busied herself with preparing the tea as Jamie hung up his coat by her cloak. Then he sat down and watched her, trying to mask both his fascination and his guilt.

It had been a long time since he and Olivia were alone together. For the first few years after her marriage that was very much his preference; the sight of her had been an arrow lodged in his heart, a nagging wound that should have been fatal but somehow wasn't, and he had avoided seeing her as much as possible. Eventually circumstances brought her back into his orbit, even though his sense of loss had only dulled. Deep in his heart, Jamie suspected Olivia would always have some hold over him. He had known her almost all his life, and loved her for nearly as long. When they met again, after she had been married four or five years, he couldn't help wondering if the same spark of affection might still burn in her breast.

He was soon set to rights on that score. On every occasion when they met and were forced into any sort of proximity—standing beside each other at a party, or waiting outside a shop for one of his sisters—Olivia kept the conversation firmly fixed on polite but mundane topics. Nothing of any intimacy was ever permitted. They might have been any pair of near-strangers, only passingly acquainted, and not two people who had once meant the world to each other.

That left him with nothing but a bitter burden of guilt. If he had been more responsible as a young man, less convinced of his ability to manipulate everything to his liking, Olivia never would have married Henry Townsend, who then never would have brought Lord Clary into her world.

The mere fact that those two men had been friends should have put Jamie on alert, once Henry died. He knew damned well that Clary was someone to avoid. But Olivia had rebuffed every tentative overture he'd ever made in the last decade, and kept her problems with Clary hidden not just from him but from his sisters as well. She hadn't wanted his help—and why should she, when she had good reason to doubt him? The fact that she had gone looking for him before she fled London, though, indicated something had changed—for the worse.

That thought made him get up and fetch his pistol from his coat pocket. "I realize the shovel was chosen on a moment's inspiration, but if you don't want to be followed, you really ought to arm yourself properly." He laid the pistol on the table as she poured tea into the mugs. "You should keep this."

Olivia shuddered, keeping her eyes away from the gun. "I don't want it."

"It's more effective than a shovel."

"Do you wish you had a hole in your chest right now?" She set a bowl of sugar in front of him. "I've no milk."

Jamie waved it aside. "I'm rather relieved you didn't have a pistol earlier, but if you must defend yourself, you shouldn't leave it up to chance encounters with shovels. Do you know how to shoot?"

"Yes." She sighed. "Mostly."

"Mostly?" The sugar bowl was nearly empty. He took a tiny spoonful.

"I know how to load a gun and pull the trigger. My aim is terrible, though, and the report tends to knock me over. In the event I managed to get off a shot, I'd probably miss and wind up flat on my back, coughing on gunpowder and completely helpless."

He darted a quick glance at her. "Then you don't really know how to shoot. We'll work on that."

"That won't draw attention to me at all," she said under her breath.

"Hmm." Jamie glanced up through his eyelashes as he stirred the sugar into his scalding tea. "And we don't want that . . ." His unspoken question hung in the air like smoke from the lamp: *Why not?*

Olivia fidgeted, looking unhappy. "You must know I don't want that," she finally said in a low voice. "Not now."

"Care to tell me why?"

She arched one brow. "Don't you know? If you managed to find me and follow me, I thought you'd know everything else as well."

He grinned at her tart tone. He did know quite a bit, possibly more than Olivia herself, but he wanted her to tell him—to trust him. This time, he wasn't going to let her down. This time, he wasn't leaving her until Lord Clary was in prison and every nasty, dirty secret of Henry's had been exposed and burned, and Olivia lost that worn, tense expression. And if she could be persuaded to give him another chance, he wasn't going to let her go, either. "Everything? How Penelope would laugh at that idea. Even I wouldn't dare claim to know *everything*."

Her lips parted, and for a moment he thought she would burst out laughing. Then the surprise faded from her face, and she seemed to subside in her chair. "How is Penelope?"

Jamie recognized the dodge, but decided to allow it for the moment. "Quite well, the last I saw her."

"Is . . . is she happy? With Lord Atherton, I mean. I—I know she was pressured into marrying him because she tried to help me, and I've been racked by guilt ever since . . ."

Ah, right. Penelope had warned him Olivia would probably be worried. A few weeks ago she had inadvertently rescued Olivia from an apparent assignation with Lord Clary, and in revenge, Clary had spread ugly rumors about Penelope that culminated in her hasty marriage to Lord Atherton. Jamie was both appalled by and grateful for his sister's fearless devotion and loyalty to her friend.

Penelope also admitted that she might have given Olivia the impression that she was not overly fond of Atherton. Jamie knew the exact opposite was true, but Olivia had undoubtedly been too caught up in her own worries to realize it. He leaned forward, happy that he could dispel one of Olivia's fears entirely. "Penelope is as happy as I've ever seen her, married to the man she loves. When I left them, Atherton had his arms around her and she looked victorious over the world."

Olivia's eyes went wide. "What? The man she loves—no, she despised him only a month ago!"

Jamie clicked his tongue sadly. "Am I the only one who pays attention? The more vigorously Penelope denies something, the truer it generally is. I daresay she said she hated him, and may have even tried to hate him, but make no mistake: if Penelope hadn't wanted Atherton, nothing on earth could have brought about that marriage. My sister would run away with pirates first."

For the first time there was no trace of anxiety in Olivia. She looked nonplussed. "Well! I hope you're right . . ."

"Hope!" Jamie snorted. "As if I don't know my own sister. Let me guess. Pen told you she despised—*loathed*—Atherton, in great detail and frequency. But somehow she always seemed to be running into him and having yet another interaction she could relate in scathing tones. We both know she would hide behind statues and climb out of windows to avoid someone she actually despised so heartily."

Olivia's lips twitched as if she were fighting off a smile. "But Lord Atherton—does he care for her?"

"I'd say he's mad for her—as any man would have to be, to marry Penelope." Olivia gasped indignantly, and Jamie laughed. "I mean it in the best possible way. Atherton is devoted to her. He jumped into the Thames and risked his life to save her when Lord Clary pushed her overboard."

The name seemed to freeze Olivia in place. The dawning smile slid from her lips, and the light in her eyes turned into stunned horror.

"Lord Stratford, Atherton's father, was very insistent they sail with him on his yacht from London to Richmond, but not until they were under way did Penelope and Atherton discover Lord Clary lying in wait for her belowdecks." He paused, but Olivia sat like a statue, hollow-eyed and still. "He wanted to know where you were, Livie. When she wouldn't tell him, Clary pushed her over the side of the boat."

"Dear heavens—he could have killed her." Her body hunched convulsively, as if she would be ill, and she seemed to age before his eyes.

"He tried," Jamie agreed bluntly. Olivia flinched, but he didn't—couldn't—relent. If she didn't know how truly dangerous that man was, she needed to. "And he very nearly succeeded. The Thames is freezing at this time of year. If Atherton hadn't spent his youth swimming back and forth across the river . . ." He lifted one shoulder. "Needless to say, Atherton and Penelope want Clary's head on a pike."

"Would that they could get it!" she said in a sudden burst of animation. "I never thought—"

"That he was so determined?" Jamie shook his head impatiently. "I think you did. Why else are you out in Gravesend, trying not to call attention to yourself, when no one in London knows where you are? Help me, Olivia. Clary tried to kill my sister. He's wanted in London for that, as well as on suspicion of causing the death of Lord Stratford." Olivia's eyes widened. "The shock of seeing his son and heir leap into the Thames, apparently to his death, was too much for the earl. He dropped dead, or so Lord Clary told people. Atherton suspects his father was in league with Clary, which puts him in position to expose Clary. But it appears you know even more about Clary's activities, and Atherton—or should I say, the new Lord Stratford—told me to implore you to help him. And since I daresay it wouldn't upset you one whit to see Clary rotting in prison or swinging from a rope, I sincerely hope you'll trust me and tell me what the devil he's holding over your head."

Chapter 6

Before he left London, Jamie had tried to answer three vital questions.

The first one involved Henry Townsend. Years ago, right after Olivia married him, Jamie had inquired just enough to satisfy himself that Olivia would be taken care of. He made sure the man had a comfortable income and no serious stains on his character, and then he quit looking. That had been his own fault, his inability—unwillingness—to think too deeply about her with another man.

This time he wanted to know everything, and there turned out to be a lot to know. Far from being the upstanding gentleman Jamie had presumed, Townsend had run with a fast crowd, which included the notorious Lord Clary. Clary came from a famous and illustrious family, the son of an admiral and the brother of a decorated commodore. He married the daughter of a duke and moved through the very best society with a commanding arrogance that earned him a great deal of deference but very few friends . . . except for Henry Townsend. And ever since Henry died, Lord Clary had been very attentive to his widow.

That had led into Jamie's second question. What could Clary's interest in Olivia be? He didn't doubt the obvious one; Olivia was a beautiful woman, even lovelier than she'd been as a girl. Despite his arrogance, Clary was reputed to be persuasive and charming when he wished to be, and many women thought him quite handsome. Their descriptions put Jamie in mind of a hawk: sleekly magnificent, powerful and ruthless. But somehow he didn't think Olivia would have begged Penelope for two hundred pounds and fled London if Clary was merely trying to seduce her.

The third question, though, had yielded the most sobering information. He knew Olivia had given up her house in the fashionable part of town after Henry's death; to make the most of her widow's portion, he assumed. But it turned out Olivia had almost no income at all. The annuity that should have kept her in comfort had been quietly canceled soon after the elder Mr. Townsend died, and Henry lost the capital at the races. Henry lost quite a lot at the races, Jamie learned, although he also spent freely on clothing and theater boxes and kept a very fine table. By Jamie's rough math, Henry had probably spent his entire inherited fortune in the course of three or four years—and yet continued to live in the same high style for two more years without accruing much debt. That alone was suspicious. When added to the mystery about Clary, it made a far darker picture. Whether Henry was coldhearted or simply feckless, Jamie couldn't tell, but there was no question that the man had left his wife penniless and at the mercy of a dangerous man.

The greater question was why. Thanks to Atherton, Jamie thought he knew the answer, but he would need Olivia's help to prove it.

"Are you ready to talk about Clary?" he asked gently.

She shoved back her chair and leapt to her feet, bending over the fireplace grate to check the warming slice of pie. She brought it back to the table and took her time arranging her cutlery and refilling both mugs of tea, even though his was almost untouched. "I don't suppose I can persuade you that this is not your problem and you have no obligation to get involved," she said at last.

"Rubbish." He leaned toward her. "He tried to kill my sister. Do you honestly believe I'd walk away and let him try the same to you?"

She flinched again at the mention of Clary's attempt on Penelope's life. James didn't care. He was relieved beyond measure that his sister and her husband were both alive and well, but he felt, deep in his bones, that Clary wouldn't leave things to chance if he got his hands on Olivia again. Pushing Penelope overboard had probably been an impulse when she refused to answer his questions. Olivia, though . . . Whatever the man wanted from her, he was willing to risk everything to get it.

"You once trusted me," he went on. "I came for no other reason than to help you, as one friend to another."

"I know." She paused as if struggling for words. "I would never forgive myself if anything happened to you because you tried to help me, though."

"Then you know how I feel," he replied. "Should I step back and let you bear all the risk? Could I forgive myself if I did nothing and Clary did you a great harm? No. Besides . . ." He winked, trying to lessen the tension. "Atherton told me things that may help us put the noose around Clary's neck. Don't forget that: I'm not just offering my manly brawn but also useful intelligence."

Slowly she smiled. As it always had, it made him want to smile back. There was something about Olivia's face that changed when she smiled; it was the spark of humor in her eyes, or perhaps the endearing little quirk to the left corner of her mouth, or even the way her chin went down a bit. Whatever it was, it had entranced him for nearly twenty years, and still did. "How could I resist such an offer?"

"Of course you can't," he agreed with a straight face. "No one could."

She ducked her head and poked her dinner with her fork, but the smile lingered. "What can I tell you? You may know more than I do."

"What does Clary want from you?"

"I don't know," she said. Jamie cocked one brow and she flushed. "Well—yes, I thought I knew what he wanted, originally. After Henry died, Lord Clary was almost kind. He offered to help sort out Henry's affairs, see that debts were paid, and so on. I had Mr. Brewster—Henry's London solicitor—so I assured Lord Clary that I was content to leave things in Mr. Brewster's competent hands."

She put down her fork and folded her hands in her lap. "Then his lordship offered me other things: his box at the theater, his carriage if I ever needed one." She hesitated. "When he wishes to be, Clary can be almost charming, in a rather overbearing way. But eventually he must have got tired of his offers being refused. He called on me one day and made a blunt proposition: he wanted me to be his mistress. He offered a house in St. John's Wood, a staff of servants, credit at the finest shops . . ."

Jamie eyed his pistol and somehow kept his mouth shut. How could Olivia not have told someone Clary was harassing her?

"I refused as politely as I could." Her eyes grew stormy. "He didn't believe it. How could anyone in my position not want him? I suspect Clary is rarely denied anything he wants, and he thought I was being coy, or teasing, and he promised me anything on earth my heart desired if only I could accept him . . . but he did it in such a way that was almost threatening. I had never before been frightened of him but that day I was, and he saw it. From then on I tried to avoid him, but he would turn up from time to time and catch me off guard. He never asked me to be his mistress again—"

Thank God, thought Jamie grimly.

"—instead he did worse. He told me Henry had owed him a great deal of money, and since we hadn't been able to reach an *amiable solution*"—she almost spat out the words—"he had no choice but to ask for it back. Of course I didn't have the sum he named, but he didn't believe me. After I refused all his offers of money, he must have thought I had a private fund hidden somewhere."

Or he wanted to terrify you even more. "Did he show you proof of Henry's debt?"

She gave a scornful laugh. "Of course not! I asked him to stop calling on me and conduct any business through Mr. Brewster. He said he would if I gave him Henry's things." She paused and tilted her head to look at him for the first time since he'd asked what Clary wanted from her. "Now why would Lord Clary want Henry's papers? Henry hardly kept any papers. Mr. Brewster paid all the bills. Henry had little correspondence; he hadn't the patience for sitting at a desk writing letters. I never saw him read anything other than the racing report or a sporting newspaper."

Clever fellow. Jamie had an idea what Henry had been up to, and scads of letters would have been dangerous.

"Lord Clary didn't believe me any more about that than he did about the rest." She returned her gaze to her untouched plate of dinner. "I still don't know what he wants, but I fear he'll hound me until I'm dead."

"Penelope said she interrupted a confrontation between you and Lord Clary in London." He phrased it carefully and spoke gently, but Olivia flinched.

"Yes." She sounded choked. "It was more of an—an assignation. Lord Clary grew more and more insistent that he'd sue me for the debt and I'd be thrown in prison. He kept insinuating I had something valuable, which he obviously felt some claim on, but I don't! Finally I agreed to meet him one evening to explain once and for all, but he clearly thought I was weakening . . ." A lock of hair fell forward to hide her face as she bowed her head. "The truth is . . . I was. I thought it might pacify him and show him I was nothing to him, or at least nothing he really wanted. But then . . . Penelope opened the door. And like a coward I fled, so fast I didn't realize until later that she had not followed. Clary hadn't *allowed* her to follow. I abandoned her to his fury, and—"

He held up one hand to cut her off. "Penelope does not blame you."

Olivia closed her eyes and looked physically ill for a moment. "Only because Lord Atherton was there to save her."

"We all need someone to save us at times," he said gently.

Hesitantly, almost warily, she raised her eyes. Jamie could only return her questioning look with one of quiet confidence and hope she believed him.

"What did Clary do that sent you fleeing to Kent?" he asked.

Olivia's deep blue gaze didn't waver from his. "Nothing directly. Unexpectedly, I received a very odd package from a solicitor in Gravesend, Mr. Armand. He wrote that he'd recently acquired the practice of another solicitor, now deceased, and in the process of sorting old files, he had discovered a diary belonging to Henry, which he enclosed. I was very startled, because I'd never heard Henry mention another solicitor. Mr. Brewster had been employed by Henry's father, and he handled everything I knew of. The Townsends came from Kent, though, so it was possible this other solicitor, Mr. Charters, handled their business in the country.

"But the diary was very . . . odd. Not only was it unlike Henry to keep a diary at all, it didn't contain the usual things a gentleman would record. Mr. Brewster had taken a holiday to his cottage outside London, but I was so curious I went to see him there. He professed not to know anything about it, though I'm not certain he was truthful." Her mouth thinned. "I missed Penelope's wedding because of that, and I learned nothing."

"Do you still have the diary?"

She nodded. "When Mr. Brewster told me nothing, I decided I should come see Mr. Armand, who would be able to tell me more. At the least, I could reclaim any of Henry's property and perhaps learn something from it. And . . . I confess I was very eager to escape Lord Clary's attention for a while." Her voice hardened. "But the vile solicitor not only told me he'd burned everything, he asked me to return the diary! He sent it in error, he claimed." She scowled. "Mr. Charters left detailed instructions for what to do with his clients' papers after his death, and Henry had agreed everything should be destroyed. He was never in the habit of explaining his intentions to me, but I can't believe he meant to leave me to Lord Clary's mercy, without a farthing to my name!"

Jamie stretched out his legs. He had a feeling Henry Townsend hadn't spared much thought at all for Olivia's situation. He'd spent a fortnight ruthlessly mining every source of gossip, rumor, and illicit knowledge he could tap. His sister Penelope, and especially her husband, had given him a good starting point, and everything he'd heard since then had only confirmed it. Nothing Olivia said tonight contradicted his research, either.

What he had to tell her was not going to improve her opinion of her late husband, and as of yet he wasn't entirely sure how it would help rid her of Clary. The only thing he was truly certain of was that he and Olivia could solve it together.

"It's a good thing you confided in Penelope as much as you did," he said. "It was another rare stroke of luck that she married Stratford's son. When the earl died Atherton suddenly became privy to all his father's secrets, and unlike Henry, the Earl of Stratford kept papers. Atherton is only beginning to sort them out, but it's clear to him so far that Clary was deeply involved in helping his father acquire a great deal of artwork by dubious means. Given Clary's interest in you after Henry's death, I suspect your late husband was part of the operation as well."

Olivia's face scrunched up in confusion. "What operation?"

Jamie smiled ruefully. "Henry was a smuggler."

Chapter 7

Olivia thought she'd heard wrong. "What?" she said again, stupidly. She shook her head before he could explain. "No, Henry barely left London. He couldn't be smuggling . . ."

"And when he did leave town, he came home to Kent, didn't he?" Jamie nodded. "To visit the family home, pay his respects to old friends . . . perhaps check on the network of people who brought his particular cargo into England."

Her heart started to pound. That diary, full of entries that looked like payments. A secret solicitor in Kent, with orders to burn everything. The generous income that inexplicably vanished at Henry's death. "What do you mean?" she whispered.

Jamie leaned back in his chair. The light of the lamp glinted off his dark hair, tousled by the wind into a wildly attractive mess of waves. An unexpected flood of longing swamped her as he tilted his head and gave her a wry smile. "I don't actually know anything for certain. Some of this is purely guessing. But it fits together, and I daresay Atherton will be able to answer more questions as he catalogs his father's collection."

"Tell me your guesses," she said.

His eyes met hers, filled with sympathy. "It's not very flattering to the late Mr. Townsend."

"It couldn't be worse than what I've already contemplated," she replied honestly. Her worst guess had been blackmail. Henry had kept company with a very fast set, and he must have known some of their secrets.

Jamie's mouth quirked. "No doubt." He nodded toward her untouched dinner. "Don't let it get cold." Surprised, Olivia looked at her food, then picked up her fork. The prospect of some answers, or at least information, revived her appetite.

Jamie was quiet for a moment, his gaze distant as if he were sorting his thoughts. "Very well. I'll start with Lord Stratford, because this is the part I heard first from Penelope and Atherton. Stratford was a well-known patron of the arts. He had an eye for promising artists, and his estate at Stratford Court is filled with exceptional pictures and sculpture. Atherton said the earl also had a private gallery, so private no one save Stratford himself was permitted to view it. Atherton saw it a few times as a boy, before his father decided his taste for art wasn't refined enough, but now of course he's master of Stratford Court and able to visit it at will. As fine as the collection around the house is, it's nothing to the works in the private gallery. One of Atherton's sisters married an artist, so he's been able to confirm that several pictures are extremely valuable, yet have no provenance. There are no bills of sale in the earl's records, nothing to indicate where they came from, which is odd for art. Normally there would be correspondence with a dealer or prior owner or even the artist himself. It's as if the pictures just appeared at Stratford Court.

"The other thing of interest Atherton told me was about a small cave, right on the river near his estate in Richmond. When Clary tried to kill my sister and Atherton jumped in after her, they made it to shore and took shelter in this cave. In the light of day, Atherton found crates suitable for holding paintings. The cave is on a piece of property the old earl acquired years ago, yet never cleared, sold, or even visited. It was let go back to wilderness, and Atherton thinks it might have been to provide cover to this cave. Any paintings could be sent by ship right into Richmond, deposited in the cave, and then retrieved by the earl or a loyal servant at a more convenient moment. No one would remark a small boat crossing the river, after all, and it's a short enough journey it could be made at night."

"But Henry didn't know Lord Stratford," Olivia pointed out. "Viscount Clary was one of his most elegant friends; I'm sure I would recall an earl."

Jamie tapped his temple. "Right you are. But Clary knew both of them—and before he pushed Penelope off the yacht, Clary said you had something he wanted, and what's more, Stratford wanted it, too. I think Clary was the conduit between the smuggler—Henry—and the buyers—such as the Earl of Stratford."

She still had trouble believing it. "Perhaps... But how did Henry get these smuggled items? How did he know what to smuggle in the first place?

He never showed any interest in art." Henry had the usual gentleman's education, which meant he'd spent a brief time abroad as a young man, but if it had made an impression, Olivia hadn't seen evidence of it. Her husband's interests had been principally ones of pleasure and comfort; he kept a cellar of fine wines and expected her to host a good table. He paid more attention to the horse races than to anything in politics or news or literature, although he was always well turned-out sartorially. Often Olivia had retreated to her room with a good book while Henry went to Vauxhall or the theater.

"This is pure conjecture, and may be utterly wrong," Jamie warned. "But Lord Clary's brother is a decorated navy commodore, and when the war ended he was assigned to Calais. The smuggling trade was still in full roar, and if an English commander of the port could be persuaded to look the other way while some contraband was loaded onto a British ship bound for England . . ." He shrugged. "An easy trip to Gravesend, which holds more than her fair share of smugglers. Once unloaded in Kent, items could be discreetly sent all over England."

"But what is this contraband?" she asked again. "That's a plausible theory for how things would get to England. Where did they come from?"

"Paris, most likely. Bonaparte's great museum, filled with the treasures of every state he conquered. Wellington ordered the plundered artwork returned, but hundreds of pieces had already gone missing by the time he made that decree. No doubt several collectors in England gnashed their teeth when he did that, and would happily seize any opportunity to get their hands on some of that art."

Olivia shook her head numbly. "You're describing a vast network of thieves and smugglers and liars. I never thought Henry was a man of unimpeachable morals, but this . . . I cannot believe it."

"I could be wrong, of course," said Jamie easily, which only convinced Olivia that he knew far more than he was telling her, and with more certainty.

"Even if I could prove any of that, what would it get me? Clary is still well-connected. It would be my word against his, and all his family's. And if you're correct that British citizens—wealthy and influential citizens—are benefiting from this smuggling, that only makes it harder to believe anything will happen. Lord Atherton might be willing to expose his father's role, but I doubt other men will be so inclined. They'll call me a wicked liar."

For a moment Jamie didn't reply. "To be quite honest," he finally said, almost cautiously, "I don't give a damn about them, whoever they may be or however many of them there are. My goals are simple: to see Clary in prison, and to free you from all remnants of Henry's scheme. Any other participants can go hang, in my opinion, or scuttle into the darkness and stay there with their stolen pictures."

She gave a despairing laugh. "Simple! I wish I shared that view."

With a sudden motion Jamie shot to his feet, sending his chair flying over backward. He braced his arms on the table right in front of her, pinning her in place with a fierce look. "Don't doubt me," he commanded. "Whatever it takes, I *will* see that man punished for what he did to you, and I swear that you will be free of this mess. If only—" He stopped abruptly, and his arms flexed as if he would toss the table aside and seize *her.* "We'll solve this, Livie," he said in a calmer voice. "I give you my word."

Wide-eyed, she managed to nod.

Jamie watched her closely for a moment, then retrieved his chair and sat back down. "You said the solicitor sent you a book. Do you have it with you?"

"I—yes."

"Shall we have a look and see if we can puzzle out anything, with this new theory in mind?"

Her heart was still thudding from his sudden intensity and nearness. Olivia slid off her chair, trying to recapture some of the distance between them, although she had a feeling things would never be the same. He'd caught her off guard and now she couldn't erase the sight of him looming over her, his hazel eyes glittering with passion, his arms very nearly embracing her. It was the closest she'd been to him in years.

She led the way to a corner of the room where a rough cabinet held dishes and linens. "I found this by accident," she said, kneeling beside the cabinet. She put her finger into a knot in one of the floorboards and lifted. It only came up an inch, but then she slid it straight out, revealing a narrow hollow in the stone beneath the house. There lay the little book Mr. Armand had sent her. She took it out and replaced the loose board.

Jamie put out his hand to help her up, but Olivia climbed to her feet without it, pretending she hadn't seen the gesture. As it was he stood much too close to her, and she thrust the book at him. "It's a ledger," she said. "Even I can see that much, but I couldn't make any sense of it."

He flipped it open. "I don't suppose Clary's name is in it."

"No." Her voice came out in a squeak. He hadn't stepped away, and she was trapped between his body and the cabinet behind her. His attention was focused on the book, but Olivia's every nerve seemed tense and alert to him. Helplessly she stared at his hands as he turned the pages. His beautiful hands that had once held her so tenderly and passionately. Out of the blue she remembered that he was adept with each; as a lad he had amused her and his sisters by writing silly messages with one hand, and equally ridiculous replies with the other. Now he absently flexed one hand every few minutes, still shaking off the effects of being hit by a shovel—wielded by her.

With some effort she tore her eyes away. Her private vow not to touch him again had been a hard one to make, but a necessary one. Even a simple touch, purely out of courtesy or friendship, would be a searing reminder that he had once been so much more than her friend.

"I believe this is going to be a godsend," Jamie murmured, startling her. While she had been trying to hide how much he affected her still, he'd been reading the diary, trying to solve her problem.

"Really?" Olivia mustered a smile. "I hope so. My luck is sure to turn soon." Too late, she winced at the words. Henry used to say that, with great confidence, and he'd been spectacularly wrong.

Jamie just grinned. "I'm staying here tonight."

She jerked backward in alarm. "What?"

"No, no," he said quickly. "Not . . . that. I should have asked. I meant to say, you shouldn't be here alone. If Clary, or anyone else, came along and discovered you, there's no one nearby to come to your aid."

"I hoped I wouldn't be here long enough for him to find me . . ." But Jamie had. He was clever and resourceful and he knew her well, but Clary was ruthless and determined. If Jamie could find her, Clary could as well. Suddenly she felt every whistling draft in the isolated cottage, and the enormity of her task loomed over her.

"Let's hope not," Jamie said, "but just in case, I would feel better if you let me sleep by the fire."

By the fire. Of course. Color flooded her face as she realized her mind had immediately jumped to the thought of sharing the only bed with him. Of course he didn't mean that. "Very well."

There was a pallet upstairs, rolled up under the eaves. Jamie carried it downstairs and laid it near the wide hearth. Olivia tidied up the remains of her dinner as Jamie organized the room to his liking. He barred the shutters and door, then pushed the table so it stood squarely between the pallet and the door. He checked his pistol and put it at the ready. Olivia fetched as many blankets and pillows as she could spare and made up the bed on the floor. She gave it a rueful glance. The pallet was surely meant for the children of the house, and it looked ludicrously small for someone of Jamie's height. "I fear it's not going to be comfortable," she said in apology.

"Out of the wind and near the fire: that's comfort in my book." He had brought one of the chairs near the fire. "Thank you, Livie."

She closed her eyes. After she'd disappeared without a trace, putting his sister in danger, then assaulted him with a shovel when he came after her—to help her—Jamie thanked her for letting him sleep on her floor.

"It's late," he added gently. "You should go to bed."

She hesitated, then nodded. It had been a long day and she was suddenly exhausted. For weeks now she had felt as if a dark cloud hovered menacingly above her, creeping closer and closer until she could barely breathe from fear of being choked by it. In the course of the last few hours, though, it had receded somewhat, driven back by Jamie's forceful confidence. He'd made her laugh. He'd eased her worries about Penelope. And now he had sworn to help extricate her from Henry's tangled affairs, whatever they might be, and sweep away that dark cloud forever. It was almost too much to comprehend in one day. Besides, she'd already read Henry's diary and made little sense of it. Perhaps it was best for Jamie to view it uninfluenced by her frustration. "I will. Good night."

She went upstairs and readied herself for bed. When she had blown out her lamp and lay in the darkness, listening to the now-familiar wind howling mournfully past the eaves, she could hear something else. His footsteps below. A soft thud, then another; his boots coming off.

Unbidden her brain called up memories of Jamie pulling off his coat, his waistcoat, his shirt and trousers. But her memories were of the stripling young man, still lean and lanky, disrobing in the hazy sunlight of a summer afternoon. Jamie of today had filled out, broad-shouldered and strong. Against all her wishes, her mind dwelled on what he would look like now, without his shirt on. How he might look at this very moment, stretched out on the pallet before the hearth, the firelight painting his skin gold. How different her life would have been if only . . .

Olivia pulled the blankets over her head to muffle any more provocative sounds—and thoughts—and somehow managed to fall asleep.

When she awoke after a surprisingly deep slumber, the sun was slanting through the tiny windows under the low roof. Something made her lie still, hardly breathing. A thud sounded faintly up the stairs, the front door opening or closing, and it all came back to her. Jamie was here.

Olivia exhaled. She was glad of it, really she was. It was nerve-racking to be alone, always worried that Clary would walk around the corner at any moment with his terrifying smile and menacing air. Jamie's presence also wound her nerves tight, but for different reasons. She had nothing to fear from him. And while he couldn't prevent Clary from finding her, his company gave her courage that she could survive such an encounter.

When she went downstairs, dressed and composed, he looked up with a grin. "Good morning."

She had to smile. He crouched before the fire, newly built up, angling bread over the flames with a toasting fork. Gratefully she came to the edge of the hearth—it was cold enough to see her breath upstairs—and inspected his cooking. "Bread with cheese?"

"No ordinary bread with cheese." He pulled the fork from the fire and shoveled the bread onto a plate. "Taste it, but beware: the cheese is hot."

Gingerly Olivia took a tiny bite. The cheese, crowned by crispy brown bubbles, had melted into the toasted bread. "It's delicious," she mumbled, taking another bite.

"I know." Jamie took the second piece of bread from the fire. "When I was a sad and lonely university student, far from my mother's table, my mates and I would roast anything over the fire when we were hungry. Apples and pears were best. Bread was also good, but the day we put cheese on top of it . . ." He closed his eyes and bit into his bread, making a throaty noise of pleasure as he chewed, his expression one of rapture.

A shiver went through her. The intimacy of breakfasting with him suddenly seemed to thicken the air. All these years, this could have been her life—this, and more. Yet again the weight of all she'd lost pressed on her heart.

Jamie opened his eyes. "Besides, there was precious little in your larder." If he felt any charge in the atmosphere, he didn't show it. "Eat, Livie."

She ducked her head and obeyed. It was disconcerting to think that she was still haunted by things he appeared to have tactfully forgotten. After all, she had been the one to insist they could remain friends, and she had been very careful to keep it so. She even wanted it to be that way. It was too late for anything else, and she would have to remember that.

"I read Henry's book last night." He paused to catch a bit of cheese before it fell from his bread. "If he wasn't a smuggler, he was engaged in some very shady dealings of another sort. By my rough tally, he paid out more than two thousand pounds over the last two years of his life."

Olivia choked. "*How* much?"

He pushed a mug across the table, filled with warm tea. "Twenty-two hundred pounds. There's no income, but I daresay Mr. Brewster has that book."

"He said not . . ."

Jamie shrugged. "I wouldn't admit it, either. If the price of transporting goods was two thousand, I imagine the income from the sales exceeded ten or twelve thousand."

She put down her bread. "That is impossible."

"We'd have to review Mr. Brewster's books to know, and I wager he's hidden them very carefully by now, if not destroyed them." He stopped at her expression. "Impossible for a man to spend ten thousand in two years? Think, Livie. You know it's not. Especially when one considers all the people who must be paid for their silence. Not that it matters now."

Her mind raced. Bitterly she thought of her canceled annuity. If Henry had that much money flowing through his hands, he hardly needed her pittance, and yet he'd taken it, too. "Why not?"

"I thought about it all night. Why would Clary come after you? It seems Henry was a vital piece of the operation and once he died, the chain was fatally broken. Every other friend of his vanished from view, you said; only Clary kept prowling around. Aside from any . . . er . . . repulsive propositions, he wanted something from you. He conspired with Lord Stratford to get my sister on a yacht where she couldn't escape his demands for information about you, and he told her Stratford wanted to find you as much as he did. Stratford himself told his son you had information he wanted. Since you never met Lord Stratford, it couldn't be something personal that he wanted. Clary and Stratford must have been referring to something else, some object Clary thinks you have." Jamie paused as the color bled from Olivia's face. "I believe Henry smuggled something into England right before his death, but failed to deliver it, and they want it."

"Oh, that's just too much!" she exclaimed furiously. "Of course I don't have anything but they'll never believe that!"

"We're not going to *persuade* Lord Clary to leave you be," Jamie retorted. "This item—if it exists—doesn't belong to him at all. Even if you did have it, you would hardly invite him to take it and wish him well."

"You're right." She calmed a bit. "But I know you must be thinking of using this mystery item in some way. How?"

"You know me too well," he said in admiration. "Or is my devious nature becoming more obvious?"

She laughed reluctantly. "The former, I hope! Although a little deviousness would be helpful now, too."

His eyes darkened and his smile slipped, and something like pain flickered over his face. But it was gone in an instant, and when he spoke his voice was the same. "I never could hide anything from you. Still, this isn't the best plan I've ever had." He held up one hand, ticking off on his fingers. "First, no such piece may exist; Clary could be utterly mistaken and as you say, it would be nigh impossible to convince him of that. Second, even if it does, we don't know the slightest thing about it. Third, we haven't got it or anything remotely close that could be used to dupe Clary into revealing himself. And fourth . . ."

"Fourth?" she prompted as he fell silent.

"Fourth . . ." Jamie avoided her rapt gaze. "Looking for it could attract even more attention. There's no telling who else might suspect Henry had things hidden away."

Oh. Olivia sat back, the black cloud billowing around her again. As if Clary weren't bad enough, there might be more people waiting to see if she had any of Henry's smuggled valuables. "Perhaps I should flee to America," she said darkly. "It can't be any more daunting than this."

"It never hurts to have a plan in reserve." Jamie pushed the book into the center of the table, where Olivia eyed it with displeasure. Perhaps she ought to throw it on the fire after all. "But I think we have good odds. What was the solicitor's name who turned you away yesterday?"

"Mr. Armand. But he said he burned everything from Mr. Charters, who was Henry's real solicitor."

Jamie nodded. "I'm sure he told you that. My father used to be an attorney. They don't destroy clients' papers blithely. If anything, most solicitors are guilty of keeping things far longer than they ought. It's tedious to sort out what should be destroyed and what should be kept, and it's far easier just to pack it all away. Even if Mr. Armand knew he had proof of illegal activity that his client wanted destroyed, he might still keep parts of the record—to prove himself innocent, if nothing else. Think of the suspicion he would be under: he bought the practice of Mr. Charters, who turned out to aid and abet smugglers. Did he know that when he bought it? Was that, perhaps, part of his desire to have it? Perhaps he wanted entree to those smugglers for his own purposes . . ."

"Well," Olivia managed to say. "That certainly *is* devious."

"With this much money at stake, never rule it out."

She simply hadn't thought of it. She could barely comprehend the sum Jamie mentioned. Her mood grew dark as she thought of all the liars and cheaters she had to deal with. Henry, the selfish, lying cad. Clary, odious and cruel. Mr. Armand and possibly even Mr. Brewster, deliberately lying to her, uncaring of the danger—and poverty—they exposed her to, all to cover their own actions.

"Livie?" Jamie's soft voice broke through the black haze of fury enveloping her. She blinked and focused her gaze on him. "You went away," he said. "Don't despair. It's not hopeless."

If not, it was only thanks to him. As wary as Olivia was, she couldn't deny that she stood a much better chance of outwitting Clary with Jamie's help. Only he believed she could save herself from this mess, and was willing to risk his own safety to help her—even after she whacked him with a shovel. A little voice inside her head whispered that she was risking all her hard-won detachment by doing this, and that she might rue this day for years to come if Jamie broke her heart again. But at this moment, Olivia thought it was worth the gamble. She had kept her head and her poise around Jamie for years, after all.

She leaned forward and fixed a determined gaze on him. "What should we do? I presume you have an idea, hopefully a very devious and underhanded one."

His brows rose with pleased surprise. "Hopefully?"

"If Mr. Armand and Clary and all the rest can deceive and bully me, I feel no qualms about lying to them. What shall we do?"

His grin grew wider. "I like the way you reason. We're definitely going to tell some lies. And they are never going to bully you again."

Chapter 8

The plan they conceived was both brilliantly simple and frighteningly brash.

Jamie had stayed up late reading Henry's diary from cover to cover. Nothing in it contradicted his theory that Henry had been a smuggler, but nothing confirmed it, either. Every entry listed a payment made to someone else, but not a single payment received. There had to be a book recording income, which must list Henry's customers. If Lord Stratford and Clary were a representative sample, that could be dangerous knowledge, but Jamie thought it was better to know than not, if only to guard against any other lurking threats.

Plumbing the depths of a ring of smugglers, though, wouldn't necessarily help Olivia. It was unlikely that Clary would take such risks if he only wanted Henry's personal papers. The logical answer was that he wanted something else, something far more valuable, but he needed the papers to find it. That meant Olivia had to get them before Clary could.

"And those are the papers Mr. Armand kept," Olivia guessed when he pointed it out.

Jamie held up one hand. "Perhaps. I still think the London solicitor knows more than he told you." Her jaw firmed, and her eyes flashed. Something inside Jamie sparked to life at the sight of her temper; it brought color and animation back to her face, and banished the anxious air that clung to her. "But Armand is closer, so we'll deal with him first. Obviously he wouldn't have sent you this book if he'd realized what it is. This documents at least two years' worth of smuggling."

Olivia threw a malevolent glance at the little book. "I still can't believe it . . ."

"I could be wrong," Jamie allowed, but he doubted it. There were only so many explanations for entries like *Ten Pounds, six shillings to Capn. B (Madonna).* Henry Townsend had been one bold fellow, openly recording his payments to local contacts who either hid or transported the illicit goods. Jamie appreciated that now, as it would make his and Olivia's task much easier.

"But you think he hasn't burned everything else," Olivia said, returning to the main point. "You think Mr. Armand still has useful information."

"If we were wagering, I'd lay a large sum he does."

She pressed her lips together. "He lied to me."

"Probably."

"He won't do it again," she vowed. "I'm going back to his office."

Jamie grinned. That was his plan, and he was pleased Olivia agreed. "We should. I think we can—"

"No." She avoided his startled gaze. "Not *we*, Jamie. I can do this."

Instinctively he scowled. "Of course you aren't going alone."

"Why not?" She picked up the diary and seemed to weigh it in her hands. "I've managed thus far."

Primed to argue, Jamie had to clench his hands into fists to keep his mouth closed. Of course she was right. Not only had she borne up under Clary's intimidation and Henry's neglect, she had taken her fate into her own hands when she slipped away from London in secret to conduct her own investigation—and then defended herself violently when she felt threatened. There was steel in Olivia, more than most people recognized.

As for him, his desire to leap to her aid and spare her any more unpleasantness might feel noble, but he had to remind himself that he had no right to overrule her. Even more, if he wanted to win her trust again, swooping in to order her about was not the way to do it. Olivia hadn't liked that when she was a child, and he had no doubt she would put him in his place if he tried it now. As little as he liked it, he had to give way.

"If you prefer," he said. She darted a wary glance at him, and he nodded in grudging concession. "It might be best to keep our acquaintance quiet. Clary doesn't know me, which means he won't be attuned to anything I do." It also occurred to him that the viscount's likely reaction to any man helping Olivia would probably be a pistol shot to the back of the head. The more anonymity Jamie had, the more useful he could be.

But that didn't leave many options for getting

anything from Armand, so in the end they decided on a bold, simple strike. Olivia put on her cloak and bonnet, looking determined and confident, and set out for town. Jamie followed her from a careful distance until she reached the edge of Gravesend, almost within sight of the solicitor's office. He might agree that she could face the man alone, but he'd be damned if he'd allow her to walk about unprotected while Clary was free. If anything happened to her, Jamie would never forgive himself.

She turned the corner, heading up the main thoroughfare into town, and Jamie went the other way, tugging his muffler higher around his face. The first thing he had to do was get Olivia out of that isolated cottage. If he could find her there, so could anyone else. Penelope had given him a little information, when he set out to find Olivia, but the biggest clue by far was that the Townsends had come from Kent, specifically Rochester. That had narrowed his search considerably, but it was hardly a great secret. It was a stroke of luck that Mr. Armand had turned out to be relatively near London, and not in one of the many smuggling villages scattered across the entire Kentish coast. But it was a stroke that could cut both ways, and the sooner Olivia quit Gravesend, the better.

He headed around town along the coast road, finally stopping at a small house at the end of a row of narrow cottages, cobbled together piecemeal and in various states of shabbiness. Jamie rapped at the door and waited. Smoke puffed from the chimney, but the paint on the door was peeling and the curtains were drawn. After several minutes a woman opened the door. She balanced a drooling toddler on one hip and looked a little frazzled, even though it was still morning.

"Is this the home of Mr. William Hicks?" he asked.

"Aye," said the woman slowly. "Who's asking?"

In reply he handed her a folded note. She looked at it sideways, then disappeared into the house. Barely a minute later the door was yanked open, this time by a man about Jamie's own age. A long scar, badly healed, ran along the side of his face from his chin, past his severed ear, into his hair. "Come in, sir," he said, opening the door wider and gesturing with a hand missing three fingers.

James stepped inside the house. It was warm but the air was thick, as if the house had been closed up too long. The woman was bundling the toddler and another small child up the narrow stairs at the rear of the large room, while two girls of about eight or ten stoked the fire and stirred the contents of the kettle hung over that fire. Limping heavily, William Hicks swept aside some schoolbooks on the bench and offered Jamie the chair at the head of the table. He murmured quietly to the two girls, and they moved the pot to a hook outside the hearth before following their mother up the stairs.

"Thank you for speaking with me," James said, taking the chair with a nod.

"Anything Lieutenant Crawford asks, I'll give," said Mr. Hicks at once, straddling the bench. He laid the unfolded note on the table. *Render this man all aid within your power, as a favor to me—Lt. D. Crawford,* it read. "You've only to ask, sir."

Jamie didn't look at the paper. "I know what he wrote, but I'm not here to ask for favors. I'm prepared to pay handsomely for your inconvenience."

"No inconvenience at all, not for a friend of the lieutenant." Hicks sat with military straightness, his gaze trained on James's face. "What can I do for you?"

"I need three things." He held up his fingers. "A closed carriage, as fast as you can find that will also allow travel with some privacy, along with a good horse or two to pull it."

"I'll have one by tomorrow morning," Hicks vowed.

"No one must know it's for me, or hear my name."

Hicks shrugged. "I don't know your name, sir."

Jamie grinned. "Exactly. I also need a hamper of provisions, enough to feed a man for three days at least. Can you stow it in the carriage?"

"I can and I will."

He nodded in approval. "And the last thing I need is information. I understand there's a solicitor named Charters in Gravesend."

"There was," said Hicks. "Dead now—must be nigh on four or five months."

"Yes. What sort of fellow was he?" He saw Hicks hesitate. "A man of discretion?"

"Aye," was the immediate reply. "That he was."

Jamie leaned forward and lowered his voice. "The sort a free trader might be able to trust?"

Hicks looked wary at the mention of smugglers, but gave a slow nod. "Might have been. I didn't have much business with him."

"But you heard things, surely." When Hicks hesitated again, Jamie dropped his voice another level. "The man is dead. I mean no harm to him or his memory. Did he leave a widow?"

From his expression, Hicks was struggling with his conscience. Jamie waited. Daniel Crawford, his friend and source of information in London, had sworn Hicks would rise to the occasion, but the pull of loyalty to home was strong. "No," said his host at last.

Damn. That cut off one main source of hope, that there could be evidence hidden with the original solicitor's family. "A brother?" Jamie pressed. "A mother? Did he have anyone at all?"

"He had a daughter," said Hicks after a moment's thought. "Out near Ramsgate, I think, but no other family I heard of."

That was a link, however slim. "Do you know her name?"

After a moment Hicks shook his head. "She married a vicar, is all I remember."

"What do you know of the man who assumed his practice?"

Hicks relaxed. "Horatio Armand. He come from Rye, I believe."

Another smuggling haven. "Is he cut from the same cloth as Charters?"

The other man's mouth opened, then closed. He lifted one shoulder, his expression unreadable.

Jamie altered his approach. "I don't intend to use this information against anyone. In fact, it helps me less if both men were upright and law-abiding supporters of the customs collector. But someone's safety, perhaps someone's life, hangs in the balance."

Hicks sighed. He frowned at the note on the table. "I can only repeat some gossip, aye? I had nothing to do with any of it myself."

"Of course not." Jamie even knew it was true. Hicks had been away at sea, a midshipman under Daniel Crawford's command, until two years ago, when he suffered his disfiguring injuries in the East Indies. He'd come home to recuperate and been unable to find a place on another ship in the navy when he was well. Daniel had spoken of him as the most responsible and capable man to have onboard, though.

"There was a good bit of free trading in this area during the war," Hick said, his voice barely above a whisper. "I expect you know that. It ain't nothing to what went on decades ago, before the Riding Officers started patrolling. Anyone who partakes of that needs a good man ashore to help cover his tracks, aye? Charters might've been one such man. I can't swear to it, but I wouldn't doubt it, either. It's hard to believe he'd sell his practice to any other sort, but I know nothing directly about Armand."

That fit with the picture coming together in Jamie's mind. "Did you ever know of a family called Townsend, from Rochester?"

Hicks frowned in thought. "Nay, can't say I do."

He hadn't really expected Hicks to say yes, but it was worth asking. "I'm also interested in knowing if a certain man has been in Gravesend, at any time in the last several years but especially in the last few months. He's an aristocrat and looks it. About my height, around forty years of age. Dark hair, pale skin, a prominent nose. He'd be seeking Charters as well, most likely, and someone called Townsend."

"I've not noticed him about town, but I can ask," said Hicks. "His name?"

This time Jamie hesitated, but it was too important to know if Clary had traced Olivia this far. "I don't want you asking for him by name. Don't mention it unless strictly necessary."

"I won't, sir." Hicks grinned. "I expect the lieutenant told you I can be trusted to hold my tongue."

"That's why I'm here." Jamie grinned back. "The man's name is Simon Clary—Viscount Clary. He's a dangerous fellow and is likely to be desperate."

"Got it." Hicks's eyes gleamed. "Are you chasing him or running from him?"

"Avoiding him at all costs. If you chance to hear anything of him, or any man who fits his description, I'd like to know it."

Hicks nodded. "Where shall I report, sir?"

"I'll come tomorrow morning for the horse and carriage." He pulled a purse from his pocket and set it on the table. "I hope that's adequate."

Hicks picked it up and peered inside. For a moment his lips moved as he counted, then he jerked up his head in astonishment. "'Tis several times adequate!"

"For your inconvenience." Jamie got to his feet. "And your discretion."

"Entirely yours, sir," said Hicks fervently. "Thank 'ee dearly."

Jamie picked up his hat, then paused. "I expect to leave town tomorrow, but if you should hear anything after that, about Clary or anyone called Townsend, would you write to your lieutenant and tell him? He'll get word to me."

"I will indeed, sir. But what if I need to contact you before?"

"I'm staying at the Stag and Hound tonight," said James. "Under the name Daniel Crawford."

Hicks started, then a slight smile touched his face. "I'll not forget that name."

Tucking his muffler higher around his neck, James said farewell and went back out into the cold. Now that supplies and transportation were arranged, he went to the inn. Olivia had told him to wait for two hours; she explained the solicitor had made her wait for hours the previous day. Not liking the idea of her sitting docilely in the very spot where Clary might seek her first, Jamie argued against that. Finally they had agreed on one hour, which gave him just enough time now to shave and change his shirt.

He crossed the busy yard and jogged up the stairs two at a time to his room. The Stag and Hound was the biggest inn in Gravesend, allowing him to come and go without much notice. The fire in his room was nothing but ash, as expected, and it was cold, but not as cold as it was in the fishing cottage. He stripped to the waist to wash and shave.

He stropped his razor and pondered the next move. How was she getting on with the solicitor? He paused to fish out his watch. Still nearly half an hour until he was to meet Olivia. Jamie soaped his face and applied the razor, hoping she returned from her mission with a stack of documents. As long as she got something useful from Armand, this would be worth it, but either way they were leaving Gravesend before Clary could catch up to them.

Just thinking of the viscount made him nick his chin. Jamie cursed and swabbed the blood away. Clary's persistence bothered him. Jamie had known many a person willing to go to great lengths to achieve their object once set upon it. If he was perfectly honest with himself, that could be said about him at times. But he had never pursued a goal beyond the bounds of reason or sanity, and Clary would be doing just that if he came after Olivia. Not only had he tried to kill Penelope and played some role in Lord Stratford's death, there was simply no reason Clary needed Olivia. If Jamie's theory was correct, and Clary was after a valuable piece of art, there had to be more discreet ways to find it than by terrifying Olivia, especially once it became clear she didn't have it.

And that only alarmed Jamie more. It meant Clary wanted her as much as he wanted the mystery object, and that made him even more dangerous.

He dried his face and changed clothes, then headed back out to meet Olivia. Just as he was about to step out of the taproom into the cold, the innkeeper hailed him. "Mr. Crawford! There's a letter for you, sir, delivered express this morning."

Jamie stopped instantly. The only person who knew where he was, and what name he was using, was the man who had lent him that name. He gave the innkeeper a nod of thanks and took the letter with him, not wanting to miss Olivia.

It took only a few minutes to reach the place where he had agreed to wait for her. There was no view of the main street from here but he found a spot that offered some shelter from the wind and a fair prospect of the street she would take out of town, not too far from where she had come at him with the shovel the previous night. He checked his watch again and finally took out his letter.

His expectation of what it would say was not disappointed.

The answer to your parting question is no. I've run every rumor to the ground and found naught. All my sources are alerted though and will report if the news changes. My sister sends her best and urges you to return to town as soon as you may.

Yr servant, Crawford

That put one question to rest. No one had seen Lord Clary since he pushed Penelope off the Stratford yacht. To Jamie's mind that meant one of two things: either Clary had taken off in pursuit of Olivia, or he was lying low in a preemptive bid to rally his connections against any charges Atherton brought. Since the first choice had dire consequences, Jamie had gone after Olivia himself while setting Daniel to finding out if the second might be true. After all, if Clary was fortifying his alliances in London, it would buy some time for Olivia to sort out her late husband's secrets.

But none of Daniel's many sources of gossip in and around London had seen or heard news of Lord Clary recently, and Jamie knew those sources included at least one member of the House of Lords. That didn't mean Clary wasn't spreading his own version of the events aboard the Stratford yacht, but it severely curtailed any relief Jamie felt at having located Olivia so quickly.

He checked his watch again. She should have come along by now, yet was nowhere to be seen. He craned his neck and looked down the lonely path toward the cottage, but they had explicitly promised to meet here. Whoever arrived first was to wait, concealed if necessary in the rambling hedgerows.

James walked down the road a hundred yards. From there he could see almost into Gravesend. The solicitor's office was a few streets down from this one, and Olivia would have only a short walk before she should come into view. Where was she?

He paced back and forth, torn between two unpleasant choices. She had insisted that she'd come this far on her own, and she could do this herself; he wanted her to trust him, and that meant he must trust her. But the note from Daniel crinkled ominously in his pocket, and the thought of Clary lying in wait for her outside the solicitor's office made his steps drift ever closer to Gravesend.

Breathing hard, he stopped. She was only a few minutes late. If he charged into the office it would blow away any chance of keeping their association clandestine. They needed every advantage they could find to stay ahead of Clary, even one as slight as the fact that she wasn't a woman alone any longer. Reluctantly Jamie returned to his waiting spot, but with his watch in hand. In another quarter of an hour he was going after her, and damn anyone who saw.

Chapter 9

Olivia pushed open the door of Mr. Armand's office with fire in her eyes and vengeance in her heart. The solicitor had dismissed her and made her feel like a fool yesterday, and she meant to pay him back in kind.

"Good morning," she said to the astonished clerk, who almost fell off his stool at the sight of her. "I've come to see Mr. Armand."

"He's not in, madam," he protested.

Olivia kept walking. Today she was not going to sit demurely and wait for anyone to deign to see her. "I'll wait in his office until he arrives."

"Madam," cried the clerk, trying—and failing—to scurry around her and block the door. "This is inappropriate!"

Olivia ignored him. Without breaking stride, she reached the door to Mr. Armand's office and threw it open. The office was empty.

The irate clerk folded his arms. "I told you, madam."

"And I told you I would wait in his office." She took off her cloak and tossed it onto the chair. "Some tea would be lovely, thank you."

With an expression of deep outrage and hostility, the clerk drew himself up. "As you wish," he sneered. Olivia just smiled at him and closed the door with a firm snap, right in his face. A few moments later she heard the outer door open and bang closed. He must be running off to fetch Mr. Armand to warn him there was a madwoman in his office.

Let him. Olivia felt a bit mad, to say nothing of impatient. The last thing she wanted to do was wait here all day.

Mindful of Jamie's warnings, she edged toward the windows, which looked east over the street. Nothing exceptional caught her eye, but she stepped well back from them anyway. She ought to sit properly in her chair and wait, and yet . . . This would be a prime moment to see if any of Henry's papers were at hand. Today the bookcases held thick legal books, and the boxes of papers she had seen yesterday were gone. Jamie, she was sure, would be rifling through everything in the office if he were here. But Olivia was still somewhat shocked her bold gambit had worked thus far, and so when Mr. Armand came thundering into the office, she was sitting calmly in the chair.

The solicitor's face was purple. "What do you mean by this, Mrs. Townsend?"

She rose and gave him her best smile. "Mr. Armand. I called upon you yesterday. You might recall it. You left me to wait for hours, then had the effrontery to tell me you had burned my husband's papers."

He blinked rapidly. "I am sorry I was unable to oblige you, Mrs. Townsend, but my predecessor—"

"Yes, Mr. Charters." Olivia resumed her seat without waiting for an invitation. Armand remained on his feet a moment, hovering in indecision, before he closed the door, cutting off the smirking clerk's observation. He strode around his desk to take his chair.

"I understand Mr. Charters was the soul of discretion."

"He was," said Armand at once.

"Utterly devoted to his clients' interest, of course."

"Of course. But Mrs. Townsend—"

"And you lied to me yesterday." Olivia smiled pleasantly at him. Her heart was pounding. She had practiced this speech during her walk from the coast, and so far, to her astonishment and delight, Armand was reacting exactly as Jamie had predicted. It sparked confidence in her breast, even though she still had doubts everything would work.

At her accusation, Armand's face filled with indignation. "You are upset and overwrought. Allow me—"

She held up one hand. "You told me you burned everything belonging to my husband. We both know you would never do such a thing."

His mouth sagged open. "I assure you, I did," he blustered, recovering.

Olivia leaned forward slightly. "Did you? I think not, sir. I think you would never destroy anything so valuable and profitable." Mr. Armand's expression went blank. Olivia straightened, making herself smooth her skirt as if she hadn't a care in the world. "I made an error yesterday in not presuming you were fully apprised of my husband's enterprise. On the chance you truly had no knowledge, I thought it would be best not to reveal it. But on reflection . . ." She smiled. "On reflection I realized your position. Of course you wouldn't assume the practice of another attorney without learning everything about it. And for that reason, I am quite certain you would never have burned all of Henry's papers. Some, perhaps . . . but not all."

Armand gazed fixedly at her. "Be sensible, Mrs. Townsend. I told you I had burned your late husband's papers because Mr. Charters requested it and Mr. Townsend agreed that it should be done."

Olivia returned his steady stare. "That would be a great pity, as I had hoped it would aid me in contacting Henry's associates who were so vital to his business."

She held her breath, even though everything had gone very well so far. Jamie believed Armand wouldn't have burned everything, either because he wanted to prove he had nothing to do with smuggling . . . or because he knew all about it and wished to conceal it, even participate in it. It had been her own idea to lead Armand into believing she wished to continue Henry's smuggling operations. If Armand only wanted to prove himself innocent, there was little chance he would hand over the papers no matter what she said or did. Jamie had suggested they could break into his office and steal them, but Olivia thought he was joking about that—probably.

Now that the scales had fallen from her

eyes, though, Olivia doubted very much that Mr. Armand hadn't known what Mr. Charters was up to; she wouldn't be surprised if the smuggling had been a chief attraction. Jamie was right: "free trading" had been a very lucrative endeavor since long before the war, and some of it still went on. And if Mr. Armand knew about it, and had been drawn to this practice because Mr. Charters had established a reputation for being friendly to free traders, then he wouldn't burn Henry's papers, and he would quite possibly leap at the opportunity to profit from it some more.

Mr. Armand's face was a stony mask. Olivia just waited, a faint smile on her lips. He was likely following the same lines of thought she was. "I'm sure I don't know what you mean."

She lowered her voice. "No? No doubt it won't surprise you to hear that my husband did not leave a fortune. I'm tired of scrimping on my widow's portion. Mr. Townsend left behind something far more valuable, though, and it would benefit more than myself if I were to . . . revive the operation."

The corners of his mouth twitched. "How do you propose to do that?"

Too late Olivia realized the flaw in her plan. If Jamie was correct, Henry had been the man in the middle, neither choosing nor receiving illicit goods. For her to run things as he had done, she would have to say she had interested buyers standing by. Unless Jamie wanted to pose as one, she had nothing. "Perhaps reviving the entire business is overdoing it a bit," she said, improvising wildly. "I should have been more specific.

It had come to my attention that some of his clients were unpleasantly surprised by his death. At their direction, Henry laid plans to obtain what they sought, plans which were some time in the making and which required great delicacy of maneuvering. One gentleman in particular had arranged for a very specific piece to be located and delivered. Sadly dear Henry caught an inflammation in his lungs and passed away quite suddenly, but he had set in motion the efforts to secure this gentleman's object. I believe his associates were so efficient, they most likely procured it and brought it to England, only to find that Henry had died and was unable to complete the transaction. No doubt it has been gathering dust since then, and I intend to deliver it and keep my husband's promises."

Olivia didn't even feel that she lied. Henry had been in the prime of life, only troubled by an affection for drink. His death had been swift and unexpected. He had surely run his smuggling ring right until the end, and that meant items would quite likely have been in transit when he died. Everything Jamie posited made perfect sense.

Slowly Armand leaned back. His expression didn't change, but Olivia could sense the calculation behind his steady gaze. "It's been a long time since your husband's death, madam."

"It has been," she agreed. "You must understand that this gentleman was quite naturally reluctant to approach me on the matter."

"Naturally," he repeated dryly. "But I've already told you, madam, I burned those papers—"

Olivia wanted to throw something at him. She

was sure he was lying. "I see. I had hoped you might have retained some part of them, as insurance if nothing else." That shot hit home, she could tell. "However, if you've truly burned everything and my husband's entire network is indeed lost, there is nothing that can be done." She started to rise, then inspiration struck. "I shall have to tell the gentleman in question that you destroyed any information that might have led to recovering his object. He may wish to speak to you himself to be certain of the matter. For your own sake, Mr. Armand, deal cautiously with his lordship. He's not the sort who likes to be denied or disappointed."

"What—I can do nothing, Mrs. Townsend!" Armand rose as she did. No longer patronizing and superior, now he sounded far more reasonable. "There is no reason you should give my name to this man."

"No, *you* don't understand," she said with all honesty. "I promised him I would do everything possible to find what he sought—I believe he advanced Henry a large sum of money, in anticipation of the difficulty there might be in acquiring it—but your actions have ruined that hope. I really wish you hadn't done it." She spoke with Lord Clary in mind. If there were any way she could divert Clary's fury onto Armand, she wouldn't mind doing it. If only her conflict with the viscount weren't so disturbingly personal.

Armand sighed. Now he was not just reasonable, but supplicating. "Mrs. Townsend, you must see that won't do any good. I cannot help him. I burned everything!"

"Did you?" She gave him a wry little smile. "The trouble is, Mr. Armand, I don't quite believe you. But either way, you have prevented me from keeping my promise. I'm not going to bear the brunt of his lordship's temper alone. You can simply explain to him that due to you, he has lost his item as well as the money he paid to procure it. Not that he wants the money, when there's a very real chance his main desire was actually obtained and merely needs to be located."

The solicitor's eyes darkened and for a moment, Olivia feared she'd gone too far. If he really had burned Henry's papers, he had nothing to give her, and she might have made yet another enemy. Mr. Armand leaned forward, bracing his arms on his desk. "Mrs. Townsend," he said in a very low voice, "I am not involved in any of that. Nor will I be. If I am able to locate any part of Mr. Townsend's papers, will that satisfy you?"

She wanted to blurt out yes and demand the papers on the spot. Instead she heard Jamie's voice inside her head: *Ask for more*. "Perhaps. If they contain enough information for me to locate this item."

"I can't warrant anything . . ."

Olivia sighed. "If you give me everything—*everything*—related to my husband, I will give my word not to mention your name, regardless of the intelligence in the papers. But if I doubt you've provided all of it . . ." She lifted one shoulder. "Please don't lie to me again, Mr. Armand."

Armand's eyes were bleak. He was caught and he knew it. He might not fully believe her threats, but he'd given away his knowledge of and complicity in hiding Henry's smuggling ring. "I am loath to break a confidence."

She smiled gently, in victory. "But you're not. My husband left me everything"—which was close to nothing—"and you are merely transferring your duty to him, to me."

"It will require some effort to locate any papers I may have . . ."

"I'll come for them first thing tomorrow morning."

Armand looked frustrated. "There is also an outstanding balance, if we're to completely settle Mr. Townsend's accounts."

"Very well." Olivia drew on her gloves. "I'll settle it for fifty pounds."

"One hundred seventy is owed."

"I'll pay one hundred and not a penny more. You would have found me far more accommodating yesterday. Until tomorrow, sir." She walked out without waiting for him to say another word. The sullen clerk was just scrambling back onto his stool, no doubt having been plastered against the door eavesdropping. Olivia beamed at him, too. "I expect to find my husband's papers neatly boxed and ready by tomorrow morning. I'm sure you know precisely where they are."

The clerk scowled as Mr. Armand appeared in the doorway. "Do as she asks, Tompkins," the solicitor said in a flat voice. "Good day, Mrs. Townsend."

Olivia gave him another sparkling smile as she let herself out. Jamie had said he'd meet her along the road to the cottage, near where she'd attacked him last night. She spent several minutes savoring how pleased he would be when he heard how well it had gone. She didn't have the papers yet, it was true, but Armand had admitted he had some. She said a brief and desperate prayer that they contained something, *anything*, useful. It would be the ultimate insult if Henry had directed his solicitor to save bills of sale or mundane letters while burning the truly important information.

She barely felt the cold outside, though the wind tugged at her cloak. It was tempting to skip and clap her hands with glee. For too long she'd had no choice but to accept what people—*men*—told her. Today she'd finally made her own demands and won her point. She wasn't a natural liar, and it would probably take hours for her hands to stop shaking, but it felt powerfully good to emerge victorious for once instead of frustrated and anxious.

On impulse she decided to stop at the baker's. She had promised one hundred pounds to Armand tomorrow, but that left her almost eighty pounds of the money she'd borrowed from Penelope. She did blush a little over the thought that Jamie would probably insist on paying from now on; all the Westons were like that. But the memory of Jamie toasting bread over the fire for her filled her with warmth. The least she could do was provide him some decent food. She slipped into the shop and inspected the tray of savory pies. Or perhaps she should get some beef fillets, or a ham.

The door opened behind her. "Have you got mincemeat pie?" demanded a male voice, just as the woman behind the counter asked, "What will you have, ma'am?"

Olivia barely heard. That man's voice was familiar. She dared a brief glance around the brim of her bonnet and almost forgot to breathe. It was Lord Clary's manservant. He'd delivered notes from his master a few times. She remembered him, tall and fair and nearly as arrogant as his employer, waiting in her landlady's tidy sitting room while she scrabbled for an answer to Clary's latest demand.

"Ma'am?" said the woman again, jolting her.

"This, please," she said softly, pointing to a loaf at random. It would seem odd to do anything else. Olivia said a desperate prayer that Clary's man didn't remember her face or voice very well, or that he was too occupied in ordering his pie from the baker, who'd come around the counter to serve him personally. Somehow she managed to count out the coins for her bread and exit the shop, trying to keep her head averted at all times. The man paid her no mind other than to move aside as she pushed open the door, and then she was outside again, already chilled before the wind hit her.

Clary must be here. Nearby, at the very least. He could be sitting in a carriage across the street while his servant bought food. The thought made her chest seize. Her breath wheezed, and her hands shook. She wanted to look but couldn't raise her gaze from the ground in front of her.

Walk, she commanded herself. Jamie was waiting for her just outside of town—at her insistence, stupid as she was. Mechanically she forced herself to move along at a normal pace. She tugged the collar of her cloak higher around her cheeks and ducked her head, a perfectly normal action to take given the wind. But the pounding of her heart drowned out the sound of her own footsteps until she could imagine Clary creeping up behind her and snatching her off her feet, bundling her into his carriage and driving off so that no one would ever find her. And her nerves were wound so tightly, there was a good chance she'd simply faint away and not be able to put up a fight at all.

The gatekeeper's house seemed ten miles away now. She kept her cloak held close around her, the cursed loaf of bread squashed under her arm. Her eyes flitted anxiously from side to side. Where was Jamie? He'd said he had errands to do. What if he was late? What if Clary had already discovered her cottage? Perhaps she shouldn't go back there at all . . . except that all her money and Henry's damned book were there. She had to go back.

By the time she reached the agreed-upon meeting point, she felt numb. Simply putting one foot in front of the other was as much as she could manage, and when Jamie stepped out from around the corner, she jumped in fright.

"There you are." He took one look at her face and his expression sharpened. "What happened?" he demanded.

Her throat worked, but her lips barely moved. "Cl-Cl-Clary," she stuttered.

Jamie seized her and yanked her off the path, into the shelter of the hedgerow and out of view of anyone coming from Gravesend. It felt almost warm here, with the thick vegetation at her back blocking the wind and Jamie's hands chafing her arms through her cloak. "Did you see him?" he asked urgently. "Did he see you?"

She shook her head. Beneath her cloak she still

clutched the loaf, which somehow restored her. As horribly frightened as she'd been, she hadn't completely fallen to pieces. "His man," she said, her voice ragged. "In the bakery." She held up the bread, which he ignored.

Jamie's fingers dug into her elbows. "Olivia, did he recognize you?"

Gradually her senses were functioning again. "I don't know. I don't think so. He came in and asked about mincemeat pies, and I left as quickly as I could, keeping my head down."

For a moment he seemed frozen, then with a start he released her and stepped back. "Right. We need to hurry. Is there another path to the cottage?"

"Along the shore, but no one uses it in winter, according to Mrs. Mason, who owns it."

"Because it's impassable or because it's cold?"

"Both."

"Good." He had unwound the muffler from around his neck, and now he looped it around hers, tucking in the ends under her collar. "We're going to the cottage and collecting everything of yours. I don't want anything left to hint that you were ever there. But we must move fast. Can you do it, or shall you stay here and I go?"

The thought of waiting here alone while Clary drew near almost made her heart stop. "I can go." She met his gaze and nodded. "I can."

Without another word he started off toward the shore, setting a pace she could barely keep up with. Olivia didn't complain. Even faster than her steps, her heart seemed to drum a quick march: *Hurry hurry hurry.* As they went, Jamie's head swiveled from left to right and back again. He was plotting any places to hide or alternate routes away from the cottage, she realized, because Clary could be driving down the lane behind them. If the viscount began asking questions in Gravesend, it surely wouldn't take long for him to hear word of a dark-haired woman from out of town, suddenly arrived and alone. In fact, he'd probably hear what her mission was, for she'd had to make inquiries to find Mr. Armand.

Armand. Her heart leapt into her throat at the thought of Clary going to the solicitor before tomorrow morning. If Clary got his hands on Henry's papers—and somehow Olivia thought Mr. Armand was much more likely to give them to Clary than to her—she would never solve the riddle Henry had left. Even worse, Clary might be able to find whatever it was he wanted before she could.

Her thoughts stuck on that idea. If Clary found it, would he just disappear? Jamie said Lord Atherton was pressing for Clary to be arrested for what he did to Penelope, which meant the viscount couldn't simply go home. If Olivia found herself in his position, she'd collect as much money as she could and flee.

Her mouth twisted bitterly; that was essentially what she had done. And now she was running harder and faster than ever. If only Clary would do the same, in the opposite direction. If he did, after all, *she* could stop running . . .

But Lord Clary had not shown himself to be the sort of man who let things go. Deep down Olivia was dreadfully certain he would keep pursuing her even if he located the most priceless work of art Henry had ever smuggled. She had refused him and thwarted him for months, and he would want revenge.

As they approached the cottage, Jamie slowed, checking for signs of disturbance. "The wool is still there," Olivia whispered. She pointed to the threadbare bit of cloth stuck above the latch.

He took the key. "Fetch everything," he said quietly. "As fast as you can. I'd prefer to leave this cottage looking as if you never set foot in it."

Olivia nodded. With one last sweeping glance around, Jamie stepped up the door and opened it. "Go," he told her.

She was already dashing across the room and scrambling up the narrow stairs. In the bedroom she grabbed her extra dresses and undergarments from the shelves and stuffed them into the valise that still sat under the window where she'd left it. Thankfully she hadn't brought much with her, although her reasoning there had been to keep the valise light so she could carry it easily. But now it paid off as she packed in a matter of seconds. Jamie had carried the pallet upstairs that morning, and she quickly put the extra blankets back into the trunk they came from. Mindful of his admonition to leave the room as if she'd never been there, she tugged the covers on the bed smooth before bolting back down the stairs, valise in hand.

Below, Jamie had already put away the few breakfast dishes and thrown dirt on the banked fire, smothering it. Winter air streamed through the wide open door, stealing the last traces of warmth. She set her valise on the table and hurried to retrieve her small purse of money hidden behind a loose stone of the fireplace.

"You've got everything?" Jamie asked, slipping her loaf of bread inside the valise and hefting it in one arm.

Olivia took one more look around the room and snatched her woolen shawl from the hook behind the door. "Henry's book," she said, turning toward the loose floorboard.

He patted his pocket. "I took it with me this morning, just in case. Let's go." She flung the shawl around her shoulders, over her cloak, and followed him out the door. Only at the last moment did she feel a pang, as she locked the door for the last time. She'd hired the cottage for a fortnight, and spent barely four days there. That extra rent money would have been useful.

Again Jamie walked almost too fast for her, but as soon as she fell a step behind, he would pause. When he raised his brow in question, she nodded to assure him she was fine, even though her shins burned and there was a stitch in her side. In silence they hurried down the dirt track, heads bowed against the wind. Only when they came within sight of the main road into town did Jamie slow enough for her to catch her breath.

"Where are we going?" she finally thought to ask.

"I've been trying to work that out," he replied, giving her an unpleasant start. "I think we've got little choice—in fact, only one."

"Where?" she asked, when he didn't explain.

He didn't answer. His eyes were fixed on a point in the distance, and she realized he was listening.

Despite straining her ears, she heard nothing but the whine of the wind and the nervous thudding of her own heart.

Suddenly, without a word, Jamie pushed her off the path. He pointed, and Olivia got the message. She ran, clutching her cloak and skirts, until they reached the shelter of the wild hedge that meandered toward the gatekeeper's cottage. Jamie pulled aside a branch of it and she flung herself through the gap. He stepped after her and let the hedge spring back, just as a horse came around the abandoned gatehouse.

Chapter 10

Jamie held his breath as the horse paused, right at the spot where Olivia had hit him with the shovel. The man astride seemed to be checking his bearings; he peered in all directions before starting his mount forward again, into the lane that led to Olivia's rented cottage.

Thank heaven she'd stopped to buy bread. All too easily he could imagine what would have happened had she not: they would have walked to the cottage, built up the fire, made some tea. They'd probably be sitting at the table, studying Henry's diary while Olivia reported on her visit to the solicitor, unaware that they were about to be interrupted—or worse, spied upon.

The horse came closer, offering a better view of his rider. The man wore a long coat, dark gloves, and had a scarf wrapped about his lower face, while his hat was pulled low on his brow. As the wind from the sea hit him, the horse shied, and the rider gave a clearly audible curse before urging his mount onward.

Next to him, Olivia crouched tense and silent. Gently he nudged her. *Was that the man you saw in town?* he mouthed when she darted a glance at him. He was fairly certain it wasn't Lord Clary himself, just from the man's nose.

She sat forward, staring intently. Her brow wrinkled and her lips parted, but then she sank back. He didn't need to see the apology in her eyes as she turned to him and lifted her hands in uncertainty.

Well. That meant they were in for a bit of a wait. He lowered himself to the ground and motioned to Olivia to do the same. The earth was rocky and as cold as ice, and the hedge wasn't doing a good job of stopping the wind. He pulled his collar up around his ears, since Olivia still wore his muffler, and settled beside her. He told himself it was for warmth and safety, but he knew it was partly also for his own selfish wishes. He leaned toward her. The scent of her skin made his stomach tighten, and he tilted a little closer. "Could it be Clary's man?" he whispered, so near her ear he could almost brush his lips against her cheek.

Olivia shivered. "Yes, but I'm not sure. I know it's not Clary."

Their gazes met. This close, Jamie could see every tiny variation in the blue of her eyes, dilated with anxiety. Running across the field had brought a bloom of color to her skin, and she was still breathing hard. Her heart must be racing, as his was—although he doubted it was for the same reason. For a moment the urge to gather her into his arms almost overwhelmed him. He wanted to pull her to him and swear he would protect her and seal his promise with a kiss . . .

But then she pulled her head back—barely an

inch, but it might as well have been a yard. He had no right to feel so desolate, but there was no other word for the feeling. Under pretense of checking the road again, he shifted away, colder than ever.

"There's nothing at the end of this road but the cottage, is there?" When she shook her head, he nodded. "It may only be someone who's lost."

Uneasily she glanced down the lane. "Shouldn't we leave while he's out of sight?"

"We can't move as fast as a man on horseback can. If he's merely lost, he'll realize his mistake and come back soon enough. If he's not . . ." He gave a wry smile. "I'd rather have a safe hiding spot to watch him go."

Her shoulders eased. "That makes sense."

It also left them exposed to the cold for longer, but it was worth the risk, if Clary had sent his servant to hunt down Olivia. Jamie wished he'd had Hicks arrange a place for them to stay tonight. He hunched his shoulders and resisted the impulse to move closer to her again. "What happened with the solicitor?" he asked to distract Olivia, keeping his voice low but calm.

"Oh!" She brightened. "It went perfectly. He admitted he hasn't burned everything, and he agreed to give me what he has for one hundred pounds. I said I would return tomorrow morning to collect it." A shadow fell across her face. "But if Clary *is* in town, he might locate Mr. Armand as well. If he gets Henry's papers first—"

"Tell me what you saw of his servant," Jamie interrupted. "Did you meet him face to face?"

"No—not really." She sighed. "I was so pleased with myself, after dealing with Mr. Armand. I stopped in the bakery, thinking I would purchase something for dinner. But then he came in, right behind me, and demanded pies. I hope he thought I was just another housewife fetching bread. I bought the bread and walked away as calmly as I could, even though I wanted to run because I imagined Clary watching me the entire way." She shivered again and huddled deeper into her cloak.

"Very good," said Jamie approvingly. "I wonder if he's here alone."

She shrugged. "He could be, although he's Lord Clary's personal servant. He used to deliver Clary's messages and he would wait outside for my response, so I couldn't avoid giving one. I can't imagine he would be far from his master for long."

There was very little reason to think that man would ride down this lonely path purely by chance. Still, Jamie wanted to see how determined he was. He made a mental tally of how long it would take to ride to the cottage and back, and slipped out his watch to see how long their visitor stayed.

"Jamie?" Olivia gazed at him with worry in her eyes. "Do you think Armand would give Henry's papers to Lord Clary?"

"I doubt it," he said, "although it's possible." Unlike Olivia, Clary wasn't above threatening people to get what he wanted. "It seems Clary is primarily searching for you, not the solicitor."

"But if he asks about me, he might discover I was looking for Mr. Armand. Clary may realize what I'm after."

He very well might, but there was nothing they could do about it now. "Armand doesn't know where you are, and we'll be out of Gravesend tomorrow in any event."

"What if Mr. Armand doesn't give me the papers tomorrow?"

"We're still leaving." Given the unpleasant surprise of Clary's servant, Jamie would be happy to leave right now. Grudgingly he acknowledged they would be much better off with Henry's things, and they didn't have a carriage yet anyway.

"Where are we going to stay until tomorrow morning?" Olivia's voice was getting tighter. "We can't sit in the hedgerow all night."

Nor could he take her back to the inn with him. For all he knew, Clary might be staying there as well. "I made some arrangements," he told her, even as he said a silent prayer Mr. Hicks could be counted on for more than he'd already asked. Jamie had really thought he was further ahead of Clary than this, and it was a rude shock to realize that the viscount was nipping at their heels already.

To keep Olivia from thinking about it, he asked more about her visit to the solicitor. By the time he saw the horse come back down the lane, he'd nearly run out of questions, and he couldn't feel his feet. Olivia must be even colder, although she'd tucked her skirts beneath her. He made a motion to her to be quiet, and they watched the horse and rider head back into town, this time at a brisk canter. Jamie checked his watch; the fellow had been at the cottage close to twenty minutes, enough time to make a thorough search, and now he was wasting no time heading back to town. Jamie's instinct was to follow and see where the man went, but he couldn't leave Olivia to fend for herself. When the rider was long out of sight, he clambered stiffly to his feet and held out one hand.

As usual, Olivia pretended not to see it as she stood up. She never took his hand or his arm. It was just another subtle but unmistakable sign of rejection, a faint signal that she didn't want him.

As if he needed another reminder.

"Did you pack a veil?" he asked, pushing away the thought. When she nodded, he opened the valise. "You should wear it until we're away from Gravesend."

She fished it out and draped it over her bonnet, wrapping the ends around to secure them. "Where are we going?" she asked, her features barely visible through the net.

"You're going to have to trust me." He pulled back the hedge so she could step out.

"Haven't I done so thus far?"

He smiled at the wry twist to her tone. "That you have."

He took her to Hicks's house, keeping a sharp eye out for any sign of Clary or his man the whole way. This time the door was opened by one of the girls who'd been tending the fire earlier. When he asked for her father, she shook her head. "He's gone out."

That was unfortunate. Before he could react, though, the door opened wider and Mrs. Hicks, sans toddler, appeared. "Why is the door open?" She saw Jamie and gasped. "Sir, come in! Grace, let the gentleman inside!"

Gratefully he urged Olivia into the house. Mrs. Hicks was sweeping slates and primers off the benches around the wide table. "Come in by the fire, sir—and madam," she added as she saw Olivia. "Grace! Put the kettle on."

"I hate to intrude on you again," Jamie began, but the woman held up both hands, her thin face wreathed in smiles.

"My husband told me Lieutenant Crawford sent you. Will's gone to see about some of your requests, sir. Anything you ask, I'll do my best to give."

James hesitated, looking at Olivia. The veil hid her expression. Too late he realized he ought to have told her his plan, but since he didn't see any other option, it wouldn't have mattered much. "It is a very great favor I've come to ask this time, but an urgent one. My friend—this lady with me—needs a safe place to stay tonight."

Olivia made a startled movement. "No—"

"I'd give you my own bed, m'lady," said Mrs. Hicks fervently. She took one look at Jamie's face and bobbed a rough curtsy. "I can see you want a moment alone. Grace, come with me, child." She herded her daughter away with a flurry of whispers.

Olivia tore off her veil. "What are you doing?" she demanded, her voice throbbing with anxiety. "Stay here? Do you know this woman?"

He held up his hand, urging quiet. "A friend—a man I trust entirely—put me in touch with her husband and vouched for him. I can't take you to the inn where I have a room, and if Clary's man is asking after a single woman in town, how long do you think it would take him to find you at any other inn?" There were only two others anyway, which Olivia must know. If she went to any of them, Clary would discover her before midnight. "We're leaving as soon as you visit Armand tomorrow; it's only for one night."

She looked away from him, toward the stairs where Mrs. Hicks and her daughter had gone. She twisted her veil in a white-knuckled grip. "You're not going to stay here, are you?"

It was a statement, not a question, but it made his heart leap. She sounded unhappy about that. "I want to find out how near Clary is, and it might attract notice if I avoid my own bed at the inn two nights in a row."

"I know." With an effort she raised her chin. "Very well. I suppose there's not much choice."

Unfortunately not. For a moment Jamie felt it weigh on him. On one hand, it seemed that he'd found her just in time, if Clary's man had traced her this far. On the other hand, he wasn't doing a very good job protecting her, forcing her to stay the night with people who were strangers to them both. He vowed to do better, beginning now. "It's safe for you here. I'll be back first thing in the morning."

She gave a jerky nod, staring into the fire. He set down her valise, then hesitated. He longed to touch her—just once, in comfort—but didn't think he could bear it if she recoiled. She looked so isolated and lonely, her arms wrapped around her waist. With a simple nod of farewell, he jammed his hat down on his head and went to the door.

"Jamie?" Her whisper stopped him. He whipped back around, taut. "Will you leave Henry's book with me?" Her pale cheeks had grown rosy in the warmth of the fire, but she still barely looked at him. "Since we're running out of time, I'd like to read it again."

"Of course." Unreasonably disappointed, he handed it over, and this time she let him leave without a word.

He headed back toward the center of town, passing by the livery stable, where he managed to intercept Mr. Hicks, fresh from hiring a traveling chaise and pair for the following day. He invited the man to share a drink in a nearby tavern, where they sat at a table away from the meager crowd and Jamie told him what awaited at home. Hicks just nodded upon hearing a strange woman would be spending the night in his home. He made a minor protest when Jamie gave him more money, under the table, but took it when Jamie said it was for a fine dinner that evening. Olivia needed to eat. The fact that he had handed over enough for a month of good dinners meant Hicks wouldn't hold back.

"It's a right spot of trouble you're in, isn't it?" asked Hicks.

James smiled grimly and tipped his mug to his mouth. "What makes you think so?"

The other man gave him a knowing look. "Not like we all haven't had our moments. The lieutenant wouldn't shy away from anything."

"No, he wouldn't."

Hicks turned his ale around and watched the foam slosh. "Is he well?"

James thought of Daniel Crawford, whom he'd known since university. Daniel had always been daring and adventurous to a fault, whether it was playing pranks on a dean or sailing into enemy fire aboard one of His Majesty's ships in the Royal Navy. Jamie had never seen him happier than when engaged in something covert or forbidden. Daniel relished intrigue and subterfuge, and a wild race to locate stolen goods and catch a murderous viscount was just the thing to pique Daniel's interest. "I'd say so."

Hicks nodded. "He was on the *Charlotte Alice* when we were sunk off Corfu. I've only got my leg still because he managed to keep hold of his pistol and threatened to blow a hole in any surgeon who cut either of us."

James blinked. Daniel had been badly wounded at Corfu, and the surgeons had most definitely cut him, removing his left arm at the elbow. "Oh?"

The other man grimaced. "It was after they took his arm. He vowed for all to hear that he was still a good shot with one hand and he'd not lose another piece of himself without payment in kind."

"That sounds like the man I know." Jamie was sure Daniel had peppered that threat with enough curses, in a dozen languages, to make the most seasoned sailor blanch.

"And now he's sent you to me." Hicks gave him a measuring look. "I haven't had steady work in nearly two years, and now I've a year's wages in my purse. No end of good turns he's done me."

"No, Mr. Hicks, you mustn't think of it that way. He's done me the favor."

"Well." Hicks raised his mug of ale in salute. "Here's to our mutual gratitude, then."

After Hicks departed, James took a walk around town. He visited three more pubs without seeing the man who'd ridden to Olivia's cottage before he returned to the Stag and Hound. He stopped to order a tray of dinner sent up to his room, and the innkeeper gave him another letter, saying it had come with the evening coach. Hiding the unpleasant jolt that gave him—it was a day full of unhappy surprises, it seemed—he was about to go up the stairs when a stranger in the taproom inquired, impatiently and loudly, where his ale was.

He dropped his glove, and took a swift look through the doorway as he stooped to fetch it. The thirsty customer was tall and fair, wore an arrogant expression, and when he turned his head to snap at the serving girl rushing by, Jamie recognized the man who had ridden out to Olivia's cottage.

He picked up his glove and continued to his room. Clary's man was staying in this very inn; how perfect. Thank the blessed Lord he hadn't dared bring Olivia here.

Upstairs he tore open the letter. It must be something urgent for Daniel to write to him twice in one day, and to send the second express. But this letter was not from Daniel Crawford; it was from his sister.

I must protest this complete and utter abandonment of our agreement. It's been a fortnight and you've not even given a hint of when you can resume work. Surely in your travels you can make time; long rides in mail coaches are endless and dull unless one is engaged in some pursuit more fascinating than

watching the scenery pass. And even if you have no compassion on society at large, think of Dan, who is greatly out of humor at being left idle. The whole enterprise sprang out of his risk and effort, and now you have abandoned him. Do not let him down, I beg you.
—Bathsheba

Jamie scowled. Bathsheba was tireless to the point of being tiresome when her will was thwarted. She'd argued, protested, even wept when he left London, and now she'd decided to try guilt. Her brother had firmly agreed that Jamie must go to Olivia's aid, though, no matter the cost or inconvenience. Jamie told himself he had nothing to regret.

It didn't quite work. The needle of remorse was sharp, and slid deep. His absence had left Daniel at loose ends, and as Bathsheba pointed out, it was also costing him money.

He shoved the letter inside his notebook. There was nothing he could do about it now, not when he had far more pressing things to worry about. Bathsheba knew why he'd left town. She couldn't seriously expect him to keep up his usual activities while riding about England, searching for Olivia, dodging Lord Clary, and trying desperately to find whatever object would put an end to Olivia's troubles.

When the serving girl brought his dinner, he took a few minutes to chat with her in hopes of finding out about Clary's servant. Apparently the man, Mr. Jakes, had already made a nuisance of himself, and she didn't mind at all sharing how abrupt he'd been with the innkeeper's wife about his bed linen, nor how he'd cuffed the boot boy.

"What a rotter," said Jamie in commiseration. "But a single gent, traveling alone, won't stay long."

The girl rolled her eyes. "His master's to follow any day now, he says. Thrust it right in Mr. Blackman's face that his lordly master wouldn't deign to stay in a slovenly place such as this. Good luck to him, I say! The Stag and Hound ain't the finest hotel, but it's the best in Gravesend. I'd like to see how he feels after a few nights in the flea-riddled beds at the Red Boar. They never air their linens, ne'er a once."

"Then it sounds the ideal accommodation for him." He winked and handed her a coin.

She grinned. "I heartily agree, sir! Good night to you."

He ate and then packed, planning on rising early. But that left him too much time to think. How was Olivia spending her evening? The Hickses would surely be kind to her but he disliked leaving her alone there. Hell, he disliked *leaving* her, especially now that she had accepted his help and company again after so many years.

Jamie paced his room, restless and out of sorts. Even after all these years apart, it was startling how easy he felt with Olivia. Despite her reserve, he could see enough of the girl he knew—and had loved so wildly—that his hopes threatened to outpace reason. Perhaps he shouldn't be surprised; while she'd been someone else's wife and strictly out of his reach, Jamie had known his best tactic was to stay away. All his efforts to eradicate his feelings had failed, which was why he'd been careful not to spend much time around her in the last decade. It took only a few hours together, even in crowded social meetings and even as she treated him with formal courtesy, and he would feel that pull, that tug toward her—and he would know it was time to leave. His family thought he was a wanderer, unable to put down roots, but that was wrong. Leaving was the last thing he wanted to do, but it was the only thing he *had* to do.

But this time . . . This time Olivia wasn't keeping him at arm's length. This time he was determined to help her, at any and all costs to himself. Last night she had wanted him to go home and leave her to it, but today she'd been reluctant to part from him. It seemed like progress, however slow. And the thought that he might have another chance at the happiness he'd once taken for granted, before losing so suddenly . . .

He cast a look at his notebook, still lying on top of his valise. Bathsheba's letter stuck out at the corner, taunting him. With a muttered oath he snatched up the notebook and flipped it open. The blank page seemed to hum with potential. Yes, damn it, perhaps he should get some work done. Almost feverishly he prepared a pen, and nearly spilled the ink as he wrenched off the top. He dipped the pen and tapped it, taking one last moment to think.

Then he set the pen to paper and began to write.

Chapter 11

Olivia spent a strange night at the Hickses' home. When the door closed behind Jamie, she felt painfully exposed. She was used to being alone—in a way she had been alone for nearly ten years—but not when thrust upon the mercy of strangers. With some trepidation she went to speak to her unexpected and unwitting hostess and apologize for the way they'd been introduced.

Mary Hicks was very kind, though. She never asked what Olivia's trouble was, or even her name. Mr. Hicks soon came home bearing a ham and a sack of turnips, which sparked an outcry of delight among his family. It didn't take much to divine that they had suffered some very hard times, probably due to Mr. Hicks's wounds. Before he arrived home, Mary murmured a quick warning, almost apologetically, and added that he'd been injured in the navy. Olivia watched him swing his daughters into his arms, beaming proudly, and suspected Jamie had given him a great deal of money. Even though she knew it had been done on her account, she couldn't feel sorry for causing it.

When it was time for bed, Mary tried to give Olivia her own bed, but Olivia steadfastly refused. In the end William Hicks brought down one of his daughters' mattress ticks and laid it before the fire. He banked the coals, asked if she needed anything at all, and when she gratefully said no, he and Mary bade her good night and went upstairs.

Alone by the fire, Olivia finally felt safe, if not peaceful. Here in this small house where no one would ever think to look for her, with a stoutly barred door and help close at hand, she could breathe easily.

It lasted only until she took out Henry's book. This time she opened it to the end, where the stream of entries ended. Jamie said he'd read it from cover to cover, but she was interested in the last entries. If Jamie's theory was right, whatever Clary wanted was most likely to be mentioned here. But no matter how many times she read it, the book never yielded more than it already had. Plenty of money, but only initials.

She set the book aside and sighed. *What were you doing, Henry?* she silently asked the glowing coals. *And why couldn't you have told me, even when you were dying?*

The answers to those questions, along with sleep, eluded her. Olivia rose and dressed before any of the Hickses stirred the next day. The sooner she collected Henry's papers and fled Gravesend, the better, especially since Clary's man was here. She made herself eat breakfast with the Hicks family, smiling at the little girls' enjoyment of sliced ham and slices of bread from the same loaf Olivia had bought just yesterday, but when there was a tap at the door, she leapt to her feet. Mr. Hicks got up to open the door and Jamie stepped inside, rubbing his hands together and stamping a dusting of snow from his boots.

For a moment she felt the room fade away. The emotion that bloomed inside her chest at the sight of his face caught her off guard. It wasn't mere hope at the prospect of solving Henry's riddles, or relief to be doing something instead of helplessly sitting around. It was nothing less, and really nothing more, than joy that it was *Jamie* who was here.

She supposed she'd had this reaction to him from the start. She had managed to repress it or ignore it for a long time, but today her defenses were gone. No man had ever made her heart soar the way he did.

Of course, no man had ever broken her heart the way he had, either.

His gaze met hers from across the room. "Are you ready?"

"Yes," she answered. For better or for worse, her lot was cast with him this time. In a few minutes she was bundled up and they had made their farewells to Mr. and Mrs. Hicks, who warmly wished them well.

They walked briskly, their steps crunching on a thin rime of ice coating the ground. For once the wind wasn't as sharp, and light snow drifted down around them. As they approached the solicitor's offices, Jamie slowed his steps. "I will be ten paces behind you at all times," he said. "As soon as you reach Armand's door, I'll fetch the carriage.

I already checked on it, and it's ready and waiting just as Hicks promised. Keep an eye on the window and do not leave until I drive up."

Her heart stuttered. "He's here, isn't he? Clary?"

Jamie's eyes were roving the streets around them, although few people were out. At her question his gaze snapped back to her. "I don't think so, but we shan't risk it. His man in staying at the Stag and Hound." He tilted his head slightly at the large inn across the street.

Olivia said nothing, her breath crystallizing on the net of the veil she wore over her bonnet. Even though it clouded her vision, she didn't feel protected by it. She strode ahead, keeping her attention on the half-timbered building that housed Mr. Armand's office. Inside her cloak pocket she clutched the small purse that held exactly one hundred pounds. The solicitor wasn't getting a farthing more from her.

In fact, he didn't even try. Today the clerk was less surly than before, and waved her toward the open inner door. "Go right in, madam. Mr. Armand is expecting you."

Olivia hardly paused as she walked through, letting out her breath when she saw the room held only Mr. Armand. With some effort she blocked all question of Clary from her mind. "Good morning, sir. You have everything ready, I trust."

Mr. Armand regarded her as if he suspected she would pull a gun on him. "I do." He nudged a package, neatly knotted in string, across his desk. "As you requested."

She smiled. "Excellent. You don't mind if I take a look, do you? I wouldn't want to walk away with someone else's papers by mistake." She felt almost rude, baldly saying she didn't trust him, but Armand had already tried to lie to her. It wouldn't surprise her a bit if he handed her a packet of worthless scraps.

"There's no mistake, Mrs. Townsend," he said, stony-faced. "But do as you please."

Mindful of the time, she untied the string and rifled through the enclosed papers, enough to recognize Henry's handwriting. "Thank you, Mr. Armand."

He pushed a paper at her. "Would you be so kind as to sign that you've taken possession of them?" When she hesitated, he gave her a flat, humorless smile. "For my records."

"Of course." She scrawled something only vaguely resembling her name, and took out her purse. "And if you'd be so kind as to provide a receipt, we can conclude our business." She had learned too well to be very watchful of her money.

By the time the clerk grudgingly wrote a receipt, Olivia had spotted Jamie in the street. He was barely recognizable, with his muffler over his face, as he adjusted the bridles of two sturdy-looking brown geldings harnessed to a traveling chaise. When she stepped out the door, package clutched to her chest, he immediately opened the chaise door and she ducked inside. The carriage swayed as Jamie vaulted into the driver's seat and they were off before the vehicle had swayed back.

The day was gray and cloudy, but Olivia ripped off the wrappings of the packet. One by one she held up the pages to the window, her eyes racing over them in search of . . . *something*. But these pages held nothing. Letters on mundane matters between Henry and Mr. Charters, receipts for expenses, and weather reports. In increasing desperation Olivia dug deeper into the packet. It wasn't thick, and it didn't take her long to reach the end, without having found a single useful piece of information.

For a moment she just sat in shock, rocking gently with the carriage's motion. Why had Henry wanted this burned? Why had Armand lied and said he *had* burned them? It was worthless—rubbish. All that wasted effort—and money . . . For a moment she considered pitching it all out the window and letting the wind carry it off to the sea.

The sound of Jamie's voice floated back to her; he was speaking to the horses, but it acted as a balm on her nerves. She couldn't despair so soon. Jamie had seen something in Henry's diary that she had not; he would read every page of this, and she had no doubt he would find something helpful in it, somehow. She pressed her fingertips to her temples and let her temper cool for a minute, then picked up the papers again. There must be some reason the solicitor had kept them.

By the time Jamie turned off the road, she had read every page twice. Unless they were using some sort of code, Henry's letters to Mr. Charters held nothing of any help. They referred obliquely to "associates" but not in terms that would identify any of them, let alone indict them, and referred only in the vaguest terms to business transactions. The expense reports were similarly bland, mere receipts. The weather reports were simply mystifying. And there wasn't the slightest indication of what items Henry had smuggled into England, let alone any that might still be missing.

The door opened. "Have you solved it?" Jamie asked.

Olivia sighed. "No."

He nodded as if that was expected. "Come down, let's have a cup of tea while they change the horses."

She gathered her skirt and stepped down, blinking at the thick flurry of white around her. "Where are we?"

"About fifteen miles from Gravesend." He squinted at the leaden sky. "The weather is slowing us down."

Nervously Olivia looked over her shoulder, as if Clary would materialize out of the swirling snow. The road behind them was empty as far as she could see—which was not very far. She shivered and tugged her cloak around her. "Where are we going?"

"East."

"Why?" Olivia glanced at him, and realized he was half frozen; snow had collected on his hat and shoulders, even on his eyelashes. While she'd been sitting snug in the carriage with a lap blanket and hot bricks at her feet, he'd been exposed to the weather. "Tell me later," she said before he could answer. "I'll secure a private parlor." She picked up her skirts and hurried inside.

But once Jamie had come in from speaking to the groom and they were settled by a fire with hot tea, she returned to the question. "Why are we going east?"

"It seemed as good a direction as any." Jamie propped his boots on the fender and cradled his tea in both hands. His cheeks were red and when he winced on a sip of tea, Olivia felt a sharp tug at her heart at the evidence of what lengths he would go to for her.

"Wouldn't it make more sense to go back to London and confront Mr. Brewster, to see if he's got the other half of the ledger entries?"

He leaned back in his chair. "Have you found something indicating him?"

At the mention of the papers, Olivia flushed. "Not yet."

"I'll wager you won't." He gave a halfhearted shrug at her expression. "Henry was quite good at this. It would be foolish to connect the two arms of the operation. I chose east because it seems more likely smugglers operated out here, bringing in shipments. I could be completely wrong, but in that event, at least we may have thrown off anyone trying to follow us."

They sat in silence for several minutes, Jamie warming his feet and Olivia feeling the dark cloud gathering around her again as they encountered yet another obstacle. Curse Henry. Thanks to his wiliness they were racketing about the countryside in winter, unsure of where to go or whom to seek, with Clary looming like a specter over their shoulders.

"What are we doing, Jamie?" she asked, staring into the fire. "We don't know what we're searching for; we don't even know where we're going."

"We're heading away from Clary," he countered. "And we'll sort out where precisely we're going from Henry's papers."

Her stomach knotted. "I haven't found anything helpful."

"No? Let's have a look. I told the groom we would stay an hour," he said.

The thought that he could divine some useful information in such a short time, after she'd spent hours poring over every page, made her want to cry. Either he would, proving her inept or stupid, or he wouldn't, and they would be no closer to finding an end to this nightmare.

What if they never found what Clary wanted? What if such a thing didn't exist? He could be chasing after them right this moment, unhindered by the snow and no doubt furious to have missed her in Gravesend. What if his servant had seen her this morning, and he and his master had followed them all day? Clary could be lying in wait for them to leave this inn. If Jamie drove them out into a snowstorm, it would be easy for Clary to shoot him . . .

Abruptly she stood. By now the viscount had assumed monstrous and supernatural powers in her mind. Even though she knew it was probably hysteria, the feeling was unshakable and she needed a moment to steady herself. "We should stay here this evening."

Jamie frowned. "I'd rather put more distance between us and Gravesend."

She shook her head. Over his shoulder the window presented a view into the nascent blizzard. The roads would be almost as dangerous as Clary. "It's snowing, and we've no idea where to go until we sort out those papers. I'll go speak to the innkeeper." Without waiting for his reply, she rushed from the room.

When she found the innkeeper's wife, the woman nodded knowingly. "I suspected as much. The snow's coming down harder than ever now, and I doubt even the mail coach will get through. Everyone's asking to stay. But I've still got a fine room upstairs, m'lady, and your man can find a bed above the stables."

The mere mention of Jamie being so far away hit Olivia like a punch. Her heart jumped into her throat and her chest felt tight, and she had to grip her hands together to stop their shaking. *No.* Last night she had endured it, but only because Jamie judged the Hicks home safe. This was just an inn along the Canterbury road, where no one would think twice about answering freely and honestly if anyone asked about her. Lord Clary might be two days behind them, with no idea where they were heading, or he might be two hours behind. He—or at least his man—had traced her as far as Gravesend and could just as easily follow her here.

She forced herself to take a deep breath. That was panic driving her thoughts again, and she mustn't give in to it. It would paralyze her otherwise. She tried to see the humor in the moment: the woman had just offered the fine room upstairs to a penniless widow, while consigning a wealthy man to sleeping in the stables with the servants. Even more amusing, Jamie would actually do it. He'd never been one to stand on ceremony or status, and easily kept company with a wide variety of people. Of course she couldn't let him sleep in the stable—it was snowing, for heaven's sake. But when she opened her mouth to explain, what came out was, "He's my husband."

The proprietress looked as startled as Olivia felt. "Oh, begging your pardon, ma'am! I presumed, since he was driving, that he must be—but I'll see that your things are put upstairs straightaway. Will you want dinner as well?"

Shocked mute by what she'd just done, Olivia nodded. She went back to the parlor, but hesitated with her hand on the door. So much for her vow to maintain a distance between them. And yet . . . did she still want to? Jamie had rushed to her aid, at no small expense or inconvenience to himself. He had sworn to protect her and help her. She trusted him implicitly—except where her own heart was concerned.

She let herself in. Jamie was waiting, on his feet and coatless. "I'm sorry, Livie," he said at once. "I should have consulted you. My only thought was to leave Gravesend as quickly as possible."

"As was mine." She rubbed her hands down her skirt, trying not to notice how broad his shoulders looked in shirtsleeves, nor how attractive he was with his hair pushed back, curling at his collar where it had got damp from the snow. Why had she said he was her husband? Hadn't she spent ten years trying to banish that wish from her mind?

"It wasn't my place to decide for you what we should do," he went on. "You've been through so much—"

An untimely urge to laugh bubbled up. "I'm fine."

He smiled. "I know you are. That's the girl I know: always strong and unbroken."

Always strong? At the moment she didn't feel strong at all. Her courage began to flag; she could still run after the landlady and ask for another room . . .

"You're right: we should stop for the night here. We do need time to figure out where to turn next, and you should have a good night's sleep."

That would be close to impossible, given what she'd told the innkeeper's wife. Sleep had been difficult when Jamie was only a few stairs away at the lonely seaside cottage. How much harder would it be to have him in the same room . . . even in the same bed?

Olivia inhaled unevenly. After telling herself for years that there could never be anything between them again, now she couldn't think of anything else. For the first time in a decade she was alone with him. No one knew where they were, and no one nearby knew who they were. Perhaps this was a chance to wipe the slate clean . . .

If it wasn't too late for that.

She pressed one hand to her forehead. She was as unsure and confused as if she were sixteen again. At least before there had only been youth and shyness between them.

"Olivia," said Jamie loudly, as if he'd said her name several times. She jerked, and met his concerned gaze. "Are you feeling faint? You've gone pale."

"There's only one room," she blurted out. It wasn't quite a lie. There was only one room reserved for them, as of now.

His expression changed. "Ah. I shall find a pile of straw in the stables—"

"No!" She flushed. "I refuse to allow that. You've been out in the weather all day."

He didn't speak for a moment. "There must be something . . ."

"I told the proprietress you were my husband," she said in a rush. "I thought it would be easier."

For a split second his face was blank, perfectly expressionless, as if he'd been struck dumb. "Right," he said after a moment. "We'll manage." Before Olivia could ask what that meant, he turned away. "We should start on puzzling these out," he said without looking at her. He held up some of Henry's papers. "They have to be important, because Charters and then Armand kept them. Did you make any discovery?"

She wilted. It was both disappointing and a relief to change the subject. By evening, she told herself, she would decide how to address the shared room. "No."

"We will." He reached for the mahogany writing case he'd brought in with him. "Let's start by aligning everything against Henry's ledger."

Over the next few hours they sorted every paper from Mr. Armand, spreading them out on the table. At one point Jamie took out a common book and began making notes. Olivia's head began to hurt; the reports seemed meaningless to her, even when correlated with the entries in Henry's ledger. Most obscure of all were the weather reports. Among the letters and receipts were inexplicably detailed reports of wind, rain, tides, and fog. "Is this some sort of code?" she finally asked in exasperation.

Jamie was frowning at one of the weather descriptions. "I don't think so, not in the usual sense. I understand the importance—anything that comes by sea, particularly covertly, relies a great deal on weather."

She sighed. "But how can they help us *now*, so many months later?" She picked up one at random. "This one isn't even for weather in Gravesend or any nearby town. It's all about the sea off the Isle of Thanet, which must be nearly fifty miles from here."

"If weather was important to Henry," said Jamie slowly, "these reports must correspond to shipments—the important ones." He ran his finger down a page of the ledger again, glancing at another weather report. "Soon after this, Henry paid twelve pounds to *Capn. P.* That's more than usual. Most of the payments are under ten pounds."

"Perhaps he took more risk."

"Perhaps," muttered Jamie, looking doubtful.

Olivia's heart sank. She'd spent half the money borrowed from Penelope to get these papers, and they only left her more mystified than ever. It probably wouldn't take Clary long to find Mr. Armand, who wouldn't waste a moment telling the viscount what had happened. The only solace she felt was the fact that Clary didn't seem to know any better than she did where to find Henry's missing treasure.

"Perhaps he paid more if the weather was dreadful," she said half in jest. "I certainly would charge more to unload a ship in driving rain or fog. I don't suppose they could sail into a harbor and berth at the dock."

He was still leaning over the array of papers on the table. "Perhaps."

"Should we make a list?" She needed something to do, to stave off the creeping feeling that Henry had hidden his tracks too well. Without comment Jamie pushed his notebook across the table. Olivia occupied herself with drawing a neat table on one page and then filled in each diary entry, weather notice, and letter. Jamie fed papers to her in chronological order, and at times got up to pace the room in thought. At some point a maid came and he ordered dinner and wine, the latter of which arrived just as Olivia finished her chart.

"What do we have?" Jamie poured the wine and handed her a glass.

She stretched her ink-stained fingers. "The only thing I notice is that all the weather reports coincide with payments." He held out his hand and she gave him the notebook.

"Yes," he murmured, reading down the page. "And Captain P was paid more than anyone else."

"If only we knew who he was," she said under her breath.

"And . . ." He looked up. "He was one of the last people paid—right before Henry died."

Which still didn't indicate who he was or what he'd been paid for. Olivia drank some wine and indulged in a few uncharitable thoughts about her late husband.

Abruptly Jamie shoved back his chair, scraping the feet loudly over the floor. "Was there a weather report for the very last payment?"

"Yes."

"From where?"

She ran her finger over the papers until she found it. "Another one from Thanet; it mentions Deal." Deal lay on the Straight of Dover, conveniently opposite the French port of Calais, where Commodore Clary was stationed.

"Ramsgate," he breathed. "Go back and add where the weather reports were gathered next to each payment, especially our Captain P."

His air of intense interest made her sit up. "Why?"

"I have an idea," was all he would say as he rifled through the papers in search of every weather document. As he read them aloud, she noted the locale of each report. By the end even she could see the pattern.

Most of the weather reports were taken between Gravesend and Sheppey, the northern coast of Kent. Every report from Thanet, though—the eastern coast—corresponded with a payment to the mysterious Captain P—which were a few pounds higher than all the other payments.

Jamie's expression was fiercely victorious. "Old Charters left no widow, but I learned he did have a daughter. She married and went to Ramsgate, only a few miles from Deal."

Her mouth fell open. "And her husband was a ship's captain?"

"No, a vicar." He saw her expression. "Who else would be better positioned to act as an intermediary with local sea captains?"

That sounded very slender evidence to Olivia. "I suppose . . ."

Jamie was undeterred. "The weather reports

could be a way of indicating something was successfully brought ashore—and weather would matter to valuable artworks, where a tumble into the water could ruin them. All of these report calm seas, fog, moonless nights, which would make it easier to unload cargo. I still believe payments were made in exchange for sheltering the goods. Higher payments to Captain P could mean he took the more valuable items. And who would suspect a vicar of being part of the operation?"

Dutifully she nodded, though not because she was persuaded. The thought of driving to the easternmost edge of Kent in search of an unnamed vicar who might know something—or nothing—about Henry's smuggling made her want to be sick. In fact, they had no proof Henry had been smuggling at all, not really. She would have put Penelope's money to better use buying a pistol to shoot Clary through the heart, and then booking passage to America, letting Henry's scheming fade into oblivion. She reached for her wineglass.

"I think we should go to Ramsgate." Jamie's eyes gleamed with renewed enthusiasm. "Let's track down Mr. Charters's daughter and see if she knows anything."

"And if she doesn't?"

He shrugged, as if her question hadn't suggested they would be wasting their time. "Then we'll know that avenue of inquiry is dead and move on to something else."

Shooting Clary in the heart would be easier, she thought, mildly shocking herself. The wine must be magnifying her anxiety; she didn't normally contemplate violence against anyone, not even Clary.

"Do you disagree, Livie?" Jamie was watching her too closely. Either that or he could still tell what she was thinking by the look on her face.

"I fear it will be a waste of time." She raised her glass, realized it was empty, and set it down with a sigh. "A long, cold drive with nothing but disappointment at the end. However, I don't have a better idea. If you're correct, that Henry left one valuable item undelivered, I suppose this is the only way to discover it."

"But you still doubt."

She twisted her empty glass. "Wouldn't Charters have delivered anything smuggled into England, even after Henry died?"

"Not if he didn't get paid for it." Jamie leaned back in his chair. "Remember he only handled this end. I presume Henry sent him funds as necessary, but we don't have that accounting. If Charters stopped receiving money when Henry fell ill, he might not feel compelled to deliver anything. He may not have known to whom to deliver it; Henry took pains to keep the receiving side—the smugglers—separated from the delivery side—possibly Lord Clary."

"What if Charters told everyone to destroy anything when he learned Henry had died? If they weren't going to get paid and didn't know whom to deliver to, why would they keep it?"

"Because they know it's worth something to someone." A knock sounded on the door, and he called out, "Come." As the maid brought in a tray of food, he gathered up all the papers, stacking them neatly with the notebook on top. "Put this out of your mind and eat," he told

Olivia in a kinder tone. "We've had enough for one day."

The maid brought a hearty stew and fresh bread, still warm from the oven, along with more wine. They ate in silence, Olivia fighting off the feeling that they had gained nothing. From Jamie's absorbed expression, she thought he was probably planning their trip to Ramsgate and how he would locate Mr. Charters's daughter. That would be like him: determined and undaunted.

Perhaps he was right. His prediction about Mr. Armand had been accurate, and whatever hunches he followed to find her had been just as good. She should acknowledge that he knew better what he was doing than she did.

Of course, it was her own actions that were keeping them overnight in this inn, sharing a room.

As if he had just thought of the same thing, he pushed back from the table. They had both finished eating and been sitting in silence for some time. "You must be exhausted. Why don't you go to bed?"

Her breathing hitched. She rubbed her palms on her skirt. "And you?"

He didn't meet her gaze. "I'll just finish the wine and see if it inspires any brilliant thoughts on where to find the mysterious Captain P." In illustration he lifted the decanter over his glass.

She should say something, explaining her actions. She should clarify what she expected, or intended, after she had taken only one room for the two of them. Unfortunately, no explanation came to mind; not a word of any kind, in fact. With a nod, she got up and fled.

The innkeeper directed her to a good-sized room upstairs, where the fire was already lit. Her valise as well as another bag that must be Jamie's were stowed neatly by the washstand. And just beyond that stood the bed, wide and inviting.

The sight of it made her stop.

For ten years she had tried to forget what it was like with Jamie. Three days in his company made her remember everything. Not only the physical pleasure—despite his youth and inexperience, Jamie had made love to her with astonishing enthusiasm and tenderness—but the joy and comfort of being loved so deeply and purely. Never had she found anyone else who cared for her that way. Abigail and Penelope were like sisters to her, but there were things she couldn't tell them. Jamie, on the other hand . . . She had always known she could confide anything to him, and she had trusted him wholeheartedly.

But as she had stood at the window that horrible day in Tunbridge Wells, brokenhearted and alone with a husband who was very much a stranger to her, watching the man she loved ride away, Olivia had thought herself the stupidest creature alive. If she hadn't been so trusting and honest with Jamie, he never would have been able to hurt her so badly. Then and there she vowed not to touch him, not to be alone with him, not to speak to him of anything beyond trivialities. She didn't even want to know about his activities; surely it was only a matter of time before he fell in love and married someone else, and Olivia wasn't sure she could bear that. It was easier to build a wall between them.

Suddenly she wished she hadn't done it. It had protected her wounded young heart, but at the cost of a friendship that had sustained her since she was a child. If she hadn't pushed him away, Jamie might have helped her endure her lonely, loveless marriage. Henry wouldn't have cared. And Olivia knew that, if she had asked, Jamie would have advised her when Clary started hounding her. The same pride that had kept her from telling him how desperate her father's finances were, ten years ago, had also kept her from telling Jamie—and all the Westons—that she was in serious trouble.

Olivia let out her breath. She wanted to solve her own problems, but by not asking for help when she needed it, she had only made things worse. And as soon as Jamie learned of it, he had come, focused and determined and willing to risk his own safety to help her.

There was no undoing the past, but she could learn from it. Olivia readied for bed, feeling a tendril of hope in her breast. It might be too late to hope for anything else, but three days with Jamie had vividly reminded her how easily they got on together. If she could manage to revive their friendship, it would be like restoring a piece of her heart. As she got into bed, she said a small prayer that he would feel the same.

Chapter 12

Jamie sat by the fire for a long time.

Olivia had told the innkeeper they were married and would share a room. Jamie had to remind himself—repeatedly—not to make too much of that. She didn't want to be alone. She had been through unimaginable strain lately. If by some chance Lord Clary forged through the snow and caught up to them, discovered what room they had, and burst through the locked door in the middle of the night, it would be a very good thing that Jamie be there to protect her.

He scrubbed his hands over his face. That was as likely as Olivia throwing herself into his arms and letting him make love to her. He'd noticed—keenly—that she wouldn't touch him, not even when climbing through a hedge. No, her actions tonight were surely motivated by fear of being helpless and alone, and he had pledged himself to protect her, not add to her anxieties. Which meant his actions tonight would be motivated by decency and honor. If he took even the slightest advantage of the situation, he would be no better than Clary—worse, in fact.

The maid came to clear away the dishes. "Will you be wanting another bottle of wine, sir?"

It was tempting. He shook his head and levered himself out of the chair. "No thank you."

"Good night, sir." She let herself out, the door propped open in her wake as a hint that he ought to go upstairs. A glance at his watch showed the hour was late. When he opened the shutter over one window, he saw a field of white, the snow still drifting down on the deserted inn yard. On the slim chance Clary's servant managed to follow their trail, Jamie had spoken to the groom who helped him stable the horses about any visitors who might come after them. With the snow falling all day, albeit lightly, it was far less likely anyone could follow them—yet. It was some comfort that they could sleep easily tonight.

Well—as easily as possible, given the shared room.

He took a deep, resolute breath. If he could endure eight years of seeing Olivia married to another man, he could endure one night in the same room with her. Still, he finished every drop of wine before packing up the papers and heading for the stairs.

The room was dark when he let himself in. A single lamp sat on the mantel, the wick turned down low to provide a bare minimum of light. It was enough to show the pile of blankets neatly folded on the table, which filled him with a mixture of disappointment and relief. He hadn't really expected to share the bed with her, and yet the possibility had lodged in his mind like a burr.

There was a rustle of bedclothes as Olivia stirred. "Jamie?"

He set his jaw. So much for hoping she might be asleep already. "Yes."

"Did you discover anything helpful?" Her voice was soft and drowsy, a little husky with sleep.

"No." His mind fixated on the image of Olivia in bed, her long, dark hair curling over the pillow, her body relaxed and clad in only a nightgown—or less. He pictured her blue eyes, clear and sparkling, as she smiled at him in the morning. With a jerk he turned his back to the bed, realizing he was staring hungrily at her shadowed form while she was still worrying about Henry's criminal past catching up to her.

"I didn't expect you would," she said, almost consolingly. "I fear it's all going to come to naught."

He took off his jacket and sat down to tug at his boots. "I don't give up that easily."

"Oh!" She sat up. He could tell by the creak of the bed ropes. "I didn't mean to suggest that. It just seems you were right about Henry; he didn't want anyone to find out, and he's made it nearly impossible."

One boot came off; he set it near the hearth. "We've only begun. Don't despair."

"I'm not despairing," she said. "Merely . . . doubtful."

Of course she would be. Olivia had had more than her fair share of things to doubt in her life—including him. Especially him, to be honest. Jamie set his second boot next to the first and went to work on his waistcoat buttons. "We're a long way from surrender. I sense those weather reports are the key to finding anything overlooked after Henry's death. A trip to Ramsgate will put it to rest one way or the other."

"Ramsgate is so far . . ."

"It'll be worth the trip if we find something. I think we should go." He said it firmly and confidently, because they didn't really have an alternative. If there was a smuggled piece of art still missing, they were locked in a race with Clary to find it first. Olivia had suggested they visit Henry's London solicitor, but they could do that at any time. Once Clary found any contraband art, it would be gone. If the man had any brains at all, he would take his illicit prize and flee, never to set foot in England again.

Jamie didn't want that. Clary belonged in prison, not in a quiet villa in Italy living off the profits of a stolen masterpiece.

She was quiet for several minutes, until he began to think she might have drifted back to sleep. That was his hope, anyway. His imagination had more than it could handle, listening to her voice in the dark and knowing he would be hearing her breathing all night long. He pulled at his cravat, not sure if this was paradise or torment.

"Perhaps you're right. I'm sure it will sound better in the morning."

In the morning. There was no question they needed to be off at first light, which would be much easier after a good night's sleep. The only problem was, how was he to get it, while listening to her every sleepy sigh and murmur?

It took only a few minutes to shake out the blankets and make a pallet on the floor in front of the fire. It wasn't comfortable but he'd slept on worse.

He stretched out his legs and closed his eyes and tried not to listen to the rustle of the bedclothes as Olivia moved around in bed.

"Jamie?" Her voice made him start. He looked up, right into her face, peering down at him over the side of the bed. "You must regret coming after me."

"Not at all," he said at once. "Don't even think that."

She laid her cheek on the edge of the mattress. The long braid of her hair swung over her shoulder, the curling end hanging right above his head. Jamie tried not to stare at it in fascinated longing. "I realize how much effort and expense you've gone to, and I cannot express how deeply I appreciate everything—you would have been well justified in walking away after I hit you with a shovel."

"That was an honest mistake."

"And you nearly froze today, driving in the snow," she went on. "You must be exhausted, and yet you want to go to Ramsgate tomorrow."

He wasn't cold now—far from it—and he wasn't sure he could sleep a wink. A flood of memories, of that one golden sunny afternoon and of all the broken dreams he'd had to survive on since then, were playing through his mind, tempting, teasing, taunting. Perhaps a gentleman would be able to repress those wicked thoughts, but he didn't have it in him, not now. "Go to sleep, Olivia."

"Of course." She sighed. "I'm sorry. I tell you how tired you must be and how much you deserve a good night's sleep, but here I make you sleep on the floor and then chatter at you."

He had to smile at that. "I've slept on far worse

floors than this, and I like your chatter. It feels so long since we really talked."

"Doesn't it?" Her voice warmed. "I wish we had better subjects to discuss than—"

"Tell me about your family," he interrupted. "I hope they are well." What he really hoped was that her family had become kinder to her in the years since her marriage. His sisters had told him little of the Herberts.

"I believe so," she said after a moment. "My sister married Lord MacLaren of Edinburgh. It was a splendid match for her. He was kind enough to grant my parents a small manor house in his possession. I believe they are quite happy there. So said my mother's last letter, a few years ago, when they took up residence."

"You haven't heard from them in a few years?"

A curious expression, somewhere between disgust and relief, flitted across her face. "They sent their condolences when Henry died."

He breathed through his nose. Sir Alfred sold his daughter to Henry Townsend for a few thousand pounds, and then abandoned her? Not even Jamie had thought that little of him. "Have they given up Kellan Hall, then?"

"I believe they took a tenant." Her voice grew a little wistful. "I haven't been there in years. Even if they were there, I wouldn't have gone."

"Because of Henry?"

The question came out before he could stop it. For years Jamie had told himself he didn't want to know about Olivia's husband and marriage. Of course, that deliberate ignorance had lulled him into thinking she was taken care of, doing well enough on her own. Even once he knew better, he had tried to confine his investigations to Henry's illicit activities, not to anything personal. He shifted on the hard floor and told himself he ought to ask more questions, even about subjects he didn't like to dwell on. He couldn't allow any more misconceptions, about anything.

"Henry had nothing to do with it—well, not directly. He wouldn't have prevented me from going, but I suppose he's the reason I never wanted to." The wistfulness had vanished from her tone. "My father used Mr. Townsend's money—my marriage settlement—to give Daphne a lovely Season. My mother told me of all the fine dresses she wore and all the suitors she had. Daphne became the beauty everyone expected her to be, and she was quite a success." She paused. "I don't think you were in London that year."

"No," he said after a moment. "I wasn't." After that soul-crushing day in Tunbridge Wells, when she wore another man's ring on her finger and told him they should keep any regrets to themselves, Jamie had gone home and told his father he wanted to be anywhere in the world except London, or any part of southeastern England. Surprised, his father had suggested he go to Devonshire and investigate reports of a coming boom in tin mining. So Jamie went and spent the next year there; his own fortune had been born, as he realized the significance of the find. Engineers had learned how to dig deep into hillsides and find deposits of tin in mines that had been abandoned for years. At the same time, a man in London had developed a method of preserving food in tin-plated boxes, which sent the demand for tin soaring, especially from the army and navy, with their thousands of soldiers and sailors in need of provisions. Jamie threw himself into it, and learned how to strike partnerships with landowners and negotiate fair wages with laborers. It all paid off very handsomely. He still owned shares of some of those mines.

And it had kept him far away from Olivia and her husband.

"So your sister married well," he said, shaking off the memories of that time. "I recall it was your mother's dearest wish that she marry a lord." Lady Herbert must have wanted the same for Olivia, once upon a time. Not that it had moved her to prevent the marriage to Henry Townsend, who was most definitely not nobility of any sort.

"Yes, our mother was very well pleased with the match: an earl, you know. MacLaren was handsome and eligible, even if Scottish, and he had a large fortune. Everything Mother and Father wanted," she said wryly. "Daphne seemed pleased with him as well. He was several years older than she, and he indulged her a great deal. I believe the only mark against him was that he preferred to remain on his Scottish properties. Daphne was certain she could persuade him to return to London for the Season every year, but to the best of my knowledge they haven't."

He frowned slightly. "You don't know?"

She was quiet for a long moment. "I wasn't in great charity with my parents. My mother would come to call, especially after Henry took the house in St. James Square, which struck her as a very fashionable part of town. She wanted me to be pleased at Daphne's triumph, but I found it . . . difficult."

Because she'd been denied any similar success, to say nothing of choice. How could Lady Herbert have expected Olivia to take joy in her sister's marriage, when it had been made possible by the ruination of Olivia's own hopes and happiness? His hands were in fists again, and it took him several deep breaths to overcome the tide of loathing he felt for himself. Even as a young man he had known the Herbert parents weren't as kind and loving as his own, but he had left her to face them on her own. What a little idiot he'd been.

"Olivia," he said very quietly, "was Henry kind to you?"

She didn't answer. The firelight flickered on her face, disguising her expression.

"I don't mean to pry," he went on, "nor to resurrect unpleasant memories. But I have always . . . wondered."

Her sigh was barely audible. "He was not unkind. If I wanted a new bonnet or a subscription to the lending library, he would agree without hesitation. He was generous with his funds. I'd no idea, of course, that he spent every last farthing during his life and left me nothing—" She stopped abruptly. "He never struck me or mocked me. In the beginning, we tried to be cordial, but before long we both knew it would never be anything more. Henry . . . He was very charming and witty, and he hated sitting at home at nights. A dinner party or a theater outing pleased him much more, and a carriage race or a cockfight would enthrall him. His father told me directly that he hoped marriage would settle Henry, but he must have been sorely disappointed. I never had the sort of influence that would have swayed him. Mr. Townsend—his father—did; until his death Henry lived within his means and was somewhat conscious of propriety. But after Mr. Townsend died, Henry lost all interest in economy or moderation. And far from being able to prevent it, I didn't even realize it."

"Do you think you could have stopped him, if you had?"

"No," she said immediately. "But it would have put me on guard for what was to come. That's the only thing I cannot forgive him. When he died, I expected to live more simply. I never expected to be—"

She stopped speaking, but Jamie could guess the next word: *poor.* "Didn't your family offer help?" he asked, hoping against hope she hadn't been too proud to ask them. The Herberts certainly owed her that much. He knew she had often resisted the help his family, particularly his sisters, tried to give her.

Her reply was so long in coming, he began to think she wouldn't answer. "No," she said at last, in a tone he hardly recognized from her: flat and expressionless. "Even if they would have helped me—something I doubt very much—I don't want it. On the day I wed Henry, I swore I would have as little to do with them as I could. My father couldn't even look me in the eye that day. He knew very well what he was doing, and I was furiously glad that it embarrassed him. It pleased me to see Lord MacLaren keep them under his thumb. He gave my parents a manor house at Daphne's pleading, but it's off in the wilds of Scotland, far from anything elegant or entertaining. My mother fretted over that, and my father muttered about MacLaren's cheeseparing ways, for he only gave them the use of the house, not the income." Her short laugh was bitter. "I find it hard to feel sorry for them. They got precisely what they wished for: a wealthy, titled son-in-law. They assumed he would be malleable and generous, but that was their mistake."

Jamie silently agreed. He knew he'd been fortunate in life, economically, but his father had been a self-made man, an attorney who used his wits to build a fortune out of very modest beginnings. Nothing had prevented Sir Alfred Herbert from doing the same. Instead the man gambled at the races and relied on his daughters' marriages to save him from penury. Jamie did not feel sorry for him at all, with the free use of a manor house and rents from his estate in Sussex.

"But how I've rambled on when you must be exhausted." Olivia sounded a little embarrassed. "And about such dull topics."

"I was glad to listen," he said honestly. "I have long been curious, and none of it was dull." Infuriating, but not dull. Talking to her was never dull.

"Truly?" She draped her arm over the side of the bed, cushioning her cheek on her hand. "You led a far more interesting life. Abigail and Penelope told me."

He scoffed lightly. "You should take anything my sisters said with a large dose of skepticism."

She smiled. "Yes, I always thought the truth must have been more risque. I daresay you never told your mother and sisters the best parts."

Jamie frowned in mock affront. "I have no idea what you're talking about."

"Penelope told me you dove into a flooded mine to help rescue the miners."

Years ago. He was surprised she knew about it. "Once. It wasn't flooded too deeply but some of the men couldn't swim."

"And that you rode a steam carriage."

He grinned. "I did. Tremendous fun it was, rolling along without aid of horses or men. I predict great things will come of steam carriages."

"Great things? They're dangerous! A normal coach won't explode!"

Jamie shrugged. "Steam carriages don't usually, either, if operated correctly. The economies are too great to ignore: one man can run a machine able to transport goods—or people—that would require a half dozen wagons. Better manufactories and skilled operators will make them safer, and then everyone will use them."

She shook her head, smiling. "I can't imagine it! But if you say it will be so, I believe it." She wet her lips. "They also told me once they thought you were in love with a French vicomtesse. Abigail said she was beautiful."

Jamie pressed his mouth closed. How had his family heard about Marie? Their affair had been very discreet. "My sisters are fond of silly gossip."

"Then you were never in love with her?"

"No," he said shortly. Never in love, not with Marie or any other woman. Not that he wanted to talk about it with Olivia. He drew breath to change the subject, but she forestalled it.

"May I ask an impertinent question?"

Warily he jerked his head yes. What could be more impertinent that asking about his lovers?

"I've always wondered," she said slowly, "why you never married."

"No one would have me," he replied at once. That was an easy answer. "I have no appeal to ladies of taste or discernment."

"The real reason, not what Penelope teases you with." There was reproach in her voice, but also something tentative and curious.

He turned his head and stared at the coals glowing in the grate until his eyes hurt. Another flippant answer withered on his tongue. Finally, very softly, he said, "You know why."

It took her a moment to react, and even then he barely heard her soft inhalation. "But I was married . . ."

Jamie closed his eyes in resignation. "It turns out that made no difference."

He braced himself for reproach or even a silent withdrawal. She had made it clear over the years that there must be distance and propriety between them. And since she had maintained that distance, she would have to be the one to breach it, either in words or in action . . .

He flinched at the touch on his shoulder. Her fingers were tentative, as if she might snatch back her hand at any moment, but it was the first time she'd touched him in years. Before she could reconsider he clasped her hand in his, as if it were a lifeline that might drift away. Her fingers were smooth and cool, and his throat felt tight. *Ten years.* For ten years he had dreamed of her, and now something as simple as the touch of her hand threatened to unman him.

"Thank you," she whispered.

Guilt pierced him to the core, stronger and deeper than ever before. "No—"

"Thank you for coming after me," Olivia went on. "If you hadn't, I would probably be at Clary's mercy by now. I couldn't make any sense of Henry's diary, that solicitor refused to help me, I would have been utterly helpless when Lord Clary's man rode out to the lonely cottage I foolishly chose—"

"Stop!" He rolled onto his side to see her better and squeezed her hand, still clasped in his. "*You* attacked me with a shovel when you thought I was Clary. *You* persuaded the solicitor to give you Henry's papers. *You* recognized Clary's servant in town and gave us a chance to elude him. You are more capable than you think, Olivia." He reached up, holding his breath in case she shied away, but she didn't move as he cupped her cheek, his fingers barely brushing her skin. "Never underestimate yourself. I certainly don't."

"You're too kind." A rueful smile curved her lips.

His heart took a bounding leap. He went up on his elbow, bringing his face closer to hers. "I am not too kind," he said quietly. His fingers stroked her cheek almost of their own volition. "You're strong, Livie. You held off Clary this long with nothing more than your wits and determination. You fled London without anyone being the wiser; it was devilishly hard to track you down. Your only fault was in thinking too well of Henry. Otherwise you would have guessed what he was up to."

She lowered her eyelashes, but he could tell his words were striking home. "I thought he might be blackmailing people . . ."

"See?" Jamie smiled. "You'd have worked it out eventually. I certainly didn't solve the mystery on my own; Atherton gave me the idea. Although I'm perfectly willing to take the credit for it, if you insist."

As hoped, she laughed, shaky but real. "But only you came after me yourself."

"Would you prefer Atherton?" he asked mildly. "I thought Penelope did her best to give you a complete disgust of him, but I can write to him . . ."

"No!" Her smile was wide now. "Of course he should stay with Penelope."

And I should stay with you, forever. The thought burned in his mind, like something branded on his very soul. He was still cupping her cheek, and only a few inches separated them. For a moment it felt as though the intervening decade hadn't happened, and he wavered. He wanted her to bridge the gap, but really, he was close enough to kiss her . . .

Ruthlessly Jamie tamped down the thought. "Go to sleep. We ought to leave early."

"Of course. Good night, Jamie."

But she didn't move. No, she turned her head slightly as if nestling into the touch of his hand.

For a moment he reveled in it, then slowly, reluctantly, he withdrew his fingers from her cheek. Braced for any sign of retreat, he clasped her hand again. "Good night, Livie," he whispered. She watched with wide blue eyes as he raised her hand and brushed a kiss on the back.

And then he released her. His heart thumped as if he'd run a mile and his skin felt alive, tingling from the touch of hers. In the dim firelight they stared at each other a moment longer.

Trust me, Jamie silently urged. *This time I won't let you down.* He hardly dared to hope she might do more than trust him, but . . . she touched him. She let him kiss her hand. She told the innkeeper they would share a room and she thanked him for coming after her. It was a start.

"Good night," she whispered again, and her face disappeared. Jamie listened to the rustle of bedclothes as she rolled over and rearranged the pillows. She must be exhausted. He, on the other hand, felt strung as tight as a bow, and thought he'd rather lie on hot coals spread over the floor next to her than sleep in the softest bed in the finest hotel in the world. And he'd give his right hand for Olivia to lean over the edge of the bed and whisper an invitation in that husky voice that had tormented his dreams since he was nineteen. *I want you to make love to me,* she'd said that glorious day by the pond. *I love you, Jamie.*

He had tried over the years to forget her, or at least to stop caring that he'd lost her. Avoiding London was easiest; the less he saw her and spoke to her, the fewer nights he spent awake and yearning. Throwing himself into work or adventure helped as well. If he wore himself out physically, his mind had less energy to wander back to her and wonder what she was doing, or if she ever thought longingly of those few happy days when they had been engaged, if she was unhappy with Henry and would consider running away with him. A string of lovers had taken the edge off his physical desires, but not the loneliness. No one ever replaced Olivia in his affections, although as an angry and heartbroken young man he had tried his damnedest to find a woman who could.

All of that was out the window now. He couldn't—wouldn't—avoid her presence until they resolved the threat Clary posed. That was also the only problem occupying his brain at the moment, and as for lovers . . . He had long since admitted Olivia was still the only woman he wanted.

An hour or more must have ticked away as he lay on the floor, listening to her breathing and trying not to imagine lying beside her, touching her, making love to her. At long last he gave up on sleep and rose silently. He might as well get something done tonight. He lit the lamp but kept it turned down as low as he could, then took out his notebook. He paged past Olivia's chart, past the letters from Daniel and Bathsheba, and opened to a fresh blank page.

Olivia stirred with a breathy sigh that made him freeze. Pen already poised, Jamie glanced at the bed, but she slept on. In the dim light he could see the shadows of her eyelashes on her cheeks, the way her fingers curled suggestively over the buttons at her neck. His heart beat a savage tattoo inside his breast, and his fingers cramped. How easily he could lean down and kiss her, slip loose those buttons, and drive away the worry and fear that plagued her for a few wicked hours, leaving them both spent and sated . . .

Don't be an idiot, he warned himself. Thinking about it was one thing; doing something about it was another, and the surest way to wreck the fragile connection growing between them again. If anything else were to happen between them, it would have to be at her invitation.

She rolled over again, giving him her back, and Jamie tapped the ink from his pen and got to work.

Chapter 13

Olivia awoke to a moment of disorientation. She was in a strange room, for the second morning in a row. She turned her head and caught sight of the table next to the fireplace, where Jamie's writing case rested, and that led her eye down to the man himself, sprawled across the floor, deep in sleep.

Quietly she slid to the edge of the mattress and drank in the sight. He lay flat on his back, his face turned away from her with one arm thrown above his head. His hair was a rich brown against the white pillow, but she knew it would glint auburn red in the sunlight. The shirt he wore was loose at the neck, gaping open and giving her a view of his throat and chest where the blankets had fallen away. Olivia's eyes riveted on that bare skin, rising and falling with his every breath, and curled her hand into a fist to keep from reaching out to touch him again.

She'd been right: being near him was dangerous to her heart. Their conversation last night in the closeted intimacy of a darkened bedroom had only revived the connection forged so long ago.

For years she had expected—hoped—it would wither away, but this morning she acknowledged it had not; she had denied it and ignored it, but it was still there.

And now she no longer regretted that. When he confessed that she was the reason he had never married, her heart nearly leapt out of her chest. When he kissed her hand, she almost burst into tears. Whatever it was that drew her to him, he felt the same thing—still. *It's not too late,* whispered a joyful little voice inside her.

She knew that didn't mean they could simply start where they'd left off. No matter what their feelings were, years of distance and regret lay between them. They might discover their longings were based on memory more than truth, that they had both become such different people, a reconciliation was doomed. There was also the matter of Lord Clary and whatever mysterious treasure he wanted, and the fact that they were running into the unknown, without any knowledge of what they sought, where it might be, or even who might help them locate it.

All in all, it was a terrible time to be distracted by matters of the heart, and yet she couldn't stop gazing at Jamie like a giddy, love-struck girl and feeling happy enough to sing.

Eventually it occurred to her that the room was cold, and if she thought it cold, Jamie might well have frozen on the floor. Carefully she slipped from the bed, thinking to get the fire going, but the first faint squeak of a floorboard under her foot made him jerk awake. "What?" he growled, bolting upright.

"Nothing," she whispered. "It's cold . . ." She gestured at the banked fire.

Jamie blinked at her, his face endearingly puzzled. He rubbed one hand over his eyes and tossed off his blanket. "I'll do it." His voice was rough and gravelly from sleep.

"No, really . . ." Her voice dried up as he rolled to his feet. His undone shirt hung loosely from his broad shoulders. One leg of his trousers had ridden up, exposing his bare foot and leg to the knee. Dark stubble covered his jaw, and his hair tumbled over his forehead as he stretched his arms and back. Then he glanced at her, standing and watching him raptly.

"Good morning," he murmured.

She had to wet her lips. "Good morning."

Neither moved. One thought pulsed in her mind: they were alone, in a bedroom, she in her thin, worn-out nightgown, he half undressed . . . and enormously aroused. Intellectually Olivia knew such a thing was common for a man upon waking, but as Jamie's gaze drifted over her, she forgot that she was cold, or that they had anything else to do today except—

He cleared his throat, looking away. "The fire."

"Oh! Yes." Blushing, she scrambled out of the way, ducking behind the narrow screen in the corner as he knelt on the hearth and clattered the poker in the grate. Cold again, she whisked a blanket off the bed and folded it around her shoulders while giving him privacy to dress—although it felt belated to worry about privacy now, after they'd slept a few feet apart and she'd stared at his bare chest and was still thinking how aroused he'd been.

Even worse, how aroused she was.

"Did you sleep well?" he asked.

She could hear the rustle of clothing. "Yes," she replied. It was true. Knowing he was near had allowed her to sleep better than she had in weeks. "And you?"

There was a thump, then another. His boots, she thought. "Well enough. I had some letters to write, I hope I didn't wake you."

"No." Letters to whom?

"I've got a friend in London who's keeping an ear out for news that might help us. I wrote to let him know where to find me next."

Olivia clutched the blanket closer. "I see . . ."

"He's completely trustworthy," Jamie added. "But if Clary does anything in London or the surrounding areas, even quietly, we'll hear of it."

She didn't say anything. If Jamie trusted the fellow, she would, too, and yet . . . Her gaze drifted to the window again, where the empty road stretched over the downs toward London, like a rope unspooling behind her, ready to reel her back at a moment's notice.

Jamie must have sensed her unease. "If the roads are clear we should be able to reach Ramsgate by nightfall. I'll send for the carriage so we can leave as soon as possible."

Olivia pressed her face to the window. Everything was dusted with white, but the sky was clear, a stark and icy blue. Her breath condensed on the windowpane, and she shivered. "The snow has stopped."

"A promising start."

She smiled nervously and dared a glance

around the screen. He was fully dressed now. When he saw her, he flashed a quick grin as he did up the buttons on his waistcoat. "I'll order breakfast. Can you manage?" Olivia nodded, and he pulled on his jacket before leaving.

The room seemed very still and quiet—or perhaps that was just her heart, reacting to his absence. As if in a daze, she moved around the room, washing her face and combing her hair, dressing and packing her nightgown back into the valise. There was nothing else for her to do; Jamie had tidied his things and left his writing case and valise by the door. As always he had been thorough and prepared, and she felt ashamed of herself for doubting him, even a little.

Her eyes landed on the pile of blankets he had slept in, and tendrils of heat went through her. With a sudden movement she scooped them up, inhaling deeply of his scent before she spread the blankets on the bed and plumped his pillow next to hers. Her hand lingered on it as she smoothed the linens.

Tonight . . . she hoped he would sleep beside her.

They drove out in a different carriage. Jamie wanted to sow as much confusion as possible about their movements, and to that end he signed the register with an unintelligible scribble. The new carriage was open at the front but it allowed him to sit beside her while he drove, and Olivia thought it a vast improvement. The air was still frosty cold and snow floated in sparkling clouds where the horses kicked it up, but the roads and the skies were clear.

Jamie had his muffler wrapped around his face, which made talking difficult. That also suited Olivia. It left her free to revel in the closeness and warmth of his body next to hers, and to daydream about what the future might hold.

As if he could hear her thoughts, Jamie took her hand in his and squeezed it. They both wore gloves, and he had to release his grip a moment later to control the horses, but the gesture made her heart flutter and sing. She looked up at him, and he winked, his hazel eyes twinkling above his scarf. Olivia snuggled a little closer to his side, feeling that this moment was the happiest she'd known in a decade, in spite of the frigid air in her face and the threat of Clary pursuing them. In fact, she deliberately blocked all thoughts of the viscount from her mind. She was too full of joy, driving through Kent in the cold, to let him steal it from her.

Thanks to a well-maintained turnpike, they reached the outskirts of Ramsgate in good time and stopped at a respectable-looking coaching inn. A neat sign proclaimed it "The Three Sails," and in the distance one could hear the faint bells of ships lying at anchor in the harbor. "Take a room for at least two nights, and a parlor for dinner," Jamie told her as he unloaded their valises. "We might as well stay here while we hunt for Charters's daughter and the mysterious Captain P, and I'm not sure I can drive another mile in this cold."

"I'll order hot tea at once," she promised. Now

that he mentioned it, her legs were numb. The hot bricks at their feet, which Jamie had replaced every time they stopped to change horses, had long since grown cold, and her boots weren't up to the Kentish winter.

Clutching the writing case, Olivia hurried inside. This time she didn't hesitate to give the innkeeper a new name: Mr. and Mrs. Collins desired a room for the next two nights. If they changed names and carriages every time they stopped, Olivia reasoned, it would be that much harder for Clary to locate them.

Given the way they'd fled Gravesend, in addition to the snow and general cold weather, the viscount must be at least two days behind them. With any luck, Mr. Armand would give him a ridiculously wrong idea and sent him on the wrong path, or refuse to tell him anything at all. Even if Clary managed to learn they had left Gravesend, he had no way of knowing which way they were heading. Thanks to the weather, the roads were nearly empty. No more than a half-dozen carriages passed them all day.

Of course the cold also worked against them. In fine weather Jamie probably would have pushed straight on to Ramsgate the day before. For a moment she considered how they might have put that time to use, finding Charters's daughter or the unknown Captain P, who might hold the key to everything. Olivia wondered what the mysterious object would gain them. Jamie was certain it would draw out Clary and lead to his arrest, but she wasn't fully convinced. For one, she knew the viscount better than Jamie did, and doubted he would fall into so neat a trap. Clary was a monster but not an idiot. He must have been quite certain there was something to find before he began hounding her. That didn't mean she and Jamie would be able to find it, though, which could leave her right where she had begun: unable to persuade Clary she didn't have it.

Jamie came in, shaking snow off his shoulders, before her thoughts could grow too grim. "Have we a room?"

"We do, Mr. Collins," she said firmly.

He didn't even blink at the name. "Very good, my dear." The porter took away the baggage, and the innkeeper, Mr. Hughes, showed them to a private parlor, followed soon by a maid with a tray of tea and dinner.

This evening was strikingly different from the last. Tonight it seemed they were on the brink of real progress. Surely it couldn't be a coincidence that Mr. Charters's daughter lived here, or that Henry had considered weather reports off this coast important enough to save when all his other papers were burned. The answers must be near.

Olivia didn't let herself think anything else.

"I hope this hasn't cost you too dearly," she told Jamie as they ate dinner. "Coming after me must have been a terrible inconvenience." She knew he traveled a great deal and had business interests all over England. Penelope had said more than once that her brother was only interested in rambling around making money. Olivia didn't think that was true, but it did nag at her that he was neglecting everything in his own life to go on this mad chase with her.

"Never call yourself an inconvenience to me." He poured more wine. "I'm sorry I wasn't in town when you went looking for me."

"Oh. Yes." She grimaced ruefully. "I hated to ask Penelope."

"She loves you like a sister," said Jamie. "She and Abigail both."

"And I do them as well," Olivia exclaimed. "Since we were children! But . . . I didn't want to involve her in any of this. Clary had already done too much to her."

"And I know my sister would never have forgiven you if you went off without asking for her help, when she was so willing to give it." He paused. "What would you have asked of me, if I had been there?"

She ducked her head and studied the tablecloth. There was a faint stain beside her wineglass, and she rubbed it with her fingernail. She had asked Penelope for money, and refused to say why she needed it. That had been for Penelope's own safety—not that it spared her Clary's wrath. "Advice," she said in a low voice. "Assurance."

The chair creaked as Jamie leaned forward. "Why not more?"

"More?" She looked up in astonishment. "What more?"

"Help," he said, his eyes intent on her. "Did you not want my help, or did you think I wouldn't give it?"

"Neither!"

"Advice and assurance would have done little," he pointed out.

"I had nothing at the time, so even a little would have been valuable."

"But you wouldn't have asked of me what you asked of Penelope."

"Money? No." She smiled ruefully. "Would you have simply given me two hundred pounds and wished me well, as she did?"

"Of course not."

"That's why I wouldn't have asked for it."

He was quiet for a long time. The firelight flickered over his face as he stared somberly into the flames. "I let you down once. Horribly. I have regretted it ever since, Olivia, more than I can ever express. I'm sorry."

She could hardly argue. His failure to secure their betrothal, even an informal one, had overshadowed her life. "Don't mention that. I don't like to think about it."

"Nor do I, stupid little fool that I was."

Olivia sat motionless. "Why did you leave?" she asked after a long moment, her voice very soft.

Jamie drew a deep breath and squared his shoulders. This was his chance to explain himself—knowing there was no excuse—but he *owed* her this. "Everything in life had gone as I wished," he began. "It never occurred to me that something would interfere with my plans—and I had so many plans. First, obviously, I would make a fortune with the funds my father promised me, then marry you, and together we would travel and make love and do as our fancies dictated." He ran one hand over his face, realizing how arrogant it sounded—how arrogant he'd been. At the exalted age of twenty, he'd thought everything in the world was his for the taking. "Somewhere along the line I pictured a country manor, a band of children, the company of intelligent and interesting people . . ." *And you,* he finished silently. All his dreams included Olivia, wrinkling her nose at him in amusement and smiling at him across the table, making love to him at night.

"You didn't even come to tell me you were leaving," she said, puncturing his thoughts and laying another lash of guilt across his soul.

"I sent you a note," he said, knowing it was no excuse at all. "I was impatient to be off; I needed an income of my own to be able to support a wife. It was the first time my father sent me to view an investment on my own, and I was eager to prove myself worthy of his respect . . ." His voice died. He didn't remember a bloody thing about that canal, which his father decided not to invest in after all. And in the end he'd cost himself something far more dear than his father's esteem.

She stirred. "I understand. That's reasonable—"

"It wasn't," Jamie retorted. "It was rude and inconsiderate."

"Well." She cleared her throat. "It was a long time ago."

"It was," he murmured. A lifetime ago. "And it taught me a very hard lesson."

Olivia seemed fascinated by her fingers. She was clasping and unclasping them together in her lap. "It might not have mattered. My father . . . He needed money quite desperately, you know. I don't think he would have waited a year, as you and I wished to do."

With some effort he repressed a snort. Sir Alfred would have said yes, no matter how he and his wife looked down on the Westons as nouveau riche upstarts. Jamie had known, with the clear-eyed brutality of youth, that the baronet was easily bought, and for that Jamie had disdained him. If he'd been even slightly worried about securing Sir Alfred's blessing, he would have gone to the man at once and begged permission to court Olivia. Instead he charged off to Wiltshire, supremely confident that Sir Alfred would wait until Jamie deigned to visit him.

But while Jamie was willing to admit his own fault—which was considerable—he refused to absolve Olivia's father of *his* fault. "You were too young to be married, to me or to anyone. No father should marry off his daughter, for any reason, when she's barely seventeen years old. He should have told me or any other suitor to wait a year."

Even in the firelight he could see her blush. "Not too young to be wed. Not too young to make love."

Lord. There it was. The thing that made his desertion unpardonable. He could have left her pregnant with his child while he roamed about the country. If he'd been man enough to make love to her, he should have been man enough to go straight to her father and do whatever it took to secure her hand in marriage. He'd behaved no better than the most heartless rake in London, taking his pleasure and leaving her to face the consequences.

Still . . .

"I can't apologize for making love to you," he said, so softly he could barely hear his own words.

Her blush deepened but she jerked up her head

and met his gaze directly. "I didn't ask you to apologize."

A firm knock on the door make them both jump. Olivia hit the edge of her plate, making the silverware rattle. "Come in," called Jamie, swiping away the wine he'd spilled at the knock. He hadn't even been aware he was still holding his glass.

The serving maid appeared. "I've come to say your room is prepared upstairs, Mr. Collins," she said with a quick curtsy. "And to take away the dinner, if you're ready to go up."

He flicked open his watch, startled to see how late it was. "Yes," he said as Olivia pushed back her chair. "We're ready."

They followed the maid, first Olivia, then Jamie. His gaze fell on her hips as she climbed the stairs in front of him. *I didn't ask you to apologize.* He wanted to know why not. He wanted to know why she wouldn't have turned to him for help. He wanted to know why she said she understood his reasons for leaving her years ago. And most of all he wanted to know what she wanted now.

The room was large and clean, sparsely furnished but with a lively fire in the grate. A desk stood by the window, two chairs sat in front of the fire, and a wide bed occupied the space opposite the hearth. Jamie went to the desk to set down his writing case. The window overlooked the stable yard. A quick glance showed no sign of any arrivals. He closed the shutters, wondering how far behind them Clary might be.

The door closed. He turned around and saw Olivia leaning against it, watching him. Suddenly all thoughts of Clary and missing treasure and smugglers vanished from his mind, and all he saw was her, looking at him with those clear blue eyes. Trustingly, he thought.

I didn't ask you to apologize.

"You must be tired." He turned back to the desk and busied himself with the lamp. "We'll start early tomorrow, with the vicar here in town. With any luck, he'll know where to find Miss Charters."

"We're due for some luck," she murmured.

Jamie nodded without turning around. The lamp was lit, but he kept adjusting the wick. "I'll step out so you can"—he cleared his throat, trying not to picture her unbuttoning her dress and sliding off her stockings—"prepare for bed."

"There's no need," came her calm reply. "I can step behind the screen."

He jerked his head. "Right." He tried to focus on his writing case, sitting in front of him. As Olivia opened her valise and unpinned her hair, he made himself dash off a quick note to Daniel Crawford, letting him know where they were. No more letters from London had reached him, although given the way they had raced across the country, that was no surprise. But Jamie expected to remain in Ramsgate at least a day or two, plenty of time for Daniel to send any news he might have heard via a fast messenger. It also gave him an excuse to leave the room while Olivia undressed. He went down to arrange for his letter to be sent express to London at first light. Then he spoke to the innkeeper about the carriage before finally heading back up the stairs.

She was sitting in front of the fire, combing

her hair. It rippled down her back and over her shoulders like dark silk, curling at the ends as she pulled the comb through it. Jamie stopped dead in the doorway. He hadn't seen her hair down in years—not since the day by the pond when he'd plowed his fingers through it while he made love to her.

Olivia looked up at his entrance. "Can your letter go out tomorrow?"

His tongue felt paralyzed, as did his brain. "Yes," he finally managed to say, tearing his eyes away from her. "First thing."

"Do you expect your friend to have any news?"

"If he does, I want him to know where to send it." He closed and bolted the door.

"Come sit by the fire," she said.

He removed his coat and took the chair opposite her, trying to keep his attention fixed on appropriate topics and not on the fact that Olivia wore her nightgown already, a garment so thin and worn he could see the lines of her legs as she moved. He also tried not to notice that there was no pile of blankets on the floor waiting for him. His heart seemed to be striking his breastbone like a hammer as he bent down and pried off his boots. His fingers were clumsy as he untied his cravat and pulled the cloth free of his collar.

I didn't ask you to apologize.

"Jamie."

"Hmm?" He flexed his arm and squeezed his fist, still wrapped in the linen, until his fingers went numb. Did she mean for him to sleep beside her in the bed? No, that couldn't be—even Olivia must know that was asking too much. He'd get more sleep sitting here in the hard wooden chair.

"I have something to say to you," she said, and finally he heard the faint note of tension in her voice.

Instantly he snapped to alertness. "What? Did you see something? Remember something?"

Her smile was a little embarrassed. "No, no, it's nothing about Clary." She was fiddling with the fringe of the thick gray shawl wrapped around her shoulders. "I have blamed you for ten years for deserting me."

It landed like a punch to the gut. Jamie flinched, feeling physical pain at her confession, this confirmation of what he had suspected—and feared—for so long. "Livie," he said, devastated all over again.

"Let me finish." She had the air of someone bracing herself, but she met his tormented gaze evenly enough. "I was wrong."

He stared. "No. No, you weren't."

"Partly wrong," she amended, with a look that reproved him for interrupting. "It was my father's doing, mostly, and Mr. Townsend's. Father wanted the marriage settlement and Mr. Townsend wanted someone to keep Henry in line. Even Henry was to blame, for he knew marrying would loosen his father's purse strings and he must have guessed I wouldn't stand up to him.

"But I was most angry at you. It was easy to think everything was your fault for not speaking to my father before you left, even though I'm no longer certain that would have made much difference."

Each word was like the lash of a whip. Jamie

sat rigidly in his chair, telling himself he deserved this. He should not be able to cling to any idea that there was a chance they could start anew.

"But," Olivia went on more slowly, "I've also been thinking of other things you've said to me these last few days, and they have made me see my own part. When my father said I must marry Henry, I went to my room and wept. You pointed out that Penelope would have run away with pirates to avoid marrying a man she didn't want, yet I walked into the church, knowing what awaited me. I could have run off—to your family, if not to hide in the woods—but I didn't even try."

"Don't." He surged out of his chair. "You were only a girl—"

"And you were barely three years older," she retorted. "Hardly older and wiser."

Jamie scowled. "It's different."

"Is it?" She raised her brows. "Because you were a man? Because you had money? Because your wishes counted for more than mine? It was my life, my person. Why should I have looked only to you to save me? You called me strong last night. It takes strength to admit I was wrong, don't you think?"

It did. He didn't care. "It's foolishness to think you should have run away," he argued. "As you pointed out, I was old enough to make love to you, and if I'd acted more responsibly, you never would have married Henry—and never found yourself in the trouble you're in today."

"My *father* made me marry Henry. Not you. It was his inability to live within his means, or to compromise, or even to take pity on his daughter's wishes, that drove him. He cared for the money, not for me; he always did. I don't think running away would have changed any of that but it would have bought time."

Time for him to come home and do the decent thing. Jamie didn't feel absolved. "I spoke in jest about Penelope running away with pirates. And in any event, you're nothing like her."

"I know." She swiped one hand across her eyes, making him feel even worse. "I don't blame you for what's become of my life since then."

Jamie muttered a curse and paced to the fire and back, the room feeling close and small around them.

"Henry and Clary are the villains there," Olivia said. Her voice cracked on the viscount's name. "But I blame myself for pushing you away, thinking it was for my own good. The problem is that it cost me more than it helped."

Still vibrating with loathing that she felt herself at fault in any way, he glanced her way, not certain he heard correctly. "How so?"

She ducked her head, and her hair fell forward, a shining curtain of curls that shielded her expression. "You've been the most important person in the world to me, almost my entire life. I never loved anyone the way I love you, and losing you hurt too much to bear."

The words seemed to echo in the still, quiet air, over and over. *I never loved anyone the way I love you.*

Love. Not past, but present.

She rose from her chair as he stood stunned, the blood roaring in his ears. The shawl slipped from her shoulders. "Can you forgive me, Jamie?"

"Forgive—?" He shook his head as if to clear it. "Livie, there's nothing for me to forgive."

"I forgive *you*."

Jamie backed up a step.

Olivia stared steadily at him. "Well? Can you?"

"Yes," he said, "if I had ever harbored any feeling that you wronged me."

"Then you don't care that I barely spoke to you for all these years."

He opened his mouth and then closed it without a word.

Olivia took a step forward. "If you don't, I will understand. I know you want to prosecute Clary for what he did to Penelope, and helping me may be secondary, or something you feel you owe me out of guilt."

He ran his hands through his hair and felt like cursing again. How could he say he forgave her, when he was the one at fault? But everything she was saying made him think—hope—"That's not it . . ."

"And if my persistence in keeping you at arm's length has ruined any chance that you could still want me—"

That thought blew away the fog that seemed to have engulfed him. Not want her? "Never," he said, and caught her around the waist, pulling her hard against him. "Never think I don't want you." He kissed her, unable to resist but meaning it to be quick because there was more to be said between them, but she put her hands on the sides of his face and held him, kissing him back in a way that almost made his heart stop.

Talking could wait.

He lifted her and walked blindly toward the bed. She clung to him, her arms sliding around his neck, her fingers in his hair, and the blood seemed to roar through his veins. He lowered them onto the bed before breaking the kiss, pushing himself up on both arms.

"Tell me to stop," he rasped even as he tugged at the ribbon holding her nightgown closed. "If you don't want me to make love to you, tell me . . ."

"Never stop," she whispered, her blue eyes glowing. "Never stop again."

Time seemed to slow. For a moment his world revolved around her, and he held her tighter to avoid being flung off into the abyss. He wanted to savor this, and drive her wild with passion . . . and he wanted to slake the years of heartache by driving himself inside her right this second, making her his so completely, no one ever would—or could—deny it again.

"I want this," she said, laying her hand on his chest. "I never wanted any man but you."

His muscles twitched. Slowly he ran one finger down her throat, over the throbbing pulse at the base of her neck, and nudged open the loose nightgown until he could see the tip of one plump breast. Olivia's breath caught, and she made a tiny sound of pleasure. His hand began to shake as he eased the linen out of the way.

In the back of his mind Jamie thought of their first time. Even then, raw as he'd been, he knew it had not been a stellar performance. Neither of them really knew what they were doing, and he was quite sure that first time was far more enjoyable for him than for her. All of the other women he'd been with since had been more experienced and talented, carnally, but nothing compared to the breathtaking joy of holding the girl he loved, or the fierce thrill of bringing her to climax. Making love to Olivia, even as a cocksure twenty-year-old boy who thought he had all the time in the world to learn her, had been the happiest moment of his life. And now he had a chance to get it right, and not squander the opportunity.

Olivia saw the turbulence in Jamie's eyes as he stared down at her. What was he thinking, she wondered. She hoped it was not about the past—she was done with the past—but he'd looked so anguished during her speech. Impulsively she cupped one hand around his cheek. "Make love to me," she whispered. Let there be no doubt that she was seducing him; let him never wonder if she truly wanted him.

His taut expression softened just a bit. "I've been waiting years to hear you say that again . . ."

She smiled. He lowered his head and kissed her while his hand stole inside her gaping nightgown and found her breast. His touch, like his kiss, was gentle, delicate, a tormenting tease of sensation. Restlessly Olivia tugged at his waistcoat buttons, then his shirt; she wanted her hands on his skin. Jamie broke the kiss at that; he sat back on his heels and stripped the garments off.

Heart thumping, Olivia scrambled backward and tugged her own nightgown off. The cool air made her skin tingle, but she didn't feel cold at all as Jamie's gaze fixed on her breasts.

"You're even more beautiful now," he said quietly.

No one else had ever made her feel beautiful the way he did. Jamie's words sent a thrill of raw desire through her. Openly she gazed at his bare chest, now more muscled than she remembered, with a sprinkling of hair. Wordlessly she shook her head; he was magnificent.

"Come here." He reached for her, and she went willingly into his arms again, settling astride his legs. His hands cupped her bottom and pulled her hips tight to his. Olivia felt the swell of his erection and let out a soft moan as he moved, grinding against her. She gripped his shoulders for balance and repeated the motion, flexing her spine so that he fit snugly in the V of her widespread legs.

Jamie's eyes rolled back in his head. "Temptress," he whispered, wrapping one hand around her nape to pull her close. "Siren."

Olivia laughed softly against his mouth. She wound her arms around his neck and her legs around his waist. "Lover."

"Love." His lips claimed hers, demanding and hungry. His hands ran over her bare skin, exploring and teasing, pressing her ever tighter against him. When his palms slid up her thighs, and his fingers swirled into the damp curls that covered her sex, something hot and bubbling seemed to explode inside her.

She pushed herself up on her knees. "I want you," she panted, tugging ineffectually at his trouser falls. "Inside me."

"I'll never last," he said through gritted teeth. He seized her wrist.

"Jamie." Olivia shook back her hair to see him

better. A bright flush covered his face, all the way down his neck, and his eyes glittered in the firelight. If she hadn't been naked in his arms, exquisitely aware of how aroused he was, she would have thought him in the grip of a fever. "We have all night."

It took a moment, but his lips curved into a wolfish grin. "We do." He undid the buttons in a flash, shoved the fabric aside, and Olivia took his straining erection in both hands, guiding it between her legs until he inhaled sharply. "Olivia . . ."

She trembled as she sank down on him. Jamie braced one arm behind himself, the muscle flexed taut and hard. His other hand slid lower between her legs, right to where their bodies joined. His head hung forward, his burning gaze fixed on the same spot.

The first stroke made her flinch. She still felt stretched and full, unaccustomed to having a man inside her, and all her nerves jumped at the deft touch of his thumb as it circled and rolled. Apprehension had left her tense and anxious earlier, and now it transmuted into a roaring desire. Jamie touched her and she writhed, riding him with short, sharp jerks of her hips.

Abruptly, just as she felt herself beginning to draw up in anticipation, Jamie flipped her off him, onto her back. He moved over her and thrust back inside her before she could form a coherent question. He curled one arm behind her shoulders, took hold of her hip with his other hand, and drove into her so hard she squeaked.

Olivia hooked one leg over his back and dug her other foot into the mattress, straining up to meet every thrust. The bed ropes creaked with every hard, heavy surge. Perspiration beaded Jamie's face as he moved. Olivia's own eyes were streaming as climax built within her, and her heart felt ready to burst with love.

And when she came, she soared, clinging to his arms and unable to make a single sound. Jamie froze, thick and hard inside her, and his expression crumbled, from anguished to rapturous as he found his own release.

"Livie." He rested his forehead against hers, his breath ragged. "My darling."

Wordlessly she put her arms around him. Darling. Love. He was all that and more—he was everything to her.

After a minute he rolled over, taking her with him. Olivia rested her cheek on his chest, smiling as the hair tickled her. "Do you forgive me?" she whispered drowsily.

Jamie was quiet. "Yes," he said at last. "I can't refuse you anything." His lips moved against her temple, and she closed her eyes, having never known such complete peace and joy.

Olivia fell asleep still draped over him. Jamie watched her sleep, absorbed in every flutter of her eyelashes, every rise and fall of her bosom. Her lips were parted slightly, and there was a sensual, sated flush on her cheeks. Gently he teased free a strand of silky hair that lay across her forehead, and she didn't stir.

He had wanted to protect her before; now he would slay dragons for her. She forgave him—and asked his forgiveness. As much as he felt himself by far the greater transgressor, Jamie realized he had no right to downplay her feelings. Perhaps there was even some truth to her words; she had kept him away to punish him. Just because he deserved it didn't mean she didn't regret it.

He heaved a silent sigh. Nothing sounded better than carrying her off to the nearest vicar and doing what he should have done the first time she said she loved him. But this time, there was more than heedless youth in his way.

When Olivia married Henry, Jamie became convinced that his chance for a conventional, happy life had slipped through his fingers. Driven by anger and a genuinely broken heart, he'd felt utterly unfettered by the typical obligations of a gentleman of good fortune. His father was still in the prime of life, fit and able to manage his own fortune and property, so Jamie had no responsibility to care for his family. There was no title or ancient estate at stake, so he had no obligation to marry and provide an heir. He took this as a sign that he was free to do as he pleased, follow any lark that took his fancy, and run any risk that appealed to him. And he had done just that, right up until his sister Penelope wrote to him that Olivia was in trouble.

Olivia knew him too well: he *hadn't* told his family half of what he'd been up to recently. Not merely the usual things that young men with money did—gambling, drinking, the company of loose women—but things that would shock everyone who knew him. This time he'd got entangled in things that could truly ruin him—and his wife . . . if he had one. Olivia had already endured one husband who wasn't what she thought, who exposed her to danger and scandal by keeping secrets. Jamie refused to do the same. Before he could ask her to pledge her heart, he had to put his life in order.

"Darling Olivia," he breathed, even though she was deeply asleep. "Tell me you still love me. Tell me you'll still have me. I won't let you go again." He wrapped the loose curl around his finger, pulling it tight for a moment before he let it slide away. "And this time I will be worthy of your trust."

Chapter 14

The next morning dawned bright and clear, the sky a cerulean blue that gave the impression heaven was smiling on them. Or at least Olivia took it as such, nursing the residual glow of happiness inside her. Jamie woke her with a kiss, and that seemed an omen of good fortune to come.

They located the local vicarage without any trouble. Unfortunately, the vicar turned out to be an elderly bachelor who had never heard of Miss Charters, although he did allow that if she had married years ago, he might have forgotten. He helpfully supplied them with a list of nearby parishes, noting which ones were held by married men.

Since the day was crisp but not frigid, and the Isle of Thanet not very large, they decided to visit as many as possible. It was a little over four miles to Margate on another good road, so they headed north with the idea of working their way south. But every vicar and curate they visited could not, or would not, help them.

"I'm not sure I believe her," Olivia said with a sigh as they went back to the carriage at the vicarage of St. Peter's, where the flinty-eyed vicar's wife watched them from her door. The woman, Mrs. Palmer, had been polite enough until they mentioned Mr. Charters of Gravesend, when her manner abruptly grew cold and dismissive.

"Nor do I." Jamie was facing the church, his gaze drifting up. Olivia followed it, but saw only the church tower, the pale gray stone stark against the deepening indigo of the winter sky. "Let's stop for a bite to eat," he said, almost absently.

It didn't take long to find a respectable-looking tavern called "The Anchor," and Jamie turned in. When they stepped inside, the smell of roasting meat and baking bread made Olivia's stomach rumble. A crowd of older gentlemen were seated by the fire, and to Olivia's surprise, Jamie chose a table quite near them. He ordered food and drink, then leaned back in his chair. "I wonder if we're looking in the proper places."

"What do you mean?" Olivia asked quietly, with an apprehensive glance over her shoulder. Jamie hadn't lowered his voice, and anyone might have overheard him.

"We've got so little information," he said, still at full volume. "But it occurred to me that we're looking for a person who must live within a very easy distance of the coast."

"Oh. Because . . . ?" She raised her brows instead of saying the rest. It was probably her imagination, but it seemed the conversation behind them had grown quieter.

"For several reasons. First, to know the weather at the coast. We know the weather was crucial. Second, to be available on a moment's notice."

She shifted uneasily. What was he doing? "Perhaps you're right," she murmured.

"It may hasten our search," he said. "Since we've got little time."

Olivia nodded, vastly relieved when the serving woman returned with plates of food. Her relief evaporated, though, when Jamie asked the woman if she knew of any neighbors who hailed from Gravesend originally.

"Nay," she said without hesitation.

"Truly?" Jamie feigned surprise. "Mrs. Palmer, of St. Peter's Church, assured me she thought there might be."

"I wouldn't know," she retorted, and walked away without a backward glance.

Her stomach knotted with worry; it felt like everyone in the room must be staring at them. "What are you doing?" she whispered.

He leaned toward her until their foreheads almost touched. "Taking a gamble. If it doesn't pay off . . ." He shrugged.

Mildly reassured, she nodded. They ate in relative silence. "Jamie," Olivia asked softly. "At St. Peter's, you looked up at the sky. What were you thinking?"

He drained his mug of ale and set it down. This time his voice was as low as hers. "There's quite a tall tower on that church. I imagine it could be seen at sea. It just made me think anew on the nature of the person we're seeking: someone who must have known, or been, a smuggler."

"You think the vicar's wife was a smuggler?"

One corner of his mouth quirked at her shocked whisper. "Not necessarily. But perhaps she was.

Whether it's Miss Charters or someone else, though, we're looking for a smuggler."

"'Tain't often an airy day blows two Londoners all the way to Thanet," boomed a hearty voice.

They both turned. A bluff gentleman, tall and white-haired, stood smiling down at them. "That's a pity," said Jamie. "This is fair country."

"Indeed it is. Although it's a trifle late for sea bathing, at this time of year."

"We are undaunted," Jamie assured him.

The stranger laughed, and nodded at Jamie's tankard. "Another ale, my friend? Patten brews a fine one." Jamie gave a nod, and the man waved one hand at the serving woman. Without asking what he wanted, she jerked her head and disappeared. "And what could I possibly offer you, lovely lady?" Their new friend fixed a pleased smile on his face and bowed very gallantly to Olivia.

She wet her lips and tried to smile, but her heart was thumping with dread. She stole a glance at Jamie, who glanced fleetingly at the seat opposite her. "Conversation, sir. Won't you join us?"

"Thank 'ee, I will." He took the seat as the woman returned with two tankards of ale. "Martha, my dear, you make my heart glad."

"It's the ale that does that," she shot back, plunking them on the table and whisking away again.

He only laughed. "That it does! As does the company of a lovely lady." He smiled at Olivia again.

"James Collins," said Jamie, inclining his head. "And my wife. A pleasure to make your acquaintance, sir." He paused expectantly, but their new companion ignored this hint to introduce himself.

"What's your purpose in Thanet at this time of year? It's a limb-of-a-way from London, which must be crying at the loss of your lady's fair presence."

"A family matter," said Jamie easily. "My wife's brother died and left some curious documents, which have wreaked havoc among the family. Naturally we are desperate to learn more, and managed to locate a solicitor in Gravesend who handled his affairs. Unfortunately, that fellow also died recently. He left behind a daughter, and we hope she may have inherited something from her father that might answer our questions about Henry's intentions."

While visiting vicars, they had decided it was better to continue the pretense that they were married, and that meant it was easier to refer to Henry as her brother. Olivia wished he'd been so easily dealt with in real life.

"Such a shame, when a fellow leaves behind trouble," said the newcomer sympathetically. "My sympathies, ma'am."

Olivia bowed her head. "That's very kind of you," said Jamie. "The only thing we know about this lady, unfortunately, is that she married a vicar near Ramsgate. Her father was named Charters but we've no idea what her husband's name is."

The other man sipped his ale. "'Tain't much to go on."

"No," Jamie agreed, "but my wife's mother is so distraught over her son's death, we had to make the inquiry."

"O' course." He shrugged. "But there be no lady called Charters here."

"It may have been years ago that she came here."

"Born and bred in Thanet, I am," was the prompt reply. "Right here in Broadstairs, as it happens. I've never known a woman called Charters." He leaned forward. "Why did you want to find her?"

Olivia tensed. Under the table she groped for Jamie's hand, which he squeezed reassuringly—or in warning, she wasn't sure which. Once again it seemed every ear in the tavern room was attuned to their conversation.

"We hope she can help us," Jamie answered.

The fellow made a low *hmph,* his gaze swinging to Olivia. "Aye, with your brother, ma'am. What were his name?"

She wet her lips. "Henry."

The older man grinned. "Plenty of Henrys hereabouts. Which one in particular?"

Before she could stop herself she looked at Jamie. Should she trust this fellow? Jamie gave a tiny nod, which somehow didn't calm her anxiety. But she did trust Jamie, so she replied, in a whisper, "Townsend. Henry Townsend."

His assessing gaze didn't waver. "He must have been up to some dangerous things, from the look on your face. You look skeer'd even to say his name."

She was. They had come all the way to Thanet without any real clues to what they were seeking, and Jamie had just reminded her they were really looking for a smuggler, not a kindly vicar's wife. A smuggler might not react well to being tracked down and questioned, to say nothing of actually helping them. It wouldn't surprise Olivia one bit to learn this room was filled with smugglers right this moment. Night had fallen, they were strangers in this town, no one knew where to find them, and there was a deep, dark ocean right down the road, waiting to swallow up any hapless person who stirred up a mystery better left long-forgotten . . .

Something of all that must have showed on her face. Before she could reply, the old gentleman gave her an abashed smile. "I can see I've brought up a sensitive matter," he said in a kindly tone. "Perhaps I should leave you in peace and not blether on like a gossipy old besom . . ." He started to push back his chair.

"No." Olivia put her hand on the table. "Please." No one else wanted to talk to them. She wasn't going to be any more at ease with one of the other local citizens, and while this fellow may have approached them to discourage them, at least he seemed friendly. "If there is anything you know that can help us, I wish you would stay."

For a long moment he just watched her, looking for all the world like a kindly grandfather as he rested his folded arms on the table. His white hair fell over his forehead, and his green eyes twinkled as he smiled at her. His clothes, she finally noticed, were sturdy and well made, and his hands were closer to a gentleman's hands than a laborer's. "I do find it terrible hard to resist the pleas of a beautiful woman, Mrs. . . . ?" He dropped his chin suggestively.

Olivia realized he knew they'd lied. Her heart pounded as she drew in a shuddering breath. *We're taking a gamble,* Jamie had said. "Mrs. Townsend," she said in a barely audible whisper. "Henry's widow."

His expression didn't change. "I thought it might be. No brother is worth that much."

Nor was Henry. "And your name, sir?" she felt bold enough to ask. If she was going to spill her secrets, he ought to as well.

"Pike, ma'am. Charlie Pike at your service."

Olivia glanced at Jamie the same moment he looked at her. He must be thinking what she was: could this be *Capn. P* himself? It would be the greatest stroke of luck she'd had in weeks.

"I—we—believe Henry left something, or lost something, that only his solicitor knew of. Finding the solicitor's daughter, Miss Charters, may be our only hope of untangling the mystery."

"Lost something?" Mr. Pike chuckled. "The only thing I ever lost to a solicitor was money, and a great mot of it, too. But I doubt you'll get a farthing back from a lawyer, ma'am. Anointed scoundrels, all of 'em."

"It's not money," she murmured. Her hands were clenched in fists in her lap, and she imagined every person in the room was eavesdropping on her words. Jamie, though, looked calm, if highly alert, so she kept her focus on the man across from her.

"Not money! What else could a solicitor have that a woman might want?"

"Something valuable. Something rare or unique. Something . . ." She lifted one hand and spread her fingers in frustration. "Something secret."

"Rare and secret, eh? Sounds dangerous. Why be you so set on locating it?" Mr. Pike leaned toward her, his bright green eyes fixed on her under his wild shock of white hair.

Olivia took a deep breath. "Someone thinks I have it," she confessed in a low voice. "And he wants it badly enough to threaten my life for it."

"The bloody blighter," said Mr. Pike in an almost genial tone. "What makes him think you've got it? Your pardon, but you don't seem to know what it is you're after."

"I don't know, precisely," she answered slowly, never taking her eyes from his. Mr. Pike knew more than he was admitting, she was sure of it. She also had the feeling that she was undergoing some sort of test, a test it was vitally important she pass. Some instinct told her Jamie couldn't help; she wondered if he felt that as well, for he had been silent for several minutes even though she could feel him beside her, listening to every word.

"But I believe it's a very valuable piece of art," she went on, picking her words with care. "Perhaps old, or the work of a great master. Nothing less than a true treasure would drive this man to pursue me as he's done, to frighten me and assault me—" Unexpectedly, her voice wobbled, and she paused to steady it. "He tried to harm a dear friend of mine because she would not tell him where I had gone when I fled town to escape him. And I fear he'll do even worse to me if he catches me before I find it."

"The dirty scoundrel," Mr. Pike said sympathetically. He still seemed remarkably unmoved by her tale. "So you plan to find this treasure and give it to him to spare yourself and others his wrath."

Her heart began to sink. Perhaps he was just an idle old chap who liked to talk, and he had no way—or intention—of helping her. Perhaps this was just an amusing story to him, and he would amble back to his mates by the fire and have a good laugh at her expense after turning her and Jamie away. Perhaps he'd be yet another man indifferent to her attempts to save herself from the trouble inflicted upon her by other men. A pox on the lot of them, each and every man in the world—except Jamie. Her temper sparked and she felt the warmth rising to her cheeks. "Mr. Pike—"

Beside her Jamie stirred, a subtle shifting of his weight. But his knee pressed lightly against hers, in warning or encouragement, she didn't know. Olivia took it as the latter. She hoped it was the latter. Still, she leaned forward and lowered her voice, even if she didn't try to hide the intensity of her feelings. "I have fled my home alone in the winter, with only what I could carry in a single valise, all the way to the very edge of England. Thanks to my late husband, who turned out to be a baser scoundrel than I ever imagined, I have no money and no place to safely rest my head. The man chasing me has cost me my friends, my home, nearly everything I hold dear. And you think I would suffer all that, only to hand a valuable object over to the man who has ruined my life? Never."

Pike tipped his head in Jamie's direction. "You're hardly alone. He's quite a strapping lad, if you don't mind my saying so."

She turned to look at Jamie. His steady hazel gaze met hers, and this time she knew he was encouraging her. "If not for him I would never have made it this far," she said honestly. "But because he's helped me, he's in as much danger as I am." She faced Mr. Pike again. "I don't want to give the treasure to the dragon, I want to return it to its rightful owner, where the dragon won't be able to touch it. But I'd sooner throw it into the ocean than let that horrible man have it."

A broad grin creased his face. "A fighting lass! I like a woman with a strong heart—and a vengeful one, too. It keeps a man on his toes." He winked at Jamie. "Very like my Mary, you are, if you don't mind my saying so. She could outface an entire regiment of His Majesty's forces and drive them back over the dunes with their heads hung in shame." He slapped one hand on the table. "Will you come along for a glass of elderberry wine, Mrs. Townsend?"

Olivia let out her breath, ready to give up and decline. As she opened her mouth to speak, though, she caught the way Mr. Pike's eyes twinkled—not with mere humor but with a wild thrill of delight, as if he found her a worthy adversary.

Or a kindred spirit.

Chapter 15

Two things flashed through her mind in the time it took to draw breath. First, that Mr. Pike definitely knew more than he had let on so far, and quite possibly a great deal more than she did. And second, that he was going to help her. She wasn't entirely sure why, but she would have bet her last borrowed shilling on it. He was simply enjoying being chased and beseeched.

So instead of a polite refusal, she said, "Thank you, sir. That's very kind. We'd be delighted."

He gave a bark of laughter. "I knew you was a witty one! *We*, indeed." He rose to his feet and offered her his hand. "I was ready to offer you my own cloak, for it's a cold walk along the cliffs, but I fancy he's got there afore me, eh?" Again he tipped his head toward Jamie.

Olivia reached for her bonnet. "I have my own cloak, Mr. Pike." Then she ruined her regal statement by catching Jamie's eye as she wound his muffler around her neck. "But he got there before anyone."

The old man laughed again and went to collect his own cloak and hat, waving one hand at his mates still clustered around the fire. Jamie leaned close to her as he dropped several coins on the table for their drinks. "You'll make me blush."

She looked into his face as she tied her bonnet ribbons snugly beneath her chin. "I told you long ago." There had never been another man who tempted her, nor touched her heart. He was the only one she had ever told *I love you*.

He tilted a little nearer. "Not from surprise," he whispered. "From joy, Livie. I'll never tire of hearing it." He darted a smoldering glance at her and Olivia swayed toward him. "It will help me bear it a little better when you flirt with our new friend."

"Flirt?" She stopped in astonishment. "Why?"

"I think it would do a world of good."

She put her hand on his arm as they turned toward the door. "Jamie . . . do you think he knows something and means to help us?"

His gaze went back to the old man, who was bundling himself up by the fire. "I rather believe he does," Jamie murmured. He glanced at her. "Either that, or he's leading us out where he can dispose of me and woo you in earnest."

Olivia blinked, then barely stifled her nervous laugh. "No!"

"I wouldn't put it past him." Jamie touched the small of her back as he guided her out of the smoky, warm pub. "He's a spry old chap and clearly appreciates a beautiful woman with some spirit and courage."

She blushed as Mr. Pike gave her a gleeful grin. "Don't be silly," she whispered to Jamie.

He only smiled.

The wind bit into them with a vengeance as

they stepped into the cobbled lane outside. A long stone wall ran down the road toward the cliffs overlooking the water, and Mr. Pike led them that way. Olivia's eyes watered as the cold gale blew in her face, and she ducked her head.

"It be right airy out tonight," Mr. Pike remarked. He threw the end of his cloak over one shoulder, but seemed otherwise unmoved by the frigid temperatures. "The darkest nights always are in Thanet."

Unconsciously Olivia glanced at the sky, where a faint sliver of moon shone above them. The heavens were thick with stars, which looked like glints of ice crackling over the obsidian sky. "You don't seem chilled by it," she said, trying to keep her teeth from chattering. Jamie, shoulders hunched, walked beside her. Olivia fancied he angled his body to blunt some of the wind's force from her, which warmed her heart if not the rest of her.

"Gracious heart alive, no," their guide replied. "Born and raised in the sea air. It makes the blood run hotter." She barely caught the suggestive look he gave her.

"And the tongue more glib," she retorted.

He nodded in appreciation. "Another very useful thing to have on the coast."

She smiled in spite of herself. He was a cagy one. He'd got her whole story—even her real name—out of her and told her nothing in return. Yet somehow she'd willingly walked out of the pub into the night with him. Was this madness? It must be that or desperation, she thought; even Jamie must be running out of ideas to pursue. "Is it a long walk?"

"A tidy few steps." He crooked his arm in invitation. "Can I offer a lady a strong arm? It can be glincey out with the ice."

Olivia hesitated, then put her hand on his cuff. Mr. Pike immediately tugged her closer to his side, although not indecently so. If it had been Jamie, she wouldn't have minded a bit.

"It's been a long while since I escorted a beautiful woman down this path," Pike said. "Ah, I miss it. You're a fortunate fellow, young man," he said without looking at Jamie.

"I feel my good fortune every day," was his reply.

Olivia thought of Jamie's suggestion that she flirt, and decided to try it. "And I feel my good fortune this very moment, as two escorts offer quite a bulwark against the wind."

Pike laughed. "Wait until you've had a nip of elderberry wine! It will take the chill right off."

They turned down a narrower lane, away from the direction of the Three Sails. Behind them the village was a cluster of stone and thatch houses, and before them the plain swept out toward the water, dotted with fishing cottages, their lit windows as bright as the stars above. When the wind calmed for a moment, she could hear the distant rumble of surf breaking on the beach.

Thankfully it wasn't long before Mr. Pike stopped in front of a gate in the low stone wall. He swung it open and led Olivia through, then waited to close it behind Jamie. A sturdy stone house stood within the walls, with a squat round tower on one end and a steeply sloped roof. Mr. Pike opened the door and went about lighting the lamps.

"Give it a firm push to close out the draft," he told Jamie, still standing in the doorway. "Come in, come in! I'll stir up the fire." He disappeared into the next room.

Olivia untied her cloak as Jamie gave the door an appraising look before carefully closing it. *Always keeping an eye on the surroundings,* she thought, then shoved the thought from her mind. She was going to trust her instinct this time. Too often she had ignored it, and told herself she was being silly to suspect other men of ignoble motives. A man of Clary's rank wouldn't stoop to harassing her. Henry wouldn't have committed criminal acts. The solicitors Mr. Brewster and Mr. Armand would tell her the truth.

She suspected Mr. Pike was also hiding something, but she thought it might work in her favor this time. It had popped into her head as they walked that their host was a smuggler himself, or had been. Raised near the coast, able to talk to strangers and draw them out without revealing himself, unruffled by her tale of stolen treasure and dragons. Instead of being alarmed or dismissive, he'd been interested.

Either way, she had nothing to lose at this point. She hung up her cloak and went with Jamie into the parlor.

Mr. Pike rose from stirring the fire as they entered, the poker in his hand. The coals in the grate were crackling back to life. He gestured at a portrait above the fireplace, of a fair-haired young woman with a direct gaze and a firm mouth. She wore the clothing of several decades ago. "My Mary," he said proudly. "Such a fetching lass she was. And a keen shot with the pistol, too."

"I envy her," murmured Olivia. Being a crack shot would have come in handy when Lord Clary grew threatening.

Pike cut a glance her way. "Do you? Every woman ought to know how to handle a gun. I'd be pleased to show you, if yon fellow hasn't done the job properly."

Jamie cleared his throat. Olivia smiled, just catching the amused twinkle in his eye. "Mr. Pike, I think your Mary must have been quite a woman, to keep you in line."

He gave a shout of laughter. "Said like a wife! Well, come sit by the fire. I'll fetch the wine, and then you can consider my offer about the gun." He winked and went out of the room.

Olivia whirled on Jamie. "He's not about to come back with a gun and shoot us, is he?"

Jamie smiled, though his eyes were watchfully pinned to the door. "I'm not worried about that." He ran one hand down his greatcoat, over the pocket, displaying the lines of a pistol. "I only hope he's not planning to keep us here all night before he gets around to telling us something useful."

She edged closer, glancing at the doorway. "I have an idea he might have been a smuggler."

"I wouldn't be surprised," he murmured as Mr. Pike came back into the room with a tray holding a bottle and three glasses.

"To take the chill from your bones," Mr. Pike said, pouring a glass and offering it to Olivia.

A cautious sip revealed the elderberry wine to be tart and rich. "Delicious," she said.

He beamed. "My own vintage. The trick is to blend in a bit of good claret wine."

She took another sip. "I never would have guessed."

Mr. Pike leaned forward. "It must be a secret between us, Mrs. Townsend. Amos Harding has been trying for years to sniff out my method. His elderberry wine is weak and thin in comparison to this."

Olivia raised her brows as she smiled. "A secret! I'm honored to be so trusted."

"I expect one glimpse of your face could make any fellow confess his darkest sin." He glanced at Jamie. "Am I right, my good man?"

"It could indeed," he quietly confirmed.

"But it troubles me greatly that you're asking after local rogues and scoundrels," Pike went on. He leaned back in his chair and fixed an admonitory look on her. "'Tain't safe to ask such questions, Mrs. Townsend. There's some who won't take it as gentlemanly as I do."

Carefully she set her glass on the table beside her chair. "I know," she replied. "But I have no choice."

"Even worse, you don't know what exactly you're asking after. It might tempt certain untrustworthy folk to tell tales, hoping to take advantage. Ask for a reward when they've nothing to give, you understand."

"It's a risk I have to take." She turned her most open and artless gaze on him. "But I think you won't lie to me—just as I think you know something that could help me."

He smiled, neither affirming nor denying it.

"Why would you think an old fool like me would know anything useful?"

Olivia didn't hesitate. "Because I don't think you're any sort of fool at all. I suspect you knew of my husband's activities, even if not by his name. I wouldn't be surprised if you know a bit about everything that goes on around here." She glanced at the portrait, where the fair Mary's gaze seemed fierce and proud. "No woman like that would suffer a fool for her husband. I daresay she'd want the most daring and intrepid man in Broadstairs."

Pike regarded her in silence for a long minute, still smiling in a kindly, slightly regretful way. "There's some as would be offended by that. It's no secret Broadstairs held a number of free traders in years past, some mighty dangerous men among them."

"And you said she wasn't afraid of a whole regiment of soldiers," Olivia countered.

Pike inclined his head. "That she wasn't."

"I hope she was just as fierce in the face of evil. I hope she wouldn't want another woman to be harassed and assaulted by any man, let alone one as cruel as the man pursuing me. I hope she would want to thwart him in any way she could."

Pike was motionless. "That she would," he said quietly, almost to himself.

"Then I believe she would help me. I would, if another woman begged my aid. And I would expect no less of a husband who loved me." Olivia waited, holding her breath and not daring to look away from him. There was an inscrutable expression on Mr. Pike's face, as if he were doing some very hard thinking. *Please,* she silently begged. *Please don't be another dead end . . .*

"Well. Perhaps." Pike slapped his knee, making her jump. "'Tis late, and you must be tired, Mrs. Townsend. Was the wine to your liking?"

"I—yes," she managed to say. "Very much."

"Excellent!" His broad grin was back. "Perhaps you'll stop by tomorrow for a cup of tea?"

Olivia stared at him, perplexed and dismayed. "That would be lovely," said Jamie beside her, giving her foot a subtle nudge. "Thank you, sir."

"My pleasure, entirely my pleasure!" He beamed as Olivia slowly rose to her feet, unsure what had happened, and he kept beaming as they went out and collected their cloaks. "Until tomorrow," he said, taking Olivia's hand and raising it for an extravagant kiss. "But you'll want to hire a better carriage, young man. It will be another raw day, and beauty such as this shouldn't be exposed to the wind for long." He still held her hand.

"Thank you, Mr. Pike," she murmured. He hadn't told her a single helpful thing, but he *had* invited them back. That must mean something—mustn't it? If only she knew what.

She waited until she and Jamie were well away from his door before she asked. "Do you still believe he will help us?"

He pulled his collar higher. "I do."

"How?" she asked anxiously.

"That, I do not know." He pressed her hand, curled snugly around his arm. "But whatever he does, it will all be thanks to you. You were magnificent, Livie."

She sighed, too tense even to appreciate the

compliment. "It will be worth nothing if he doesn't have anything of import to tell us."

"He told us a great deal," Jamie replied. "He married a fierce woman who could—and may have—faced down soldiers, which a smuggler's wife might do. He likes you, perhaps a little too much. He plays the part of an old fool but he isn't one. Not once did he question the charges of smuggling, or deny he knew anything about it. It looked for all the world as though he was testing you, to see if you truly know something or are merely asking questions. It's been almost two years since Henry died, after all, and presumably no one's been asking about those activities since. I would be cautious, too, if someone suddenly turned up asking about it."

They headed back toward the Anchor and their carriage, walking so briskly they were almost running. The wind howled and tugged at their clothing, and Olivia kept as close to Jamie as she could without slowing her stride. "And his invitation to tea?"

"If he has nothing to tell us, why would he ask us back?"

"Because he's enjoying the attention."

"Possibly," Jamie conceded. "But at the moment he's our main hope."

There it was in words: they were running out of clues. If Mr. Pike was merely toying with them, it hardly mattered. They had nowhere else to turn.

Jamie must have sensed her thoughts. He stopped abruptly, turning to face her. "Either way, this is not the end," he said, cupping one gloved hand around her cheek. "It may take us a while to find a new possibility, but we shan't despair."

She leaned into his hand, and for a moment the wind seemed to stop. "You're so confident . . ."

He grinned, his teeth white in the darkness, then gave her a quick, hard kiss on the mouth. "And you should be, too. Between the two of us, we're more than a match for Lord Clary—or Captain Pike."

Jamie had taken many risks in his life, but never one where so much hung on the outcome.

On one side, he was pleased—elated—that his gamble in the pub had paid off. Charlie Pike was exactly the sort of fellow he'd hoped to flush out, and he would have bet heavily that Pike knew far more about Henry's activities than he'd let on so far.

On the other side, though, just because he knew didn't mean he would tell them. Understandably reticent, Pike might tell them the whole operation had ceased at Henry's death, whether or not it was true. He might give them another clue, another lead, and following it would take time Jamie worried they didn't have. And if Pike warned them not to stir waters that had gone quiet, Jamie didn't know what he'd do.

When he bet on a horse, it was only money at stake. When he traveled off the beaten path, he felt able to defend himself. When he invested, he had plenty of time to investigate and weigh his options, as well as negotiate a reasonable bargain.

This time, though, he had few options and even

less time. Jamie knew with horrible certainty that nothing would ever persuade Lord Clary that Olivia couldn't lead him to the treasure. He probably believed she had it already. And Jamie didn't doubt that Clary would be all too pleased to vent his frustration on her in numerous vile ways if she didn't give him *something*.

And while Jamie thought Clary was ultimately after money, the viscount was also motivated by a sinister obsession with Olivia herself. He had a strong foreboding that it would take more than a missing treasure for her to be free of the man.

He told her none of that. By the time they returned to the inn, she had begun to believe Pike did mean to help them in some crucial, even if small, way. There would be time enough to worry about Clary once they had the treasure in hand. For tonight they could focus on that first pressing matter, and each other. He took her to bed and held her close. She fit so perfectly against him. She responded to his kiss as if the last decade had blown away like the vestiges of a bad dream. She forgave him. She trusted him again—perhaps could even love him again. Jamie held her in the dark and felt his heart twist to think that he might not be worthy of that—again.

Chapter 16

The next morning broke cold and blustery, wind rattling the panes of the windows, along with infrequent bursts of rain. Olivia woke up when Jamie slid from the bed. She heard the light crack as he broke the ice in the washbasin, smiled at the muffled curse he uttered while splashing his face, and then snuggled deeper into the mattress as she listened to him stoke the fire. By the time he got back into the bed, she could feel the first tendrils of warmth from the hearth—which did not erase the shock of his chilled hands as he reached for her. "You're cold," she gasped.

"Not for long," he whispered, slipping his hand inside the loose neckline of her nightgown. Olivia squeaked as his palm found her breast. Her nipple surged under his cold fingers. "I thought you were asleep."

"I was!" She writhed in his arms, though not in any real attempt to get away from him.

"Then let me be the first to wish you good morning, my love." He nipped her earlobe between his teeth and Olivia shivered, but not from the cold this time. His knee nudged hers, and she parted her legs at once. He wrapped himself around her, his erection hard and insistent at her back.

When he tugged up the hem of her nightgown, she started to roll over, but he kept her pinned in place. "Don't move," he breathed against her shoulder. "I like the look of you this way, still soft and dreamy with sleep. Let me imagine you asleep so I can wake you properly . . ."

The first touch of his fingers between her thighs was so gentle she caught her breath. If she had been asleep, it wouldn't have disturbed her. Again his fingertip dipped, gliding lightly through the dark curls. Olivia didn't know how he could think she looked soft with sleep now; she felt wide awake and tense with anticipation.

As his fingers slowly teased her, his mouth whispered kisses across the back of her neck. Part of her wanted to melt with happiness at the worship, and part of her wanted to push her hips against his hand for more intense pleasures. Every time she shifted, though, he held her still, trapped in the cocoon of his arms and legs.

She quivered as his fingers finally touched her, still lightly but with purpose. He groaned, his breath hot against her skin. "Already wet and hot . . ."

"Yes," she whimpered as he stroked, far too leisurely. "Please, Jamie . . ."

He laughed softly. "Patience, my sleeping beauty."

Olivia closed her eyes and gave in. He wanted to wake her; if only he knew that he already had. She'd finally roused from the deadened state that had dulled her heartbreak. It felt as if she'd been wrapped in a dozen blankets to shield herself from feeling anything, and in a matter of days Jamie had peeled them away. Even with the threat of Clary chasing them, even with the shock of discovering Henry's criminal acts, the world had an unwonted sharpness and clarity now. It felt as if she could see and hear and think more clearly; all her senses were keener.

Especially when he was touching her. When she began to tremble from the delicate teasing of his fingers, Jamie shifted. "So beautiful," he sighed. "So bewitching." He nudged her knee farther forward and then his erection was against her, pressing inside her. Olivia arched her back and he sank deeper. This time his breathing stopped, and for a moment neither moved, caught in the moment of being so completely joined.

With a growl Jamie pulled her thigh back, lifting her leg up until he could hook it over his. He paused to lick his fingers, then resumed stroking her as his hips began a hard, driving rhythm against hers. Again she tried to twist, and his fingers bit into her shoulder as he pulled her against him, until her body was arched and open. The bed ropes creaked as he surged forward, again and again, until tears ran down her cheeks. She could only grip handfuls of the bedclothes as a whirlwind built within her. She tried to hold it back, tried to wait for him to join her, but he refused to allow it. He sucked at the skin behind her ear and he plucked at her nipple, all while his cock thrust inside her and his wicked, insistent fingers wrung a brilliant, almost blinding climax from her.

She broke with a long, gasping sigh and a

tremor that shook her body. Jamie barely paused as he grabbed a pillow and stuffed it under her hips before he rolled her over onto her stomach. Still buried inside her to the hilt, he took hold of her hips and began thrusting hard and deep. Still reeling, Olivia tucked her hands beneath her chin and let him ride her. Every jolt of his body into hers set off another tremor inside her. And when he finally stiffened and groaned in his own release, a truly dreamy smile curved her lips.

Jamie bent over her. His lips touched her shoulder, and she realized he was trembling. "Good morning," he said in a ragged voice. "I trust you're well and truly awake."

Olivia smiled and stretched beneath him. "And if I'm not?"

He was quiet a moment, then gave a raspy laugh. "I would try again. In a few minutes." He eased away and collapsed onto the mattress beside her, facedown on the pillow.

She flipped onto her side and scooted closer to him, smoothing the damp hair back from his forehead. Her heart gave an unsteady thump at the faint smile that appeared on his face when she touched him. *I love you,* she thought. *Always have and always will*. It must be written on her face, shining in her eyes. Love felt like a cozy fire in her breast, warming her from the inside out.

But as had been the case for too long in her life, shadows hovered at the edges. She and Jamie weren't any ordinary couple, free to fall in love and live a carefree happy life. Not yet, and perhaps not ever. *It would kill me if Clary hurt him because of me.*

As if he could hear her, his eyes fluttered open. For a moment they lay side by side, gazing into each other's eyes.

"Don't be anxious," he said softly.

Olivia rolled her eyes sheepishly. "You read me too well."

He moved one shoulder in something resembling a shrug. "You're my favorite subject to study."

That could hardly be true, after the last ten years. She looked away, trailing her fingers over his back, broad and strong. "I never could keep a secret from you."

"Why must you?" He rolled up on one elbow and caught her hand, bringing it to his lips.

"A lady must always have her secrets."

Instead of grinning at her lightly spoken reply, his face grew grim. "Right. I suppose we all do."

Olivia waited, puzzled, but he said no more. "Do you think Mr. Pike will be helpful?" she ventured.

"I—" Jamie stopped. His expression was serene, but Olivia knew him too well. He was keeping something from her. "I certainly hope so."

"I hope so, too," she said firmly. "But if we never find Henry's lost treasure, I will blame Henry—not you. If Lord Clary continues to hound me, I will blame him—not you. If Mr. Pike is only toying with us . . ." She forced a smile. "I shan't be surprised."

Jamie let out his breath. "I don't know what we'll do next, if he can tell us nothing."

Olivia paused. It was the first time he'd admitted doubt about their chances. But of course he must have been making those calculations all along, she realized a moment later. He simply hadn't shared them with her. Even though his unflagging confidence had buoyed her through the last several days, she was glad that he had been honest.

And perhaps she could pay him back. She kissed his knuckles again, then released his hand. "I feel lucky today. Don't you?"

Cautious surprise flickered in his eyes. "I do."

"Let us believe Mr. Pike will help us. If he can't, we'll worry about that tonight."

The smile that slowly spread over his face was wondrous: fierce, proud, and determined. "We will." He kissed her once, hard, and tossed back the blankets. "Let's be on our way."

By the time they had dressed and eaten, the storm had blown out to sea. The wind was still brisk but the sun began to emerge from the clouds as they set off in the carriage. With hot bricks underfoot and Olivia's hand tucked into his pocket for warmth, Jamie drove out of the inn yard and headed up the coast toward the far side of Broadstairs. It was a small village, but it had taken them a while to walk from Pike's stone cottage to the tavern. He retraced their steps, hoping fervently that today would bear fruit.

Mr. Pike opened the door in his banyan, a matching cap on his head. "Come in, come in! Forgive my informality, my old bones were cold last night." He slapped his hip and grinned, but Jamie noticed he didn't have a trace of limp.

The table was already laid in the parlor where they'd sat last night. Pike had obviously been waiting for them. He turned to Olivia. "Would you mind preparing the tea, my dear? I find a lady always does it ever so much better than any man could hope to."

She gave him a twinkling smile. "Of course, sir." Today she wore her blue dress, the one that made her eyes glow and set off her dark hair and fair skin. Pike looked as dazzled as Jamie felt. If he got her into silks and jewels, Olivia would set London on its ear.

"It will be a fine day for sailing," Pike said as Olivia served the tea. "Are you a sailing man, Mr. Collins?"

"Only for sport." Jamie didn't add that he considered sailing a summer sport.

Pike nodded philosophically. "Better than naught, I suppose. Spent my life upon the sea; most everyone in Broadstairs has. I never saw what made a man want to stay on a farm. The earth is the same, day after day. The ocean, now . . . The ocean is a new world every time you venture out, calm one day, fierce and dangerous the next."

"Were you ever in grave danger?" Olivia asked. She gazed at Mr. Pike with rapt interest, and Jamie could almost see the older man puff up under her regard. No doubt about it, Pike was a lonely old chap with an eye for the ladies.

"Every time, Mrs. Townsend, every time!" He winked. "That's the appeal of it."

For the next hour he regaled them with tales of his adventures on the sea, although without ever quite saying what business took him to sea. Olivia poured several cups of tea, as if to keep his tongue well lubricated, and gradually enough details crept in to assure Jamie that their guess was right: Pike had been a smuggler. An enthusiastic and crafty one, from his telling.

The time he dove overboard to secure loose barrels. The time he ended up swinging over the ocean on a rope in a storm when they needed to haul down a sail in quick order. The way he described the customs men who would sometimes board his ship and harass his men. "Not a brain among the lot of those revenue chaps," Pike said disdainfully. "Idiots all, fond only of causing trouble."

Olivia nodded earnestly. "Oh yes. I read in the newspapers about a man who outsmarted the revenue men so often, they stopped arresting him."

Pike chuckled. "That would likely be Joss Snelling. A luckier chap you'll never meet. Once, the revenuers set a trap for him. Left their horses at the top of the cliff and went down to lie in wait at the bottom. Old Joss come ashore to find they was buried when the cliff gave way, and he could walk home unhindered." He shook his head admiringly. "He'll outwit the devil himself, when Beelzebub comes for his soul."

"He's still smuggling?" Olivia said in surprise. A horrified look crossed her face, as if she hadn't meant to say it aloud.

"'Till the day he dies, most like," said Pike comfortably. "It's bred in us in Thanet."

Ask him now, Jamie thought suddenly. He fixed his gaze on Olivia and tried to communicate it to her. She had Pike eating out of her hand. The right question now could unlock the mystery . . .

She caught his eye. In a charged second, a whole conversation seemed to pass between them. It was another gamble, Jamie knew, but they had run out of safe bets.

Olivia wet her lips before looking up at Mr. Pike again. "Right to the bone, Mr. Pike?"

"Aye, Mrs. Townsend."

"Then you must know something about the object I seek."

Jamie realized he was holding his breath. Mr. Pike was reclining in his chair, hands clasped over his stomach, the genial expression still fixed on his face. For what seemed like an hour, he simply sat there, smiling at Olivia. "I wonder, have you got a plan for what you'll do with this lost item if you find it?"

"I want to return it to the rightful owner."

He made a face and flipped one hand. "Some Frog?"

"Perhaps a Frenchman," she acknowledged. "Perhaps an Italian, or even an Austrian. The Duke of Wellington says England's honor compels us to return what Bonaparte took."

"I don't support returning anything to a Frog," he warned. "Trophies of war, I say. The duke can say what he wants; it's our men what bled and died fighting his war, and I'll not be handing back anything won, fair or not."

Olivia drew an unsteady breath. Jamie could see the pulse pounding at the base of her throat. He tried to hide his own anxiety, even though his muscles felt so taut he wasn't sure he would be able to move. "I fear that if I don't find it, the man pursuing me won't stop until he has it. He deserves it far less than any Frenchman alive, I promise you. He already tried to kill my friend . . ." She glanced at the portrait above the fire. "Penelope looks very like your Mary, sir, with beautiful blond hair and blue eyes, and an indomitable spirit."

Pike didn't look at the painting. "And how do you know that you'll be able to do as you say? How can you be certain it will solve your problem with this unworthy scoundrel?"

"If I return it to the rightful owner, Lord Clary can never get it."

Oh no. They had agreed not to use the viscount's name. Olivia realized her mistake at the same moment Jamie did. Her color faded, and he saw her fingers curl into fists in her lap.

"Clary," repeated Pike. His expression didn't change, but there was a note of satisfaction in his voice.

Olivia looked agonized, but she obviously reached the same conclusion Jamie did: they had nothing to lose by telling him all now. "Yes, Lord Clary is the man after me. He feels entitled to—to whatever it is! Even *he* doesn't know because he's not the person who wanted it, nor is he the man who paid for it. But that man is dead, and Clary wants it now."

Pike leaned forward. "So Clary thinks to seize his chance now the original client's dead, and he'll get it without paying for it?" He gave a *tsk*. "No one likes a man who won't pay."

"He thinks I have it and he's demanding I give it to him." Olivia shook her head, her face imploring. "Please, Mr. Pike, *please* tell me you know something that can help me."

"I?" He raised his brows. "Mrs. Townsend, I know plenty that could help you. But just like sea legs, secrecy's bred into every Thanet man as well. You're a fetching lass, but it takes more than a pretty face to cozen a Thanet man of all his secrets." He rapped his knuckles on the table. "Let me show you something, though."

Olivia's shoulders sank in defeat, but she rose. Mr. Pike offered his arm, and she took it with a strained smile. Jamie, though, had been watching Pike. Their host looked too pleased with himself. Pike wasn't going to *tell* them anything, but Jamie would have bet a large sum, right this moment, that he *was* going to help them.

"I can't abide seeing a woman in trouble," Pike said as he led them through the house, up a flight of stairs. "No man should raise his hand to a woman unless she's holding a knife to his throat. But when that man's a cheat as well . . ." He shook his head and opened a door.

It was an ordinary study, in Jamie's quick assessment. A desk stood near the windows. The view outside overlooked the cliff and then the sea, where the waves glittered blindingly bright in the sun. A pair of sparsely populated bookcases and a worn settee were all else that occupied the room. Pike closed the door behind them.

"A man's oath is his bond," he said quietly, "but when a fellow dies . . ." He shrugged. "I allow some duty is owed to the chap's widow." He went to the wall near the fireplace and bent down. "I left the trade years ago—too hard on the back.

But it's a hard thing to give up, like drinking, and when a profitable opportunity arises, well, there's no need to be a fool." Jamie couldn't see what he was doing, but after a moment Pike rose to his feet. He pushed on the paneling of the wall, and then slid open a section.

Jamie barely heard Olivia's gasp. In the narrow space behind the panel hung a painting. As Pike pushed the panel farther open, the light illuminated an armored knight on horseback, sword raised in battle over a crouching, snarling dragon. The beast's scales were green-black, its teeth gleamed white; its long tail glistened with small spikes. The knight's sword shone like polished silver, and he wore a cross upon his breast as he regarded the dragon with implacable resolution. Even the horse was fierce, its front hooves pawing the air before the dragon's face.

"St. George," said Pike, studying the painting with his hands on his hips. "Quite fond of him, I am. Most times I di'n't look too close at the shipments, but when no more instructions come regarding this one, I had a look. Then come word Townsend was dead and everything was over." He shrugged again. "No one ever asked for it. My fee was paid, so I kept him."

"Then he's been here for two years?" Olivia asked in a choked tone.

"Nearly," Pike agreed. "Two Februarys past."

She wet her lips. "Henry died two years ago this January."

"I expected as much. And if Clary thinks to intercept him . . ." Pike noticed Olivia's start. "I know of Lord Clary—or rather, Commodore Clary, whose lax inspections allow the trade to flow free. Coincidence, that a man of that same name thinks to catch a shipment paid for by another."

"Who . . . ?" Olivia's voice shook. "Who painted this?"

Pike squinted at her. "One fellow called him Teezun. Not sure who that is."

Titian, the great Italian master. Jamie barely kept his mouth from falling open in shock. He and Olivia had called their missing object a lost treasure without any idea of how great a treasure it really was. Jamie had no great eye for art, but he'd traveled on the Continent and dutifully viewed the masterworks of every country he visited, so he had a passing familiarity with most prominent artists. This painting wasn't familiar to him, but even he could tell it was very like other works by Titian.

This had to be what Clary wanted. A true Titian would be priceless.

"I don't fancy him being sent back to France, if that's what you've got in mind, but I always kenned he weren't mine to keep." Pike reached into the open panel and lifted the painting off the wall. "Even free traders know what's fair." He held it out to Olivia, who seemed transfixed. Reverently she took it and held it to the full light of day.

It was painted on a thin panel of wood, a little over two feet in height and a little less than that in width. The colors were subtle but rich, and every line was precise and strong. The frame was primitive but protected the work perfectly.

"Are you giving it to me?" Olivia's wide-eyed gaze jumped from the painting to Mr. Pike.

"Aye." He folded his arms across his chest and

smiled ruefully. "I think you'll do right by it. It shouldn't be hidden in a closet where only an old goat such as myself can see it."

"I haven't much money," she began, but Pike waved his hand.

"I was ne'er promised anything beyond a fee to hold it. Others brought cargo in, and others come to collect it. All I did was mind it for a bit." He winked again. "Never say smugglers haven't got any honor, Mrs. Townsend."

"Thank you," said Jamie quietly. Olivia looked overwhelmed, holding the painting at arm's length as if it might be dangerous.

"Truthfully, I'm mighty glad to send it on at last," Pike confided. "A man always sleeps a bit better when the cargo is out of the house."

Jamie could believe it. Even now he felt the tension of searching give way to anxiety about the next steps. They were far from through with this endeavor.

"It took me a while to conclude whether the greater kindness was giving it to you or denying anything about it." Pike paused until Olivia looked up and met his gaze. "But you're a stalwart lass. I couldn't leave you to face your dragon unarmed." He chuckled. "When you said you didn't want to give the treasure to the dragon, I thought you must know what you sought."

Slowly a smile crossed her face. "Mr. Pike, I had no idea—none at all."

"I realized that. And that's why I thinks you should have it." He gave her a small bow. "May St. George guard and protect you, Mrs. Townsend, all the rest of your days."

Chapter 17

They returned to the inn in an ebullient mood. "I can't believe it," said Olivia for the fourth time as they drove into the yard of the Three Sails. The painting was wrapped in oilcloth in her arms, too precious to release even to store in the carriage boot.

Jamie laughed. "But you felt lucky!"

"Not because I thought he had the painting," she protested. "Because I couldn't believe it existed at all! I was so sure—"

"What?" he prompted when she stopped. He pulled the horse up as a groom came running.

"I was so sure Henry would have taken steps to prevent it." She shook her head. "It seemed he'd done everything else to keep me from discovering anything."

Jamie jumped down and then helped her alight, carefully. "He couldn't have planned for everything." He turned his head and spoke to the groom about the horse, then led her toward the inn. "Remember that: no plan is foolproof."

Olivia just shook her head. "Yours seem to be! Have you been wrong a single time?"

He grinned. "As much as I enjoy dazzling you, I'm as astonished as you that my guesses turned out to be correct. Well—it must be admitted I was utterly wrong about the necessity of finding Miss Charters."

"Only in that we found Captain P himself instead—and he had what we hoped he had." She lowered her voice as they reached the inn door.

"And thank God for it." Jamie opened the door. They headed directly for the stairs, to spirit the painting out of sight. Olivia hunched her shoulders, draping her cloak over the oilskin, and Jamie stayed close beside her. Just as they reached the stairs, though, the innkeeper stepped in front of them.

"Good day, Mr. Collins." He nodded at Olivia. "Ma'am."

"Good day, Mr. Hughes." Jamie gave the man a nod, impatient to be upstairs.

"Was your errand successful?" The innkeeper's eyes were fixed on Olivia—too fixed. It brought Jamie's guard up, even before the man glanced pointedly at the panel peeking out of her cloak and added, "Did you find what you were looking for?"

Olivia's cheeks were red. Her mouth opened but no words came out. "We did indeed," said Jamie evenly, giving her a gentle nudge of warning. "A fine memento of our trip to Thanet."

"Hmm." The innkeeper squinted at Olivia. "Are you well, madam?"

"Oh yes." She flashed a nervous look at Jamie. "Why wouldn't I be?"

"I can't say. But you look rather pale and upset,

Mrs. Collins." He paused, and Jamie braced himself instinctively. "Or perhaps that's not the right name?"

As pale as snow, Olivia whispered, "Collins. Our name is Collins, sir."

For the first time in a minute, Mr. Hughes looked directly at Jamie. "I'd like a moment alone with the lady."

He put a protective hand on Olivia's waist. "For what reason?"

"I have reason to suspect you're not her husband." The man crossed his arms, showing off well-muscled forearms. "Has this man abducted you from your family, ma'am?"

Olivia gasped, as if letting out a breath she'd been holding for hours. "What? Of course not! This is my husband!" She stepped closer to Jamie. "Why on earth would you think otherwise, sir?"

"And is he your husband of your own free will?" Now the innkeeper bent a dangerous glare on Jamie.

"Before God, he is!" Olivia's voice rang with conviction as she recovered from her surprise and alarm. She stripped off her glove and thrust her hand forward to show the gold ring she still wore. "See there? Well worn to my finger, where it's resided many years! What is the meaning of this inquisition?"

Mr. Hughes's expression eased. "I beg your pardon, ma'am. I had to be sure. If you weren't with him of your own will, it would have been my duty to step in and restore you to your family."

"Where did you get the idea she was not my wife?" asked Jamie quietly. The door was at their back and no one had come in, but anyone could be lurking in the taproom or around the corner in one of the private parlors. He slid his hand into his pocket and curved his fingers around the butt of his pistol. He probably wouldn't have time to cock and fire it, but it was a heavy piece and would make a good cudgel, if need be.

"The lady's brother was here, searching for her. He said she'd been persuaded to run off with an adventurer and he wanted only to be certain she was safe."

Bloody hell. It could only be Clary. Jamie eased backward a step, taking a swift glance into the taproom. "Is that gentleman still here?" If they could catch the viscount by surprise, this might not be a disaster. He didn't see any sign of the man, though.

"No, sir, he waited for you a half an hour, then took his leave, saying he would return later."

"What did he look like?" asked Olivia, her lips barely moving. The indignant flush had faded from her face. "Mr. Hughes—I do not have a brother, nor a brother-in-law. Whoever that man was, he lied to you."

Doubt shadowed the innkeeper's face for the first time. "Not meaning any disrespect, ma'am, but are you sure? He described you in every detail; said you were his younger sister Olivia, a genteel and reserved lady who disappeared from the family home. He said your parents were frantic and feared a fortune hunter had persuaded you to run off."

"All lies," whispered Olivia, shaking her head in tiny, jerky motions. "I have no brother, nor have

I lived in my parents' home for many years. Was he tall—about my husband's height? With dark hair combed back? A prominent nose and a lordly air?"

"Aye," said the innkeeper slowly.

"Did he say where he was staying?" Jamie demanded, gripping his pistol. Perhaps he could still catch Clary. "How long ago did he leave?"

"Close to an hour ago," said the innkeeper, to Jamie's disappointment. "He didn't say where to find him, only that he would return tonight to see . . ." He hesitated. "To see Mrs. Collins."

Olivia inhaled, almost like a whimper. Jamie released the pistol and threw his arm around her, pulling her against him. "No," he whispered fiercely. "Do not. He will never touch you." Still trembling, she gave a tiny nod.

Now the innkeeper looked uncertain. "Who is the fellow? I take it you know him . . ."

"We do," said Jamie over Olivia's head. She pressed her face into the front of his coat and gripped his jacket. "To our everlasting dismay."

Mr. Hughes cleared his throat. "I . . . I let him wait in your chamber."

Jamie's eyes narrowed. Even if Clary had been a friend, the innkeeper had allowed a stranger into a guest's room. "How odd," he said in a frigid tone. "I distinctly recall paying for the *private* use of that room until tomorrow at the earliest."

The innkeeper flushed. "I didn't want any shady business in my inn," he muttered. "And the gent insisted on seeing if his sister might have stayed behind. When I knocked on the door and got no reply, he commanded me to open it, and then he pushed in . . . Perhaps I ought to have asked him to wait below."

"Perhaps, indeed." Jamie glared at him. "Did you wait with him? How did you know he wasn't a common thief?"

"No," the innkeeper confessed after a long pause. "He didn't look like a thief . . ."

Jamie jerked his head toward the stairs. "Let's go see if I've been robbed and ought to summon the local constable."

Realizing now that he was fully in the wrong, Mr. Hughes kept talking as he led the way upstairs, trying to explain his well-intentioned though perhaps, in hindsight, mistaken actions. Jamie barely heard a word the man said, nor did he much care. Thank God Olivia held the long-sought prize in her arms, still concealed beneath her cloak. If Clary had come this evening, or if they'd found the painting yesterday . . .

In the corridor outside their room he nodded at the innkeeper again. "Open the door."

Mr. Hughes cast an alarmed glance at the pistol Jamie drew from his pocket, but after one look at Jamie's expression, he turned and put his key in the lock. Gently Jamie pushed Olivia to the side, directly behind the innkeeper. Quietly he cocked the pistol and raised it.

The door swung ajar under Mr. Hughes's hand. Jamie slid inside, scanning the room from side to side, neither surprised nor disappointed that it was empty. He uncocked his pistol and threw the door open all the way. "Do you still think the fellow was my lady's brother?" he said grimly.

Mr. Hughes blanched. Everything in the room

had been thrown about. Two of Olivia's dresses lay on the bed, ripped into ribbons; the crown of Jamie's spare hat had been punched through. His writing case had been smashed open, leaving the polished mahogany splintered and the ink bottle broken, and papers were strewn across the floor.

Olivia peered around him and gasped. Jamie gave her a warning glance, and she went quiet. "Go fetch a constable," he snapped at Mr. Hughes.

"Oughtn't you see if something is missing first?"

"I'll do that while you fetch the constable." Jamie shoved him out of the room and closed the door. Then he ran his hands through his hair and cursed vividly.

"What are we going to do?" Olivia whispered, staring at the wreckage. "He was here—he tore apart my clothes—Jamie, he must have read all of Henry's papers—"

"Perhaps." He stepped over those papers and took the painting from her. "But he didn't get this, which I suspect is why he vented his frustration on our possessions. Olivia, he did not touch either one of us, and he *will* not," he repeated.

"But he's *here*," she said in anguish. "In Ramsgate. We weren't clever at all—he managed to find us—Jamie, how can we make it back to London ahead of him? How can we hope to slip out of town without him pursuing us? What if he's come back and is below at this very moment, waiting to finish what he began?"

He set the painting on the floor and dropped the bar across the door. Then he laid his gun on top of the chest of drawers and took out the pistol case. He opened it and began loading the second pistol. "By God, I hope he is. I'm ready to be done with that man once and for all."

"No!" She grabbed his arm. "The constable is on his way! You can't shoot Clary without being arrested."

Jamie stood rigidly for a moment. It was still tempting. But that would leave Olivia alone at the outermost reaches of Kent, in possession of the painting that made her a target. Clary might not be the only person who wanted it. He sighed. "I won't shoot him unless I must. Gather up what can be saved and leave the rest. Mr. Hughes is going to spend the rest of the night replacing what we need most urgently, or I'll see him prosecuted for collaborating with a thief."

With a nod, Olivia began picking through the remains of her clothes. Aside from his hat and writing case, nothing of Jamie's had been touched; it seemed Clary had bent his destructive impulses on her belongings. Jamie packed his things into the valise and was gathering up the scattered papers when Olivia's voice made him freeze.

"Jamie." She sounded like she was choking.

He dropped what he was holding and lunged to catch her, thinking she might faint. But she held up a paper. It had been torn from his notebook, Jamie realized, but the writing was not his own. In large, jagged handwriting was a threat:

You know what I want. Don't make me hunt you down again. Deliver it to my home in London within one week's time, or you will be very, very sorry you tried to cheat me, dearest Olivia.

"Does that mean he isn't coming back tonight?" Olivia gripped his arm. "Are we safe for tonight?"

"Perhaps." And perhaps not. Jamie didn't trust a word Clary said. "But we *will* be safe tonight—if not here."

In silence they finished packing. Olivia left her ruined dresses where they lay in stark testament to Clary's violence. Jamie flipped through his papers, trying to think of anything that might aid Clary in tracking them again. Daniel's letters were still there, as was Bathsheba's, although both were phrased obscurely enough they must have seemed insignificant to a third party. The letters of credit from his banker were still in his coat pocket, next to Henry's diary; Jamie said a silent thanks to his father, who had advised him never to leave important documents like that lying around. The bundle of Henry's papers was gone, but Jamie had expected as much. A grim smile crossed his face. Those papers were useless now, but he hoped Lord Clary tore out his hair trying to make sense of them.

He picked up his common book, from whence Clary had torn his note, and riffled through the pages. There was Olivia's chart, with the dates of Henry's letters and the location of the weather reports. That would have helped Clary more than the rest, if the viscount had only realized what it was. Of course, since Mr. Pike no longer had the painting, even the chart was worth little.

He was about to shove the book into his valise

with the rest of the papers when it fell open to a place near the back. Several pages had been cut out, but roughly. Ragged scraps bore traces of handwriting, and his heart seemed to turn to stone as he realized what those pages held.

Clary had taken all his work.

Chapter 18

The only way Olivia was able to keep her composure as she sorted through her ruined clothes was to take periodic peeks at the Titian, sitting propped up against the bureau. The oilskin cloth had fallen off, revealing the painting. Even in the fading winter sunlight, St. George's figure glowed with righteous glory, and the dragon's scales had an unearthly sheen. As long as they had that painting, she told herself, Clary had not won; he had not beaten them. He had caught them off guard and given them a nasty shock, but nothing more.

Still, her hands shook as she picked up a chemise, one of her favorites that she had embroidered herself with small pink flowers on the hem. It had been ripped to shreds. So were her two extra dresses and her nightgown. Clary had left her stockings and garters untouched, but otherwise she had only the clothes she wore. If it weren't so cold out, causing her to wear every petticoat and her shawl, she would have lost even more, she thought in a burst of bitterness. Clary seemed determined to steal everything she valued and tear it to pieces.

"I think that's all," she said to Jamie, throwing the ruined chemise behind her onto the bed. She didn't even want it now that Clary had touched it.

He was staring at his common book, which lay open in his hands. At her words he jerked up his head and looked at her with something like . . . horror. "Right. Good."

"What is it?" she asked, her pulse jumping in worry. "Did Clary write something else?"

"No. He stole some work of mine—notes about a business proposition I had made with a friend." He stuffed the book into the valise and closed it. "But it's nothing, a minor inconvenience. Stay here. I need to have a word with Mr. Hughes and see if he's fetched a constable yet."

Anxiety made her stomach lurch. "Let me go with you—"

"Someone needs to stay here," he said with a pointed glance at the exposed Titian. "Bar the door behind me, and don't open it for anyone except me. And keep the pistol at hand."

She wet her lips. "You never did show me how to shoot it, you know."

He flinched as if she'd slapped him. "I know. I wouldn't leave you if I thought you'd really need to use it. Just point it away from you and pull the trigger; the noise will bring help."

"All right." There was nothing else she could say. He left, sliding one pistol back into his pocket on his way out the door, and she put the bar in place. For a few moments she occupied herself collecting their baggage into a neat arrangement near the door, but they had only the two valises.

She put Jamie's pistol case into her valise, now almost empty, but left out the gun itself. He'd bundled all his papers from his writing case into his valise. A shiver went through her as she studied the damage to the finely crafted wooden box. It hadn't been locked; Clary could have turned the key and read everything inside. But it looked like he'd smashed it with the fireplace poker, like a wild beast might do. Olivia laid it on the bed next to her torn clothing.

She pulled up a chair near the door and found herself facing St. George again. The saint wore a noble but fierce expression as he poised his sword to meet the attack. The dragon, its gleaming green and black scales standing up like polished plates of armor, coiled like a cat preparing to spring on its victim. It was a stunning painting. She wondered who the true owner was. Mr. Pike had scoffed at the notion that the French had any claim to it, but it must have only been in France because Napoleon demanded it in one of his punitive peace treaties. That meant it had been taken from its rightful owner years, perhaps decades, ago. Would anyone even *know* who rightfully owned it after all these years?

But then, that was not her problem. Olivia rubbed her brow. Their plan was merely to deliver it to the Duke of Wellington, or some other appropriate person who would know how to return it, and reveal Clary's murderous pursuit of it. Then, with any luck, the viscount would be arrested, prosecuted, and sent to prison. Neither she nor Jamie nor Penelope would ever need to think of, or see, the man again.

Of course, that relied on their ability to return to London safely with the painting undamaged, and persuade people in power that their story was the true one, rather than any lies Clary might tell. Now that the viscount was in Ramsgate, breathing his sulfurous breath down their necks, that seemed far more difficult than it had this morning.

Her gaze fell on the note, that horrid, taunting note that exuded Clary's cruel confidence that he could reach her at any time, that he could bend her to his will by force of his name, his personality, his position, and wealth. Even when she held the painting he wanted, he threatened to ruin her if she didn't surrender to his demands.

"If you're so good at killing dragons," Olivia softly told St. George, "I wish you would put your sword through Lord Clary's heart."

By the time Jamie reached the taproom, Mr. Hughes had summoned the local constable. It appeared the innkeeper knew where the officer liked his midday pint, and he clearly wanted to present his side of the story first. Jamie put a stop to that at once.

"I wish to swear out a complaint against Mr. Hughes," he said, "for allowing a man into my chamber for nefarious purposes."

"I did no such thing!"

"A man who has taken an unhealthy and criminal interest in my wife," Jamie went on. "A man who sliced every item of her clothing to ribbons and rifled through my personal papers, no doubt for the purpose of future harassment. Mr. Hughes had so little care for his inn's reputation that he admitted a man wanted for the attempted murder of my sister, the Countess of Stratford, and gave him leave to search a guest's room."

"Murder!" Mr. Hughes's eyes bulged. "He was a gentleman, professing his concern for his sister!"

"And yet you didn't summon the constable when you believed that 'sister' may have been in grave danger." Jamie glared at him. "You didn't even bid him wait in your parlor until such time as the lady could be found and queried about her circumstances."

The constable was on his feet now, hands raised. "Now, now, gents. Let's sort this out. Is the lady in any danger at the moment?"

"No," said Jamie. "I told her to bar the door while I was away."

"Good, good." He turned to the innkeeper. "Did you allow a man into this gentleman's rooms while he was away?"

Mr. Hughes heaved a bitter sigh. "Aye."

"Not good practice, Tom," said the constable in commiseration. "Now, was anything stolen, sir?" he asked Jamie.

"Some papers of mine are missing, and every article of my wife's clothing was cut to shreds. She has nothing but the clothes she wore today."

"That's not right. Tom, I expect you'll have to replace what the lady lost." The constable gave the innkeeper a stern glance, and Mr. Hughes nodded once. "And you know who this fellow is, sir?"

"I do." Jamie checked that the door was closed,

then lowered his voice anyway. "He left a note for my wife, confirming he knows her. His name is Viscount Clary. For months now he has been harassing my wife, whom Mr. Hughes will attest is a reserved and proper lady. Several weeks ago Lord Clary pushed my sister, the Countess of Stratford, overboard while boating on the Thames. If you inquire with the magistrate in London, you'll discover that my brother-in-law, the Earl of Stratford, has sworn out a complaint against Lord Clary for attempted murder."

"Murder! An earl! A viscount!" Mr. Hughes sank onto a bench, staring blankly in front of him. "I can't believe it . . ."

The constable looked grave. "That's very serious, sir. By the time I send to London, I expect the man will have disappeared, but I don't like the thought of a murderer loose in town."

"You could arrest him for theft or damage," Jamie suggested. Anything to keep Clary confined and away from Olivia. "He must have stayed at a nearby inn."

After some more talking—the constable was a man of many words, it seemed—it was agreed that a pair of men would be sent out to look for Clary. Privately Jamie thought they wouldn't find him, if only because the constable seemed more concerned about making sure there were no murders in his town than in actually apprehending Clary. But Mr. Hughes did promise to replace at least one set of clothing for Olivia by night, and he made one other valid point.

"You'll be safe tonight in my inn," he vowed. "Now I'm on guard against the villain and he'll never step over my threshold again. I'll set the grooms to keep watch through the night. No one will come near you or your wife, I swear it. Let me atone for my mistake, sir."

Jamie wasn't entirely sure, but without knowing where Clary was, there was a risk in going to another inn. "Very well. But we'll want a different room."

Mr. Hughes agreed at once, and Jamie went up and told Olivia. Once he saw her settled, still shaken, in the new—larger—room, he told her he had to go out again. This time he took a horse from the stables and rode back to the Anchor. Charlie Pike was in his usual spot near the fire, and he looked mildly surprised when Jamie stopped in front of him.

"I have another favor to ask, Captain Pike," he said, deliberately using the title for the first time. "Of a business nature."

Pike hesitated, then a broad smile crossed his face. "Fetch up a chair, young man."

Chapter 19

They reached Richmond late the next day. As she watched the red brick towers of Stratford Court come into view, Olivia quietly marveled at what money could accomplish. When she'd left London, on her own with only two hundred and thirty pounds—and most of that borrowed—it had taken her days to reach Gravesend, via public coaches and inns.

By contrast, when Jamie wanted to get somewhere quickly, he found a boat to sail them up the Thames, directly from Broadstairs to the stairs at Stratford Court. A journey that would have taken her at least three days, most likely in chilly, uncomfortable conditions, was over in a single day of fairly elegant travel. He'd said something about Mr. Pike advising him, but Olivia knew this was all Jamie's idea. Despite the cold, he had spent most of the voyage at the rail, studying the passing shore with interest, even pointing out where he thought her hired Gravesend cottage must lie.

But now they were here. Mr. Pike waved from his position near the helm. It was his boat, a small racing schooner, and he seemed as pleased as pie to be sailing today. Olivia wished she could enjoy it as much as he did. But then, an older gentleman whose swashbuckling days were behind him might find the sudden race to Richmond exciting, while she still felt her future hanging in the balance. Could they beat Clary back to town?

Jamie had dismissed the idea of returning directly to London; he wanted to confer with Lord Atherton—*Stratford now,* she reminded herself. It certainly couldn't hurt to have an earl at their side when they lodged charges against Clary, and Olivia knew she owed Penelope an explanation. Because of her, Penelope and her husband had almost drowned.

Unfortunately, until Lord Clary was locked in the deepest, darkest dungeon London had to offer, Olivia wouldn't feel any of them were safe from him.

They made it ashore with little trouble. The late Lord Stratford had owned a racing yacht of his own, and there was a proper dock. Mr. Pike shook Jamie's hand and heartily wished them the best. "Soonsever you be in Ramsgate again, do come by for more elderberry wine," he added.

"We will," Jamie told him. He lifted their baggage while Olivia cradled the painting, now packed between layers of linen and the makeshift wooden frame beneath the oilskin. They climbed off the schooner and onto the dock, and waved as Mr. Pike went about adjusting his sails for the return trip.

"It's a long walk," Jamie said as they turned toward the house. "Can you carry it?"

She nodded. "I'm not letting go of it for an instant."

The wind wasn't as strong as they got farther from the river. Their footsteps crunched along the gravel drive and Olivia kept her cloak pulled close around her. Still, she was grateful to see the wrought-iron gates loom in front of them, with the impressive front of Stratford Court just beyond.

When the butler announced them, Penelope flew across the room to throw her arms around Olivia. "Are you hurt?" she demanded. "Did you kill that awful Clary? Where have you been?"

Olivia smiled. "I'm well—thanks to your brother. But you—Clary tried to kill you! And all because of me. Penelope, I've been waiting to beg your pardon—"

Her friend shushed her by laying her fingers on Olivia's lips. "Don't. I'm so happy to see you again! And you, Jamie. You did it! You found her!" She spun around to embrace her brother.

"Just a moment, Pen." Jamie had left the valises with the butler and now held the painting. He shifted it to accommodate his sister's hug. "This needs to be handled with care."

"What is it?"

"I'll show you, never fear," Jamie told her. "Is your husband about?"

Penelope nodded. "In the gallery. He and Gray have been there every day."

They found the new earl in his study. A door stood open into a larger room, and Olivia could see paintings covering every inch of those walls. Benedict, Lord Atherton—*Stratford now,* Olivia reminded herself again—looked up as Penelope led them in. "You're back!" He strode across the room to clasp Jamie's hand. "And successful, I see. It's a great pleasure to see you again, Mrs. Townsend." He bowed.

Olivia smiled back, a little dazed. The earl was a spectacularly handsome man, with wavy dark hair and vivid blue eyes. The only other time she'd met him, he and Penelope had been glaring daggers at each other, quite unlike the intimate glance they exchanged now. Penelope went to her husband's side and he slid his arm around her waist. "They found something, Ben."

Benedict's gaze focused on the parcel Jamie held. "Indeed. Gray," he called.

A tall, lanky fellow with untidy brown hair stuck his head around the door. "Yes?"

"My sister Samantha's husband, Lord George Churchill-Gray," Benedict said in brief introduction. "He's an artist and has been helping catalog my father's private gallery. Gray, here are Penelope's brother, Mr. James Weston, and the elusive Mrs. Townsend. They've found something."

Gray came into the room still holding a small picture, which he set down on the wide mahogany desk. "What?"

In answer, Jamie laid the painting on the desk and began unwrapping it. "I believe this is what Lord Clary wants."

For a moment there was silence as St. George was unveiled. When the dragon appeared from beneath the protective cloth, Gray inhaled sharply. He made a motion toward the painting, and Jamie stepped aside, letting the artist finish uncovering the piece.

"It's definitely an Old Master," said Benedict after a moment. "Even I can see as much."

"It's Titian," said Gray reverently. He lifted the panel and carried it to a side table near the windows, where he propped it up. Slowly he sank down on one knee, gazing raptly at the painting. "Look at the strokes—the light—the definition. Where did you get this?"

"Near Ramsgate." Jamie glanced at Benedict. "Would your father have pursued this?"

"To the end of the earth and beyond," replied Benedict without hesitation. "He had four by Raphael but only one by Titian, and that one only a lesser study. Gray has nearly completed the catalog." He looked at Gray. "Do you know this painting?"

Slowly Gray nodded, still absorbed in the painting. "Titian didn't usually paint so small. This is rare, most likely a commission for a patron. St. George is English, so it could have been a gift." He looked up. "I've never seen it personally, only a sketch. I knew a fellow in the Strand who made a point of copying every Titian he could locate; spent years in Italy tracking them down. He admired the technique tremendously. He kept a sketchbook of his drawings and showed me." His eyes went back to the painting. "I remember the dragon."

"How did you get it, Olivia?" Penelope sounded dazed. "How did you *find* it?"

Olivia shifted her weight. "That's a long story."

"The more important question is what we ought to do with it," Jamie said. He turned to Benedict. "You were right, by the by, about the smuggling."

"I grew more certain of it by the day," was the grim reply. "You brought it back to London, so I presume you have some ideas about what to do with it."

"It's more about *how*." Jamie caught Olivia's eyes. "The rest is a *very* long story."

"If there's a long story to be told, we should sit down and have something to eat." Penelope took her arm and led her down the corridor to a spacious drawing room. The gentlemen followed, Gray trailing at the rear and carrying the Titian. "Tea," Penelope directed the servant who emerged almost instantly through the doorway when she rang the bell. "And sandwiches and cakes."

By the time refreshments arrived, Benedict's sister Samantha came in with her mother. Olivia had heard all about the Stratford family, from the evening several months ago when the Westons had been invited to dine at Stratford Court. Then, Penelope had called the dowager countess a beautiful but cold and distant lady, and Samantha she described as quiet and reserved. Today neither appeared anything like that; Samantha was laughing when she came into the room, her cheeks pink and her blond hair ruffled by the wind, and her mother was smiling fondly at whatever amused her.

Both women stopped short at the sight of guests. Penelope leapt to her feet. "Samantha, Lady Stratford, this is my brother, James Weston, and my dear friend Olivia Townsend."

"Welcome to Stratford Court," said Lady Stratford. She held herself very gracefully erect, but a cordial smile curved her mouth as Olivia bobbed a curtsy and Jamie bowed.

"I'm very glad to meet you at last," said Samantha warmly to Olivia. "Penelope has told us so much about you."

"They've brought news, Mother," said Benedict before Olivia could recover from her mortification at the trouble she'd brought on everyone. He came and took the countess's arm and led her to the painting. "I suspect this is what Father was pursuing when he died."

The color leached from the countess's face as she stared at the Titian, and for a moment she looked frozen. "Oh my," she murmured at last. "It is something he would covet desperately." She turned anguished eyes on her son. "Is this what caused him to endanger you and Penelope? My dear, I am so sorry—"

Penelope hurried to her side. "My brother thinks this painting will help us see Lord Clary chained in the bottom of a prison. Isn't that right, Jamie?"

"I'd like nothing better," her brother agreed.

"Then you are very welcome, today and for all time," Samantha said fervently. "That man tried to kill Penelope. I could lock the chains on him myself."

"I still prefer the hangman," said Benedict with a covert glance at his wife. "But where on earth did you find this? And how?"

Jamie's eyes met hers. Olivia read his unspoken question there. After all she had done to avoid telling anyone her suspicions about Henry or how menacing Clary had become, including fleeing London without a word to anyone, he didn't know how much she wanted to reveal now. Olivia knew that if she gave any sign of distress, Jamie would keep her secrets.

But she was done with that. There was no way they could destroy Clary without revealing Henry's illegal activities, and even though Olivia hadn't set out to ruin her late husband's name, he had brought it on himself. Her loyalty lay with the people in this room now, her real family. She gave a decisive nod.

"This painting was smuggled into England," Jamie said. "It most likely came from France, where it may have been looted from Bonaparte's grand museum." Benedict said nothing but his brilliant blue eyes were fixed on Jamie. "We think—with good evidence—that Lord Clary was part of the operation, most likely as the man who located buyers for the smuggled art."

"Including our father," whispered Samantha. She, too, listened raptly.

Jamie nodded. "I believe so."

"I'm quite sure of it," Gray interjected. "The late Lord Stratford made entries in his ledgers indicating substantial payments to Lord Clary, although not why. The dates correspond to when certain paintings were entered in his private gallery, but nothing else exists to demonstrate where those paintings came from."

Olivia felt Jamie's satisfaction. It fairly radiated off him as his guess was proven right once more. And it made her strangely elated as well—not merely the facts of the matter, but the fact that he was pleased. "The smugglers brought their cargo ashore in Kent. Local people were paid to hold the works until a buyer was found, when the paintings would be brought into London or sent anywhere in England. In Lord Stratford's case, they could have been delivered right to his door. We came today on a small sloop from Broadstairs, courtesy of a gentleman who was extremely helpful to us. As for how the works were brought out of France . . ." He lifted one hand. "I can only remind you that Lord Clary's younger brother is a navy commodore, stationed in Calais. That may be utter coincidence, of course."

"I'm convinced." Benedict looked fierce with triumph.

"How did you get caught up in this?" Penelope asked Olivia in a stricken voice.

She took a deep breath. "Henry was the leader of the ring." Penelope's mouth dropped open. "He arranged everything, with Clary's help. I knew nothing about any of it," Olivia went on. "But I believe this is why Lord Clary was so persistent in his . . . attentions. He discovered this painting—or one like it—was smuggled into England but never delivered, and he wants it."

"The Duke of Wellington ordered all looted artwork repatriated," said Gray, frowning. "Are you certain?"

"No," said Jamie. "But many pictures disappeared in spite of the duke's order. And I daresay some collectors wouldn't hesitate, if offered something like this which couldn't be traced."

Gray conceded that. "Of course there would be some. But if you bring this to the duke—that is your plan, isn't it?" Jamie nodded once. "It could cause an international incident. You're saying not just this painting, but several pictures of equal rarity and value, were stolen and smuggled to English citizens with the aid of an English naval officer."

"I don't give a damn about any of them except Lord Clary."

"Nor do I," muttered Benedict.

"That helps." Gray returned Jamie's annoyed look with a shrug. "Wellington has other concerns now; he may consider the matter of the art done with and not want to resurrect it over Lord Clary. You should be forewarned. My older brother is in the Home Office and they've got plenty more to worry about than one smuggler."

Jamie said nothing, but Olivia saw the lines of worry settle on his forehead. Her own stomach seemed to drop into her shoes. And suddenly she didn't feel nearly as confident that they were any closer to a solution.

She didn't have a chance to speak to him until late that night. Jamie was quiet through dinner, listening as Gray and Benedict argued about the best way to proceed. He barely looked up at her when the ladies left the dining room, and when the gentlemen rejoined them later, he wasn't with them. Olivia murmured an excuse to Penelope and went in search of him.

She found him in a small closet near the earl's study. The door stood open but Olivia hung back a moment. The Titian was propped up against the wall on the sideboard. A single lamp burned beside it, shedding golden light over the dragon, who glistened like a monster from hell. St. George was lost in the shadows, more a silhouette than a portrait now. His upraised sword looked spindly and insignificant in the face of the dragon's bared teeth and spiked tail. Jamie had drawn a chair up directly in front of the painting and now sat, elbows on his knees and chin propped on his clasped hands as he gazed broodingly at it. Tentatively Olivia knocked on the door.

Jamie glanced over his shoulder. "Come in."

She came to stand beside him. "I thought finding it would solve everything. I feel very naïve."

"You shouldn't."

Olivia stared at the painting for a moment. If Wellington wouldn't be the instrument of justice she had hoped, what did that leave them? What were they to do with this priceless work of art? "Perhaps we should hack it to pieces and deliver it to Lord Clary thus."

He grunted. "That would be one way to thwart him."

"I take it you don't see many other good choices," she said after a full minute of silence.

"Good choices? No." He sighed, flexing his fingers without taking his eyes off the painting. "But I expected all along we'd face bad choices. The only problem is, which one should we take?"

"What are the less dreadful options?"

He reached for her hand and pressed it to his lips. "Anything that allows Clary to go free. I fear Gray is right: Wellington won't be terribly motivated to call for the prosecution of one man over one painting, especially not if it could lead to evidence of more smuggling. The people who paid

Henry are likely to be influential and wealthy in their own right."

"But Clary tried to kill Penelope!"

"He did," Jamie agreed. "But that's a separate matter." He pressed his lips to her palm. She sagged against the chair as his tongue traced a delicate circle on her skin. "I suppose I shan't share your bed tonight," he murmured.

"No . . . ?" Her voice quivered as he continued making love to her hand.

"My sister cannot keep a secret. If she saw me slipping into your bedroom, the whole household would know by breakfast."

He didn't want anyone to know they were lovers. Olivia thought of the nights—and mornings—they had spent in each others' arms, naked and uninhibited. He hadn't shown any hesitation then. But as soon as they returned to London, where anyone of consequence might discover it . . .

She forced the thought from her mind. Secretly or openly, she loved him. She wanted him. "Who says we must share a bed? I think we can make do very well with only this chair . . ."

Jamie gave a slow smile, his glittering gaze making her skin prickle with anticipation. "You're right. Lock the door."

The ground was hard underfoot, the grass stiff and brittle in the cold. "Over there," Jamie said, his breath white puffs on the frosty air. He pointed to a clearing in the woods. The two Stratford servants, both with rifles on their shoulders, nodded and stamped off through the brush to make sure they were alone.

"Are you certain we have to do this today?" Olivia rubbed her hands together. She wore a luxurious cloak over a fur-trimmed pelisse, and thick woolen stockings under stout new boots. Penelope had opened her wardrobe and insisted Olivia borrow whatever she needed, which turned out to be warm clothing. Jamie was going to teach her how to shoot.

"I should have done it days ago." He put down his pistol case on a large boulder nearby and opened it. "The first day, in fact, when you had to resort to using a shovel to defend yourself."

"I'm very glad I didn't know, or have a pistol then," she retorted. "I'd have shot you!"

"I hope you never need to use this, but you should still know how. Come here."

Reluctantly she joined him. "The only person I want to shoot is Clary."

"Then you'd better be able to hit him." He tipped up her chin and kissed her. Dimly Olivia thought she shouldn't let him do that; after he kissed her she found it hard to argue with him about anything. "Although I would much prefer that you never have to lay eyes on that man again, it will set my mind at ease knowing you could defend yourself."

For the next hour he taught her how to load the pistol and prime it, making her do it over and over until she could manage it with her eyes closed. While they were working the servants set up a dummy, stuffing an old coat with straw and wedging it onto a sapling. Someone stuck a hat above it, and Jamie picked up the primed and loaded pistol. "Shoot."

Olivia took a firm grip on the stock and held the pistol out. It was a beautiful gun, but heavy. She squinted at the dummy and pulled the trigger. With a flash and a bang, the gun fired, and she almost toppled over backward.

"Load it," Jamie instructed, standing behind her with his arms folded.

Olivia strained to see the dummy. "Did I hit it?"

"No."

She gave him an aggrieved look and went to the pistol case. "You see now why I didn't bother taking a pistol."

"You can learn this. A little more powder, please."

She tapped more powder into the muzzle and rammed home the ball and charge. "If I learn how to shoot, will it change how we deal with Clary?"

"What do you mean?"

Once more she stepped into position and aimed at the dummy. "Shouldn't we put it to use?" She pulled the trigger, and this time the dummy's sleeve fluttered. She lowered the gun with a pleased smile. "I hit it!"

"You hit the sleeve. Load again."

"The sleeve is what I aimed for," she protested, doing as he said.

"Aim here." Jamie tapped the middle of his chest. Olivia paused, picturing the damage a shot to that spot would cause. "I mean it, Livie. Aim for the center. If you miss, you're still likely to wound. If you aim for the arm and miss, the shot goes wide and you're defenseless." When she didn't move, he came forward and took out the second pistol. "There's a reason a man travels with two pistols. There's not time to stop and reload if you're in danger. If you feel you must fire, do it seriously." As he spoke he loaded the second pistol, his actions smooth and practiced. Without hesitation he raised his arm, pulled back the hammer, and fired. To Olivia it seemed he barely glanced at the target, but the dummy recoiled, and a dark hole marked the coat, just left of center, when the sapling stopped swaying. "If Clary comes at you, he won't be so delicate," Jamie said gently, putting the pistol back down. "He'll mean to harm you. Aim for the center."

She raised the pistol, hesitated, then lowered it. "How?"

He stepped up behind her and put his arms around her. His hands closed over hers on the pistol stock, and he settled his cheek next to her. "Imagine him pushing Penelope into the freezing cold river," he murmured, guiding her to raise her arms. "Picture him catching you unawares. What would his face look like?" Olivia's hands started to shake as the image filled her mind. "Now picture him coming at you," Jamie whispered. "Right there, in the dark green coat." Her fingers twitched on the trigger. The flintlock snapped closed, and the pistol fired. This time the dummy lurched sideways. "Better," said Jamie in approval.

Olivia stood holding the pistol. Her ears rang from the percussion of the shot, but the image of Clary coming at her stayed in her mind, a grotesque specter looming over her. "We need to set a trap for him, don't we?"

Jamie didn't say anything. She turned around. He was still right behind her, and she looked up at him until he sighed. "I don't know what sort of trap."

"We have the painting," she pointed out.

He looked away. "I'm afraid that's not enough. Benedict is certain Wellington will be outraged. He may be, but Gray is probably right that the duke won't be eager to prosecute the case. Without Wellington's firm support, the outcome is far from certain. Clary has connections, after all. I don't want to risk him going free."

"But if we give the painting to Wellington—" she began.

"Clary would be even more enraged at you, for putting it out of his reach," Jamie said softly. "And he would still be a free man." He framed her face in his hands as her stomach knotted at the thought. "That only means we need a tighter trap—one he cannot escape. The painting is part of it. You must be part of it. It's the rest I haven't got worked out yet."

What could ensure Clary's conviction? The answer came to her quite quickly: Henry's other diary, the one that showed his income. The smuggling diary hadn't been in code, just ordinary abbreviation. If she could get that other book, it should show who had paid Henry for the stolen art—and, if Jamie was correct, it should also show commissions paid to Clary for his help. Surely that would persuade Wellington that Clary had been an integral part of the plot and should be prosecuted.

And she knew who had that diary.

Chapter 20

They returned to London the next day, to the Weston home in Grosvenor Square. Olivia had been a visitor many times in this house, but never a guest. She'd batted aside every invitation, saying that it was silly when she lived so near. But this time she was installed in a large, elegant bedroom overlooking the square, and when she peered out the windows, it was hard not to marvel at the view.

"Will it do?"

"Of course," she said with a smile. Jamie leaned against the doorway, his arms folded. "You must be glad to be at home again."

He shrugged. "This is my parents' home. But it's safe and convenient. No one will be admitted without my permission, and the footmen will be watching the doors."

"Where is your home?" She had never known where he considered himself home. It might not even be in London. He certainly left the city enough not to need a permanent residence here.

"I haven't got one," he said. "I never stay in one place long enough to need one."

Stay with me, she thought in longing. But Jamie hadn't said a word about the future. Olivia had ordered herself not to expect that, when she told him she loved him; it was quite possible their chance for a happy life together had come and gone years ago. But every moment she spent in his company, every night she spent in his arms, made her more certain than ever that he was the only man she would ever love. He was the person she wanted to see every day for the rest of her life. It was only as time went on that she became unhappily conscious of the fact that he might not feel the same about her.

"I need to return to my lodging," she said, shaking off those worries. "To retrieve some fresh clothing and personal items."

"Didn't Penelope give you gowns?"

Olivia fiddled with a button on her dress—a dress borrowed from Penelope. "She did, but I would like my own." Penelope's clothing was a bit tight in the bosom and a little short in the skirt. Lady Samantha had offered to share her clothes as well, but she was even slimmer than Penelope. Even though everything Penelope lent her was far nicer than anything Olivia owned, she wanted to feel normal again, even if just by wearing her own undergarments.

"Of course," said Jamie after a pause. "We'll have to be quick, though. I'd rather not make our presence known to all of London just yet."

"I understand," she promised. "I only need a quarter hour."

Two hours later they went. Jamie hired a plain closed carriage, and Olivia wore a veil over her bonnet. The weather in London was far milder than it had been in Kent, but she still bundled herself into Penelope's thickest cloak. She got out her key as they turned into Clarges Street, and gripped the handle of her empty valise. Most of what she wanted would fit inside, and she didn't have the time to pack up everything anyway.

She jumped down almost before Jamie had stopped the carriage, and had unlocked the door by the time he tied up the horses. Her rooms were on the first floor, but the short, plump figure of the landlady came hurrying down the hall before they had made it up three stairs.

"See here," cried Mrs. Harding. "Stop, I say! Stop where you—oh! Mrs. Townsend!"

"Yes," said Olivia nervously. "I've only come for a moment, Mrs. Harding . . ."

"Well, it's about time! If I didn't know better, I'd think you were involved in something unbecoming."

Jamie was nudging her to keep going. "It's a very long story, ma'am, but I haven't got time to explain now," Olivia said, climbing another step.

Mrs. Harding waved her hands. "So many callers you've had since you left! Will you want your letters?"

Olivia froze. "Letters?"

Her landlady nodded. "A good number of them. I've put them all aside in my parlor, for I didn't know—"

"Who delivered them?" Jamie interrupted.

Mrs. Harding frowned at him in affront. "That is none of your concern, sir. And who are you? Mrs. Townsend, are you in danger?"

The letters had to be from Clary. What was he sending her? Or was he simply trying to find her? Olivia gave Jamie an anxious look, and he responded with a firm nod, his gaze steady. "This is my trusted friend, Mr. Weston. Will you show him the letters for me? He's entirely respectable and honorable." It would save time if Jamie looked at the post. Already she felt her time ticking down. Merely being back in this house, where she had spent so much time parrying Clary's increasingly persistent advances, was making her tense.

Mrs. Harding looked doubtful. "I don't know, Mrs. Townsend, it doesn't seem right. I don't keep that sort of house."

Jamie bounded back down the stairs and gave her a charming smile. "A pleasure to make your acquaintance, ma'am," he said with a bow, "but Mrs. Townsend is in a frightful hurry—did you say she's had a lot of callers recently?" He guided the older woman down the corridor, waving one hand over his head at Olivia: *Go.*

She ran. Her fingers shook as she unlocked her door on the upstairs landing, but the rooms looked just as she had left them. She hurried into her bedroom and stuffed as many things into the valise as she could. Jamie hadn't come up to fetch her yet, but it felt like she'd been here an hour already. She went back into the sitting room and opened the top drawer of the chest. She needed another thick shawl to replace the one Clary had ruined in Ramsgate.

Tucked inside the drawer, a bundle of pamphlets caught her eye. She paused. It was probably best to leave her collection of *50 Ways to Sin* here, but on the other hand . . . It was a notoriously naughty story about a widowed lady who recounted her amorous adventures across London. Even when she found them shocking, Olivia felt a keen interest in, and even an odd affinity, for Lady Constance, the authoress. Constance was never afraid, never bullied by men, and she pursued her own desires without regard for their impropriety. More than once Olivia had wondered what someone like Constance would have done when Clary began making lewd propositions; laughed at him, most likely. And then there were the men Constance took to her bed, for adventures that were ever more erotic. Before she could talk herself out of it, she pushed them deep into the valise. *Just something to read at night,* she told herself, to take her mind off her troubles . . . and perhaps inspire more pleasurable activities.

The only warning she had was the sound of a single footstep in the doorway. "My dear Olivia," said the voice that had dogged her nightmares for months. "How very delightful to see you again."

Olivia whirled, clutching a shawl defensively. Her heart shot into her throat and her hands started shaking. She felt like a fox, staring down the barrel of the hunter's gun as Lord Clary strolled into the room, his dark eyes gleaming and a smirk twisting his lips.

But no. She was not a helpless fox, and she was not going to let this man terrify her. Deliberately, even though it felt like her bones were cracking as she unclenched her fingers, she laid the shawl on the chest behind her. "Lord Clary. I didn't hear the maid announce you."

"As if I'd wait for that stupid girl to come upstairs when I've been searching high and low for you for weeks now. How fortunate that I happened to be passing by when you finally returned home." He started toward her, flexing his hands. His dark gloves made those hands look like talons, and Olivia repressed a shudder.

"You may call me Mrs. Townsend, out of respect for your bosom friend, my husband." She knew he had no respect for her personally.

"That's right: Poor Henry, so sadly dead before his time, leaving behind a pretty, young . . ." He paused in front of her. "Helpless . . ." He leaned closer, his black eyes boring into hers. "*Foolish* widow."

She forced her shoulders back, hoping she looked more poised than she felt. Just being this near him made her skin crawl, and she had to fight down the urge to flinch away. Of course he wanted that—he wanted to see her try to escape because he liked the chase . . . followed by the kill. Clary was the sort of man who fed on conquest. He wouldn't mind if she simply surrendered, but he'd be even happier if he had to overpower her.

"How flattering," she said evenly. "Not many would call a woman of my age young."

One side of his mouth curled. "And yet you act like the greenest girl." He clicked his tongue in a pitying way. "Did you really think you could run away from me?"

"I think she did quite well," said Jamie's voice from the doorway. "Given that you've only now set eyes on her, when she returned to London on her own."

Since his face was so near hers, Olivia saw how the viscount started, how his eyes flared. But the flash of fury was gone in an instant. He straightened and turned on his heel, raking a cold and dismissive glance over Jamie. "The accomplice. What is your name—Westly?"

"James Weston." Jamie stared brazenly back. "Your reputation precedes you, sir."

Clary's smirk returned. "I hope so. I hope you both keep it in mind." He took a few steps away from Olivia, and she made herself exhale slowly, to keep him from hearing her gasp in relief. "I grew tired of waiting for you to answer my message, so as you see, I have been forced to come to you." He eyed Jamie coolly. "Hand it over and we'll part on amicable terms."

"Amicable?" Jamie raised his eyebrows, looking genuinely astonished. "How gracious. Particularly after shredding so much clothing."

The viscount almost smiled at that. "We all have momentary passions. Sometimes one gives in, don't you agree?" He darted a glance at Olivia. "Perhaps by traveling as a man and wife, when you're no such thing."

"Are you certain about that?" Jamie asked.

Clary's smirk vanished. Now he looked coldly furious. "I want it."

"It," repeated Jamie in the same mildly curious tone he'd used before. "What, precisely, do you mean? Since we're being so open and frank with each other."

"You know what I want," snarled the older man.

Deliberately Jamie looked right at Olivia. "I do.

And you shall remain disappointed for all eternity on that score."

Clary inhaled, and Olivia braced herself for a furious outburst. Jamie appeared untroubled, but in spite of herself she measured the distance to the door, and the location of a heavy candlestick she could use in defense. But then Clary let out his breath and his shoulders eased. "Not *her*," he said dismissively. "Henry's contraband. I know you fetched it from Thanet. Produce it at once."

"If it was Henry's, by right it's now his widow's property."

"Don't try to be clever," snapped Clary. "It's mine."

Jamie rocked back on his heels. "On the other hand, I seem to recall seeing a bill of receipt, in the Earl of Stratford's own hand, detailing a claim to the very same item you seek. So if anyone other than Mrs. Townsend has a right to . . . *it*, I believe it would be the new Lord Stratford." He smiled. "My brother-in-law, as it turns out."

A muscle twitched in Clary's jaw. "All right," he said in a venomously soft voice. "That's the way of it? How unfortunate he survived."

"Yes, he'd like to speak to you about that incident on the river," Jamie said. "As would a magistrate."

Clary sighed. "Such a waste of time that would be. What would he accuse me of? Murder? It's a capital crime. As a peer, I would be tried—if it ever came to that—in the House of Lords. Ponder my chances, for a moment. Who could accuse me? The new young earl, who has few connections? He saw nothing with his own eyes. His wife, the nouveau riche heiress he married as a result of some scandal?" His smile was terrible in victory. "We all know I would never set foot in a prison. Even those who might wonder will look to my lineage and family and assure themselves that such a gentleman, one of them, could never be guilty of such a thing. You're a bigger fool than you look if you don't acknowledge the truth of all this."

Olivia felt sick. Dear God. He was right—every word of what he said was true, just as Gray had warned them. She had feared Clary would call her a liar, but it was even worse. He would call Penelope and her husband liars, too, and all the pompous lords in Parliament would believe it. Jamie had worried about setting the right trap for Clary, but now Olivia saw that it didn't matter; they could set any trap they pleased, and Clary would still walk right out of it. And then he would be free to harass and bully her for the rest of her life.

But all Jamie said was, "Perhaps. Let's see how it goes."

"On the other hand," Clary went on as if Jamie hadn't spoken, "if you deliver the item to me, I shan't take out any humiliation on your family." He clasped his hands behind his back and paced across the room toward Jamie. Both men looked calm and composed, but Olivia felt as if her insides had been twisted up like a spring. Again she eyed the candlestick and gauged how much force it would take to swing it like a cricket bat into Lord Clary's head.

"And I believe you're a man of business," the viscount said, stopping in front of Jamie. "A man who knows a good deal when he's offered one."

"Money plays no part in this," said Jamie quietly.

"No?" Olivia just caught Clary's dangerous smile as he glanced at her again. "Perhaps you're a stupid fellow after all." With a sudden movement, he charged, shoving Jamie backward with two hands to the chest. Jamie almost caught himself—one hand gripped the door frame before Lord Clary viciously banged the door on it, once, twice, until Jamie released it with a howl of pain. Quick as anything the viscount slammed the door shut and turned the key in the lock, and then he swung around to face her.

Olivia already had the candlestick in her hand. Seeing him hurt Jamie like that had jolted her out of all fear and anxiety. She was ready to kill this man, and she raised the heavy candlestick in threat. "If you try to touch me I'll bash in your skull," she vowed. And her hands did not shake in the slightest.

Clary came a step closer but no more. From outside the room, Olivia dimly heard Jamie shouting, and Mrs. Harding's worried shrieks. She kept her focus on Clary.

"I'm not going to take you here and now, my dear," he said. "But I *am* going to have you. You're going to come to me, bare yourself, and go down on your knees. I've spent too long panting after you, and by God I will not be denied."

"I'd sooner drown myself in the Thames."

He sneered. "We both know that's not true. We both know you want to live a long, happy life with your own Sir Lancelot outside the door there."

There was a dull thud against the door.

"He's going to give me the painting to spare his sister from being exposed as a manipulative little whore," Clary said, "and you're going to give yourself to me to preserve whatever is left of your reputation."

Olivia snorted in disgust. Something hit the door again, this time with a great cracking sound. Jamie was going to break the door down, and it couldn't happen fast enough for her. Her fingers flexed around the candlestick.

"Because if you don't . . ." Clary took a step nearer. "I'll unmask you for the debauched purveyor of sin that you really are. Very careless, my dear, to leave the evidence about for anyone to find. And when Sir Lancelot discovers that the quiet widow leads a scandalous double life . . ." His eyes traveled over her once, lingering on her breasts before moving lower. "Well. Let's just hope you learned enough on your wicked adventures to persuade me not to tell everyone your little secret."

Olivia blinked, confused. Unmask her as a purveyor of sin? What did that mean? He had been in their room in Ramsgate. She was quite sure Clary had ripped up her clothes because he suspected that she and Jamie were lovers, which would cause a minor scandal if everyone knew, but it was hardly a sign of wicked debauchery.

But that was the moment something struck the door once more, and this time the wood exploded. Splinters flew everywhere, and when Olivia looked to the doorway, there stood Jamie with a fire axe in his hands.

"Lord Clary," he said, breathing heavily, "if

you're not out of my sight in the next minute, there will never need to be a trial in Parliament."

Clary eyed him for a moment. "No matter," he said coolly. "I'm done here." He glanced at Olivia, then walked out the door. Jamie stepped aside for him, but not much, and he raised the axe as the other man brushed past him.

Neither of them moved until they heard the door below. "Mrs. Harding," called Jamie sharply.

"Yes, yes, sir, he's gone," called the landlady, her voice fluttering. "Oh my, is Mrs. Townsend hurt?"

"No," he replied before shoving the ruined door shut. It bounced off the jamb and hung ajar. "No thanks to you," he added under his breath. "I suspect your henwitted landlady has been encouraging him to hang about waiting for you to return. Christ!" With a sudden movement he flung down the axe. Olivia jumped as it crashed to the floor, skidded across the floorboards until the blade bit into the leg of a table and arrested its slide. "Did he touch you?"

She set the candlestick back on the table. "No. But he threatened me."

Jamie's eyes had an eerie, deadly glow about them. "How?"

She took a deep breath. "I don't quite know. He said he would expose my scandalous secret as a purveyor of sin. I've no idea what he means, but he said he would ruin me unless . . ."

"Unless we give him the painting?"

She wet her lips. "No. He wants . . ." Jamie wasn't going to take this well. "He wants me to surrender to him."

For the first time his gaze focused on her. "What?"

"He wants me to . . ." She made a suggestive motion. A corner of paper sticking out of her valise caught her eye, and suddenly it dawned on her what Clary meant. Her mouth dropped open in astonishment. "Oh! Or else he'll tell everyone—I think he believes I'm Lady Constance, who writes those naughty stories!"

Jamie seemed turned to stone, his face a blank mask. Olivia couldn't keep back a gasp of laughter. It was more hysteria than amusement, but still. She clapped one hand over her mouth and turned her back.

"The hell he will." Jamie stalked across the room and spun her around. He took her face in his hands. "I'm sorry—I never thought he would be sitting here waiting for you—Livie, he could have hurt you—"

"He didn't." She wrapped her hands around his wrists, feeling the tension in him. It was strange; normally she would have been the one unable to breathe and stricken with alarm at Clary's threats. But Jamie had come to her aid with an axe. He chopped down the door to get to her. Even now he was taut and furious and would probably go after Clary with the axe again if she bid him to. It was so unlike the Jamie she knew, unflappable and always ready with a plan or an idea. "Thanks to you."

For a moment raw emotion blazed across his features. He pulled her to him and kissed her as if he thought it might be the last time. His hands shook and he held her almost roughly. Olivia surged against him, thinking what would have happened if he hadn't come with her today. "I could have killed him when I saw him in here with you," he said, his voice a dark growl. "And I would have."

"I know." She ran her fingers into his hair. "Thank heaven you didn't have to."

"Right." He exhaled and hung his head for a moment until his forehead touched hers. She could almost feel him gather himself, and when he spoke his voice was noticeably lighter. "So. He plans to denounce you as Lady Constance? I don't imagine that would go any better for him than the last bloke who tried it."

"Someone already tried it?" she said incredulously. "I never hear the best gossip . . ."

As hoped, Jamie grinned. The tension dropped from his body, but not the intensity or focus. "Some poor fool thought he'd sorted out Constance's true identity. He accused a woman in front of a ballroom full of people."

"Did people believe it?" she said anxiously.

Jamie snorted, but with a hint of laughter. "Not for a moment! He'd been set up, of course, but he made himself a laughingstock and slunk out of town the next day."

"What happened to the lady so unjustly accused?"

"You'll enjoy the story," he said. "She received a marriage proposal that very night—and accepted it. It caused quite a stir."

It brought a wistful smile to her face. "I certainly approve—provided it was accepted with delight and not in shame, to repair a stained reputation."

"By all accounts she could only have accepted because her brain was addled by the deepest love. You'll have heard of the gentleman; his sister is fast friends with Abigail and Penelope. Mr. Douglas Bennet."

Olivia gaped. She thought he'd been teasing about the marriage proposal. But she did indeed know of Mr. Bennet, who was one of the most notorious—and elusive—bachelors in London. How many times had she listened to Abigail and Penelope giggle with their friend Joan about her brother's lack of interest in decent women? "And who was the lady?"

"Madeline Wilde. She'll not be bothered by a little scandal. Lord Clary, on the other hand . . ." He put his hands on his hips and stared out the window. "That's his great threat? You, Lady Constance!"

Olivia drew back, pretending to be insulted. "Well, I'm not sure I like that you find it hard to believe. Constance is regarded as a very adventurous and capable lover. Lord Clary seems sure everyone will believe I'm she. "

He grinned, almost restored to his normal humor. "Never doubt my appreciation of you as a lover. I merely meant you would never write such unbelievable stories."

Her face warmed, thinking of the pamphlets hidden in her valise. "I quite enjoy some of those stories," she murmured. What did he mean, unbelievable? He certainly didn't mind her interest in that sort of thing when they were in bed together.

But Jamie had begun pacing, his expression distant yet focused. "Perhaps that's an idea, though," he murmured.

"What?" Olivia put her hand on his arm. It was almost alarming how unafraid she was of Clary. He'd threatened to do much less before, and she'd fled London, terrified and desperate. Now she felt only a deep certainty that somehow she and Jamie would prevail. Even if every word Clary said was true—no magistrate would bind him over for trial, and no peer in Parliament would believe Penelope over him—Olivia felt strong enough to defy the viscount now. He could point at her in front of all society and call her out as Lady Constance, and somehow she felt she would only laugh.

A cunning smile stole over Jamie's face. "His lordship has given me an idea for how we can bring him down."

"What is it?" She seized his arm. "Jamie, what?"

He started at her touch. "Ah—he wants a painting. He doesn't know exactly which painting. Perhaps all we have to do is give him a painting."

"I doubt he'll be fooled by an ordinary picture. It must be old, or a famously valuable work—" She stopped, remembering the conversation at Stratford Court. "Or a *copy* of a famously valuable painting."

His smile grew hard and fierce. "Exactly."

Chapter 21

After Clary surprised them at Olivia's rooms, Jamie spoke to all the Weston servants, strictly warning them about Clary or anyone else who might try to gain entrance to the house. Thankfully Olivia didn't seem terrified by the encounter—in fact, when Penelope arrived the next day, she wanted to go shopping.

"Shopping?" Jamie frowned. He knew women, especially his mother and sisters, were fond of shopping, but now? He hadn't thought Olivia was as devoted to the pursuit of new bonnets.

"I need a few things," Olivia said.

"It's perfectly safe," Penelope put in. "Benedict has armed the footmen, if you're worried about Clary."

Jamie continued to frown. He didn't like it, but he had no good reason to protest. It wasn't as though he had been able to prevent Clary from getting close to Olivia and threatening her. And she looked so eager to go; both she and Penelope were sitting on the edge of the sofa, hands clasped in identical poses of supplication. It would probably be good for her to get out and do something normal with one of her closest friends, and he knew Penelope was right. Benedict had informed him before they left Richmond that all his servants were under strict orders to keep Lord Clary far away from Penelope, and that any servant who happened to shoot the viscount in the course of protecting the countess would be neither sacked nor punished, and might well receive a reward.

"I can't stay locked up in the house all day, afraid to set foot outdoors," Olivia said gently, proving she could read his thoughts. "I refuse to let that man ruin my life, and I feel very safe with Penelope and her servants."

"Of course not." He had no right to keep her in Grosvenor Square, Jamie reflected. Trying to do so would do him no good. "Buy something handsome."

"Splendid!" Penelope beamed. "We'll take care, I promise."

Olivia gave him a brilliant smile. She must be ready to see a face other than his, he thought with a pang. The two women left in a swirl of cloaks and happy chatter, leaving the house quiet and empty when they had driven off in the Stratford coach. Jamie stood at the window and watched it roll toward Bond Street, the footmen standing tall on the back.

And while Olivia was enjoying a day of shopping with his sister, he should get to work on the plan he hadn't felt like sharing with Olivia.

He went to see Daniel Crawford. He hadn't heard from Daniel in several days, which could mean anything, or nothing. No one answered his knock at the Crawfords' house, so he went around the corner to the Blue Boar tavern. There he found his friend, a tankard of ale in front of him.

"Well!" Daniel gave him a lopsided grin. "Welcome back to town at last."

Jamie pulled up a chair. "I hope you haven't been here since I left."

"Not entirely." Daniel swirled his ale before taking a long sip. "But there's little else to do."

He felt that dig. He and Daniel had been friends since university, but only recently become business partners. Then Jamie had hared off after Olivia on only a moment's notice, and instead of bellowing at him for abandoning his responsibilities, Daniel had wished him well and offered to help. "I know. I've been working—"

"Thank God." Daniel leaned forward, and some of his lethargic veneer slipped away. "It's been over a fortnight, sellers are clamoring at my door. Bathsheba persuaded me to fill any orders we can get, but . . . When can I tell them we'll have something new?"

"Not that," Jamie muttered. "Well, not entirely that. Did you know Lord Clary was back in London?"

Daniel sighed, the sharp eagerness fading from his face. "I heard a rumor. By that time, you'd sent word you were leaving for Richmond, so I knew I'd be seeing you soon."

"Tell me everything."

His friend gave him a long look. "First I have to know—*have* you been working? I understand this matter trumps all else, but it would help—"

Jamie pushed his hands through his hair. "I was," he said in a low voice. "But Clary stole it.

He tracked Olivia to the inn where we were staying and ransacked the room. So I have nothing to give you, and every reason to want to see Clary destroyed."

Daniel cursed. "How many pages?" He cursed again when Jamie told him. "That ruddy sod!"

"Exactly," he agreed. "But it's given me an idea. I need to know what Clary is doing, though."

The other man huddled over his ale again. "He's staying very quiet. I've heard he's been to visit a few people—largely family connections—but he's not staying at his house. No one is quite certain where he's living, but it's not at home with his wife, who continues to profess that he's gone to Wales. I daresay she knows very well that he's in London, but her servants are every bit as tight-lipped as she is."

Visiting family connections. That sounded like Clary was taking pains to assure his allies that he was innocent of anything Benedict might say about him. Jamie didn't care about that—he'd never expected to persuade Clary's own family of his guilt—but it meant he needed to put things in motion soon, before public opinion had hardened. So far Benedict had persuaded a magistrate that Clary should be brought in for questioning, but that was a far cry from a conviction. "Any word of him in the gossip? Anything about his finances or personal habits?"

Daniel shrugged. "It's not hard to find rumors of financial trouble, so I've heard a few things, but nothing ruinous. Personal habits . . . I presume you mean women? I haven't found a mistress yet. He prefers brothels and none of those girls want to talk about him. It hardly reflects well on the man, but neither does it convict him."

Jamie brooded over that. What was driving Clary to pursue Olivia so fixedly? It wasn't just the painting. Clary wanted the Titian *and* Olivia.

"What is your idea?" Daniel's voice punctured his thoughts. "You said you had one, thanks to this bloke. What?"

He was still working it out, but it was starting to become clearer. "I'll let you know."

With only a brief stop on the way for supplies, Jamie went back to Grosvenor Square. He was glad his parents were out of town and had given him the use of the house. The elder Westons had gone to their country home, Hart House in Richmond, to be near their daughters. Penelope, at Stratford Court, was only across the river, and Abigail was even closer, as her husband owned the neighboring property, Montrose Hill. Jamie knew his mother loved life in town, but even more she loved her family. He walked through the spacious, elegant hall and wondered if they would give up this house and take a smaller one, if they meant to spend more time in Richmond. His father wouldn't want to; Thomas Weston liked a big house, and Jamie knew he had his eye on hosting fashionable society parties as well as family gatherings, with grandchildren running up and down the stairs.

Slowly he ran one hand over the banister railing. It was wide and smooth, curving gracefully toward the upper floor. If they'd had this house when he was a boy, he would have mastered sliding down it. When he had a son, he'd have to show the boy how it was done . . .

Twice already he'd barely stopped himself from asking Olivia to marry him. He knew she would say yes; even worse, he knew she was waiting hopefully for him to ask. If only he had known sooner that she would feel that way. It could have saved her from Clary, and him from entanglements that now tied his hands and kept him from falling to one knee. If only he'd been able to dispatch Clary quickly and permanently, proving that at least he was capable of protecting a wife.

His hand balled into a fist on the banister as he castigated himself. What sort of maudlin idiot was he to stand here regretting things instead of trying to right them? He released the banister and took the remaining stairs two at a time. There was work to do.

Olivia returned to Grosvenor Square that evening breathless with excitement and pride.

"I hope this helps," said Penelope for the sixth time as they rolled up to the Weston house. "It must! It was so exciting!"

"Wasn't it?" Olivia laughed. She still couldn't believe everything had gone so splendidly. She peeked out the window and watched one of the Stratford footmen bound up the steps and ring the bell. "Thank you for helping me, Pen."

"Of course! How could I not?"

"I hope Jamie's not too upset that we lied to him."

Penelope rolled her eyes. "Trust me, Olivia, he'll forgive you at once. Hasn't he always?"

No, thought Olivia with a tremor of doubt. Nor had she always forgiven him at once. But it was too late for that now; the deed was done. She hoped her success would mitigate any disapproval Jamie might feel.

The butler opened the door of the house, so she gave Penelope one last hug and climbed down. "Good luck!" her friend cried from the window as the coachman drove off.

Olivia waved back, then hurried into the house. "Is Mr. Weston at home?" she asked the butler, removing her cloak and bonnet.

"Yes, ma'am. He has been working in the library all day."

"Thank you." Clutching her prize, she headed for the library. She tapped at the door, then turned the knob, too eager to wait. The Weston library was a grand and impressive room, with a high ceiling and tall windows that overlooked the garden in the rear of the house. The sconce lamps were all burning brightly, illuminating the room. The long velvet drapes had been drawn already, and fires crackled in the grates of both fireplaces, warming the long room. A wide table near one fire was covered with papers and held Jamie's battered writing desk, still bearing the scars of Clary's attack, but there was no sign of the man himself.

Disappointed, she came into the room. He must have spent the day here, catching up on correspondence and other business matters, from the sheer volume of paper. Some of it was clearly drafts, with parts marked out and blotches of ink in the margins. Olivia drifted toward the fire, still chilled from the long carriage ride. It felt delicious next to the fender, and she turned to warm her backside, too.

For several minutes she indulged in the warm glow of the fire and the anticipation of Jamie's reaction when she showed him what she'd located. Olivia let the small, leather-bound book fall open in her hands and read the scrimped writing with deep pleasure. Henry's payment diary, kept in Mr. Brewster's own hand, indicated exactly which members of society had paid for smuggled art from France.

Olivia had warned Penelope it would be a gamble when she proposed the plan, before they left Richmond. But once her friend heard the complete story, Penelope agreed it was a gamble worth taking. Benedict was vowing to hunt Clary down and kill him, if a magistrate couldn't be bothered, and Penelope did not want to see her husband in jeopardy of prison. Both of them agreed that neither Benedict nor Jamie needed to know about the mission until after it was over.

Mr. Brewster had been very startled to see her on his doorstep again. Even more startling, judging from his expression, was the way Olivia calmly laid a pistol, borrowed from one of the footmen, across her lap. She marveled at how well the gun focused his attention and changed his demeanor. Within an hour Mr. Brewster had completely reversed his course, from blustering that he had no idea what she was talking about to handing over the diary. This time Olivia read it right there, to be certain it held useful information.

Jamie, of course, was right again. Lawyers didn't throw out valuable papers.

Olivia was sure they had enough to hang Clary now. Unlike the abbreviated notations in the other diary, Mr. Brewster had meticulously documented every penny Henry received and spent. One thousand pounds for a Madonna and child. Six hundred twenty for a painting of St. Sebastian, two thousand two hundred for a statue of Venus, one hundred fifteen for a bronze figurine of Apollo. Great artists were listed along with ones she'd never heard of, and some of the pieces were presumably so old, no one knew who had crafted them. *Ancient*, read the notation next to those. And every expense was documented, from five shillings for canvas to wrap pictures to the hundreds of pounds paid to Lord Clary, always noted as *Commission*. Even doing very hasty arithmetic Olivia could see that Henry had raked in a fortune, and that Clary had shared in it.

She was sure Jamie would forgive her for lying to him about shopping when he saw the diary. It hadn't escaped Olivia that this was taking a toll on him; the guilt on his face when Clary caught her unawares still ate at her. The night he slept on the floor, he had told her she was stronger and more capable than she knew. Olivia wanted that to be true, so much that she decided to make it true.

Happily she closed the cover and leaned forward to put it on the desk. When she dropped the diary, it dislodged a stack of papers close to the edge. One, then another page drifted off, down toward the hearth. Olivia grabbed them on instinct. But as she moved to put them back on the desk, her eyes caught on the words.

Dear Reader,

If nothing I have related thus far has shocked you, I regret that my story on this occasion may very well leave you speechless. This time I write of my encounter with two men: one the very best sort of gentleman, and one the very worst . . .

Olivia was stunned speechless. Wide-eyed, she read that page twice, then the other. It was unquestionably an issue of *50 Ways to Sin*, written in a neat, unfamiliar hand. Where did Jamie get this? And how?

The door opened as she stood there, confounded. "Livie," exclaimed Jamie. "I didn't know you were back." She looked up in time to see his eyes lock on the pages in her hand, and his expression go curiously blank.

"Yes." She shook her head in mute question. "What is this?"

"What do you mean?" He pushed the door closed behind him.

"I mean—" She blushed. *50 Ways to Sin* was a clandestine pleasure of hers, one she didn't quite know how to discuss with Jamie. But it turned out he not only read it, he was able to get advance copies. She had never read this one and it was handwritten. "I know what it *is*. This is an issue of *50 Ways to Sin*. But how did you get this?"

"Oh. It's just a copy someone gave me," he tried to say, but Olivia snorted.

"I know it was never published! I would remember reading it!"

Jamie's expression changed to one of astonished interest. "You read them?"

"Everyone does! Of course I do." Her face heated as she spoke, and without thinking she glanced at the pages in her hand. She should have read all of it before saying anything.

"Do you . . . enjoy them?" he asked cautiously.

Now her entire body was burning hot. "Yes. Oh *yes*. They're so . . . free. So bold. So—" She broke off at the sight of his face. "Don't say you have anything against a woman pursuing pleasure."

He raised his hands in surrender. "Not a thing."

"Why do you have this?" She shook the pages. "Where did you get it? It's a draft of the next issue, isn't it?"

He swallowed. "Perhaps."

"But—Jamie!" She laughed incredulously. "You must know who Lady Constance is!"

He didn't say anything. He didn't have to.

"Who?" Olivia demanded, agog with amazement. "Who is she? You do realize all of London is wild to know."

"All of London? Hardly." He made a face, but avoided her fascinated gaze.

"Well, much of London, and nearly every woman." Every woman of Olivia's acquaintance, at least, especially including Jamie's own two sisters. It was Penelope who had introduced the notorious story to her and Abigail. Penelope had overheard her mother discussing it with some friends, in terms titillating enough for her to spend a fortnight searching surreptitiously for it. From then on both Weston sisters were devoted readers, along with their friend Joan Bennet. Olivia didn't know, or want to know, how they had procured it. She did hear that Penelope had once been caught reading it and was punished severely by her mother, but also that Abigail blushed and said reading it hadn't impeded her romance or marriage—rather the contrary, in fact.

She looked at the pages again. From what she'd read, this looked to be another deliciously shocking issue where Constance indulged in a cooling swim in a secluded pond, only to be discovered—and surely pleasured—by a passing local gentleman. Olivia could only imagine how heated it would become, for those pages were missing. This draft had no number, but she knew they must be nearing an end. Of the fifty ways to sin the title promised, nearly forty had been published.

And now it turned out Jamie, of all people, knew the identity of the mysterious Lady Constance. How astonished Penelope and Abigail would be! And Jamie—what a sly one, to keep such news secret all this time. He must know it was hotly debated around London. Some gentlemen had even offered bounties to anyone who could discover her true name. "Who is she?" she asked again. "And how do you know her?"

Jamie took his time replying. "I know the fellow who publishes them," he finally admitted.

Her brows went up. That was nearly as interesting, and just as unknown. "Who?"

"A mate of mine from university. He was

wounded in the war and struggled for a good while when he returned home. These have provided him a tidy income."

"I don't doubt it. I heard they sell five thousand copies of each issue."

"More like eight, actually," he murmured.

Incredible. She shook her head in admiration. "I don't begrudge him the success. I applaud him for taking the risk, in fact—I've never read anything where a woman's pleasure was so boldly celebrated and pursued." With a faint groan, Jamie sank into a chair and hung his head. "Is something wrong?" she asked with a flicker of concern, taking a few steps toward him. "Are you unwell?"

He shook his head.

"If you fear I'll reveal Constance's true identity, I swear I won't."

His shoulders hunched. "It's not that. I trust you."

She was perplexed, but still desperately curious. "Then who is Constance?"

Jamie scrubbed his hands over his head. When he tilted his head to look up at her, his dark hair stuck up in ruffled waves, as it used to do when he was a boy. But his expression was that of a man bracing for a blow, and his eyes were wary. "I am."

Part Three

But true love is a durable fire,
In the mind ever burning,
Never sick, never dead, never cold,
From itself never turning.

—Attributed to Sir Walter Raleigh

Chapter 22

For a moment she didn't react, and Jamie allowed himself to imagine that he hadn't said it. It was his most closely guarded secret, and the one he'd sworn he would absolutely deny to the death if anyone ever suspected. That had been his bargain with Daniel: *No one must ever know.*

But Olivia had him dead to rights. She was trusting and loyal enough that she wouldn't push him if he denied it, even though she held the damning proof, written by his own hand. After all the promises he had wrung from Daniel and Bathsheba not to tell a single person, he was the one who gave himself away. So much for all that; he'd left his half-written issue lying out on the desk. How could he have been so stupid, to leave the draft where she might find it?

The only solace was that it was Olivia. Of all the people in the world, he did trust her the most. He couldn't fathom that she would unmask him in public, not even for the rather large bounties a few idiots had placed on learning Constance's real identity. But that didn't mean she wouldn't be appalled or horrified to discover it was he who had written those erotic stories in a woman's voice, and the longer she stared at him blankly, still clutching the pages, the more he feared she was.

"You," she said faintly. "*You?* Jamie . . ."

Damn it. He lunged to take the papers from her, but she leapt backward. "Forget I said it, Livie. It's over anyway."

"Over?" She put the pages behind her back as he made another halfhearted attempt to reclaim his draft. "It's not over until there are fifty. Everyone is expecting fifty!"

"No," he said in a low voice. "It's over."

Still looking dumbfounded, she came and sat in the opposite chair. For a moment she studied him, her head tilted slightly to one side as it always was when she was thinking. "You've truly written them all?"

Resigned, he nodded.

"How . . . ?" She shook her head in amazement. "This isn't even your handwriting."

He sighed and held up his left hand. His right hand, the one Clary had slammed in the door the other day, was still swollen and sore. Writing with his right hand was easier, but strangely his left-handed writing was neater.

Olivia knew he could write with either hand. She accepted it without argument. "Why?"

"It was a lark," he said, knowing how awful it sounded. "My friend and I got into an argument about whether women were capable of the same . . . desires as men. He insisted not, I thought yes." He dared a glance at her, to see if that struck a chord with her. If so, he couldn't tell. Her blue eyes were still wide and stunned, and a thin, puzzled line divided her brows. "There, ah, there might have been a wager of sorts on the answer. Wanting to win, and a little bit the worse for drink . . ." He cleared his throat, remembering the bottle of fine Douro port that had helped inspire the first issue. "*Much* the worse for drink, I wrote one to prove my point. I slid it under his door, thinking we would share a good laugh over it, he would acknowledge his loss, and that would be the end."

"Obviously it went further than that," she said.

He sighed. "I didn't expect that his sister would find it first. She read it and . . . er . . . enjoyed it. She took it to her brother and demanded to know where he got it and if there were more. He recognized my handwriting, of course, and came to pound down my door. I explained it wasn't meant seriously but by then he'd come to agree with his sister. They wanted to publish it; they both thought many ladies, and even gentlemen, would find it . . . stimulating."

Pink washed up her cheeks. "Surely you didn't doubt that."

"I didn't think much about it at all! It was a *joke*, Livie." He ran one hand over his face. "But the truth was, Daniel—my friend—needed money. He lost his arm in the war and thus his rank in the navy. His father left him a newspaper press, although the circulation had fallen off after the war and it was barely allowing them to survive. He persuaded me to let him try publishing it."

That, Jamie knew, had been his downfall. Daniel was scraping by financially, yet offered to print it entirely at his own risk. To keep his friend from throwing away his last shilling, Jamie had bought the paper for the first edition, fully expecting it would prove a terrific waste and put the whole mad idea out of Daniel's head. More fool him. "It sold well, and soon he was back at my door wanting another story."

Another understatement. Daniel had laid out a strong argument that they would be good partners, but Bathsheba had begged. Not only did she see an opportunity, she wanted to read more about Constance. "I wanted to help him get back on his feet so I agreed to write a few more." He raised one hand and let it fall. "I never suspected it would get out of hand."

"Out of hand!"

"Popular," he amended. "In demand. I never thought many people would read it, let alone clamor for more. But once I started, it became impossible to stop. It gave my friend a purpose, after months of struggle and melancholy. It put food on his table and warm clothing on his back. I couldn't say no."

She just stared at him in amazement. He held out one hand. "May I have it back?"

As if she knew what he meant to do, Olivia drew back, holding the pages protectively. "Why?"

"So I can burn it," he answered honestly. "It's rubbish."

"No it's not." She looked down at the papers. "It's wonderful."

His face felt hot. God, he was blushing like a girl, partly in humiliation at being discovered and partly, secretly, in a bit of white-hot arousal that Olivia liked it. She'd been reading his words all along. She called the stories free and bold and found them erotic and engaging. If he'd ever wanted any sort of encouragement or approval, that was it.

"How did you think of them?" she asked, head still lowered. "How did you decide what would happen?"

He imagined a widowed woman, free of any guilt or fear or anxiety. He thought of a woman who deserved pleasure, but who kept love at bay. Then he thought of all the ways a man might tempt such a woman into forbidden ecstasies and help her embrace the sensual creature who lived inside her. In his imagination, he was every mystery lover, given one night of wicked abandon with a woman who would never allow him more.

He thought of *her*, the one woman he'd always loved but thought he would never hold again.

"Bathsheba," he said instead. "My friend's sister. She suggested modeling the gentlemen on members of the *ton*. It amused me to skewer men who often took themselves too seriously, and when I ran short on ideas, Bathsheba was all too happy to venture out into society to gather some new piece of gossip or tawdry rumor to fuel another story. I embellished very liberally, not wanting to stray too close to any man in truth."

"Bathsheba," she repeated slowly.

"And her brother, Daniel Crawford."

Olivia started. "The name you used in Kent!"

James gave a limp smile. "He gave me leave, I swear it."

"Then he knew where you were?"

He heard the subtle note of alarm enter her

voice. "He was the only one. Even Bathsheba didn't know. I needed someone who could ask questions in London and carry out any other useful tasks for me."

She swallowed. "Does he know why you went?"

"Yes," Jamie said evenly. "It was his network of reporters and informants who helped me locate you and discover what Clary might be up to."

A faint shudder ran through her. "Then he knows everything?"

"No, he knows only what I asked him to learn, which was mostly about Clary."

"And Henry." Her head was still bowed.

"Yes."

Olivia still clutched his handwritten pages in both hands. Jamie closed his eyes to avoid seeing them. He'd had a thought, a mad, momentary idea, that he could use *50 Ways to Sin* to help put away Clary. Now that his secret was out, though, there was no choice but to end it. Later tonight he would burn everything and make it official. Daniel would be unhappy, and Bathsheba would probably rail at him for days, but Jamie meant to keep his word. He wasn't precisely ashamed of what he'd done, but he was very well aware that he would be ridiculed and mocked forever if he were ever exposed as the author. He didn't want to do that to his family, but especially not to Olivia—Olivia, whom he still wanted desperately to marry.

On the other hand . . . This was his chance. If he put an end to Constance here and now, it would leave him in the clear to propose marriage to Olivia at long last, and this time see it through . . .

"Why did you say it's over?"

Olivia's quiet question startled him. He felt a flush creep up his neck. "That was my only condition," he muttered. "If anyone ever discovered my part, I would never write another word."

"So it's my fault."

"No." He sighed. "Yes. But don't blame yourself. I'm not sorry."

"I am!" She smoothed the pages. "I don't want it to end. What were you planning for this story?"

Saying it out loud might make it seem even more foolish. Use a fictional strumpet to catch a very real villain? Jamie flexed his fingers and studied his knuckles. "I had an idea that Constance could help sway public opinion against Clary."

Olivia started. "How?"

He was blushing now, he knew it. The only person who ever commented on the stories, to his face, was Bathsheba, and her comments were far more often critical. "The gentlemen Constance has affairs with are based on real men, disguised but recognizable. There's no reason I couldn't make Clary one of those men, but make him cruel and indecent to her." Olivia nodded expectantly, neither laughing nor gaping in shock. "I hear a lot of gossip. It won't take much to turn people against Clary. He's not widely admired or liked, and if he assaults Constance . . ." He shrugged.

She sat in silence for a long time. Twice he saw her read the page in her hand again. One moment Jamie would wonder desperately what she was thinking, and then the next he would think he didn't want to know. She read his stories—and enjoyed them—but that was when she thought a woman wrote them.

Nothing had surprised him more than the evident fact that no one suspected a man wrote them. Jamie liked women too much to let his lead character seem weak or insipid, and of course he made her the most uninhibited, licentious woman in England, so she had to be strong-willed and capable as well. What would Olivia think of him now? It was an odd feeling to have the dark corners of his imagination exposed, and Jamie felt a real fear that she would be so appalled or shocked that she would never see him in the same light.

"I think it will work," she said in a very low voice. "It's a good idea. You should keep writing."

His head jerked up. "What?"

"Everyone reads this. If Clary is a villain in the piece, people will think of him so. We need everything we can marshal against him, don't we?"

"Yes, but—" He rolled out of his chair, onto his knees beside her. "Are you disgusted that I did it?"

She smiled, a little nervously. "No. You wrote a woman unafraid to pursue what she wants, unashamed of her own desires. How could I be disgusted? I already told you I like the stories for—for a number of reasons."

He thought about telling her that most stories had come out of his fantasies about her, then discarded the thought. For now. "You're a rare woman, Olivia Townsend."

"I also have something to confess," she said. "Since we're telling secrets. I was going to tell you anyway—I came here as soon as I returned home—but I didn't go shopping with Penelope today."

Oh Lord. Jamie tensed. "What did you do?"

She got up and went to the desk. "I went to see Mr. Brewster. He was our London solicitor, and he handled all Henry's money. Every bill we ever had was sent to Mr. Brewster. He told me weeks ago that he had no idea what that diary from Mr. Armand meant, but I knew even then he lied to me. So today I told him that I knew, and that I wanted the diary *he* kept for Henry." She turned around and held out a leather book.

His eyes riveted on it. Great God. He had been absolutely certain Brewster would have destroyed that, after Olivia had put him on guard with her first visit. But she had it, the record that could prove everything about Henry's smuggling ring and close the shackles on Clary's wrists. "How did you get that?" he asked stupidly.

"Penelope and I went to Bethnal Green and demanded it." A guilty blush stained her face but she didn't lower her gaze. "The footmen were armed," she added. "Liars deserve to be confronted and made to admit their lies. For two years Mr. Brewster lied to me and told me not to worry about anything regarding Henry's estate, when he knew all along there was trouble lurking."

"Does it show—?" he began, but Olivia was already nodding.

"Hundreds of pounds paid to Lord Clary for smuggled art." She smiled, less nervous and more hopeful. "And thousands more paid to Henry by members of the *ton*. It turns out Mr. Brewster kept very good records."

Jamie came to his feet and swept her into his

arms with one motion. She opened the book and showed him a few pages, pointing out entries indicating payment to Lord Clary, right next to payments received for paintings of Diana at the hunt and sculptures of Nike. Jamie let out a whoop and swung her in the air. Olivia threw her arms around his neck and laughed.

"What a pair we make," she said as he set her down, still laughing. "Sneaks, the both of us!"

He grinned and kissed her. "A perfect match."

Her face glowed. "How are we going to catch this villain?"

Jamie looked at the desk, where his notes and drafts were scattered. He knew what he wanted to do with the story, and if Olivia agreed with him, he felt lucky enough to take the gamble—and win. "I have to tell Daniel. And I think you should meet him, too."

Chapter 23

It looked like any other house, narrow and a little run-down, in Totman Street on the outskirts of respectable London. Jamie rapped the knocker twice and stepped back down beside Olivia. "This is going to give Daniel quite a start," he predicted.

"Your plan?" Her blue eyes shone. "I think it's brilliant. Although I wish there was more I could do."

"As if you haven't endured enough. Allow me to turn this foolish lark of mine into something worthwhile." He grinned, and was rewarded with a smile. It warmed his heart to see Olivia's confidence returning. For that alone, everything had been worth it.

Of course, her confidence was yielding other benefits as well. The diary she had pried out of Mr. Brewster's hands held a trove of information. That morning they'd sent a letter to Benedict, urging him to come to town as soon as he could—and to bring his solicitors. Jamie had realized at once that they should attack Clary on two simultaneous fronts: legally and socially. The diary meant they had a real weapon legally, and

Benedict, the Earl of Stratford, was better poised to lead that fight. Jamie had no doubt that his brother-in-law would be in Grosvenor Square by the next morning.

However, he was less certain of Daniel's reaction. Thus far he had written thirty-eight issues, which gave him only twelve more. Jamie himself had been the one to insist on a limit of fifty; he hadn't thought it would last that long, but as the joke became a prosperous venture, he realized it could go on forever. Before conceiving the plan to ruin Clary he'd been more than a little tired of it, and reiterated his desire to stop soon.

But now . . . What if it took more to turn society against Clary? He was already breaking his vow to stop writing immediately if anyone learned the truth. Daniel would be amenable to more issues, Jamie knew. He'd already begun hinting that he saw no need to stop at fifty; *That was only a title,* he'd said in casual conversation before Jamie left London. *If people enjoy it, why should we deny them?* The only question was whether Daniel would approve of what Jamie wanted to do with those issues.

The door opened. "Back at last!" cried Bathsheba. She must have been working, judging by the cap pinned over her hair and the large, ink-spotted apron she wore. Then she spotted Olivia. "Oh. I beg your pardon . . ."

"This is Mrs. Olivia Townsend," Jamie said. "Olivia, Miss Bathsheba Crawford. May we come in?"

"Of course!" Blushing, Bathsheba swept open the door. "Come in, ma'am."

Jamie led Olivia down the servants' cramped stairs. Instead of a kitchen or other storage rooms, though, the arched hall below held a printing press. The walls were lined with cords strung the length of the room, and pages hung from every inch of them. Olivia's lips parted in wonder and she craned her neck, trying to take it all in. Jamie felt a bit of surprise as well. The issues must be selling better than ever, judging from the number of pages drying. Early on, they could hang an entire order on half this many cords. The press, a giant wooden apparatus that occupied the center of the room, was making a dull groaning noise as Daniel operated it, but that ceased when he caught sight of Jamie.

"Ho there!" He spun the lever back, then came around the press, wiping his hand on the stained apron he wore. His other sleeve was rolled up and pinned closed below his elbow, where his left arm ended.

"Daniel," Jamie greeted him. "Still at it, I see."

He laughed. "Someone must. We decided to print back copies, and the orders flooded in. Bathsheba's near wrung her arm off, trying to keep up." He darted a quick glance of veiled curiosity at Olivia.

"Olivia, this is my friend Daniel Crawford. He's responsible for tempting me into wickedness. And this, Dan, is Mrs. Olivia Townsend."

Olivia bobbed a curtsy. "How do you do, sir?"

"'Tis a pleasure to make your acquaintance, Mrs. Townsend," said Daniel Crawford gravely. He bowed just as Bathsheba came in.

She'd swiped the cap from her head and removed her apron, and now she came forward with a wary look. "Welcome back, Jamie. I hope everything turned out well on your journey."

"So far." Jamie went to close the door, although there was probably no one else in the house. Daniel gave his two servants the day off when there was printing to be done. He told everyone he was printing volumes of poetry for private collections, to explain the quantities of paper and ink. Jamie wondered if anyone believed that anymore. "I've come to talk to you about that. Shall we sit down?"

Daniel and his sister exchanged a glance as they took seats on the battered collection of chairs at the back of the room. Bathsheba's mouth set into a grim line, and Daniel seemed to be bracing himself. "Do you need further help?" he asked, almost resigned. "More information? I've put out the word on your queries to everyone I can."

"Today I've come to talk about Constance." Both Daniel and Bathsheba froze, their expressions mirror images of alarm. As one they looked at Olivia. "She knows," Jamie told them.

Bathsheba inhaled. "No! Not now! Orders are coming in every day—Danny and I can hardly print enough to keep up, even though we work at it all week long! It would be foolish to stop now, no one need know. You must understand how important this is," she appealed to Olivia. "You must keep it in the strictest confidence—"

"Of course I will," said Olivia in surprise.

Jamie shook his head. "We're not stopping. I've got twelve issues left and I need every one of them. Constance is going to help us destroy Lord Clary."

Both Crawfords stared at him, Bathsheba's mouth still open in protest. "Er . . . What?" Daniel finally said.

Jamie looked at Olivia, and she gave a firm nod of approval. The Crawfords already knew about Clary, after all. "You know I've been keen to know what Clary does and where he goes. The reason is that he's been harassing Olivia. When she wouldn't agree to become his mistress, he assaulted her. It turns out her husband ran with a fast set and didn't always follow the law of the land. Clary knows this—because he was part of that same crowd—and he's threatening her. When she left town to avoid him, he tried to kill my sister because Penelope refused to tell him where to find Olivia. This man deserves to be locked in a prison, but he's got connections." Jamie smiled darkly. "And since he doesn't intend to play honorably, neither do I."

"How is Constance going to help ruin him?" asked Bathsheba slowly.

"People tend to believe Constance is telling the truth, or something close to the truth. Every gent who gave a sly wink and a nod when people whispered that he was the man Constance described has established her credibility better than I ever could. Therefore, if a villainous man named . . . Lord Brarely starts harassing and hurting Constance . . ." Jamie shrugged. "I think he might even try to kill her."

Again the Crawfords exchanged a glance. "Is there part of this plan that prevents us being sued?" asked Daniel.

"Sued?" Jamie raised his brows. "You mean,

will Lord Clary publicly admit he's the murderous rapist in the story?"

"He's a lord," Bathsheba pointed out. "Lords are wealthy, and you said this one has connections. He'll drive us out of business, if not see us put in prison for obscenity."

"We're going out of business in twelve issues anyway."

Her mouth firmed into a flat line. "We'll have no choice if members of Parliament swear out warrants for our arrest!"

"It's all fiction," Jamie said. "Lord Clary must have a guilty soul if he recognizes himself in the villain of a tawdry little pamphlet."

"Tawdry!" Bathsheba scowled at him.

"It's not so little," added Daniel under his breath. "But more to the point . . . How do you know anyone will believe it? Gents who wink and nod when people ask if they've known Constance are one thing, when Constance is . . . er . . . complimentary." He avoided looking at either woman. "Now you're going to portray a gentleman as a monster. People won't be so eager to believe that."

"Everything else will be the same," he assured them. "Constance will meet a man and find pleasure. It will merely happen after she escapes the clutches of the villain."

Bathsheba continued to glare at him. "Must you? Any Minerva Press novel will give that story. This is special—Constance doesn't need to be rescued! She's perfectly capable of looking after herself and now you want to make her a fainting, delicate woman. I think readers have taken to her because she's strong and able and because there is no villain she must be saved from."

"She's right," said Olivia. He glanced at her in surprise. Her blue eyes gazed solemnly into his. "Don't make Constance weak."

"Have faith." He covered her hand with his. "I'm too fond of Constance to let her helplessly suffer abuse or indignity. But she's led a charmed life thus far; she's got her way in everything she's decided to do, and has never suffered censure or unwanted attentions. We both know that is virtually impossible for any woman. Facing adversity will demonstrate her strength, not destroy it. How much more inspiring will it be when she triumphs over the villain in the end?" He paused, looking from Bathsheba to Olivia. Bathsheba still looked angry, and Olivia worried. "Dare I mention once more that she's fictional, and not some actual woman I intend to subject to cruelty?"

Olivia blinked, then smiled ruefully. Bathsheba colored and threw up her hands. "Very well. Do what you will."

"And this will help spare a flesh-and-blood woman real harm," Jamie went on. "Isn't that enough reason to do it?"

"It is." Daniel put his hand on his sister's arm. "You know it is."

"I do," she agreed at once, with a penitent glance at Olivia. "Of course."

Daniel exhaled. "What is your plan?"

They were with him. Jamie hid his surge of relieved elation and quickly outlined what he intended to do. By the time he finished, Daniel's forehead had developed the deep groove it got when he was thinking, and Bathsheba was staring at the floor, tapping her fingers against her skirt. "How rapidly do you want to publish these?"

"As fast as I can write them."

Daniel and his sister exchanged a glance. "It takes a full week to print one edition now."

"We'll have to work faster," said Jamie impatiently. "I want two or three a week."

"Three a week!" Bathsheba threw up her hands. "We've got orders for nearly nine thousand copies of the next issue. Since you left, and there are no new issues, the booksellers have been ordering older issues again. We can't print twenty thousand copies a week. We can hardly print six thousand."

Jamie didn't say anything. His eyes traveled over the reams of paper hanging from what looked like miles of rope. At the beginning, they'd developed an efficient system. Each issue could be no more than eight pages long, so they could print all the pages on one sheet of paper. The first day they printed the first side, the second day the second side. The third day they cut and bound the pages, and then the pamphlets went out to the bookstores and shops. If all three of them worked on it, they could deliver several thousand copies a week. But Bathsheba was right; there was no way the three of them, or even the four of them, could produce twenty thousand copies or more every week.

Bathsheba put her hands on her temples. "Perhaps it won't take long to sway opinion. If this man is as evil as you say, surely you can do it in two or three issues."

"No," he said slowly. "It must be more than that. People will fear for Constance's life. I intend to show Clary for the monster he is, not some reckless or impulsive fellow who is easily brushed aside. It will last all twelve issues remaining, and we have to keep a steady stream of them. I want everyone in London to be talking about it. We'll have to get help."

"Help." Daniel burst out of his seat. "Where? From whom? You were the one so crazed with secrecy you swore you would stop if anyone discovered it!" He glanced at Olivia and held up one hand in apology. "Not that I regret your change of heart. But because of that I never hired anyone. Bathsheba has been forced to work down here every day with me, and it's still a struggle to keep up."

"Well," said Jamie evenly, "I did offer to stop many times before this."

Daniel flushed. "And I persuaded you not to. I know. But—who are you going to find to help us? I presume you still don't want the secret out."

Absolutely not. Constance had become the means of salvation and his greatest vulnerability at the same time. The safest thing, for his good name and social future, was to stop writing at once. He had to be free of Constance before he could marry Olivia in good conscience. The uproar if he were revealed in public was too dreadful to contemplate.

But he would give everything he had to bring down Lord Clary. Constance had begun as little more than a joke to him, then become the means to help a friend. Now she had the power to serve justice to someone who might otherwise escape unscathed, and save the woman he loved. Even at the risk of ruining his own name, he was determined to press ahead.

That reminded him of something. "It's quite possible my name will come out anyway," he warned them. "I told you Clary stole some pages from my book in Ramsgate," he said to Olivia. "They were notes for future stories."

Her mouth opened in a perfect O. "That's why he said he would denounce *me* as Lady Constance!"

Jamie cleared his throat, aware of Bathsheba's avid gaze. "Erm. Yes. But if I write stories featuring Clary, he'll either believe it's you, or suspect it's me."

"Why?" Bathsheba asked.

Everyone looked at her. She just shrugged. "There's a half dozen imitators already. I daresay even if Clary showed your notes to people, they wouldn't believe it was by the real Constance. Don't forget, I've read your first drafts, Jamie. They all improve markedly after I make some changes—"

"Yes, I see," he said testily. Her changes were minor and they both knew it. "Well, I certainly will act astonished if anyone accuses me, and Olivia can deny it with complete honesty. But then we're all agreed?"

Daniel nodded, Bathsheba pursed up her lips but didn't demur, and Olivia declared a stout "Yes."

"We need a partner," he repeated. "Someone who understands the need for secrecy, someone who might even revel in it. And of course someone who grasps the reward associated with success."

"I could hire an illiterate boy," said Daniel after a moment. "He'd only be able to work the press, not set the type."

"The pamphlets look distinctive," Bathsheba pointed out. "Even an illiterate boy would notice. Besides, one boy won't speed us up very much."

"No, we need someone who knows his way around a press." Jamie frowned in thought.

"A newspaper printer," said Olivia. The other three looked at her. She nodded. "Newspapers know how to print quickly."

"They also don't know how to keep a secret," replied Bathsheba.

"Well, there must be some who can. The *London Intelligencer* has anonymous reporters. The lady who writes the scandal page for them has never been identified."

"How do you know it's a lady who writes that page?" asked Daniel in surprise.

Olivia looked startled. "Oh! I thought it was obvious. She must attend all the parties, to hear the things she writes of, and men never listen to gossip the way women do . . ."

Jamie raised his head. The *London Intelligencer*. He knew that name. He knew that paper. He also knew the man who printed it, Liam MacGregor, was a bold and ambitious Scot with nerves of polished steel. And Olivia's words made him recall one curious fact he'd learned over the last year. Every week MacGregor had an appointment at Wharton's Bank. Jamie did some business there, and more than once he'd seen the man arrive and be shown into a private office. And on one occasion earlier this year, MacGregor's appointment had been with Mrs. Madeline Wilde.

The lady who had been publicly accused just a few months ago of being Constance.

Waiting idly while a bank partner fetched the papers he needed, Jamie had seen both of them arrive and go into the same office. That didn't prove anything, but Mrs. Wilde had been the subject of rumor and fascination even before the scandalous accusation . . . because she moved in the very best society circles but cultivated an air of aloofness. Or she had, until accepting Douglas Bennet's marriage proposal in front of one hundred and fifty guests at Lady Cartwright's midsummer ball.

Jamie, knowing the truth, had found the entire thing wildly amusing. Mrs. Wilde didn't seem perturbed by the uproar—in fact, she gave every appearance of being blindingly happy with her new fiancé—and after Mr. Bennet thrashed a couple of fellows who called her Lady Constance, even that rumor died down.

But Liam MacGregor . . .

It might be pure coincidence, but if anyone would employ a female writer, it would be MacGregor. And the man who accused Mrs. Wilde must have had some reason to suspect her. She was well-known for attending society events, after all, where she must hear all the gossip. And either way, MacGregor had managed to keep his scandal page author a complete secret.

"I'll find someone to help run the press," he said abruptly. "We're going to meet this schedule, and Lord Clary will be reviled across London by the time we're done."

Chapter 24

Jamie set to work with a vengeance. He moved all his writing to his bedroom and told the servants he wasn't to be disturbed. Olivia soon learned to stay out of his way, too. He would sit for an hour, staring out the window with a small frown knitting his brow, then reach for his pen and cover pages and pages. Sometimes he stopped halfway through and cursed, wadding up the paper and throwing it onto the fire. Other times he would cross out a word or a paragraph and write on without pause.

At night he still came to her. She supposed he waited until the servants had gone to bed, but every night, often very late, he would let himself into her bedroom and slide beneath the blankets and draw her close. Many of the regular servants had gone to Richmond with the elder Westons, which made it easier on Olivia's conscience. Jamie seemed as comfortable doing for himself as she was, so they were left in peace unless they rang for someone. The house in Grosvenor Square became a small private world, where Olivia at times felt nearer to being married than she had ever felt with Henry. She and Henry had inhabited the same house but never shared a life. Even when Jamie spent hours working in the next room, she felt close to him.

In part, she knew, it was because they were both working on the same cause. While Jamie was writing, Olivia made lists of Clary's habits, tastes, and foibles for use in the stories. They both wanted everyone who knew Clary, in any degree at all, to recognize him immediately. And when a shudder of fear or disgust rolled over her, as she thought about the man who had terrified her for the last year, she thought of him being humiliated and scorned by the very society he took refuge in, and the words came easily.

One night Jamie came in as she was getting ready for bed. "Here," he said, handing her a stack of paper.

Intrigued, Olivia turned up the lamp on her dressing table. So far he hadn't let her read anything, even though he'd told her bits and pieces of what he planned to write.

He sank down on the nearby chaise as she read. Within minutes he was stretched out, one arm hanging off the side and one hand behind his head. He stared up at the ceiling, looking exhausted. Olivia stole a glance at him over the pages. "Has Constance worn you out?" she teased quietly.

One corner of his mouth quirked. "It's a fine line to walk: too much about Clary and it will lose all appeal. Too little and it won't serve our purpose."

She laughed and read on. Within a few lines

she was able to forget that Jamie had written every word, and let herself become absorbed in the story. He had handed her not one but four issues, a third of the total left, and she read straight through to the end.

In the first one, Lord Brarely, a dark and imposing man with powerful connections and a very advantageous marriage, began paying Constance attention. She refused him, as she had refused all other married men, and instead turned her favor on a distinguished gentleman of some scientific renown. Olivia shivered at the delicate way he "scientifically" probed Constance's skin for points of particular pleasure.

The second story saw Constance stop for a cooling swim in a secluded pond during a trip, only to be discovered by Lord Brarely. She accused him of following her and he replied that no one would believe she hadn't enticed him. Fortunately, a handsome country squire passed by, and Constance explored the pleasures of making love in the water after Brarely went on his way.

The third story featured letters from Brarely, trying to coerce Constance into being his mistress. Constance, who had long since avowed that she would never belong to one man, burned them, but the specter was already clearly shaped. The fourth issue took place at a ball, where Brarely did nothing more than stare at Constance the entire evening. Even though Constance landed in the arms of a notorious rake who was only too pleased to spirit her away to a secluded and secure bedroom, Olivia felt her own stomach knot at the description of Brarely's dark, hawkish eyes following Constance around the room. Jamie had perfectly woven that unease, as well as the urge to dismiss it as womanish fear, into Constance's words.

"Well?" asked Jamie when she lowered the pages, her heart thudding.

"It's good." She cleared her throat to rid her voice of its husky quality. "Very good."

"Excellent. Now come here."

She moved to sit on the end of the chaise. Jamie sat up and slid one arm around her waist. "I don't want to disappoint my loyal readers," he murmured, tugging down her nightgown and brushing his lips against her bare shoulder.

Olivia smiled. "As one of those readers, I can safely promise you have not." In spite of Lord Brarely's ominous presence, Constance still indulged in her customary erotic interludes, all the sharper for diverting her mind from him.

"As the most important reader, yours is the most important opinion." He caught the end of the ribbon that tied her nightgown closed. "Which one did you enjoy especially?"

She inhaled as he pulled the ribbon. There was no doubt the issue set at the pond struck deep, and roused a hundred memories. "There's something to recommend them all . . ." She looked down at the pages in her hands. "How do you think of this?"

"A gentleman shouldn't say."

She very much wanted this gentleman to say. She wanted to know what inspired his ideas. He'd said Bathsheba offered suggestions from time to time, but Jamie hadn't spoken to Bathsheba in days; he'd been closed up in his room, writing. Everything on these pages sprang from his own imagination, and Olivia was desperate to know more about that. Did he imagine similar encounters between himself and other women? Was this interlude of theirs doomed to end, once he'd had his fill of her? Olivia could not ignore the fact that Jamie had been a healthy, virile man during her marriage. He hadn't married anyone else, but she was keenly aware that he had had several affairs. Thankfully Penelope and Abigail had only mentioned such things in passing—the beautiful French vicomtesse being the most notable instance—but it would have astonished Olivia more if Jamie hadn't had lovers.

"Is Constance based on a particular woman?" she asked.

He stopped kissing her shoulder, and his hand, now nestled inside her nightgown around her breast, went still. "No."

She wet her lips. "More than one person has remarked that Constance goes through lovers like a dedicated rake might. Is—is she based on you?"

He didn't reply for a long time. Olivia smoothed the pages of his draft and let them drop to the floor. "I never thought you lived like a monk," she said, trying to explain. "I could hardly blame you if you did have numerous lovers. I *don't* blame you, in fact. I . . . I am just curious. You know what my life was like with Henry, but I only know of you what your sisters told me." That sounded dreadful, and she cringed. "Never mind. You don't owe me an explanation."

"There were other women," he said in a low

voice. "Yes. In the first years of your marriage. More than one, although I wouldn't say numerous. It drove me a little mad, thinking of you with Henry. I wanted to scrub you from my mind and forget how you felt in my arms—I wanted to forget *you*, even though I knew that was impossible. But it didn't work." He sighed. "Every time I took another woman to bed, I wished she could be you, or enough like you to fool me for a night. It never worked. Finally I gave it up as a hopeless cause and stopped trying."

Her breath caught. "Stopped trying?"

He lifted one shoulder awkwardly, not meeting her gaze as she twisted to see his face. "I haven't had a woman in almost two years."

"Oh." She felt her heart give a little leap, then suddenly wrinkled her nose. "Only two! That leaves eight years of other women!"

His mouth curved. "Well, it took me a while to realize the truth." He paused. "Some of them lasted a while, some only a few nights. I knew none of them would last longer, or be more than a brief liaison. I was no good for any woman then, Livie. But I did learn something from all of them."

She knew he didn't mean erotic acts, although she had a feeling that was also true. "I don't doubt it."

"But as to what inspired Constance . . ." He shifted his weight, angling closer to her. "I thought of you."

Olivia jerked. "I never—!"

He touched one finger to her lips. "No, not in that way. I know you better than that. But in other ways . . ." His finger trailed down her chin and skimmed her throat, pausing on the point where her pulse pounded. "I imagined a woman able to explore her deepest desires, even those she thought dark or unseemly. I wondered what she might do, if she were freed from any worry about scandal."

Her heart was slamming into her ribs. Hadn't she done just that? From the moment she first told the innkeeper that Jamie was her husband, Olivia had given in to more and more of her deepest desires. She wanted everything from him—every smile, every secret, every shattering climax. She wanted him to know that she was his, completely, and always would be.

"And I think you've proven me right," Jamie breathed against her neck, his lips teasing the skin below her ear. "There is a far more sensual woman inside you than you even realize, Olivia, and the thought of drawing her out drives me wild." His finger traced loops and whorls across her bosom, as softly as a butterfly's wing, before catching the gaping neckline of her garment. "Tell me you agree . . ."

"Yes," she whispered as he slid the sleeve down her arm. "With you I am . . ."

"And you like what Constance does." The other sleeve fell away from her shoulder, leaving her bare to the waist.

"Yes . . ."

"What did you like best?" One by one he tugged her arms free of the nightgown. "Was it the whip? Was it the blindfold? Do you long to tie me up while you make love to me?"

She opened her mouth, then closed it. Her face burned. "What are you suggesting?"

"Have you ever thought of doing that?" he asked again. "Or of being tied up? It can be quite arousing."

She sat like a wide-eyed statue, barely breathing. "Tied . . . with what?"

He raised her hand and brushed his lips over the fluttering pulse in her wrist. "For you? Silk ribbons. As blue as your eyes and soft enough not to mar your skin, even as they hold you exposed and defenseless against a lover's ravishment."

"Tied to what?" she asked faintly.

His teeth nipped her shoulder, and her whole body spasmed. "My bed. Completely open and vulnerable, hiding nothing . . . denying nothing."

Her throat worked as she swallowed hard. "I haven't denied you . . ."

"It's the ultimate trust, to give yourself into your lover's hands and cede all power to him. Or to her," he added. "All pleasures go both ways. Would you prefer to tie me?"

Olivia gulped for air. It was one thing to read about such a thing, and another to do it herself. But the image of Jamie bound and in her power . . . "No."

He growled in satisfaction. "Not at all?" He unknotted his cravat. "Not even a little?"

Olivia watched in dazed disbelief as he pulled the linen loose, unwinding the long cloth as if to deliberately show off the length of it. He wanted to tie her up and ravish her. Or for her to tie him up and ravish him. She should be shocked, and yet her pulse throbbed and she had to press her knees together to keep from sliding off the chaise.

She should not find this arousing or exciting, but God help her, she did.

It was all Jamie's fault, too. Olivia rued the day she'd ever begun reading *50 Ways to Sin*. Everyone had been talking about it, and the way it recounted one very loose lady's erotic adventures with various gentlemen of London. It was completely ridiculous and yet . . . well, widowhood was lonely. Discreetly, feeling somewhat embarrassed by her own unhealthy interest in them, Olivia read every one. And now she was reaping a full penance, as sinful images and ideas bloomed in her mind while Jamie whispered provocative things to her. Even worse, they were *his* images and ideas . . . inspired by her.

"Do it," he murmured, dropping the cravat in her lap. "Tie me." Calmly, deliberately, he unbuttoned his cuff and rolled up his sleeve before extending his arm, wrist bared and fist clenched.

She stared. Slowly she plucked the cravat from her lap and wound a loop around his wrist. At his sharp intake of breath she paused. Jamie's face was set in stark lines and his eyes blazed with hunger. He didn't say a word.

She wound another loop.

You're mine, she vowed silently. *Mine to seduce, mine to love, mine to hold. I will do everything to persuade you of it.* Her heart raced and she felt wild and powerful. She twisted the cloth around his wrist again, but when he raised his other hand and held it to the first, inviting her to bind his wrists together, she pushed it away.

"This way," she whispered, clasping her own fingers through his. Jamie's eyes widened but he made no protest as she coiled the cloth around their entwined hands, binding her hand to his. One-handed, she couldn't make a knot, so she pulled the loose end down between their wrists.

"Now what?" His voice was deep and guttural.

She put her free hand on his chest and pushed him until he sprawled back into the pillows on the chaise behind him. "You're mine."

His eyes drifted closed as she worked at the buttons on his trousers. "I always have been, Livie . . ."

It took longer than it should have, working with only one hand, but finally she pushed the tail of his shirt out of her way. His abdomen flinched as she ran her palm down the length of his erection, circling her fingers around the head and taking his measure in a firm grip. Jamie swore under his breath but he stayed still and taut. The hand bound to hers trembled as she lowered her head. Olivia stole a glance at his face and saw him watching her through half-closed eyes. "Mine," she said again, feeling as reckless and wicked as Constance.

He gasped as she flicked her tongue over the head of his cock. She smiled and braced herself more comfortably. Slowly she closed her lips around him, marveling at the response of his body. She had heard of this act before *50 Ways to Sin* featured it in one issue, but never before had she realized the intimacy of it. Even though she was on her knees pleasuring him, it was obvious that Jamie's entire being was focused on her; his muscles trembled with rigidity and his breath hissed between his teeth with every stroke of her tongue.

With a sudden movement, he yanked on her hand, dragging her on top of him. His kiss was dark and desperate, and Olivia reveled in it. He broke it off and sat up, turning her around until she sat on his lap, her back against his chest. Their bound hands pulled his arm around her, giving him leverage to pull her hard against him. With two hard shoves he pushed her twisted nightgown down and off, leaving her naked in his arms.

"No," she panted. "I want to please you . . ."

His laugh was harsh. "You do, darling. Now open your legs and let us please each other." Straddling the chaise, he draped one of her legs over his knee, exposing her quim, as Constance would call it. Olivia felt wicked just thinking the word; her eyelids fluttered open for a moment and she realized they were facing the mirror. She blushed deeply as she saw herself reflected there, her eyes glittering, her hair wild, Jamie's strong arm wrapped around her middle and his hand on her knee, urging her to spread her legs farther open . . . and his face, hard and fierce with want as he watched everything in the mirror over her shoulder.

"Jamie," she squeaked, her voice melting to a sigh as his fingers stole up her thigh.

"Livie," he breathed, his teeth playing at the delicate skin where her shoulder met her neck. "Be wicked with me." His fingers swirled through the dark curls between her legs before plunging between the dark pink folds there.

Olivia moaned and writhed. He knew just how to touch her . . . But she wanted him to feel the same exquisite ache. She dug her toes into the carpet and rolled her hips. With a whispered curse, Jamie moved, holding her tighter, and then he was inside her. His breath caught as he went still, and she realized he couldn't move.

She spread her knees wider and pushed. His fingers paused. Olivia watched his face in the mirror as she sank down. She felt him tremble. His grip on her hand, still bound to his, tightened until his knuckles went white. Olivia slid her free hand down her belly, insinuating her fingers among his. "I'm always wicked with you."

"Show me." He tugged his hand free and clasped her shoulder. His gaze remained fixed on her hand, but he seemed to stop breathing as she stroked herself.

Olivia knew quite well how to pleasure herself. For the last few years of her marriage to Henry, it had been her only way to climax, and her bed had been just as lonely after Henry died. But she had never touched herself so openly, so boldly, and certainly never with a man's cock deep inside her while he watched with a burning fascination. *Be wicked with me.* She focused on his face and circled her finger just so before finding the rhythm she knew would send her over the edge.

It built faster than ever, almost taking her off guard. When she felt it rise up and take hold of her, she barely had time to gasp before the floor seemed to fall away from beneath her feet. Jamie crossed his free arm over her chest and bowed his spine, forcing himself deeper inside her before he jerked in the throes of his own release.

For what seemed an eternity neither moved. Olivia opened her eyes a slit and marveled at the decadent picture they presented, she sprawled wantonly across him with her hand still between her legs, Jamie with both arms wrapped around her and his forehead on her shoulder. A tiny satisfied smile tugged at her lips. Wickedness had never been so wonderful.

"Livie," Jamie rasped, his breath hot against her neck. "Olivia, I love you. I'll love you till I die."

The same emotion was flooding her, a tidal wave of love that swept everything else away. She kissed him, her heart too full for words. She knew he loved her, as surely as she knew that she loved him—and always would.

But he never said anything more. And later, when he slept next to her in bed, one ink-smudged arm thrown over her waist, Olivia couldn't help wondering if that omission meant something.

Chapter 25

Winter descended in force on London, gray and dismal and so cold Olivia could see her breath in all but the warmest rooms of the house. Jamie wrote and wrote. Every now and then he would put on his hat and coat to go for a walk, but otherwise he spent his days shut up in the house, hunched over his desk.

Although society was smaller at this time of year, there were still a few parties and public balls. Bathsheba went out as usual and reported back via penny post on what she heard. The first of Constance's stories involving Lord Clary caused barely a ripple, but as the issues came out, Bathsheba heard more and more whispering about the horrible man stalking Constance.

"It's working," she wrote in one note, "although not as rapidly as one might like. At present people are not sure if he is a real threat or a future lover. I really think several more issues will be required . . ."

Jamie threw it on the desk. "More! That woman is determined to drive me mad."

Olivia smiled. "You cannot fault her. They're

selling better than ever." It was true. Every print shop and bookseller within fifteen miles of London was wild for copies, it seemed. Even more crucially, Daniel was meeting that demand. He'd persuaded Mr. Hicks to come from Gravesend to help, and somehow Jamie had engineered a partnership between Daniel and Liam MacGregor, who published the *London Intelligencer* newspaper. Olivia had been as startled as anyone to hear that, but at this point nothing Jamie did should surprise her. MacGregor took a third of the profits, and in return he enabled them to more than double production.

"Just these may drive me into a sickbed." Jamie stretched his arms overhead.

"Take a rest," she said, overcome with remorse. "I wish you would let me help. I sit here doing nothing, and you're going to go blind from writing."

He held up one hand. "Not one word of that. You're providing a vital service." He snaked an arm around her waist and pulled her close. "I'm in desperate need of inspiration . . ."

Olivia laughed and let him pull her into his lap for a searing kiss.

Her part, they both knew, would come. Every trap needed bait. Clary wanted the painting, but it would be easier to draw him out if he thought he could also catch Olivia unawares and alone.

Jamie didn't need to tell her this. She also didn't intend to let him keep her hidden away for protection. Clary had violated everything Olivia held dear: her freedom, her happiness, her friends, and her love. There was no doubt in her mind that Clary viewed Jamie as an obstacle, the man who was keeping her from him. That made him a danger not just to Olivia herself but to Jamie. For both their sakes, Clary had to be dealt with—and Olivia knew she had to be the one to do it.

It took just over three weeks for Jamie to write, and Daniel to publish, eleven issues of *50 Ways to Sin*. As Jamie had planned, Lord Brarely grew more and more menacing. Constance grew more and more alarmed by his sinister hovering. Bathsheba reported that everything she heard indicated people were appalled by Brarely's intimidation and beginning to worry for Constance's safety. She wasn't privy to as much discussion of the stories as Olivia might have been, but Olivia hardly left Grosvenor Square. Jamie had suspicions that Clary was watching the house. In any event, MacGregor was able to monitor most gossip, thanks to his still-unknown columnist, and his word on this was most satisfactory: there were several open bets about Brarely's identity, and Clary was the runaway favorite.

But they knew it was time to spring the trap when Jamie came home from one of his walks late one frigid evening. "Clary's furious," he told her as he brushed a light dusting of snow from his greatcoat. "He's finally told someone he thinks it's you blackening his name."

"Where did you hear it?" Olivia had known it would happen if their plan worked, and yet her heart skipped a beat in apprehension anyway.

"A coffeehouse. I ran into a fellow I've done business with, and he said Clary was spewing slander about you." Jamie handed his coat and hat to the waiting footman, who melted into the far recesses of the hall. "Are you worried?"

Yes. With Clary, she would always worry. But Olivia forced the thought down and gave a firm nod. They had a plan, and she wasn't about to shy away from doing her part.

He gave her a smile that was part reassurance, part promise of vengeance. "Good. I think it's time."

Two nights later Olivia put on her old blue cloak and walked out into Grosvenor Square at twilight, late enough for the streetlamps to be lit but not yet dark. The footman hailed a hackney and directed the driver to Mrs. Harding's lodging house, then helped her inside. The bulky valise she carried held only a few items, but she held it close for comfort. Jamie had gone out several hours earlier to make final arrangements, and Olivia only now realized how accustomed she had become to his presence.

In Clarges Street she paid the driver and ran up the steps. Mrs. Harding popped out of the back of the hall as she came in. "Oh! Mrs. Townsend."

"Yes." She started up the stairs.

Mrs. Harding followed, a worried frown on her face. "I am not pleased by this. You can't come and go as you please—I don't keep that sort of house—and the gentlemen! There are to be no gentlemen upstairs, Mrs. Townsend!"

Olivia stopped at the top of the stairs. "Mrs. Harding," she said firmly but quietly, "I shall be quitting my rooms after tonight. I suspect you know why." After her last visit here, she had formed the idea that Mrs. Harding, or perhaps one of the servants, was reporting to Lord Clary when she came and went. It was too striking a coincidence that the viscount would have been so close at hand the one time she returned to Clarges Street.

Mrs. Harding flushed deep red. "I'm sure I don't know what you mean, but I've half a mind to call the constable about this. I do not approve of the way you comport yourself!"

"Very well," said Olivia, knowing the landlady would do no such thing. "Call the constable." She turned and opened her door.

The rooms looked the same, undisturbed and waiting. She went into her bedroom to be sure all was prepared, then returned to the sitting room and lit the lamps. She unpacked the valise, setting the box on the table and the painting on the floor by the cold hearth, just out of sight behind the worn armchair. St. George seemed to be gazing right at her, approvingly. *Protect us all,* she told him silently.

The tap at the door made her jump. Telling herself it could be Mrs. Harding, but knowing it probably was not, she opened the door.

"There you are." Clary shoved at the door as she instinctively tried to push it shut.

Olivia backed up, her heart pounding so hard it hurt. She had planned to lure him here, but now that he was in the room, there was no chance to reconsider anything. "Please leave, Lord Clary."

"Not yet. We have some unfinished business to attend to, you and I."

"No, we do not," she exclaimed, her voice rising.

He closed the door behind him, turning the key in the lock. Watching her, smiling grimly when she took another step backward, he slid the key into his pocket.

"Where is my landlady?" Olivia demanded. "I am not receiving guests—"

"I didn't ask the old besom's blessing. Nor do I need your permission!" snarled the viscount. As he came forward into the lamplight, Olivia saw signs of strain in his face and figure. There were shadowy circles under his eyes, his black hair was mussed out of its normal smoothness, and his clothes bore signs of inadequate laundering.

Good.

They weren't glaring signs of ruin, but to Olivia, who knew how precise and demanding Clary normally was about everything, including his person, they revealed a man whose grasp on his world was slipping. That was exactly what she and Jamie had set out to do, but it also made the viscount even more dangerous.

"Once I asked," Clary went on, recovering his quiet, deadly voice after the moment of anger. "Once I begged you, my dear. But you were troublesome and obstinate. I'm not a man to be refused, yet you did so . . . several times." He took off his greatcoat and set it aside. "Not again, Olivia."

She wet her lips. "I do not want to have an affair with you, sir," she said, making sure her voice was firm and strong.

Clary's smile was terrifying, and even though he stood on the opposite side of the room, it made her pulse leap with anxiety. "Did I not make myself clear? I'm not asking this time." He paused and Olivia inhaled a shuddering breath. "First, tell me where the painting is. I'll be gentle if you tell me. If I have to search for it . . . you will not enjoy what comes next."

"Why?" Her voice shook. "Why do you want me? It's unnatural . . ."

A look of surprise crossed his face. "Why? I don't completely know, my dear. The usual reason, of course. You took my fancy. Not strongly enough to warrant upsetting my arrangement with Henry, but once he was gone, there was no reason I shouldn't enjoy you." He shook his head and clicked his tongue sadly. "But you were so cool and polite. Such a challenge! I knew it wasn't grief—no one mourned Henry that much, especially not the wife his father bought for him." He stopped at Olivia's flinch of shock. "Oh yes, everyone knew. His father kept a tight leash on him, and the only way to loosen it was by accepting a wife's gentle influence. How fortunate for Henry you had no interest in settling him! He did appreciate that. It made his later activities so much easier." Clary closed the distance between them as Olivia stood rigid with humiliation. Henry had told everyone he married her only to placate his father. She wasn't surprised that he'd felt that way, but the revelation that he had told all his elegant friends . . . that took her off guard. Even her belief that her husband was gentleman enough to keep the truth of their marriage discreetly secret was false.

"Speaking of those activities, tell me where it

is." Clary's dark eyes burned. "I know you have it."

Olivia shook her head.

"Tell me." His voice sharpened. "All the way to Thanet and back. Henry kept that side of things to himself—at times I thought he must not trust me. But I know the cargo came ashore off Ramsgate, and you fled directly there. Such daring, Olivia. As much as I appreciate your desire to find the last shipment for me, your choice of accomplice was poorly made. As if taking another man to your bed would make me less determined to have you." With a sudden movement he pushed her. Olivia gave a startled yelp. "I haven't got all night to indulge you. Tell me where the painting is, and this will be a pleasant experience for both of us." He shed his jacket and began unbuttoning his waistcoat.

"There." Olivia backed up and pointed a shaky finger. "There it is. Take it and leave me alone."

At her words Clary spun on his heel, searching. The painting was on the floor, slightly hidden by the wingback chair next to the hearth, but he saw it. His breath hissed, and he crossed the room in three strides to lift it. For a few moments he studied it, even flipping it over to see the back. "My God." There was a pulse of excitement in his hushed whisper. "My God, he got it . . ."

"You can have it," Olivia said again. "Just take it and go."

Slowly he raised his head and turned to look at her. The familiar cold smile appeared. "Not yet. You've wrought too much mischief lately, and you're going to pay for it." He set the painting down on the chair, carefully propping it up. The dragon snarled, coiled to attack. Its scales shone in the lamplight.

"No."

"No?" He flexed his fingers. Olivia knew he didn't want her to acquiesce. He wanted to force her. "You've said no to me one too many times." He started toward her.

Olivia raised the pistol. While Clary had gone to the painting, she had sidled to the box on the table, screened by her valise, which held two loaded and primed pistols. These were smaller pistols than Jamie's, but no less accurate at close distance. Jamie had bought them just for her, and she had followed his advice to keep them both ready. "Stop, sir."

He laughed. "You aren't going to shoot me." He took another step, and Olivia pulled the trigger.

Clary howled and clapped one hand to his chest. With an expression of disbelief he shoved back his waistcoat to reveal a sticky smear of blood near his shoulder. He turned on her with murder in his eyes. "That seals your fate." He charged toward her.

Olivia ran, the second pistol clutched in both hands. Clary caught her skirt but she wrenched loose. Frantically she twisted the doorknob, but he had locked it. She pressed her back to the door and aimed her gun.

Clary froze. For the first time something like fear flickered in his face. "Don't!"

Olivia kept the pistol trained on the painting. "You need it, don't you? I heard your wife has left you and her father has cut off her funds. That was most of your income, wasn't it? Now that Henry isn't paying you to help him sell smuggled artworks."

"Put down the pistol," Clary ordered.

"You're ruined in London," she went on, trying to keep her voice from shaking and her words from running together. "You need that painting so you can flee London and sell it overseas, to someone who doesn't know it's stolen. Don't you?"

"Olivia," said Clary with a voice like steel, "put down the pistol. You might accidentally fire, for God's sake!"

"That painting is your salvation," she accused, "but you won't just take it and leave! You want me for no other reason than that I refused your advances. You've chased me and assaulted me and you tried to kill my friend Penelope—"

"The lying little whore should have been more accommodating," he snarled. "Just as you should. I will not ask again, Olivia. Give me the pistol!" On the last word he lunged at her, and Olivia pulled the trigger.

The report knocked her arm backward into the door and she almost dropped the gun. Clary swiveled to stare in shock. The bullet had drilled right through the painting, leaving a smoking hole where the dragon's head had been.

"No," he choked. "No—you've spoiled a priceless masterpiece!"

Sensing he would turn on her in a moment, Olivia threw the pistol. It struck the painting, and the thin wooden panel splintered into several pieces. Clary gave a hideous scream but Olivia had pushed past him and was running, straight across the room, through the door of her bedroom, and right into Jamie's arms.

"You'll regret—" Clary's raging growl was cut short as he reached the doorway, two steps behind her. Jamie thrust Olivia behind him. Benedict, Lord Stratford, stood at his side. Behind them, three other men were coming to their feet.

Feeling that there was no more persuasive argument than a confession from Clary's own lips, Jamie had invited a magistrate to join him in quiet darkness in Olivia's bedroom while she waited for the viscount to arrive. Benedict had declared he was going to be there as well before Jamie could even ask him, and Gray insisted on the same. Gray, in fact, offered to bring his father, the Duke of Rowland, and that had sealed the magistrate's agreement. All four of them had slipped into the room some time ago, sneaking up the stairs while Jamie distracted the flighty Mrs. Harding in the parlor.

Clary gazed in horror as the magistrate stepped forward. "Viscount Clary, you need to come with me, sir."

"That woman shot me," said Clary. He gave Olivia a look of pure hatred.

"She did," agreed the magistrate, "and I have to commend her aim. You tried to force yourself on her, and I cannot fault a widowed lady for protecting herself."

After that Clary refused to speak. The magistrate made him hand over the key, and sent for Mrs. Harding to tend the viscount's wound. The constables who had been waiting nearby arrived and they escorted Lord Clary to a closed heavy carriage in the mews.

"Thank you for your patience," Jamie told the magistrate.

"My duty, and nothing more." The man's gaze traveled past Jamie. "Will you require anything else, Your Grace?"

"Not tonight," said the Duke of Rowland. "Hopefully we shan't have anything like this ever again."

The magistrate bowed. "I trust not, sir. Good night." He let himself out.

A wild, fierce grin split Benedict's face. "We've got him! He'll never wiggle out of this."

"I doubt it," said the duke in agreement. He bent down to pick up a piece of the shattered painting. "You did this, George?"

George Churchill-Gray looked over his father's shoulder. "I did."

The duke examined it a moment. "Very fine work."

"Thank you." Gray frowned. "Except there—I did not have time to get the shadows exactly right, you can see they don't line up as well as they should . . ."

Rowland chuckled. "Next time you'll get it." He cocked his head and gave his son an appraising look. "There's a very fine portrait of Cupid and Psyche in Ashby's collection. Perhaps you could—?"

Gray's expression indicated they'd had this conversation before. "I don't like to copy paintings, Father."

"But your mother's so fond of that one, and

Ashby won't sell the damned thing," the duke complained. "Just once? For your mother?"

Gray shook his head and walked out, followed by his father still cajoling him. Benedict started to follow them, then stopped. "I have permission to tell Penelope everything, don't I?" he asked Olivia. "I understand if you would rather I not, but she'll be wild to know. It took all I had to persuade her to stay home in Margaret Street."

Olivia laughed—shaky, but happy. "You may tell her. And Lord Stratford—" She put her hand on his arm. "Thank you."

Benedict glanced at Jamie. "It was neither my idea nor my effort that arranged this. And it was solely your bravery, ma'am, that made it succeed."

"Thank you just the same," she said softly. He smiled, and followed Gray and Rowland.

That left her alone with Jamie.

"Is this really the end of Clary?" she asked hesitantly. "Did we do enough?"

"The magistrate heard every word. With both of Henry's books and the proof of the real Titian, that should be enough to keep his lordship in prison for a long time."

She let out her breath, her shoulders slumping. "I hope so."

Jamie gathered her close. "It is so," he whispered. "For us."

"I can't believe this worked," she said, her voice muffled against his chest. It had seemed the maddest scheme she'd ever heard, but Jamie carried it off. Not only a magistrate but a duke had heard Clary confess.

"Thanks to you. Never underestimate how

much a villain wants his victim to realize how clever he's been."

"And I shot him." Her laugh was unhappy. "I didn't like that . . ."

His arms tightened. "Think of it as retribution for what he did to Penelope."

That did help. And even though Olivia had aimed for the center of Clary's chest, as Jamie had instructed, she was deeply relieved she'd only hit him in the shoulder. On no account did she want to feel guilty for Clary's death. But if she'd aimed for his shoulder she would have missed, and who knew what would have happened then.

"It was much easier to shoot the painting." She raised her head to look at the remains. "Although it is a pity to destroy Gray's work."

"No, I think he's glad." Jamie grinned. "His copy fooled Lord Clary. That was reward enough."

"Entirely! It was a beautiful fraud."

The real Titian was still at Stratford Court. Benedict had put it with the other paintings from his father's gallery that were probably stolen, and had set his solicitors on the task of determining who the rightful owners were. Now that Clary was caught by other means, he could do it quietly and spare his family any unpleasant scandal. More than once he'd said he was willing to expose his father, but Olivia suspected he would be even happier not to, for his mother's sake.

"That leaves only one urgent issue," Jamie said, breaking into her thoughts. "Olivia my darling, will you marry me?"

Her eyes widened. "After all this?"

He smiled slightly. "You did accept me once.

I hope you can do so again." He grew sober. "I had to rid myself of that other woman. If not for Constance I would have asked the vicar in Ramsgate to do the job, the first morning after you said you still loved me. I had feared I would never hear those words again . . . But now I stand before you a free man, even more deeply in love with you than ever. I swear I will always be by your side when you need me; I vow to protect and defend you with every resource I possess. Say you'll still have me, my love."

Olivia placed her hand against his cheek. Her smile deepened. "You misunderstood me," she said gently. "I meant, after all that we've been through, you still have to ask? My heart has been yours since I was ten years old."

"I never take you for granted," he promised, and kissed her hand. "Say yes."

"I have never said no to you." She slid her arms around his neck and lifted her face. "Yes. For the rest of my life, *yes*."

Chapter 26

Christmastide
Richmond

It took some doing to build a fire in the cold, but Penelope Lennox, Lady Stratford, was adamant that it must be done, and done by them, without the aid of servants. Her sister, Abigail, swept the snow from a patch of earth, then dumped out the bucket of kindling she'd brought from home and arranged it into a pile.

"Why couldn't we burn them in the fireplace?" asked Joan, Lady Burke. She sat huddled in her fur-trimmed cloak on a fallen tree nearby. Only recently returned from her wedding trip to Italy, she was rarely without her cloak, even indoors, and insisted England had grown colder and darker in the months she was away.

"Penelope wants a ritualistic sacrifice," said Abigail, fussing with the kindling.

"I didn't want to be discovered," replied the lady in question.

"We're only a few hundred yards from Hart House," Joan pointed out. "A gardener may see the smoke and come running to douse us all. Then you'll have to explain why we were building a fire in the woods when the house is full of perfectly good fireplaces."

"Countesses don't have to explain themselves."

Abigail sat back on her heels and raised her eyebrows. "Oh, don't they? Then countesses can light their own fires, thank you very much."

Penelope drew back a step and cradled one hand around her belly. It had begun to show her pregnancy, and she wasn't shy about invoking it to excuse herself from anything disagreeable. "Benedict made me swear not to do anything dangerous."

"Like walk in the snow in the woods?" asked Abigail soberly. "Where you might slip and fall into abandoned grottos—"

"Or be chased by wild animals, or hit by falling trees," chimed in Joan in dire tones. "Not to mention freeze to death. It can't be good for your health to be out here, Pen."

Penelope glared at both of them. "Neither of you have any imagination or sense of drama—none. I'm reconsidering my fondness for your company."

"Then you'd really have to light your own bonfire," muttered Abigail, lighting a spill of paper from the lantern and holding it near the kindling she'd arranged. Unlike her companions, she had not married a wealthy man, and had learned how to light her own fires through necessity.

As wisps of smoke drifted upward, Penelope's

tone brightened. "See? I told you I had no talent for it, but Abby's got it lit on the first try. Well done!"

Abigail climbed to her feet and dusted off her skirt. "It will be your job to snuff it at the end, since you made us come out here."

Penelope gave her an outraged look. "And with good reason!"

"I still say we could have locked the sitting room door and burned them in perfect comfort," Joan added. "And with hot tea at hand."

"Not to mention sandwiches and biscuits," said Abigail slyly as she fed more wood into the fire. It was going rather briskly now, and she reached for the thickest pieces of wood to arrange above the leaping flames.

Penelope shot her a filthy look. Pregnancy had doubled her appetite. "Traitor." She made a show of taking out a stack of papers from the basket she'd carried into the woods. "I'll just get started, then, since neither of you have any fortitude or sense of the moment." She picked up the topmost item and held it over the fire. "I apologize to my mother for stealing this one from her dressing room," she said somberly, and stooped to ignite the corner. Hungrily the fire latched on to it, consuming the cheap rag paper with ease. Penelope dropped it onto the flames and they watched it burn, the words *50 Ways to Sin* blackening as the paper crumbled.

"Go ahead, Abby," Penelope prodded.

Abigail picked up the next issue. "I really can't believe he did it."

Her sister shuddered. "Do not speak of him! I

don't want to know, I don't want to think about it."

"You can hardly forget." Abigail bent down and ignited the pamphlet, tossing it into the flames without any of Penelope's theatrics. "You must admit, it was impressive how secretly it was done."

Joan snorted as she took the next pamphlet from Penelope and threw it into the fire. "And how brilliantly!"

"None of that, please." Penelope held aloft another issue. "I deeply regret lying to obtain this one."

"You didn't at the time," pointed out Joan.

"That was before I knew *my brother* wrote it." Grimacing, Penelope dropped it into the flames. A piece of wood broke and sent up a shower of sparks.

"I find if I try very hard, I can forget that." Still, Abigail threw another issue onto the fire before Penelope could prompt her.

"It's too bad, really," said Joan thoughtfully. "They were quite popular. It seems a shame simply to end it . . ."

"But Constance found her own happiness," said Abigail. "Once assured of that, I find I can let her go quite contentedly."

"She was never real," said Penelope through gritted teeth. She threw two more copies on the fire. "She was a figment of Jamie's imagination!"

"And you always said he had none." Abigail grinned. "If only you could apologize to him for that."

"No, I most certainly will not apologize! Better he should apologize to us, for being such a—a sneak!"

"Wait." Joan sat up straighter. "I thought you said Olivia told you in strict confidence."

Abigail looked blank, then colored. "Penelope," she growled. "Did you tell Jamie we know?"

Her sister's face was cherry red. "No. Not really. I—I told him I knew what he'd been up to and that I did not approve!" She averted her face and burned more issues of *50 Ways to Sin*. "I'm sure he had more than one inappropriate activity to be ashamed of."

"Oh Lord." Joan covered her face. "I shan't be able to look him in the eye tonight."

Penelope snorted. "No need to. Mama's invited everyone to dinner. It will be easy to avoid him—if he even comes."

After the uproar over Lord Clary, Mr. and Mrs. Weston had judged it best to stay in Richmond for a few months. Benedict had had to spend so much time sorting out the contents of his father's picture gallery, he'd been only too happy to accept when invited to escape to Hart House. Joan and her husband were invited upon their return from Italy, because there was so much news to tell Joan after her sojourn abroad, not least of which was the shocking news about *50 Ways to Sin*.

Everyone had known it was ending, of course. The building suspense over the terrifying man threatening Lady Constance had gripped London. With a new issue every few days, it was all anyone could speak of. Even in Richmond, Mrs. Driscoll's shop had carried a good supply, with more arriving every day. For once the printer seemed able to keep pace with demand. It had not taken long for belief to permeate society that Viscount Clary was the man pursuing Constance. All the particulars matched, and Clary's reputation and demeanor did not help him. When a member of Clary's circle blustered that it was all rubbish and libel, the *London Intelligencer* pointed out that many of Constance's stories had been quietly confirmed by the gentlemen described in them, and why should this one be different?

The gossip column of the *Intelligencer* waxed eloquent about the helplessness a widowed lady without connections might feel in the face of Clary's lascivious demands, and reprimanded society for being so willing to believe and savor her previous tales, but not to believe her in her hour of need. Since no one could condemn Constance as getting her just deserts without revealing their extensive knowledge of her prior actions, it was discussed as avidly as any other issue had been, and slowly but surely opinion swayed against Lord Clary.

Compounding it was the news that Lady Clary had left London without her husband to return to her parents' home, and soon Clary himself was arrested—although he did not stay long in prison. The *London Intelligencer* reported that the viscount had been released on account of a festering wound he'd received to his chest, and had fled town to set sail for the East Indies. The newspaper also noted that Commodore Clary, the viscount's younger brother, had recently been demoted to captain and sent to a post in the Bay of Bengal, and wasn't it a coincidence that the two of them had left England just as the Clary fortune was revealed to be gone?

Abigail, Penelope, and Joan had been as transfixed as anyone by the unfolding scandal. As married ladies, now there was no check whatsoever on their reading or discussion. Given Penelope's experience with Clary, they had all considered it a superb ending to a brilliant story.

Then the day after Olivia married Jamie by special license—coincidentally on the same day the very final, triumphant issue of *50 Ways to Sin* appeared in bookshops, wherein Constance's mystery lover helped her vanquished the Clary-like nemesis and secured Constance's hand in marriage as well as her heart—Olivia took her new sisters-in-law aside. "I have something to tell you," she began. "It must stay a secret between us forever."

Penelope had been wary. "I vowed I would never keep another secret from Benedict."

"This one, you'll want to keep. It harms no one, but . . . I think you'll understand once I tell you."

When Olivia said his name, Penelope laughed. Abigail stared in doubtful astonishment. "Are you certain?"

"Quite," was Olivia's reply, her face as pink as a rose.

Penelope quit laughing. "That's impossible!" She turned to her sister. "Abby, you can't believe this nonsense!"

"But Olivia's not a liar," said Abigail slowly, still looking perplexed. "Why would she say such a thing? She knows how we followed *50 Ways to Sin*. If it turned out our brother—our very own *brother*—was writing them . . ."

Penelope made a choked sound. "He can't be!

And even if he were, why would you tell us such a thing?" she demanded of Olivia.

"Because we're family now. Because I don't want to keep it from you." She hesitated. "Sisters shouldn't keep secrets from each other."

Abigail and Penelope exchanged a look expressing doubts on that point, but neither pursued it. "You're truly serious?" Abigail asked again. "It was Jamie all along? Every issue?"

Olivia nodded.

Penelope had leapt to her feet. "Right! Well, if that's the truth I'm glad to know it. Thank you, Olivia!" Seizing Abigail's arm, she'd pulled her from the room and immediately announced that they had to burn every last copy of *50 Ways to Sin*.

So here they were in the woods, in the middle of winter. Joan's husband, Tristan, had gone to see some of the contraptions at Montrose Hill House. Sebastian, Abigail's husband, had invited him to see his late father's inventions, and nothing fascinated Tristan more than innovation. He'd quizzed Sebastian at dinner the other night and got the idea that some of those inventions might be practicable after all, given some capital investment. Benedict had gone back to Stratford Court, across the river, to fetch his mother for dinner. Jamie and Olivia were expected to arrive from London later in the day, which left this one afternoon when the three of them were unoccupied and could slip away for an hour.

"Joan," Penelope prompted. "Your turn."

Joan hesitated, smoothing the copies in her hands. "I think I ought to be able to keep a few issues. He's not my brother, after all."

"All of them," said Penelope darkly.

"Just three." Joan slid them under her cloak. "I can't think of Constance as a man, I can't!"

"There *is* no Constance!"

"Just because she's not a flesh-and-blood person doesn't mean she's not real!" Joan appealed to Abigail. "Don't tell me you don't feel a true connection to the characters in your favorite books."

"That is true, Pen," Abigail replied. "Just because they aren't real people doesn't make characters less . . . real."

"You realize neither of you are making any sense, don't you?" Penelope threw up her hands and began stuffing pamphlets into the fire without ceremony. "Constance is not real. Therefore, none of what she wrote was true."

"And yet you took great pleasure and enjoyment from her stories, and—dare I say it—found much truth in them," said her sister slyly.

"Close your mouth," ordered Penelope, flushing deep red.

"Just because it wasn't an accurate recounting of actual events doesn't mean they weren't entirely possible." Joan clutched her pamphlets close as Penelope advanced on her, a dangerous gleam in her eye.

"Give them to me."

"You're being ridiculous about this," Joan declared. "I wouldn't be so upset if *my* brother turned out to be the author."

"Oh?" Abigail arched her brow. "Then you weren't upset when his bride was accused of being Lady Constance, and Douglas proposed marriage to her anyway in front of a large crowd of people?"

"Of course I was upset," said Joan indignantly. "I wasn't there to see any of it! We came home and he was all but married! My mother could barely speak for days, she was so astonished."

"It was quite shocking," agreed Abigail. "Mrs. Wilde was always so quiet! So mysterious! So elegant and sophisticated. Who knew *Douglas* would be the one to win her?"

"Oh, she gave him many a setdown." Joan's eyes shone with delight. "They all bounced off Douglas's thick head, of course, and then she fell in love with him anyway. I do adore Madeline—she knows how to say all the impertinent things I long to say, only she manages to say them with wit and style and no one ever scolds her for them."

"She's married," Abigail reminded her.

"So am I!" protested Joan.

"It must be the style," said Penelope. "Or perhaps the wit. Regardless, hand over that pamphlet you're trying to hide under your cloak. I can't believe you want to keep it."

"I enjoyed this one very much." Joan held it out of Penelope's reach. "So did Tristan."

"And what would he say if he knew who wrote it?"

Joan's eyebrows went up. "Tristan? He'd think it the best joke in all of Britain and ask your brother to read it aloud, with spirit and commentary. Shall I tell him at dinner tonight?"

Penelope's face was brick red and screwed up in frustration. "Don't you dare. Oh Lord, the humiliation if everyone knew!"

"If everyone knew that Jamie had pulled off one of the greatest clandestine operations in recent history?" Abigail came to stand behind Joan in a show of support. "Not only enthralled London but served justice to a man in sore need of it. And made a fortune along the way, too. I expect he'd be made a Lord of the Treasury, or appointed to the Home Office."

Penelope's fury cooled a little. "That is true," she said in a quieter tone. "He did run that monster Clary out of England. Which is not as good as seeing him left to rot in chains in prison, but at least now there's a strong chance he'll die of malaria or cannibals."

"I hope it's malaria," said a new voice. Olivia stepped out of the trees and walked toward them. "I can't wish Clary's flesh on anyone, not even the most savage of cannibals." She shuddered.

"You're here!" Abigail hurried to embrace her new sister-in-law. She glanced behind Olivia. "Is—?"

"Jamie's at the house," Olivia said with a smile. "I told him I could find you on my own." She tilted her head and looked curiously at the fire.

"Penelope wanted to build a bonfire," explained Abigail.

Her sister flushed. "Welcome home, Olivia." Then a huge smile burst across her face. "And how many years I've been waiting to say that! I'm so glad you finally made Jamie see reason and marry you."

Olivia's face glowed with happiness. "So am I. Although I'm not sure it happened quite that way . . ."

Penelope waved one hand. "Near enough, I'm sure. You remember Joan?"

"Very well." Olivia bobbed her head. "A pleasure to see you again, Lady Burke."

"Congratulations on your marriage," said Joan warmly. "I wish you great happiness, Mrs. Weston."

Olivia laughed. "Thank you—very much." Being a Weston at last still brought a thrill of incredulous delight whenever someone called her by her new name. Jamie's parents had welcomed her with open arms, declaring that they couldn't have chosen better for their son if they'd done it themselves. Abigail and Penelope had reacted with cries of delight and a flurry of hugs. It was nearly the opposite of her first marriage in every way. Even her own parents had sent a note of congratulations. Olivia thought that was probably due to their interest in any largesse she might share with them, but nevertheless she responded politely. Nothing was going to cloud her happiness.

"I'm to summon you to dinner soon," she told her new sisters-in-law. "Are you done with your bonfire?"

"Yes!" Joan leapt up from the log she sat on.

"No!" said Penelope at the same time. "Er . . ." She glanced from Joan to Olivia and looked torn. "Almost."

Olivia turned to Abigail, only to see that she was having trouble hiding her amusement. "I think you'd best give in, Pen. Let Joan have her way."

"Abby!" Penelope widened her eyes impatiently. "Whose side are you on?"

"The side of peace and happiness," her sister answered. "As long as you keep quiet, there will be peace. There's no need to ruin the happiness Joan might have."

Olivia's gaze narrowed on the fire. A stack of blackened paper smoldered in the ashes, and when she leaned forward she caught sight of enough uncharred paper to realize what the three were doing. "Oh—oh my!" She burst out laughing. "You're burning them?"

"Every one, by Pen's edict." Abigail grinned widely.

"What a waste!"

"See?" In a flash Joan hid some more pamphlets inside her cloak and hurried to Olivia's side. "Shouldn't we go to dinner? I think it's much colder now as well."

"If we feed the fire it will be warmer," Penelope retorted.

"It will also be warmer if we go back to the house." Joan turned toward the house, then paused. She leaned close to Olivia and whispered, "There really won't be any more, I suppose . . . ?"

Olivia hid a smile and shook her head. Jamie had sworn he was done, with no interest in writing more, and she believed him. She also hoped they would be too busy building a life together and loving each other. As much pleasure as it gave Olivia to read *50 Ways to Sin*, it was a hundred times better to experience the pleasures Constance wrote of in her own bed, with the man she loved so desperately.

Joan heaved a sigh. "I feared as much." She lowered her voice even more. "Tell him it was truly

›rilliant and inspirational. Really." Without wait-
ng for a reply, she headed down the path. Abigail widened her eyes in amusement and gave her
sister a shrug before joining her friend.

Penelope stared after them, openmouthed, then
nuttered something under her breath. She tossed
he few pamphlets left in her hand onto the dying
ire. "Traitors."

"And you wouldn't have kept your copies if
you'd never known?" Olivia helped her kick dirt
onto the last flames, then stamp on the embers. It
had recently rained so there wasn't much risk of
he fire spreading. When they had extinguished
he fire completely, Olivia linked her arm with Penelope's and they started toward Hart House.

"It's just *wrong* for him to write stories like
hat," Penelope said as they walked. "What was
he thinking?"

"I believe it was to help a friend." Then Olivia
added, in the spirit of truthfulness, "It may also
have begun as a wager, after some drink."

Penelope snorted. "Of course. Men and their
drunken wagers."

They wound their way along the path through
the trees into the gardens. As they reached the
end of the Fragrant Walk, neatly graveled and bor-
dered by shrubs that perfumed the air in spring
and summer, Hart House itself came into sight.
Both Abigail and Joan had disappeared, but two
gentlemen were standing on the terrace behind
the house, and one of them lifted an arm in greet-
ing.

"Ben," exclaimed Penelope in delight. She
picked up her skirts and hurried toward him.

Benedict caught her in his arms and held her close for a minute before they went into the house, his dark head bent near her blond one. Olivia wondered if Penelope was telling her husband what she'd been doing out in the woods, and then decided it wasn't her concern.

Jamie strode out to meet her, opening his arms as he drew near. Olivia ran into his embrace, marveling again that he was hers—at last. "Where were you?" he whispered, nuzzling her ear.

"Penelope made a bonfire."

He pulled back to give her a shocked look. "Penelope? How did she manage that? Are the woods burning to the ground as we speak?"

"Abigail may have started the fire," Olivia amended, "but Penelope was the one who wished it. And I helped her put it out, so the woods are safe."

His hazel eyes narrowed and she could tell he saw right through her. Not that it bothered her; she didn't plan to keep secrets from Jamie, either. "You told them, didn't you."

Olivia gave a guilty smile. "How could I keep such a secret?"

"By not telling anyone." He shook his head in mock dismay. "I'm gravely disappointed, Mrs. Weston."

That name gave her a thrill of happiness. "Truly? It doesn't give you any pleasure to hear that Lady Burke thought they were brilliant?"

"None."

"Nor that I did, too?"

Jamie scoffed. "I thought you would be above such rubbish."

"Oh no. I assure you, I found them utterly entrancing." She slid her arms around his waist. "Especially the one in the pond. And the one in the carriage. And also the one with the two brothers."

Jamie, who was fighting off a grin, suddenly scowled at the last. "No."

She shrugged. "Of course, you haven't got a brother, so I presume that was Bathsheba's suggestion."

He burst out laughing. "It was! I shudder to think what she would have written."

"Perhaps she will, now that you've quit the field." Olivia thought about it. "I expect she'd do quite well."

"If Bathsheba wants to be Constance's heir, she may take the crown with my blessing." Jamie kissed her. "As much as I owe Constance, I'm happy to bid her farewell."

"You won't miss her, even a small bit?"

"Hmm." He pretended to think even as his hands slid under her cloak. "She kept me company when I was alone. And she did develop my imagination in many wonderfully lascivious ways. You liked the story in the pond, did you?"

"Above all others," she said unsteadily, arching against him. He was running his hands up and down her back and sending shivers over her skin.

"And what about it particularly pleased you?" he murmured.

Olivia took a deep breath. "Because it was very like the day I knew I was hopelessly, irrevocably in love with you. That was the happiest day of my life, until recently."

Jamie lifted his head. "I could say the same.

Except that I knew you were the one for me long before that day." He twined his fingers through hers and raised her hand to his lips. "That day was the day I knew *I* was the fellow for you, and *that* made it the happiest."

There was no reason to argue; it was all true. She went up on her toes and kissed him, reveling in the spark that went through her at the touch of his lips on hers. "I love you, James Weston. So much that I can even bid Constance farewell without any grief."

He laughed, a low rumble in his chest. "I feel no grief—not since I have you to replace her. You are infinitely better in every way, my darling."

Olivia beamed. The smile felt permanently etched on her face these days, and she thought it would be forever. "As long as I'm with you, I feel that way, too."

Epilogue

The house in Totman Street hadn't been so quiet in months. Bathsheba Crawford wandered down to the vaulted-ceiling room where she had spent so many hours laboring—setting type, inking the plates, working the press, cutting and binding pages. Now there would be no more of that. The press stood silent, and nary a sheet of paper hung from the ceiling. It could almost be a normal servants' hall again.

She knew *50 Ways to Sin* had been a raging success. Even now Daniel was dining with Liam MacGregor and talking about more joint ventures, new printing opportunities for both of them. During the frantic printing of the final issues, MacGregor himself had come to help man the press, and in the space of a few days he and Daniel had become friends. Bathsheba was immensely pleased to see her brother become almost the same man he had been before losing his arm: purposeful, confident, thriving on the high stakes of their work. And all of it paid off handsomely.

For the first time in years they had plenty of funds for coal and food and new clothes—the last being especially fortunate, to replace all the garments ruined by ink. Bathsheba knew she and her brother owed a huge debt to Jamie Weston. He hadn't taken a single farthing of the profits. If only he hadn't wanted to end it. Bathsheba was sure the people of London, indeed all over Britain, would have kept buying issues long past number fifty. Surely there was so much more for Constance to do . . .

There was certainly more Bathsheba wanted to do.

She went back upstairs into the clean and tidy sitting room. Now that they weren't printing day and night, they had servants again, and the house was much neater. Daniel's desk was there, and she opened the front. The slots that had been filled with overdue bills just months ago were empty, and the sight gave her great pleasure. Almost idly she pulled out a sheet of paper and twirled a quill between her fingers. Was this how Jamie had begun? How did one come up with story ideas? As clever as she knew Jamie to be, plenty of people, some of whom were complete idiots, wrote poems and stories and gossip columns and even complete novels.

Bathsheba took out a penknife and sharpened her pen. She eyed the blank page. She had a healthy imagination, even if her own life had always been utterly mundane and even dull. More than once she had suggested adventures for Constance. Jamie had used some of them, but not all. Before she was aware of it, she had uncapped the ink and dipped her pen. Constance had made her farewell, but not before entrancing all of London with her adventures. Surely that audience would be eager to read another, similar tale . . .

This was just for her personal gratification, she told herself. No one had to read it, after all; she could even burn it and no one would ever know she wrote anything. Carefully she set the pen to the paper and wrote:

Dearest Friend,

Recently someone told me that an interesting life is of little note if one leaves no record of it. Although I had never thought to record some of the most daring of my youthful exploits, I have reconsidered, and so set my pen to paper to tell you, first, of my most extraordinary adventure: the night I saved the Duke of W's life and was rewarded with a passion that seared itself into my memory . . .